ACOUSTIC

Patrick Kendrick worked an entire career in the fire service before retiring to write full time. He also worked as a freelance writer, publishing articles and short stories in newspapers and magazines. One assignment brought him into contact with a serial killer that he corresponded with for several years… until the killer began to threaten him and launched a series of lawsuits against him. The killer was eventually murdered in prison but his frightening and graphic 'diaries' describing his crimes became the basis of *Extended Family*.

Kendrick was knighted by the Fraternal Order of Police for his articles on crime. He's won honourable mentions from the Mystery Writers of America and the Beverly Hills Film Festival, the Opus Magnum Discovery Award from the Hollywood Film Festival and the Florida Book Award for his first novel, *Papa's Problem*.

He lives in South Florida and when he is not writing, spends as much time as possible in, on, or under the ocean.

Also by Patrick Kendrick

Papa's Problem
Extended Family

ACOUSTIC SHADOWS

PATRICK KENDRICK

an imprint of HarperCollins*Publishers*
www.harpercollins.co.uk

This is a work of fiction. Any references to real people, living or dead, real events, businesses, organizations and localities are intended only to give the fiction a sense of reality and authenticity. All names, characters, places and incidents are either the product of the author's imagination or are used fictitiously, and their resemblance, if any, to real life counterparts is entirely coincidental.

Killer Reads
An imprint of HarperCollins*Publishers*
1 London Bridge Street
London SE1 9GF

www.harpercollins.co.uk

This paperback edition 2015
1

First published in Great Britain by
HarperCollins*Publishers* 2015

Copyright © Patrick Kendrick 2015

Patrick Kendrick asserts the moral right to be identified as the author of this work

A catalogue record for this book is available from the British Library
ISBN: 978-0-00-813969-8

Set in Minion by Born Group using Atomik ePublisher from Easypress

All rights reserved. No part of this publication may be reproduced, stored in a retrieval system, or transmitted, in any form or by any means, electronic, mechanical, photocopying, recording or otherwise, without the prior permission of the publishers.

This book is sold subject to the condition that it shall not, by way of trade or otherwise, be lent, re-sold, hired out or otherwise circulated without the publisher's prior consent in any form of binding or cover other than that in which it is published and without a similar condition including this condition being imposed on the subsequent purchaser.

MIX
Paper from
responsible sources
FSC" C007454

FSC is a non-profit international organisation established to promote the responsible management of the world's forests. Products carrying the FSC label are independently certified to assure consumers that they come from forests that are managed to meet the social, economic and ecological needs of present and future generations.

Find out more about HarperCollins and the environment at
www.harpercollins.co.uk/green

For Bill – I'll see you on the ocean again, one day.
~PK

ONE

Erica Weisz strode up the sidewalk to the Travis Hanks Elementary School in the tiny town of Frosthaven, Florida, a bounce in her step. It was a sunny autumn morning, and Erica loved the weather and this rural area she'd moved to only six weeks ago.

Frosthaven was a rural town of less than 3,000 full-time citizens, surrounded by freshwater lakes and a diminishing citrus business that was losing ground to imported fruit. The groves stretched out over small hills that rolled on for as far as the locals wanted to see. The scent of orange blossom wafted in the air as Erica squinted at the surrounding citrus groves. From far away they looked green and lush. But, like the 'FOR LEASE' signs on the downtown buildings, the diminishing groves echoed the slow decline of a dying place. Most people living here were firmly ensconced in the federal poverty level. The only exceptions were the remaining citrus and cattle processing plants and fertilizer manufacturers, who employed nine-tenths of the town's population.

Though Erica was not completely comfortable with her new job, she enjoyed working with the children at the town's solitary elementary school. She felt she'd gone back in a time machine to an era when people were simple and friendly and communications not so obscure. She had been working *per diem* as a substitute for the past three weeks, coming in last minute when they'd call her in the morning. Then, just yesterday morning, Dr Linda Montessi, the principal, pulled her aside in the hallway.

'Good morning, Erica,' she said, her tone professional, as was her appearance; blunt cut hair that brushed her shoulders and framed an oval face that showed kindness weathered with caution. 'Got a minute?'

'Uh, sure, Dr Montessi,' said Erica, her mind on other, more personal matters, as usual.

'I recently got a budget item approved, one that allows me to hire a permanent substitute. I was hoping you might take the job?'

'I . . . well . . . are you sure? I mean, I'd love to but . . . '

'And we'd love to have you. So, you'll accept the offer?'

'Well, to be honest, I'm not sure how long I'll be staying in Frosthaven.'

'Oh?' replied Dr Montessi, her eyebrows arching, as if searching for an explanation.

Dodging the unspoken enquiry, Erica said, 'Gosh, I'm sorry. May I think about it and let you know tomorrow?'

Dr Montessi smiled warmly. 'Yes, of course. That's fine. Sleep on it, and let me know.' She walked away and back to her hectic schedule.

Erica thought about the offer now, as she neared the school gates. She knew she should consider accepting it. The school was a nice place to work, and the best part was that it was within walking distance to her boxy, hibiscus pink, cinder-block home on Barney Avenue. It might be a poor community, but the people seemed genuine and welcoming, and this offer was just another example of that. For the first time in a long time, she had begun to feel comfortable with where she was. But, there was a persistent, creeping worry that loomed over every decision she made. If she stayed longer, her background check would come up clean, but how long could she keep her secrets from these people?

Dr Montessi was a warm, motivated educator who often dressed up in funny costumes to amuse the students, whilst making significant learning points. For Halloween, she had dressed up as a witch and shared the cautionary tale of the unfortunate Salem Witch Trials. She turned the story into a parable about people bullying others who held beliefs different from their own. The children adored her. She and Erica had hit it off right away. They both had backgrounds in science, and enjoyed similar pastimes such as cycling and CrossFit. Erica decided she wouldn't allow her usual dark thoughts to trouble her this day. She would focus on the positive offer instead.

Like all schools in Florida, Travis Hanks Elementary had experienced budgetary problems. The facilities definitely showed years of use, but everyone worked together to keep it clean and tidy. Colourful banners were hung promoting positive affirmations and anti-bullying campaigns.

Striding through the main office, Erica said hello to the school nurse, Nora, who cared for children with sniffles or scraped knees or tummy aches. And to Sally Ravich, the front office lady with the purple, horn-rimmed glasses, who commented on Erica's blue, flowered dress and matching, oversized purse.

'That blue matches your eyes,' she said in her lyrical, southern drawl. Then, noting Erica's running shoes, added, 'I saw some nice flats that would match your purse at Payless yesterday.'

'Thanks, Sally,' said Erica. 'I'll stick to my running shoes.'

When Sally asked what she kept in a purse that big, Erica replied with wide, exaggerated eyes, 'Everything.'

Lynn LaForge, the assistant principal, another excellent educator, who doubled as soccer mom and cheerleader coach for her daughter's middle school team, also greeted Erica.

'You have Mrs Miller's class again, today, Erica,' said Lynn. 'Still has the flu. Did you perm your hair?'

'No,' said Erica, absently putting her hand in her shimmering, black hair. 'I left the house with it damp, and it curls if I don't blow it out.'

'Is that your natural colour?' asked the inquisitive administrator.

Erica's cheeks turned red. Her hair was as dark as a coal bucket and though she was a brunette, with natural sun-kissed highlights, she dyed her hair the lustrous black it was now. When she was a child, she'd been hit in the head by a swing and had to get sutures. It healed fine, but the hair over the scar turned white. Such an anomaly was too distinct, too memorable, and she couldn't risk standing out.

Lynn smiled. 'I'm sorry, hon. I didn't mean to embarrass you. You look great,' she said, then cautiously added, 'Still haven't met any locals?'

Erica turned the corners of her mouth down. 'If you mean men . . . no. But, I can't say I've really been looking.'

'I've got a brother-in-law . . . '

Erica smiled benignly and shook her head. 'I'll let you know.' Changing the subject, she asked, 'Do you know if Mrs Miller left me any new lesson plans?'

'Sure,' said Lynn. 'She emailed them to me, and I ran off a hard copy for you.'

'Thanks,' said Erica.

'I think she'll be out the rest of the week,' Lynn added. 'She's pretty sick.'

'Oh, okay,' said Erica, sorting through the plans Mrs Miller had sent her. 'Thank you, Miss LaForge.' First names were fine at this school, but Erica did not need, or want, people to know her that well, so maintained a friendly, but slightly aloof manner.

The janitor, Mr Swan, was ambling down the hall, his gait slightly hitched from the prosthetic leg he'd earned in Vietnam. He was carrying some fluorescent replacement bulbs, wearing a worn leather tool belt around his waist, as he dodged children running for their classes.

'Slow down,' he admonished, 'or someone's gonna get hurt.'

'Hey, Mr Swan,' said Erica. 'How are you today?'

'Oh, hi, Erica,' replied the old handyman, beaming. 'Couldn't be better. And how are you?'

'I'm very well,' she said.

'Good, good, good. Well, have a great day, young lady,' he said, grinning, a tooth missing from his smile.

Erica continued to class. She had about eight minutes to prepare for the day – not nearly enough time – before the children started pouring in. Many of them were children of Guatemalan field workers, or welfare kids, their tattered second-hand clothes hanging from their thin frames like battle flags. She welcomed the third graders, and told them Mrs Miller was still sick. They were going to make jack-o'-lanterns today, with construction paper and paste. But, first, there was a reading lesson they needed to finish: *The Legend of Sleepy Hollow*.

'You'll like it,' Erica promised. 'It's scary.'

After a few moans and groans and shuffling of papers and books, pencils being sharpened and whispers hushed, the children fell silent and began reading to themselves.

Erica was in the back of the room, looking for the orange construction paper that was supposed to be in the closet, when she heard the first popping sounds. *Firecrackers? Inside the school, or from the nearby woods?* It was 8:20 a.m.

One of the little boys in the class asked, 'is that fireworks?'

More popping sounds.

Erica knew, now, they weren't firecrackers. *Acoustic shadows*, she thought. *That's what he had called them.* She went to the window near her desk and looked out through the blinds, sweat breaking out on her neck. The school was in the shape of a giant 'U', so the view from any window yielded a view of the other side of the building. She caught a glimpse of a man dressed in black, suited up like a SWAT team member, carrying an assault rifle, bands of ammo wrapped around his torso, pistols on his belt. A late model van was parked in the pick-up lane in the parking lot, its doors left open, puffs of oily smoke coming from the tailpipe.

'No,' Erica said to no one, her heart now in her throat. 'Not again.'

'What do you see, Ms. Weisz?' asked Rachel, a little girl with an almost comical mop of blonde curls.

Suddenly, there was a sound of shattering glass, more popping sounds getting louder. And screams. Erica froze, considering her options; her training had never taught her how to protect anyone other than herself. Now, she wasn't sure she could even do that.

The PA system came on. The class stared at the old box speaker on the wall as it brought them terrifying noises. There was a humming, then the sounds of things banging and shuffling. A rough voice, indistinguishable, then Dr Montessi's voice, pleading. 'Please don't hurt the children.'

'We're not going to hurt them,' declared a high-pitched, male voice that ended with hysterical laughter. 'We're going to *kill* them!'

'Just kill *them*,' said another voice, calmer, in control, and the shooting resumed. Rapid and, loud, *blam, blam, blam*. The firecracker sounds replaced by unmistakable, up close, booming gun blasts.

Then silence. A groan. The meaty sound of a body hitting the floor, hard. And the gun blasts started again. A door slammed. Steps growing fainter. Silence.

They're coming here, Erica thought, fear briefly immobilizing her. Inside her chest, her heart beat so fast she thought it might burst. The children stared at her, quietly expecting *something*, but Erica's eyes locked on Rachel's. The little girl's lips began to quiver, and a tear sneaked down her cheek. More kids began to sob. 'I'm scared,' said one of them. One little girl urinated as she sat at her desk, crying silently, a puddle forming at her feet. None of the other children noticed.

Gunshots echoed in the hall. *Pa-tow, tow, tow. Pa-tow-tow-tow*. 'You sons of . . .' came Mr Swan's voice, then more gunshots, louder and closer.

Erica couldn't breathe as she listened, adrenaline sharpening her senses.

Silence again. The giant clock above the teacher's desk *clicked* as it turned to '8:23'.

Footsteps coming down the hall; now closer.

More screams. More gunshots.

Finally, Erica found the courage to move. She ran to the door and locked it.

'Quick, class. Everyone to the back of the room. Now!' she ordered.

The children scurried to the back like bait fish fleeing a predator. Erica heard a thud and glanced at the window in the door to the hall. Suddenly, Lynn LaForge appeared in the frame, her face a mask of horror. She peered in the window for an instant, her eyes wide and wet with terror. Her hand rattled the door urgently. She opened her mouth when a bullet ripped through her face, blood spattering the window, and she was gone. That fast. Alive one second, gone the next.

'Inside the closet,' Erica ordered, trying to calm her voice.

The kids began pushing and shoving to get inside the small space. *It would not hold them all.* Erica packed in as many as she could and closed the door, her mind racing, her breath ragged. She sprinted to the front of the class again, grabbed her purse, then hurried back. She began frantically piling desks into a barricade.

The doorknob rattled, then violently shook. A masked face appeared in the bloodied window. The gunman banged his rifle butt against the door handle, once, twice. Erica turned to the kids who couldn't fit into the closet; they were huddled behind the overturned desks, whimpering, fear transforming their faces. She put a finger to her mouth to shush them. She clutched her purse and tried to squeeze in with them behind the makeshift barricade, but couldn't quite conceal herself.

An abrupt burst of gunfire sent parts of the door flying, glass spraying. The smell of sulphur crept into the room as the barrel of a rifle came into view where the door had been, slowly revealing a black, gloved hand on its grip. Then, the man was in the room. A ski mask covered his face but his eyes were wide and wild through the openings. The weapon he wielded was an Armalite AR-15, semi-automatic. With a thirty-round clip, it weighed only 8.8 lb. It was light, manoeuvrable. Deadly.

Erica could see his eyes hone in on the pile of desks where she and the children were hiding, and realized her leg was sticking out.

'C'mon outta there,' he commanded. She reached for her purse, her heart now in her mouth. She stuck her head up.

'Please,' she said. 'I . . . I sent the kids out to the playground . . .'

'SHUT THE FUCK UP!' he screamed, wincing, as if he were in pain. He stared at her and pulled his mask up, sweat running down his face, his breathing hard, laboured. He was in his forties maybe, with a blunted, street-worn face: twisted nose, cauliflower ears, scarred brows. He squinted at Erica. 'What's your name?' he hissed, sweat dripping off his nose.

She stared back at him over the top of the overturned desks 'Wh . . . what?' she asked.

A whimper issued from the closet, followed by some rustling. The door began to creep open. The gunman swung the rifle in the direction of the noises, aimed high, and pulled the trigger. Flames spat out the barrel as bullets sprayed across the room, splintering wood from the closet door and bursting the windows, sending glass flying through the air like thrown diamonds. The noise was deafening. Now hysterical, the kids screamed.

Erica stood up. 'It's Mil . . . Millie,' she said, realizing now with a paralyzing fear, *he isn't here for the students*. 'Please,' she added, 'don't shoot the children.'

The gunman nodded his grisly head as he removed the empty clip, plucked a new one off his belt, and shoved it into the rifle.

Rachel stepped out of the closet, her face pale, blood pouring down her arm, her mouth hanging slack.

Erica ran to the bleeding girl. A bullet had nicked her upper arm. Only a flesh wound, but she was in shock: her colour blanched; her skin cold and sweaty. Erica's emotions morphed from paralyzing fear to unequivocal rage.

The gunman grinned after reloading the bullet clip and looked up at Erica, whose back was to him.

'Turn around,' he said, pulling the bolt back on the rifle, chambering a round.

'She's bleeding,' she said, her voice trembling with rage. 'Let me help her. I just want to stop the bleeding. I . . . have a scarf in my purse.'

The gunman coughed and spat on the floor.

Erica retrieved her purse and came back to Rachel. She pulled out her scarf, tied it around the wound, and brought her over to the pile of desks.

'Stay down,' she whispered to the little girl. Their eyes locked and Rachel robotically obeyed the command.

Erica reached into her purse again, her hands shaking. This time she came up with a small, almost toyish-looking Bersa Thunder .380 automatic pistol, with matt nickel finish. She had taken a deep breath and now let it ease out, exhaling slowly, her hands locked together, steadying them as she stood and swivelled back to the gunman – who stood transfixed – and squeezed the trigger.

There was a bang, amplified in the small room, and a red vapour puffed out the back of the gunman's head. A small, dark hole appeared in his forehead, then blood began to flow from the hole and poured over his still open eyes. He blinked once and fell to the ground as if he was a marionette and someone had cut the strings.

Erica sat down with the children, her legs shaking, trying to swallow, but her throat was too dry. She settled for a deep breath and closed her eyes, her ears ringing from the gun blasts.

The children behind the desks stared at her with their mouths open. One by one, the other kids began to slip from the closet. No one said anything. Some began to sniffle, some cried, some were ominously silent. Several of them came over and hugged her.

She took another deep breath, trying to calm herself.

'Everyone, please . . . sit down,' she pleaded.

She stood, extricating herself from the swarm of children. Holding her gun pointed at the fallen man, she approached cautiously. She noticed he was still breathing, just as she heard more gunshots coming from down the hall. Then more screams. She looked back at the children.

'Get in the closet,' she whispered, harshly. 'There's another one out there.'

They pushed inside, silently but quickly. Erica looked over at the kids behind the desk pile. 'Close your eyes,' she told them, calmly. 'It's going to be okay.'

She stood for a moment, her mind racing, but she could not arrive at a different conclusion. She aimed her gun at the gunman and put another bullet into his head. The shot took off a section of his skull and stopped the breathing.

One of the boys jumped up from behind the desk pile, trembling, his mouth an 'O'.

She recognized the boy from another class and felt the need to try to reassure him.

'I'll be back, Ricky. Please stay down until then.'

The boy slumped as if deflated, his white, spiked hair giving him the appearance of having seen the devil himself.

Erica pushed past the remnants of the door and peered into the hall. It was dark and there were huge holes in the ceiling and walls; evidently, the other gunman had shot out the lights. Oily smoke hung in the air like pale spectres raised from the recently slain. She saw poor Mr Swan lying at one end of the hall, sprawled out, his prosthesis angled, blood spilling from his body. She wanted to go check for a pulse, but stopping the other gunman before he killed anyone else was her first priority. She stepped over Mrs LaForge, trying not to look at her face. Holding up her gun, she kept both hands on it, just as she'd seen actors do in police dramas, just as she practised between rounds at the gun range. She had just killed a man for the first time in her life. There was no time to reflect on it. She could – no, *would* – do it again. There were no other choices.

She eased down the hall toward where she could still hear occasional pops of gunfire, staying close to the wall, making herself a smaller target.

She came to the part of the building that was the bottom of the 'U' shape and peeked around the corner. Another blast, this one a cavernous, exploding sound, and the other gunman emerged from one of the classrooms carrying a seven-round, Remington 870 Express, pump shotgun. He stopped and began pushing more shells into the gun. Like the first man, he had removed his mask. She could see he was younger than his accomplice, with long, curly, unnaturally red hair. His face was pale and covered with inflamed acne.

Erica stepped away from the wall. She was maybe fifty feet from the shooter in a wide-legged stance, one eye closed as she aimed the gun at him.

He was quick. He pulled the shotgun up and fired at her from hip level. The blast took a row of lockers off the wall, but some of the buckshot found her, striking her left hip and abdomen. She fired as she fell; the round hit his chest. He stumbled, surprised, and pulled open his shirt. Erica saw he was wearing a bullet proof vest and was unhurt. It slowed him temporarily, but he grabbed the Remington and pumped another round into the chamber.

Erica was lying on her back, her side on fire, blood soaking her blue-flowered dress as she craned her neck and again squinted one eye. When she tried to lift it, the pistol seemed to weigh as much as a sledgehammer. It wavered in the air. She wasn't sure she had the strength to pull the trigger.

The gunman took a step closer, levelled the rifle, a crazed, loopy smile on his face.

Her breath was ragged, but she held it again as she aimed and fired the gun once more. This time, the round caught him in the neck and his head dropped to one side. The shotgun clattered to the floor as the ginger-haired gunman crumpled.

Erica lay still, listening, her ears ringing from the gun blasts, the usually noisy school utterly quiet. The eerie silence was almost as frightening as the gunfire. Her eyes drifted toward the ceiling and it began to spin, go out of focus. She tried to get up, and slipped in her own blood. She vomited as she tried to pull herself back to the room, back to the children. Make sure they were safe.

A whining siren echoed in the distance, growing slowly louder. A door opened. Sounds of children whispering, crying, their tiny feet hardly making any sounds as they came to her like cherubs from heaven.

TWO

The on-scene reporter was a bottled-blond man, with an actor's angular jawline, and a steady, dramatic voice. He held the microphone to his mouth as the camera showed glimpses of the elementary school over his shoulder.

'Details are still coming in,' he advised, 'but we are providing exclusive coverage right now of yet another school shooting; this one, in the small town of Frosthaven, Florida, where, once again, a close-knit community has been ravaged by gun violence. These people are friends, co-workers, and fellow worshippers at the nearby 'Tween Lakes Baptist Church.'

The camera panned over to show the church, which had become a makeshift command post, with policemen from several local agencies swarming around it like bees. Blue and red lights flashed harshly. Streets were crammed with cars parked at odd angles, doors left open, hysterical parents huddled together, screaming into cell phones, held back by yellow crime-scene tape, and reassuring, but guarded, troopers from the Florida Highway Patrol. Across the bottom of the televised broadcast from THN (Televised Headline News), a banner read: **Initial reports: 10 dead. 4 wounded in Florida Elementary School.**

The reporter continued. 'These are humble people of modest income. Hard-working, simple people who, like the rest of us, are wondering, why did this happen here? When will these shootings stop? And, as authorities begin to bring out the wounded and the dead, we are left to question, who did this and why? How did Travis Hanks Elementary School fall in line with Columbine, Virginia Tech, Aurora, and Sandy Hook? What causes these *human tornadoes*, if you will, to visit these innocent communities, and disrupt and devastate them as we all watch in horror and disbelief? Gail, back to you.'

The camera lingered on the reporter, as the news anchor, Gail Summer, turned to her producer, and whispered, 'Did you get that? The human tornado thing? That's brilliant. I'm going to keep it going.' The producer nodded enthusiastically.

'Well, Dave, it's clear that this tragedy is tough for you to report, but I think you've made a significant analogy with your reference to human tornadoes. That's very descriptive of exactly what these mass shootings are. They happen without warning, like a tornado, and literally tear apart the fabric of the community, not just figuratively, but physically and psychologically as well. No one can predict them or stop them, and they seem to be growing in number. And, speaking of numbers, we're getting some additional numbers from the police spokesman right now . . . Can you and your crew catch that, Dave?'

The camera panned back as a police chief pushed through the crowd and took his place on a small dais. Coils of black electrical cables ran like snakes up to the makeshift podium to feed the dozens of cameras and microphones; to feed America's insatiable interest in this obscene phenomenon.

The police chief was from a nearby municipality: Sebring, home of the 12-hour Grand Prix race. Frosthaven did not have its own law enforcement agency, but was covered by several surrounding city and county departments. The Calusa County Sheriff's Office normally had jurisdiction, but the Sebring Police Chief was the first ranking officer on scene, so he was stuck with the command assignment. This included talking to the media; a job he did not like and for which he felt ill-equipped. He stood before the cluster of microphones, staring at them as if they were gun barrels pointed at him, sweat glistening on his pate.

'I'm uh, Chief Dunham with the Sebring Police Department and . . . uh, want to assure everyone that, uh . . . the school grounds are now secure.' He paused to brush sweat off his brow with his sleeve. 'All of the children have been gathered at the Baptist Church, and their parents are collecting them now. Initial entry was made by some of Sebring's PD and Calusa County Sheriff deputies at approximately 8:42 this morning, following an emergency alert made by a staff member at the school. I . . . we . . . have assessed the deceased and wounded, and the injured parties have been transported to nearby hospitals. There are, at this time . . . ,' he paused again to refer to his notes, 'ten school employees that were killed, the names of whom we cannot release at this time, pending notification of their families. I also want to say, though one child is being treated for a minor wound, by some miracle, it appears none of the children were killed. Now, that is all the information I have at this time . . . '

Dave Gruber jumped in. 'Chief Dunham, can you tell us if it's true that one of the teachers had a gun and shot the intruders?'

Chief Dunham looked as if he was punched in the stomach. Wearily, he leaned back toward the bank of microphones. 'I . . . I'd rather not . . .' he began, but as he glanced around the crowd, many of whom were parents who had just picked up their children, he felt he had to say something. 'It does appear that, possibly, one of the teachers was able to obtain a gun and was able to shoot the, uh . . . shooters.'

Questions were hurled like Frisbees at the Chief from the myriad of reporters who were still showing up by the dozens. They were in vans with giant telescoping antennae being manoeuvred and raised. There was a helicopter flying overhead. Chief Dunham felt dizzy.

'Are you saying there was more than one shooter, Chief Dunham?'

'It … appears, at this point, that, uh, there were two shooters.'

'Can you tell us who they were?' asked another reporter.

'I'm sorry,' said the Chief, 'but this is still an ongoing investigation. The last thing I can tell you is that I will be working with local and state law enforcement agencies, and we will let the news media know more as soon as we know more. Now, I have to go.'

Gruber threw in one last long-shot question. 'Can you confirm that one of the shooters survived?'

Chief Dunham looked back at the reporter, frowning. 'No comment,' he said, as he pulled himself away from the crowd and pushed his way back through to the command post, his cell phone ringing audibly.

Gruber whirled back to the camera dramatically. 'There it is, Gail. Police Chief Dunham, from the Sebring Police Department, issuing a statement where, at this point at least, it appears there were two gunmen, one of whom may still be alive. And, more importantly, his statement confirms stories of some heroes arising out of this … maelstrom, if you will, particularly, this unknown teacher who, evidently, was able to wrestle a gun away from one of the shooters and stop them before they killed more today. Gail, back to you … '

Gail Summer's eyes were large and moist, pupils dilated, excited. This was a story that was just going to keep giving.

'Well, okay, thank you,' she said as the camera focused back to her. 'Thanks to Dave Gruber, our reporter with local affiliate, KBFT, Channel 7, out of Orlando, who was first on the scene with coverage for us. We will keep you posted on this … tragedy, yet another school shooting in a tight-knit community located right in the middle of Florida, really, in what some people might call idyllic, small-town America, typical of where so many of these types of incidents are occurring. Once again, we must ask ourselves, why is this happening and where will the next *human tornado* vent its fury? We have to take a break right now, but stay tuned as our coverage of this tragedy continues.'

Governor Scott Croll watched the broadcast in his office as his private plane was being readied for departure. He would be on the ground and at the school in less than an hour. Next to him was Commissioner Jim Bullock, the chief of the Florida Department of Law Enforcement – the FDLE – and one of his top investigators, Special Agent Justin Thiery.

Thiery was a broad-shouldered former quarterback for the University of Florida's Gators, who maintained his upside-down triangle figure with a steady regimen of weights, running, and sparring. He'd originally been with the Capitol Police, the governor's own dedicated police force, but as budgets shrank over the years – *streamlined*, as politicos called it – the CPs were 'absorbed' by the FDLE in the 1990s. Thiery was not happy about being *absorbed*, but what's a guy going to do when he's halfway to a pension? He stayed put, and kept his mouth shut, and did his job. He did it well.

Croll strode over to Thiery and, though the crown of his head barely reached the level of Thiery's coat pocket, he stuck out his hand and shook Thiery's with robust enthusiasm, his persuasive grip conveying a veiled challenge that belied his diminutive size.

'Good to see you again, Agent Thiery. How's the family?' His wide-eyed gaze was engaging, yet unsettling.

Thiery had no idea what Croll was talking about. His wife had left him long ago and his two sons were grown and gone. 'Everyone's fine,' he replied. 'Thank you. And yours?'

Croll cocked his head. 'Where does that accent come from, Agent Thiery? South Georgia?'

'Close enough. I'm a Gainesville native, sir.'

'Ah. Don't meet many of those.' Croll nodded and pursed his lips as if trying to recall something. 'My eldest daughter just made the USA tennis team. We're very proud of her.'

'Outstanding.'

'Yes,' said Croll. 'Did Jim, er, the Commissioner go over our expectations?'

'Yes, sir. I'm to take the lead in the school shooting investigation.'

'That's right. Jim says you're the best man for it.'

Thiery glanced at Bullock, who simply raised his eyebrows.

'I'll do my best, sir. But, can I ask why you want our department to handle this?'

Croll looked at Thiery as if it was obvious. 'We're consolidating our efforts. Trying to increase our efficiency; something I've been asking all of our departments to do. Frankly, there are so many departments on scene down there now, they're tripping over each other. You caught the police chief from Podunk, right?'

Thiery had seen the small town chief on the news, felt bad for him, but there was no way he was going to knock another cop just to cater to a politician. He asked, 'What about ATF or the FBI? One of my associates in Lakeland said the young shooter, what's his name? Coody? Said he'd heard the kid had his apartment booby-trapped.'

'As a matter of fact, the FBI has sent an agent from their WMD office in Miami. A woman named Sara Logan. Know her?'

Thiery took a long breath, let it out slow. He knew her well, though it had been a few years since he'd seen her. He knew her personally. 'We've worked together on some cases.'

'Problems?' asked Croll, noting Thiery's sudden uneasiness.

'No,' he replied.

Croll stared at him now, his lidless eyes like a gecko's. 'If I didn't know better, I'd say you were trying to get out of this assignment, Agent Thiery.' His smile was a painful grimace.

Thiery returned his stare. 'Not at all, sir. I just don't want to get knee deep, then have the case pulled from me by the Feds. Besides, they seem to have resources we don't, anymore.'

Croll forced a laugh. 'You believe this guy, Jim? I thought you'd be thrilled to take part. We need a hero to rise out of this, fellas, and frankly, the FDLE could use one, too.'

'I'm flattered and very interested, sir. It's just … it's going to be a huge case. Complicated. If we're going to follow the Feds' lead, I'd rather it be up front and avoid a hostile takeover, or turf war. That's all.'

Bullock spoke up. 'I think that's all he's trying to say. Right, Justin?'

'That's all I *did* say,' said Thiery.

Croll stopped smiling. 'Well, okay. When you're in the position to make those kinds of decisions, maybe you can go that way. For now, you're the man, the SAS, the Special Agent Supervisor. Our man. Pull this thing together so Florida doesn't continue to look like a bunch of morons who can't even vote right. Do the job you're supposed to be so good at, *capiche*?'

Thiery nodded, but said nothing.

Bullock's face turned red. If he weren't so close to retirement, he'd tell the governor to go fuck himself. He had no right talking to one of his men like that, especially Thiery, a solid cop who'd raised two boys by himself after his wife walked out on him ten years ago.

'I'll be in Washington,' he said blandly.

Croll looked at him as if trying to remember if he'd given him permission to leave the state, his eyebrow arched.

'For the National Police Commissioner's meeting?' Bullock asked.

'Of course,' said Croll, then turned back to Thiery. 'You want to fly down with me, Agent Thiery?' Like he was offering a gift.

'I should probably drive down. If I'm taking lead, I'll need my car to get around.'

'Nonsense. Fly with me. I've got a limo picking me up. It'll be the fastest way. If you need a car, you can check out a cruiser at your Orlando office, right?'

Thiery's jaw muscles flexed. 'Sure,' he said.

In a penthouse suite at the Bellagio Hotel in Las Vegas, eighty-year-old Emilio Esperanza watched the live coverage of the shooting at the Florida elementary school on one of the three big screen

TVs. Another TV was set to the stock market, the sound turned off; banners of numbers flowing across the bottom of the screen reflecting in Esperanza's eyes. The last TV was showing an old black-and-white gangster film. Esperanza picked a speck of tobacco from an unfiltered cigarette off his lip with his bony, blue fingers, and flaked it to the floor, then reached over and turned up the oxygen that ran into his nostrils via a plastic nasal cannula.

'You should have a nurse doing that for you, Papa,' said his son Julio, himself over fifty years old. His thick hair looked like a coiffed chrome helmet on his head. Tanned skin. Teeth like polished porcelain chips. His collar button was open on his starched, maroon shirt, Rat Pack-style, under his tailored, bone-coloured, linen suit.

The old man's eyes slid over to his son's like those of a Komodo dragon eyeing its prey. He raised his wrinkled upper lip as if to spit.

'That didn't work out too well last time, did it?'

Julio cast his eyes to the ground. One way or the other, it would all be over soon. He wished he had the balls to strangle the old man himself, save them both a lot of trouble. But he didn't.

'Time for you to do *something*, Julio.'

'Sure, Papa. Anything.'

'Get that fucking marshal on the phone, *numero uno*. And, *dos*, get your little posse together and get down to Florida. This thing stops now.'

THREE

Erica Weisz lay in a private room in Lakeland Regional Hospital dreaming of fire. She saw only bright orange light and felt searing heat all around her, at once welcoming her and, conversely, pushing her back with its intensity. Then it was gone, as if sucked into a vacuum, taking her life with it, but leaving her body and an all-encompassing emptiness as cold as any Arctic region on earth.

She woke up sweating, strands of hair stuck to her face, tears streaming down her cheeks. A feeling of post-operative nausea and dizziness enveloped her. She sat up with great difficulty and felt pain in her side and lower abdomen. The room spun to a stop, and she was able to see her surroundings in the late afternoon light that filtered through the window: an aseptic hospital room painted a vague green, an uncomfortable-looking vinyl chair for visitors, her chrome-railed bed with unwrinkled sheets as if laid over a corpse.

Her mouth was dry. A small folding table next to the bed held a yellow plastic pitcher of ice water, a clear cup, and a plastic straw. She peeled the paper off the straw, stuck it directly into the pitcher, and drank deeply. She looked at the IV in her arm and up to the bag that fed it. Lactated ringers in a one-litre bag, piggybacked with a half-litre of normal saline, a red tag on the bag that read Amoxicillin on its side. Both were dripping at KVO ('keep vein open') rate. She reached down with one hand and pinched the skin on the back of the other hand. It made a small fleshy tent that lingered for a few seconds before slowly laying back down. She was extremely dehydrated. She glanced up again and saw an empty plastic IV bag, its insides coated with blood. Must be pretty bad if they had to give her blood, too. She reached up and turned the drip rate up on the bag of ringers, and forced herself to drink more water.

She wondered if she'd said anything while under anaesthesia and wondered how long she'd been out. *What happened to the red-haired man after I shot him? Was he dead?* She recalled the urgent jerk of her body as the buckshot caught her in the side and spun her around. She remembered the look of surprise as she fired and caught him in the neck.

Fear crept through her as she thought there might have been other gunmen and that some of the children – those precious children – might now be dead. She hoped she had stopped them all in time. Before they could get to the kids. She remembered being consumed with that goal: *stop these bastards before they hurt anyone else*. She remembered waking up briefly in the recovery room, a doctor speaking to her and she back to him, but she couldn't remember what the conversation was about. Probably previous medical history, current meds, etc. Standard medical questions. *Had she revealed anything?*

The plastic name band on her wrist read: Weisz, Erica. *I didn't tell them everything*, she thought. It gave her relief, made her feel safe, at least for now. But that wouldn't last long. She needed to make a plan; first, she needed to make a phone call.

The phone rang at Robert Moral's home. Moral was in his office, on the computer, playing *Slots Jungle Casino*. Netbet.org had given it a '#6' rating, so he dived right in. Let his wife answer the phone. He heard her banging around in the kitchen then shuffling over to pick it up.

'If it's those vultures from MasterCard,' he hollered to her, 'tell them I already sent a payment, and it is *illegal* – make sure you tell them it's *against the law* – to call a debtor's home and hassle them.'

'But ...' she began.

Moral lost two hundred dollars on his opening bid at a double-down blackjack game. It infuriated him. If he hadn't been distracted ... 'Just fucking tell them!' he roared.

His wife padded to his office as quiet as a cat, her hand over the phone receiver.

'It isn't MasterCard,' she said, trying to ease the bitterness she found in her own voice. 'I think it's that woman. I think she's called before. I recognized the area code.'

She handed him the phone abruptly, glancing at the on-screen gambling site as if it were child pornography. She whirled and left the room; a woman with a heart of gold encased in a two-hundred-twenty-pound bag of cellulite that assured she would hold little regard for herself and forever put up with shit from her husband.

Moral licked his lips with a scotch-dried tongue. He tried to clear his throat, then helped himself to another gulp of booze: J & B's. He winced. No more Johnny Walker Green Label. Hell, not even black or red label these days. *These* days. But he'd get back there. Right after the next big day at the track. Or the tables. The *real* tables. Not these virtual games that were probably rigged to begin with.

'This is Deputy Moral,' he said. Nothing. But, he could hear breathing. It was her. It had to be. And *she knew*. Guilt welled up in him like a longing for another hit at the table.

'Mildred?' He listened for a moment. 'Are you okay?' he tried. 'Can you talk?'

Just the breathing.

'Millie,' he said, gathering his courage after another swig of cheap scotch, 'I'm working on another plan. Don't worry. Stay where you are, and go to safe haven 'B'. We're going to send in an extrication team. You're safe. I'm coming down myself. Okay?'

There was a cough; someone clearing a throat. Then, a click on the other end of the line, a dial tone that seemed to grow louder with every beat of Moral's heart. He felt an icy sweat form on the back of his neck and lower back. He realized, with growing trepidation, that the caller might not have been the woman. *Oh fuck!* he thought.

'Honey?' he pleaded. 'Did you recognize the area code on that call?'

'I think it was from Las Vegas, dear.'

But she wasn't in Las Vegas anymore. His voice quivering, he said, 'You better pack me a bag. I'm going to have to leave. It's … uh, work.'

FOUR

'We have breaking news,' said Gail Summer, looking wearier than she had earlier in the day. 'It has now been confirmed that one of the shooters, nineteen-year-old David Edward Coody, was critically wounded, but has survived. He is currently in a medically induced coma; a decision made by doctors that will allow him to recover if they can control the swelling in his brain. Evidently, a bullet, possibly fired by one of the teachers, hit him in the neck but travelled up and pierced part of his brain. If he does survive, this will be an unusual twist to this recent surge of school shootings where most of the gunmen end up dead, usually by their own hands.

'Adding to this tragedy,' she continued, 'is the discovery of two more bodies, found at the home of Coody's mother, Shelly Granger. It appears, at this time, before going to the school, Coody stopped at his mother's home early this morning and shot her. Evidently, Coody did not live with his mother. He lived with his father, Ellis Coody, who divorced Shelley Granger seven years ago. A second body, thought to be Shelley Granger's husband, Ernest Granger, was also found. Both of them had been shot multiple times.

'We also now know, from several law enforcement agencies' sources, that the second gunman was 41-year-old Franklin Michael Shadtz, a man David Coody recently befriended. Not much is known about Frank Shadtz who, apparently, up to six weeks ago, lived in the Chicago area. It is unknown how the two gunmen met, or exactly what their relationship was.

'Agents from the ATF and FBI responded to David Coody's house after some non-detonated explosives were found at the Granger home. They were met by an uncooperative Ellis Coody, the father of the shooter, who was arrested for interfering with a police investigation. Forensics teams have seized computers at the home, but reports have come back saying the hard drives may have been erased or destroyed.

'And, in another breaking story from Florida,' she went on to report, 'a six-year-old boy shot and killed his four-year-old brother last night, after finding one of his father's loaded guns in the bedroom. The father, a former firefighter, owned sixteen guns. Police say all were loaded, and none had trigger locks. The six-year-old is in the custody of Florida's Department of Family and Children's Services as of this morning. Police officials say the father has been arrested and may be charged with manslaughter ...'

Bullock pulled Thiery off to the side while the governor briefed his press secretary.

'Justin, I know you don't care for the man, but you're smart enough to know who butters your bread. I'm almost out the door, but if you handle this case as well as I know you can, they might look at you to replace me.'

Thiery frowned at him. 'That's supposed to be some kind of incentive?'

Bullock shrugged his shoulders, sweat beginning to bead on his shining black scalp as he cooked under the sun. There were bags under his bulging eyes, and his jowls hung like leather satchels on a big, beefy Harley-Davidson.

'I can't be a politician like you, Jim. I still like being a cop too much.'

'Thanks, man. Why don't you just kick me in the balls?' Bullock said, allowing a slight smile. 'Well, if you don't want my job, try to keep cool so you don't lose yours.'

'I'm sorry, Jim. You were a good cop, too, but you know how it is; I can't stand someone up my ass.'

'You knew there were going to be increased responsibilities when you came to work with me. Don't blow it now. You can last a few more years, can't you?'

Thiery looked at the ground, his hands in his pockets. 'Sometimes, I think I can't last another five minutes when I get around this governor.'

'Oh, c'mon. Hang in there. Show him what you can do. Hell, at the rate he's going, he won't be in office another term.'

'We can only hope. Okay. Sure. You know I'll do my best.'

'You going to be able to work with Logan again?' asked Bullock.

Thiery chewed the inside of his cheek. '*Working* with her was never the problem.'

'I know,' said Bullock, his tone consolatory. 'You had a tough enough time raising the boys after Adrienne left. Then, the shit you got from your own department … '

'You mean when my co-workers started gossiping that maybe I'd done away with my wife? Shit. Why would that bother anyone?'

'I know, I know. You got the crappy end of the stick, for sure. I was just saying, you didn't need Logan doing you dirty, too.'

'It takes two to tango. I should'a known better. She was married. Still is, I think. It was a mistake made by a stupid guy feeling sorry for himself. My bad.'

There was nothing else to say as Thiery allowed to guilt to envelope him. After a moment, Bullock broke the silence.

'All right, then. When I get back, you come over to the house. I'll get Helen to make some of her fried chicken and collard greens,' he offered, then added, 'or some other redneck favourite of yours; friggin' hillbilly.'

Thiery laughed. Bullock making fun of his southern accent was a joke they'd shared for years. Grinning ridiculously, Bullock squeezed his shoulder.

'That's better. Now, I gotta get going, too. I'll see you in a few days. Okay?'

'You bet,' said Thiery, just as the governor came back.

'Ready to go?' asked Croll.

'Absolutely,' replied Thiery, and he managed to give Bullock a wink, unseen by the governor. 'See you, boss.'

Once on the plane, Thiery sat quietly as the governor pored over documents. After a half-hour, he looked up at Thiery, his face taking on a countenance of supreme knowledge. As if just remembering something, he reached into his tailored and severely pressed slacks and pulled out a silver dollar. He handed it to him.

'My father gave that to me when I started my first business. Said he wanted to give me my first dollar *earned*.' He paused like a preacher considering the next words of his sermon. 'I've always believed in that: a man *earning* what he wants.'

Thiery nodded and looked out the small window of the private jet. He guessed where Croll was steering the conversation, but he wasn't taking the bait.

'I went on to *earn* over a half-billion of those,' Croll bragged. 'I'm not bragging. Just wanted to let you know where I came from. What's important to me.'

'I know where you're coming from, Governor,' said Thiery.

He leaned forward, a slight smile on his face. He held out his hand, palm up, the coin flashing in the light through the cabin window. Thiery waved his other hand over the coin, once, then again. The coin vanished after the second pass.

'Well, I'll be damned, Agent Thiery. I didn't know you knew magic! You should do that for my grandson sometime.'

Thiery nodded and went back to looking outside. He could see Croll staring at him in the reflection of the plane's window, wanting his dollar back. He saw him blinking nervously, his Adam's apple moving up and down, like a snake swallowing something, trying to figure out a way to ask for his money back without seeming as if he needed it.

'I, er … uh …' Croll mumbled. 'That coin has some sentimental value.'

'It's in your top pocket,' said Thiery, calmly.

Croll reached in – too quickly – and found it there. He beamed, but Thiery noted the sweat on his forehead.

Thiery physically had to bite his tongue as the governor's words echoed through his head: *Now you know where I'm coming from.*

FIVE

Robert Moral grabbed the first flight he could find out of Ronald Reagan National Airport going to Orlando, Florida. He had watched the news unfolding about the school shooting. He knew that Erica Weisz had been shot, but when he tried to call the hospital, they wouldn't let him talk to her. Moral felt as if his guts had turned to water, and it was all he could do to keep them from running out his ass. He called the Sheriff's office, found the shift supervisor, and identified himself as a US Marshal investigating a person of interest to their department. That's all he had to say as a federal agent. After calling a number to verify who Moral was, the supervisor called him back and confirmed that Miss Weisz had been shot, but was stable. They had not been able to talk to her yet, but she was under guard at the hospital. If she woke from her surgery, they intended to ask her some questions about the event at the school. Moral gave the supervisor his phone number, and asked him to call him as soon as someone from the Sheriff's department made contact with her. No, he couldn't elaborate but, please, he pleaded, just do this.

Gail Summer's eyes were glassy. She was as tired as an Iditarod sled dog, and she looked as if she might have been crying, but she wanted to use that look, so she had told the producers of THN she would stay on for another four-hour shift. They applauded her willingness, professionalism, and perseverance.

'This just in: the victim toll from this morning's school shooting in Frosthaven, Florida has officially reached twelve dead; a number that now includes the mother of David Edward Coody, Shelly Granger and her husband Ernest, as well as the second gunman, Franklin Michael Shadtz. The number of wounded stands at four, and includes one child who was treated and released with minor injuries.

'The school's front desk receptionist, Sally Ravich, is one of the wounded survivors. She has been credited for possibly saving dozens of lives by activating the school's intercoms and alerting the school of the attack. The other two wounded are Coody, one of the gunmen, and, finally, Erica Weisz, a teacher who, by some accounts, was responsible for saving, not only the lives of the students assigned to her, but quite possibly many others. She was, reportedly, the teacher who armed herself and fought back against the heavily armed intruders. On scene and giving us live, exclusive coverage of this tragedy is Dave Gruber. Dave, do you have anything new for us about Erica Weisz?'

The camera shot switched to Gruber, the Lakeland Regional Hospital in the background. The reporter held his hand against his ear, the mic to his mouth, as he continued the story.

'Yes, Gail, we're here at the hospital where not only some of the survivors were taken but one of the gunmen as well. We've been trying to get an interview with Erica Weisz, the brave young teacher who, it's been reported, was able to obtain a gun and shoot the gunmen, in a strange twist of fate we don't usually see at these tragedies. It's been reported that she has undergone surgery and is recovering, but that's all we've been able to get from the hospital's public information spokesperson. Now, the alleged gunman, we've learned, is still in a medically induced coma, but we've also learned that David Edward Coody was a troubled young man. As we've seen in other cases like this, Coody was a loner who seldom talked to classmates and, in fact, did attend classes at Travis Hanks Elementary School several years ago. More recently, he was a student at the University of Central Florida where he was majoring in agricultural science, until he dropped out about six weeks ago. There have been sporadic reports from fellow students that he'd been seeing a psychiatrist, but we don't have a specific diagnosis as to what he was being treated for. We'll keep you informed as we get new information. This is Dave Gruber, reporting for THN. Gail?'

'Thank you, Dave. We'll get back to you soon. Now, we have to take a break but please stay with us for live, up to the minute coverage of the Tragedy at Travis Hanks, and, later, please tune in to my own show, *The Summer Report*, where I'll be discussing the Human Tornado Phenomenon with our guest, celebrity psychologist and best-selling author, Dr Jay Gill.'

Before cutting to commercial, they ran a video clip showing a seriously concerned-looking Dr Gill, who was commenting, in his pseudo-southern drawl, 'I agree, Gail, these *Human Tornadoes*, as you call them, come in like a wrecking ball and destroy so many lives, and it's usually because they come from destroyed lives themselves. They're looking for what we are all looking for: love and acceptance … '

Thiery accepted Croll's offer to drop him by the FDLE offices in Orlando, where he had called ahead and arranged to pick up a loaner cruiser. The governor went on to meet the media at the school while Thiery filled out the necessary paperwork and picked up the navy blue fleet car; a gas-guzzling Crown Vic that smelled like cigarettes, and was home to an army of black ants that lived in the Burger King detritus littering the floor.

The drive from Orlando to Frosthaven was soporific. The air conditioning in the car held the shimmering outside heat at bay, but made Thiery's eyelids heavy. He felt as if he was dreaming as he drove into the nightmare ahead. Crows stood along the arid road as if too tired to fly, their beaks parted, pointed tongues jutting out as if issuing a silent warning. The topography was mostly flat; wildlands turned into cattle pastures or citrus farms. A cow's skull hung on the gate of a ranch he passed. One stretch of highway looked exactly like the last, but Thiery grew more anxious with each passing mile. There was a segment of I-4, then on to US 27, a two-lane road that provided a singular hopeful moment when it snaked through Lake Wales where the old Bok, or 'Singing' Tower stood, its bells tolling as Thiery drove by. The area's small hills and moss-covered oaks reminded him of his home in northern Florida and made him long to be there.

He listened to the carillons playing, a melancholy sound that reminded him of the music from *Phantom of the Opera*. He slowed the car and opened the windows to hear the haunting sounds better, then found himself thinking of masked gunmen bearing assault weapons, strafing their way through a small schoolhouse filled with frightened children. He became filled with an empty sadness, then anger, considering the incongruity of the beautiful music and the atrocious event that had brought him here. He never had to worry about such tragedies when his boys were at school, and he wondered what was happening to society as a whole. *Was it lost? Could it get any worse?* In just over a year, the country had gone through the Aurora theatre shootings, the Sandy Hook shootings, and the Boston Marathon bombing, all perpetrated by young men, most, barely out of their teens.

He thought of his sons, Owen and Leif, and wondered how they were doing. He tried to call them, just to check on them, but neither answered. He made a mental note to try again when he got settled in to whatever cheap motel he could find.

Thiery stopped at a convenience store to get a soda. While browsing the shelves, he watched a couple pull up to the gas pumps. They both got out of the car. The man had no arms and his wife placed something in his top shirt pocket before grabbing the pump handle and inserting it into the car. Thiery noted she had huge biceps and wondered if it was because she had to do more with her arms because her husband could not. The man came into the store. He nodded to the clerk and leaned forward, obviously a regular customer there. The clerk withdrew a credit card from the armless man's shirt pocket and looked out the window to see which pump he was at. Thiery marvelled at the symbiotic relationship the trio shared. His loneliness bore down on him again, and he tried to shrug it off as he got back into his car and onto the road.

Thirty minutes later, he arrived in Frosthaven. It was easy to find the only elementary school in town. The governor had beaten him to the scene by about fifteen minutes. Thiery was pleased with that. He didn't want to arrive together and appear to be Croll's gopher boy, though in truth, that was exactly what he was. Thiery was comfortable talking with the press, but didn't want to try to talk over the governor as they searched for the right words to address a community undoubtedly in shock and looking for answers that would not be easily forthcoming.

He parked the car and saw the governor already talking to the media. Generator-fed lights beamed bright spots into his face before the sunset. Croll looked like a small nocturnal creature caught in the shadows. Thiery knew he should go over and stand next to him as he, in turn, would designate the FDLE as the organization that would be taking over the investigation. But the thought of asking the local police chief to step aside while he and Croll bathed in the limelight did not appeal to him. He decided, instead, to take a quick look at the school, first. The governor was in love with the cameras, and it would be a perfect opportunity for him to remind everyone what a wonderful, caring man he was. Thiery expected he would milk every second of it.

He noted dozens of memorials had already been placed on the sidewalk: pastel teddy bears, bouquets of flowers, signs made up with words like 'God Bless you, Dr Montessi' and 'We will never forget you, Mrs LaForge', written with magic markers in a rainbow of colour. 'So long, Mr Swan', 'Thanks for taking care of us, Nurse Nora. Now, God will take care of you'. Candles lined the path and flickered in the slight breeze. Crude, white crosses made out of pressure-treated furring strips stuck in the grass. Several children, embraced by their parents, sang softly as they rocked back and forth, comforting each other.

Thiery pushed past the yellow plastic crime-scene tape that surrounded the school and identified himself to the phalanx of Calusa County Sheriff deputies who stood guard. One of them radioed his supervisor for the okay to allow the FDLE agent inside.

Thiery entered the main office first, as the shooters had. The reception desk had been shredded by bullets. Walls were pocked with holes. There were blood stains on the tile floors, marker tape where bodies had fallen, a red smear on the wall, ending in a handprint. Thiery noted something he couldn't quite make out, lying on the desk in a dried pool of blood. He produced a small Mag light he kept with him and shone it on the puddle. Bone fragments and broken teeth. He wondered if the person they belonged to had lived, and if so, what did he or she look like, now?

He caught himself holding his breath, trying not to inhale the death-filled air, as if by doing so, he was in some metaphysical way taking something from the victims. He shook off the feeling and tried to breathe through his mouth, so he wouldn't smell the burnt scent of carnage.

He proceeded slowly down the hall, passing another taped outline next to a janitor's work cart and another blood stain, its edges smudged, probably from the victim rolling around in pain. He continued on.

Around the corner, he saw yet another taped outline and began to feel anger building up inside. He tried to push it away and remain objective, professional, but he'd always been a man ruled by his emotions and not his intellect. True, it was a detriment as a law officer, but people are who they are; with very few exceptions, that can't be changed.

He focused on a ceiling light, blown off by a shotgun blast. Hanging precariously from a piece of electrical conduit pipe, it swung slowly back and forth, like a metronome, the acoustic ceiling tiles around it dotted like Swiss cheese.

Thiery began to look into the classrooms. Nothing of note in the first few. Then he came to one where the door was battered and its window shattered. Entering the room, he discovered another taped outline and scattered bullet casings with small, numbered notes next to them. *Had to be one of the gunmen.* He looked around the room, observing the devastation: the closet where the children must have taken refuge, a pile of overturned desks. Plywood had been affixed to the blown out windows, but a steady, cool wind crept into the room. Thiery shivered as he saw a small pink shoe with a single drop of blood on it. His eyes grew moist and his jaw muscles flexed involuntarily. He thought of his sons again, remembering them as school-age kids, confused and angry about a mother who had simply left them behind one day. Dropped them at school and disappeared. They directed their anger at him for being a cop who worked all the time, but couldn't even find his own wife. In spite of that, they'd grown up okay, if a bit distant from him.

Thiery looked down, surprised to see his fists clenched.

He exited the classroom and resumed his tour of the hall, past more taped outlines, more emptied cartridges and shotgun shells, more numbered tags next to them. More blood. The smell of gunpowder had permeated the walls and ceiling, and the coppery scent of blood assaulted his nostrils.

Via email and texts on his tablet, Thiery had been getting updates throughout the day from the local police agencies involved and had finally received the names of all the victims. With the exception of the janitor, they were all women. He wondered about that. *Were there no men teachers? If so, why weren't some of them shot? Wouldn't they be more likely to confront a shooter?* Typically, one doesn't find many male teachers at an elementary school, but it seemed to him there should be *some*.

He completed his initial reconnaissance of the school and followed his path back through the U-shaped building, jotting down notes on his iPad and checking for any new reports coming in. As he went back through the main office he came to the nurses' station. The window of the door was blasted out; another taped outline on the floor, more blood stains. The mailroom had been sprayed with bullets, but the cubby-holes where teachers picked up their messages were relatively unscathed. He read the names on the boxes, mostly women's names, but a few belonging to men, too. He checked the contents in the boxes that were clearly male: Ed Bremen, a teacher, stored documents from the Calusa County School Board referencing special needs children; Tim Cress, the coach, had stowed a whistle and a stack of after-school soccer flyers; Randy Perry had lunch schedules and dietician reports, indicating he supervised the cafeteria staff.

So there were, indeed, some men who worked in the school. But the only one shot was James Swan, the janitor. Thiery tried to accept it was just a numbers thing; the ratio of men to women was such that it was logical more women would be shot. But, as he left the school and walked back to the church that the authorities were using as the command centre, he couldn't let it go. Did the shooters have a problem with women? Were they men who hated their mothers and decided to make these women pay for their angst? Did they come home one day, as he and his sons had, to find their wives or mothers gone?

Governor Croll was pontificating to the media as Thiery arrived at the church.

' ... as we send these special people – our friends, family, co-workers, protectors, and teachers of our children – to be with God, we must reaffirm our intent to *never* let this happen again.' He banged his fist on the podium to accentuate his message. 'I say we do *not* allow these people to die in vain. Let's utilize their ... ultimate sacrifice to make our schools, our communities, and our lives safer. I've been on the phone today with governors from around this great nation, and with the President, and there is a groundswell of support for this community, and for newer, tougher laws to protect innocent citizens from harm. Please stand with us and help make the changes we need in order to protect our children and our children's children. Be safe, be strong, be better. Thank you, and may God bless and keep you.'

A moving speech until Thiery remembered the last line, 'Be safe, be strong, be better,' had been used as Croll's campaign slogan. That was all he was doing: campaigning. Thiery wondered what the governor's NRA backers would think of him now. He'd previously run on a platform of protecting Second Amendment rights and, by so doing, had amassed an unprecedented campaign war chest. While he had not said the words 'gun control' in his speech, he was certainly suggesting it. This, coming from a governor whose first order of business was to walk a bill through legislation called the Stand Your Ground Law, allowing ' … Florida residents to justifiably use force in self-defence when there is reasonable belief of an unlawful threat, without an obligation to retreat first … ' Now, here he was, suggesting just the opposite. *What a chameleon*, thought Thiery.

Croll stepped off the dais, but continued to address the barrage of cameras stuck in his face. As he spoke, he saw Thiery standing nearby and waved him over.

'This is Special Agent Justin Thiery,' the governor announced to the hungry media, 'from the Florida Department of Law Enforcement. He will be taking over as lead in this most important investigation. Police Chief George Dunham and Sheriff Conroy have done an excellent job responding to this community's emergency needs today and coordinating the initial command. But,' he continued, 'as this tragedy affects so many people in nearby communities, and there are a myriad of law enforcement agencies involved, I felt it in the best interest of justice for the investigation to be placed under one umbrella. One directly under my *personal* supervision, and so the FDLE will be that lead. Agent Thiery?'

Thiery shot a quick glance toward the police chief from nearby Sebring and hoped the governor had given him some notice before pulling the rug out from under him. He was a smaller man, maybe hitting five foot seven with his work shoes on, a ring of premature grey hair nesting around an otherwise bald head. He appeared even smaller in his oversized uniform, though he kept it sharply pressed and neat. Next to him was a tall man with thick, dark hair on his head and arms; the latter were crossed as if he were angry. The five o'clock shadow on his massive jaw looked as if it had been drawn by a cartoonist. His eyes were black and glinted in the media lights, as did the huge gold badge and name tag on his formidable chest. Thiery could barely make out the man's name: Sheriff A. Conroy.

Thiery looked over at Dunham. Rather than indignation, Thiery thought he spied relief. He could almost see him sigh and was, once again, mindful of stepping on a fellow law enforcement officer's toes. He approached and extended his hand. Dunham took it and gripped Thiery's huge paw with a ferocity that quietly said, *I'm glad you're here.*

Conroy jutted his chin up, but did not extend his hand. Thiery could feel the turf protection and accompanying resentment from him, big time.

'Thank you, Chief Dunham,' said Thiery. 'I've been inside the school, and it looks like your men did a very thorough job.' He said it loud enough for the reporters around them to hear. The short, balding, and oh-so-humble police chief nodded, accepting the affirmation. Thiery fielded questions from several reporters before finally ending with, 'I still need to meet personally with Chief Dunham and his officers, the Calusa County's Sheriff Deputies, and several other involved agencies. The FDLE will be collating all the information from each of the very professional departments that responded today to assess what we know and what we need to learn to move forward with this investigation. Now, if you'll excuse me, I have considerable work to do.'

Thiery stepped away from the crowd, and Croll immediately grabbed him by the elbow and ushered him to the side as reporters, still ravenous for some sound bites, lighted on Chief Dunham. Thiery watched as Dunham was forced to struggle through a few more questions about what he first saw, what his officers first saw, what they thought was happening, *et cetera*. Thiery thought the police chief held up well for a man who had been on his feet for twelve hours.

Conroy stepped over, obligatorily, and said, 'I'm Sheriff Conroy,' and handed his card to Thiery. There was a lump in his lower lip where he held a chaw of tobacco that made his teeth brown and syrupy looking.

'Did you …' began Thiery, but Conroy held up his paw like a STOP sign.

'We've just been supplying the manpower. It was my SWAT that came in but all the vics and perps were down by then and we didn't fire a shot. The little chief over there was first on the scene and that's why he has command.'

Thiery took the hint. He didn't have the patience or the temperament to come down here, sort through a mass tragedy with all its witnesses, reports, media, and evidence collection, *and* deal with some cowpoke cop's ego. He'd be professional and polite, but work around the man whenever circumstances allowed.

'Hey there, Alton,' said a voice from behind Thiery. 'Sorry we didn't get a chance to talk earlier.'

'Understood, Governor Croll,' said Conroy, smiling for the first time, though it looked painful for him to do so.

'You've met Agent Thiery, then?'

'Uh, yeah. More or less. I was just tellin' him, we wish we'd handled more of this, but it was, unfortunately, over by the time we got here and sent in our SWAT.'

'Understood,' said Croll. 'Well, sooner or later we'll get the county consolidated. It only makes sense, right? Need to have everyone under one umbrella with one strong leader, right? It's a waste of resources to keep all these ma and pa departments separate. Taxpayers won't stand for it anymore.' He stopped and looked around as if to see if anyone was listening to him. 'Can't believe it's happened here. I would've thought if one of these events happened in Florida, it would've been in Miami. How are Janine and the girls?'

'They're fine, thanks,' said Conroy. 'Oldest is married, now, and the youngest is a junior up at UF. I'm glad they're not around here for this. Both of them used to go here when this town used to be a nice, quiet place. Now, we can barely keep up with the ghetto people moving in, people making meth in their garages.'

'Yes, it's a shame,' Croll added dolefully. 'You let Agent Thiery know if you or your men need anything. He has direct access to me. Now, where is my car? I've got to get gone.'

Croll and Conroy shook hands and Conroy drifted off, back through the masses that drew away from him, like Moses parting the Red Sea.

'You did well, Agent Thiery,' said Croll, when the two men were away from the crowd. 'That's what I was talking about when we discussed earning rewards earlier today. Outstanding. You show great confidence.'

'Thank you, sir, but we still have a lot of work to do.'

'Oh, of course,' said Croll. 'But, you'll get it done. Get with these other departments. Alton's a good guy, and the other fella, Chief Dormer, or whatever his name is, seems all right. Put together a report and let's move on. There'll be gun control fanatics and hordes of media people trying to wring every story out of every poor soul that lives within ten miles of here. The quicker something like this is put behind us, the sooner the town will heal. So, give it a few days, and get back to Tallahassee.' He grasped Thiery's arm like a father making a point to his teenage son. 'You know, Jim, er, uh, the Commissioner is going to retire in less than a month, and I'd like to have his successor in place before he leaves, so he can mentor him. How'd you like Jim to give you his best on the way out the door?'

Thiery shook his head. 'I can't even think about that right now, Governor.'

Croll gave him the gecko look, again, and said, 'Don't look a gift horse in the mouth, *Mister* Thiery.'

'I'm not trying to be disrespectful, sir, but I see this investigation lasting weeks, maybe months, as we put together a prosecutable case.'

Croll scrunched up his face. 'Investigation? What's to investigate? We know who the shooters are. Not much in the grey area there, would you say, Agent Thiery?'

They walked in silence for a moment as they made their way toward the governor's limousine, Thiery's blood pressure rising with each step. Then Croll broke the uncomfortable void.

'Do you know Brian Ahearn, the Fire Chief, up in Tallahassee?' he asked.

Thiery shook his head. 'No, sir. Can't say we've met.'

'You should meet him some time. Smart guy. We go golfing every Thursday afternoon; he has a great swing. He's a man looking to move up, maybe take an appointment somewhere. I bet you'd hate to have a former *firefighter* take over that commissioner job.'

Thiery listened to the threat but he did not respond.

'Anyway, you know what he told me? He told me about when he used to be out in the streets, when he went to a multi-car accident, a ten-car pile-up say, on the interstate, or wherever. He said the worst thing he and his men could do was stay on the scene too long. The best thing to do was to *clear the scene* as quickly as possible. He told me the longer they were there, the more dangerous the scene could get with traffic backing up and such, and once the initial patient care was taken care of, if they didn't get off scene quickly, more and more motorists would come up and say they were hurt. It was as if these people would convince themselves that they must be hurt, too, if they were just *near* such an accident. Most of them were opportunists looking to get their name on an accident report so they could sue somebody. People want to blame somebody for something, then lawyer up and make money off it.'

They were at the limo now, the governor's driver holding the back door open for him. Thiery didn't know quite what to make of the governor's soliloquy, but he refused to play into his hands. He pulled back his jacket sleeve and looked at his watch. Almost ten o'clock. He felt his neck stiffen from fatigue and not a little bit of anger. *This governor is an asshole*, he reminded himself. *Just let it be.*

'By the way, Agent Thiery, I talked to the President today. He's going to come down here, talk to the families of the deceased. He's fascinated with this woman; the teacher who shot the intruders. He's going to want to talk to her, in particular. Better get to her quickly, before she lawyers up, too.'

'I'm doing my job, sir,' said Thiery, dryly.

'Good,' said Croll, regaining his shit-eating grin. 'Keep it moving. Let's clear the scene, *capiche?*'

Thiery was looking around for his innocuous sedan when he saw Sara Logan standing among the parked cars, watching him, tapping her lower lip with her cell phone. He hadn't seen her in three years. She looked the same. Blonde, short-cropped, spiky hair, green eyes that slanted up at the corners, a nose that looked fragile, mocha skin. She had a scar on her chin from running through a glass door when she was a teenager. She'd been banging the neighbour's son when her father came looking for her. She ran through the glass like Bruce Willis in an action film. Still, the scar didn't detract from her exotic looks. Gorgeous, but the word *carnivorous* came to Thiery's mind. His stomach filled with crawling things and he drew in a breath.

He'd weaned himself off her after she'd dumped him, let her come back to his bed from time to time, until it was more painful to see her than get laid, then swore off her. She took it with a shrug of her shoulders. She'd made it clear she wasn't looking for a relationship. She was looking for a hard, sweaty lay, and that's what she used Thiery for. She and her much older husband, a contractor who built bridges, had made the choice not to have children. He had grown-up kids from a previous marriage. He wanted to travel, eat out every night, and have an attractive young lady on his arm. She could fulfil that obligation and still maintain her career, which she loved because it validated her professionalism and allowed her certain freedoms.

Thiery had just been a glorified dildo for her.

'Hi, Sara,' said Thiery, trying to find his voice.

She used that smile that was warm, welcoming, and as disingenuous as a Coach purse sold on the streets of Bangladesh. She stepped closer, placing her hand on his shoulder and pushed herself against his chest. A light kiss on his cheek – very, very near his mouth – then she pulled away, leaving a cloud of musky scent that made him want to throw her in the back seat of the nearest car.

He hated himself for that.

'Hi, Justin,' she said, completely aware of what she did to him, to most men. 'Bad day, huh?'

He cleared his throat, attempting to regain some semblance of professionalism. She was looking him over again, assessing him.

'What's your role here, exactly?' he asked.

She let her eyes roam over him without hurry, or embarrassment. Her pupils were dilated. 'Whatever you need,' she said, the double entendre dripping off her words. That smile again. 'I'm here for federal presence in case there's something beyond what it looks like.'

'Well,' said Thiery, 'on the surface, it seems like most school shootings. One of the perps used to attend the school years ago. Not sure about the other one, yet. I don't see anything that would lead me to believe this was a terrorist act, domestic or foreign. I heard the explosives they found were just pipe bombs and homemade crap.'

'So were the pressure cooker bombs in Boston.'

'Understood. I just don't think you'll find much that demands you or your department's time.'

Logan shrugged. 'So, I hang out and assist as needed. Maybe liaison with ATF, take one monkey off your back. Okay? I'm not trying to interfere.'

Thiery knew this to be true. She might be a horny woman with a questionable moral compass, but she was a damn good investigator, too. She was insightful, and she had helped him on several huge and legally tricky cases in the past.

'One of the teachers reportedly shot the intruders,' Thiery continued. 'Her name is Erica Weisz. Maybe you could look into why she had a gun in a public school. Did she have a permit to carry and, if so, why? I'll let you know if I need anything else,' he ended, knowing full well how she would interpret those words.

'Where are you staying?' she asked, lowering her chin but raising those cat eyes back up at him.

He hesitated before telling her but figured she probably knew already. She'd once told him that she'd looked up his credit rating, knew which Internet sites he visited most often, and what grades his kids made in school. She was a Fed, so what was alarming about that? It was creepy, but not surprising to him.

'I'm at a little cheesy joint up the road, The Sun Beam Motel. There's nothing else nearby unless you want to go up to Lake Wales or Orlando.'

'I'm in Orlando, at the Gaylord Palms. You know I couldn't stay somewhere I had to worry about my feet sticking to the carpet.'

'Of course not,' said Thiery.

Her Blackberry rang, and she put up a finger as if asking him to wait, then put the phone to her ear and turned away. He watched her walk to her car and felt his heart sink. Her blue FBI windbreaker failed to cover the ass that filled out her tactical pants. It taunted him like a schoolyard bully.

'Ah, shit,' he said to no one.

SIX

Erica couldn't sleep. They offered her pain medication, but she refused it. She wanted to be alert. The news covering the shooting was on; she tried not to watch it, but almost every channel had coverage of it. She was pleased none of the children had been killed, and terrified when they kept flashing a picture of her on the screen as they played up her role as a hero. They must've obtained it from the Calusa County School Board from her identification badge. It wasn't a great picture, but it was good enough for someone looking for her to recognize.

The photo popped up again, this time in response to one of the mothers of a student being interviewed. The reporter asked what she'd like to say to Erica Weisz, the hero of Travis Hanks Elementary. With a microphone in her face, her deep southern drawl making it difficult to understand, the woman said, 'Yeah, I s'pose she is a hero.' Her emphasis on HEE-row mortified Erica and she wished the reporters would just stop. 'I mean, she saved the kids' lives, right?' the mother continued, 'but, what would I like to say to her? I guess I should say thank you. But, to be truthful, I'd like to ask why she had a gun in a public school.' The footage stopped with the woman's face framed on screen mid-sentence, her mouth twisted, and her hair driven back by the wind making her look severe and angry.

The reporter for a THN affiliate, a woman whose hair didn't move when the wind blew, returned her attention to the camera and said, 'there you have it, a thankful parent. But, as we've begun to hear, there are questions about where the gun came from that Erica Weisz used to slay the shooters. Initial reports came in saying she had wrestled the gun away from intruders, but police are now saying it at least appears she may have brought the gun onto school grounds, which, according to school officials, is strictly forbidden.'

Erica turned off the television, her anxiety growing. She noted the nurses had left the syringe that inflated the bulb in her Foley catheter next to the bed. She used it to deflate the Foley and drew it painfully out of her urethra. When she looked at the collection bag, she saw she wasn't producing much urine. An ominous sign.

Keeping intact the electronic monitoring devices hooked up to her, so as not to alert the nurses, Erica pulled the IV out of her arm. They had used a large bore, 14-gauge catheter, and the hole it left behind started to bleed. She held a tissue on it and used the tape that held the IV in her arm to secure the tissue over the wound. Then, she slowly got out of the bed, her abdomen so sore it took several attempts to simply sit up. Finally, she made it into a semi-erect posture, crossed the room, and peeked outside the door. Thank God for long electrical cords and beds with wheels.

Her legs were trembling from the loss of blood and the freezing air conditioning. A wave of nausea swept over her, but passed as she took a few deep, calming breaths. Icy sweat frosted over her forehead and lower back, but warmed slowly as her circulation began to flow again. An empty chair was outside her door, a walkie-talkie sitting atop a folded newspaper. The Calusa County Sheriff's deputy assigned to stand guard at her room had moved to the nurses' station and was flirting with the one of the women. She would have only a few minutes.

She looked under her hospital bed and found a plastic bag with her name scribbled on it in block letters. Inside were her underwear, running shoes, and purse, *sans* the pistol. The dress had probably been taken by the police to examine the blast pattern. Her side felt as though it might rip open as she bent over and retrieved her belongings. She gritted her teeth and wondered if she would be able to maintain consciousness. After a few deep breaths, the pain subsided, and she looked around the room. On the back of the door was a long, white lab coat with a name tag. It would have to do.

She brought her purse over to the sink in the disability-equipped bathroom adjoining her small room. She quickly washed her face, brushed her hair, and spruced up her sallow complexion with a little make-up. She wasn't going to win any beauty pageants, but she might pass for something other than a bloodless zombie. She peeked out the door one more time and saw the deputy was still preoccupied. At the very last moment, she took a deep breath then pulled off the pulse oximeter cord, blood pressure cuff, and the EKG electrodes. It would take a moment for the lights to indicate a problem at the nurses' station, another minute or so for one of the nurses to notice, and another moment for them to convince themselves the patient hadn't accidentally pulled the monitors off rolling over in her sleep. In all, she could expect a minimum of three minutes before they would come in to check on her.

Erica pushed open the door and turned quickly down the hall without looking back. She walked with purpose, sucking up the pain, not hurrying, but assuming the role of an efficient nurse looking for something for one of her patients. It had been a familiar role at one time.

She found the room where nurses kept their personal belongings in lockers with names taped to the front. Only two or three were locked. Evidently, most of the nurses knew and trusted each other. Erica tried to remember when last she could trust anyone; it seemed a lifetime ago. Feeling guilty but having no choice, she found some women's clothing: a pair of jeans and a Lady Antebellum concert T-shirt. She rolled them up and shoved them into her purse, then noticed the door to the supply closet adjoined the dressing room.

She wanted to simply leave – ASAP – but it might be worth her while to take a quick glance.

Erica stepped into the supply closet and looked around. She noted the narcotics were locked in a refrigerated glass case, as they should be, but most of the non-narcotic drugs were on the shelves. She threw a bag of normal saline into her purse, some bandaging and IV materials, and was just reaching for the Amoxicillin when the door opened behind her. She turned to find a young doctor standing there, fumbling with his keys, trying to find the one that opened the narcotics cabinet. He looked up at her.

He frowned, obviously not recognizing her. She hoped that the hospital had enough part-time nurses that her being there wouldn't draw curiosity. The doctor smiled and held the bunch of keys in his hand.

'I can never find the right key to open this thing.'

Erica smiled back and nodded, but her heart was racing now. She felt sweat forming on her upper lip and swallowed dryly. Then, she felt something move down her arm. She glanced down and saw blood beginning to seep through the lab coat where the IV had been.

'Haven't seen you around here before,' he said, as he fumbled with the keys.

Erica swallowed dryly. 'I'm … I work *per diem* … you know, with a registry. I … uh, usually do private duty but the registry called me today and said the hospital needed more staff, so … '

The doctor stared at her for a moment, his eyes meeting hers, as if contemplating what she told him. He turned his attention back to the keys and finally found the right one that opened the cabinet. He withdrew a vial of morphine, jotted his initials on a form attached to a clipboard inside the cabinet and was about to close it when he turned back to her.

'Need anything out of here before I close it?'

'Uh, no,' she managed, trying to keep her voice from breaking. 'No, thank you. I was just getting some Amoxicillin.'

'Oh,' he said. 'For the patient in 309?' His eyes went to her sleeve and saw the spot of blood. She could see him staring at it.

Erica's mind began to race. She thought she might lose it, but managed to hold herself together.

'The teacher with the gunshot wound?' he added, his eyes now locking with hers. 'Not too many other trauma patients here right now.'

Erica stared at him for a moment thinking she'd been discovered, then nodded slowly.

'She's some lady, huh?' the doctor continued. 'Poor thing, they had to take some shotgun pellets out of her abdomen. A few nicked her spleen, but they managed to save it. She's got some healing to do, but I heard she is going to be fine. Good thing that she had that gun. Probably saved every kid in that school. That's a hero in my book. Take good care of her, eh?' He turned to go out the door, then stopped and turned back to her. 'Grab a coffee later on?'

'Uh … okay,' she said.

'I'm sorry,' he said, coming back into the room. 'I'm Doctor Spirazza. Todd,' he said, extending his hand. 'And you are …?'

Erica couldn't look down at the name tag on her coat without giving herself away.

'Susan,' she said, smiling broadly.

The doctor frowned. 'Nice to meet you … Susan.' He stood there for a minute as if he were waiting for her to say something. 'It says "Melissa" on your name tag.'

Erica looked down at it, feeling her face flush. 'Oh, shoot. Mel and I came on the same time tonight. We were so busy gabbing that we must've accidentally grabbed each other's coats.'

The doctor stood gazing at her for another moment, then smiled. 'I've got to finish my rounds, but I'll be looking for that coffee in about an hour, or so. Think you can break away then?'

Erica licked her lips, trying to be a little sexy, but her tongue was as dry as her lips, and it was like licking flypaper. 'An hour, sure,' she gulped. 'Meet you at the nurses' station then?'

He winked at her as he left the room, then hesitated again. 'You've got some blood on your sleeve,' he said.

Erica looked down, again, as if surprised, and could see the stain had spread.

'Oh, damn. Must be from the gunshot patient. I was changing her dressing. Melissa will have a tizzy fit if I don't get that out. Thanks for telling me.'

The doctor smiled again, turned, and sped off toward his rounds.

Erica had to sit down for a moment or she would have fainted. She put her head between her legs and breathed slowly. She rolled up the sleeve and wrapped some gauze around the IV site.

When she stood up this time, she made a beeline into the hall and hung a left. She found the elevators and pushed the button. As she waited, she looked back down the corridor. The cop that had been flirting with the nurse was walking back to Erica's room, the nurse accompanying him. The nurse was with him. Erica's heart began to race again. She looked at the elevator light above the door that indicated which floor the car was coming from. Three more floors to go.

The cop and the nurse entered her room. She was screwed. Within thirty seconds, both emerged. She heard the nurse say, 'I can't imagine where she could've gone with her injuries, or why she would've removed her IV. It doesn't make sense. I'll look to the left, you go to the right. I'll notify my supervisor, too.' They weren't panicky yet, but it was clear they wanted to find her and get her back where she belonged. The cop started in Erica's direction. She held her breath.

Ding. The elevator finally arrived at her floor. The doors stayed shut for what seemed an eternity. She wanted to dig her nails into the crack between them and pry them apart. When they finally opened with a sucking sound, Erica darted inside. Then, the doors took forever to close. As they finally began to inch toward each other, she saw the cop walk past, looking both ways, but not into the elevator.

Once in the lobby, Erica practically ran out of the hospital and into the parking lot. She walked away into the darkness, feeling safer with every step, but her side began to throb with pain. She leaned against a car and tried to catch her breath. Looking into her purse, she took out the stolen clothes, kicked off her Nikes and began to pull the jeans on. As she was doing so, she noticed a lump in one of the hip pockets and stuck her fingers in to investigate. Car keys. With a remote door lock. She finished sliding into the pants, then discarded the lab coat, and pulled on the T-shirt. The jeans were huge in the waist, the shirt baggy, but they would do for now. She squeezed her shoes back on without untying the laces. She noticed dots of her own blood on them and was grateful the inquisitive doctor had not noticed in the supply room.

She moved into the middle of the parking lot and pressed the red button on the remote, the one with the picture of a horn. A piercing *HONK* from behind momentarily scared the crap out of her. She turned to see which car's lights flashed.

'No way,' she whispered aloud. It was a squatty, black, Chevy Camaro SS. The SS stood for Super Sport. That meant it was fast. Erica smiled and got into the car.

SEVEN

Thiery gathered officers from the various departments that had responded to the scene and questioned their involvement. Answers ranged from, 'we arrived and responded as a tactical SWAT unit', from the Calusa County Sheriff's Office, to, 'by the time we got here, it was all over and we just helped with traffic', from the Lake Wales Police Department. They all met in the offices of the parish hall at the church as parents and teachers from the school began to filter out and make their way home. It would serve as a temporary command post until a mobile unit was brought in.

There were numerous departments involved, plus the school board sent their internal police. Thiery delegated assignments to each department, based on their involvement, and dismissed those representatives from departments with little to no involvement. He requested reports from all in attendance, then asked Chief Dunham to head the interviews with the families of survivors and victims. Though he didn't say it aloud, he felt Dunham had a natural compassion that made people more comfortable talking to him. Dunham nodded his head graciously and accepted the assignment.

Thiery asked Sheriff Conroy to have his department do the most extensive reports, the scene diagrams and initial entry reports, and to follow up with the county dispatch system to get an accurate account of any calls they received, the times they came in, were dispatched, units arrived, *et cetera*.

Conroy almost sneered as he said, 'that's what I was going to do anyway.'

Thiery was in no mood for his callousness. 'Good, Sheriff Conroy, then you're probably as concerned as I am about the reports I'm hearing on the response to the school.'

'What's that supposed to mean?' asked Conroy, pushing himself off the wall he'd been leaning against.

Thiery's jaw muscles flexed as he pondered the quandary of calling out the local sheriff in front of his peers, or swallowing his own pride and looking weak in front of the same group. He was about to say something not very nice when Logan stepped in.

'I think what Agent Thiery was saying is, it's very late, and we all know what we have to do.'

All eyes turned toward her. She'd come into the meeting later than the others and had stayed hidden in the back of the room until now.

'Hi, I'm Agent Sara Logan, with the FBI. Agent Thiery asked me to follow up on the guns used in this morning's incident, and I've accepted that assignment. So, if any of you have questions or comments regarding the subject, please don't hesitate to contact me.'

Thiery nodded. 'Thanks, Agent Logan. Which reminds me, I need to ask you all to get with your administrative staff and, when your officers have completed their reports with whatever system you use, have them send them to me in a PDF format, okay? And, before we leave tonight, I need to get everyone's contact information on a piece of paper we can duplicate and share with each other.'

'I, uh, already have that, sir,' said Dunham. He stood up, no taller than anyone's shoulders in the room, walked to the front, handed a copy to Thiery, then began handing them to other officers.

'Thanks, Chief,' said Thiery, nodding his gratitude.

Fatigue permeated the room like a Port-O-Potty air freshener. The combined scents of gun oil, leather, Kevlar, and sweaty bodies covered in polyester uniforms wafted about. Thiery could hear stomachs growling and watched officers rubbing tired, red eyes. Most of them had been there for fifteen hours, or more.

'Okay, people,' said Thiery, 'let's wrap it up for tonight. You have my number. Please call if you think of anything pertinent. I'll touch base with all of you tomorrow. Try to have a good night, and get some rest.'

Everyone filed out of the room and headed to their cars. Thiery saw Logan talking to Conroy off to the side and paused, then decided to keep moving. At that point, he didn't want to talk to either one of them.

It was three o'clock in the morning at the tiny Sun Beam Motel, a clean but dated motor court that offered HBO, free Wi-Fi, a swimming pool, and close proximity to Legoland. After settling in, Thiery called his sons. Both lived in California: one in the Navy, twenty-one-year-old Leif, stationed in San Diego; the other, Owen, a twenty-three-year-old firefighter in San Francisco. After seeing the devastation at the school, Thiery ached to tell them he loved them.

Neither answered their phone. He tried not to take it personally. He wondered if they'd heard about the shooting, wherever they were. It would be midnight in California. They were both young and probably partying. Maybe they were both on shift at work.

He had felt a distance develop as they had grown up with him, their only parent. It was difficult to be both loving caregiver and disciplinarian, and he'd wished he had someone to tag team with. He believed, at times, they blamed him for their mother leaving them so young. They were there, in the house, when some of his co-workers, FDLE agents, stopped by, from time to time, to ask him more questions about her disappearance. She had packed a few items – enough for a weekend away – then vanished.

For a while, Thiery was the primary 'person of interest' in her disappearance. Newspapers printed the story of the cop whose wife was missing, and it had created problems for his sons at school. It was no secret to anyone that surviving spouses were the first suspect in missing or murdered partners. He felt people thought he was guilty of something and the burden weighed heavily on him.

When Adrienne hadn't returned after a few weeks, Thiery's initial reaction was to assume the worst: she had left him, but something bad had happened along the way. Following that instinct, he'd gone to New York, where his wife had grown up in Brooklyn, the daughter of Albanian immigrants. Though he hadn't spoken to Edona Manjola since he and Adrienne were married – Adrienne's mother had never cared for him, for reasons he didn't understand – he located her apartment, but it was empty.

He learned Adrienne's mother was dead. When he made further inquiries, neighbours told him that, a few weeks earlier, she had killed herself by leaping from the building. The suicide reinforced his notion that something had happened to Adrienne, but a check with every hospital in New York, and even the coroner's office, turned up nothing. With no other living relatives, Thiery hit a dead end.

After she'd been gone for over two years, after Thiery had spent every waking moment trying to find her, and then hired several private detectives to continue the search, he was no longer a suspect. He was just alone. Case closed. There was no formal announcement as to his innocence, any more than there had been that he was a suspect. The case, like his wife, just faded away. After seven years, he finally had her declared deceased, allowing him to collect a small life insurance policy she'd carried. He'd placed the funds in an account for his sons' college savings.

He often wondered if he should have remarried, but that wasn't something he was going to do just to have a built-in babysitter. In any case, it was too late, now. His sons were who they were, and, to them, he was who he was. All the regret in the world wouldn't change that.

By four o'clock, Thiery was in bed, poring over reports he'd gathered from the Sebring and Lake Wales Police Departments, as well as the Calusa County Sheriff's Office, whose SWAT had yielded the most reports.

The reports from the departments who'd arrived first on the scene, Sebring PD and the School Board police, stated in dry, legal terms how and what they did to secure the building, set up a command post, and assist in the evacuation that was underway when they arrived. The Sheriff's SWAT team recorded the team's entry at 8:42 a.m., immediately followed by the discovery of both the victims' and perpetrators' bodies.

The Fire Rescue reports comprised brief medical statements that included patient treatment – four treated for wounds and six more for chest pain, shock, or trouble breathing – and recorded which hospitals the patients were transported to. There were reports from each forensic team that entered the building and dealt with each of the bodies, the location, nearby weapons, bullet casing trajectory, and various gun blasts. All in all, the local law enforcement agencies had done an outstanding job, doing what they were supposed to do. The problem was that reports were just that: reports. Facts, times, data. There were no leads in them that would take the investigation to a point of conclusion. It was all paperwork formality, but, as lead investigator, he had to read every one of them thoroughly, in case something popped up.

Thiery wondered again about the response time. According to the dispatch log, *Calusa County SWAT arrived at 8:42. The initial call came in at 8:26. A sixteen-minute response? Maybe that was normal for this area, but Dunham had arrived at 8:38. Technically, the Calusa County Sheriff Office was 'outside the city limits' but it was still in very close proximity to the school. How did a police chief from a neighbouring city several miles away beat a SWAT located a few blocks away? Maybe protocol had them meet at the main department before responding? Maybe they had to go there for their SWAT gear? In most cities, officers kept their response gear in the trunk, but it might be different here.* Thiery made a note to himself to audit the dispatch tapes and call times.

Deadened by fatigue, Thiery wondered if he was making something of nothing. *Maybe the governor was right*, he thought. Maybe there wasn't an investigation, other than to determine what triggered the two men to do the shooting. What was their common fuck up? Abused as children? Bullied in school? Too many violent video games? Could anyone ever really know what caused these – *what had they called them on the news?* – Human Tornadoes?

Still, something bothered Thiery. Something that, every time he began to doze off, woke him like a new lover trying to sneak out of bed. *Why was a forty-one-year-old man hanging out with a nineteen-year-old kid?* How and where did they meet? And what about Erica Weisz? What was *her* story? How did she get a gun? Why would she chance taking a loaded weapon to school? And what gave her the wherewithal to aim and shoot it? Most people couldn't do that, even once. She managed to do it twice. He made a note on his iPad to check with the school board's human resources department to see if her employment background revealed anything.

Thiery's head slumped to one side. The reports and his ever-present iPad slipped from his hands as sleep overcame him. He welcomed the coming slumber and managed to slip off his loafers and slide his feet under the covers, though still dressed. The mattress was too soft for his liking, but felt like a mother's embrace as the window-banger AC unit hummed a soft lullaby.

His slumber lasted about one minute before his mind, as weary as it was, clicked back on, repeating the questions: *What did Frank Shadtz and David Coody have in common? A mature, adult man from out of town and a nineteen-year-old, pimple-faced, hayseed kid. How had they met and joined together with the common idea they should shoot up a school?*

'Shit,' he said aloud, rolling out of bed, his head swimming. 'Goddamnit, man! Turn it off,' he admonished himself. He got up, went to the bathroom, and unwrapped a tiny bar of soap. He washed his face and rinsed, then looked at himself in the mirror, though he had to squat to do so. His brown eyes were bloodshot, his face salt-and-pepper-whiskered, and his hair greasy. Someone once told him he looked like George Clooney on steroids. Right then, he was closer to Mickey Rourke on a bender.

He shuddered and looked at his watch: 5:15. He couldn't talk to the dead Shadtz and doubted if Coody was out of the coma yet. Maybe he would never come out of it. He needed to talk to Erica Weisz and Sally Ravich, the adult survivors, as well as some of the children. It kept coming back to that. But, it was so frigging early, or late, or whatever and he was just too damned whipped.

He went back to bed and drifted off. This time, he slept almost seventy minutes before his cell phone rang.

Away from his father, Julio Esperanza was the man. No one would have ever guessed he cowered under the glare of his father's gaze. Few people had seen what his Papa did to those who crossed him. Just the thought of his father's displeasure turned Julio's blood to ice.

When he was eighteen, his father had told him to pack a bag; they were taking a trip out to the ocean. Just the two of them. They drove from Ciudad Juarez, a city his father literally *owned*, all the way out to the coast in his fancy new American car, a Lincoln Continental.

They travelled to a small town called Puerto Penasco where Emilio owned a rather large beach house neither Julio nor his mother had known about. There, the father told the son he was now a man, and he allowed him to drink his very fine, aged tequila. Julio had never felt so close to his father, sipping the golden liquor on the warm sand overlooking the blue ocean. He felt as though they were buddies for the first time in his life.

One morning, Emilio told his son he had friends coming from Tijuana. They were bringing Julio presents in honour of his birthday, because they respected Don Emilio. The men arrived, oddly, driving two beat-up vans. One man got out of his van and, grinning, went to the back and opened the side door. A half-dozen perspiring but beautiful women emerged from the back, as if a genie's bottle had tipped over and spilled its lovely contents: blondes, brunettes, even a redhead who looked like the American movie star, Ann-Margret. They wore lots of make-up, and low-cut blouses that pushed their breasts up into nice, plump, fleshy pillows. A couple of them wore fishnet stockings. Julio almost drooled looking at them and found himself becoming both excited and a little nervous.

The sun was setting, casting a warm, welcoming, orange glow over the ladies and the idyllic beach setting. Emilio told the women to go inside the house and freshen up. They walked close to Julio. He could smell their perfume and their sweaty sex. A couple of the *mujeres* winked at him. One brushed by him, slowed, and dragged her hand across his still hairless chest, letting her fingers linger on his nipple and giving it a little twist. Goose bumps broke out all over his body and an erection grew, noticeably, in his swim trunks. The men laughed good-naturedly.

From the other van, two more men got out. Both of them had automatic rifles and pistols and stayed near their van. No one got out of the back.

Julio was not frightened, or even surprised. He had seen the men who worked for his father carry guns before. In fact, most of his father's 'friends' had one in a belt or shoulder holster, under their jackets. He knew his father's businesses made lots of money, so it made sense these men armed themselves, particularly in Mexico, where kidnapping and murder were very common.

'Go in the house, Julio,' his father ordered. 'The girls are sweet. They will take care of you.' Julio grinned as if he'd just given him the best present in the world. No one had to tell him twice. He was ready to bust.

For the next couple of hours, Julio lost his virginity to a variety of willing women – all pros – using a variety of positions, angles, and tricks that aroused and satisfied him over and over again, until he thought he would die from exertion. They had gathered in the bedrooms upstairs, showered, and played until everyone worked up a voracious appetite. A few of the women had gone downstairs – tired of the insatiable needs of the boy toy – and helped Emilio cook a grand dinner for everyone there. They gorged themselves on paella and homemade sangria.

After dinner, Emilio told the women to clean up the dishes. He and the men were going outside for a walk and a cigar. Julio was exhausted, but his father insisted he come along.

'The initiation of your manhood is not complete,' he said. Julio grinned wearily and tagged along behind his father and the other men.

They strolled down the drive and approached the van the other men still guarded. Julio had forgotten about it and wondered what was inside that was so important as to keep these men out here while the others had enjoyed such a sumptuous meal and the company of the ladies.

Emilio nodded to the men and told them to get some dinner. They nodded back, gratefully, and one of them said, 'The tools you need are in the front.' Emilio said, '*Bueno*,' then went to the back of the van and opened the doors.

Inside, hidden in the shadows, were three men, all bound, their hands behind their backs. Bandanas wrapped tightly around their eyes. Sweat-soaked clothing stuck to them like a second skin. Emilio reached in, grabbed one of the men by his arm, and guided him out, telling him to watch his step as he climbed out of the van.

Julio grew uncomfortable now, but said nothing. A warm wind came off the ocean like the breath of a killer whispering in his ear and he felt sweat form in his scalp, then trickle down and hang on his chin for a moment. When it fell, he thought he could *hear it* hit the ground.

Emilio went to the front of the van and looked around in the cab. He came back brandishing a machete. He approached Julio and put his hand on his shoulder.

'These men stole money from me.' he said, gesturing with the blade. 'When I tried to get it back, they threatened me and my family. We cannot allow this. Do you understand, son?'

Julio nodded, but a lump of fear grew in his throat, and he could not swallow, though he desperately needed to.

Emilio pushed the blindfolded man to his knees, his once pressed, linen suit, dishevelled and filthy as a beggar's. The man began to cry and plead for his life. The other men inside the van began to whimper like puppies in a sack that was weighted down for the river.

Emilio brought Julio over to stand with him and said, 'Watch what I do to men who try to hurt me.'

He brought the machete up and to the side as if he were shouldering a baseball bat. When he brought it back down, it struck with a wet, meaty sound, and stopped hard against the man's neck bones. Blood spurted and sprayed Emilio and Julio. Emilio tugged at the blade and dislodged it from the man's cervical spine. The man began to convulse and fell forward. Before he hit the ground, Emilio swung the blade again, catching it in the wound from the first swing. This time, it went clean through. The man's head came off, hitting the ground with a thud.

Julio stood transfixed, his mouth wide, lips quivering. He could see the man's face and watched his mouth open and close, like a fish gasping on a hot, dry deck. He turned and retched into the grass, his legs shaking under him like saplings caught in a hurricane.

Emilio pulled another man from the van. The man sobbed and made promises and excuses, but it was as if Emilio could no longer hear him. He pushed him to the ground near the body of the first man, then turned to Julio.

'It's your turn, Julio. You must help kill our enemies.'

Julio shook his head. 'No, Papa, I cannot do this.'

Emilio reached over and slapped him. The blow hit him in the ear and made it ring so loud he could barely hear what else his father was saying. But he heard enough. 'If you don't do this,'

Don Emilio declared, 'one of these men will shoot you. Do you understand?'

Julio nodded, tears streaming from his eyes. *How had this happened?* One moment, he was happy and sated, full of wine and women. Now, his father was threatening him and he was being forced to murder a man he did not know, and in this most brutal way.

'Stop crying,' said Emilio. 'You won't be able to see what you're doing.' He placed the sticky handle of the machete into Julio's hand.

Julio looked at the blade, shining black in the moonlit night. Before he had gone downstairs for dinner, he had made love with the red-haired whore and, as they lay there in post-coital bliss, he had noticed his phallus, still shining from their sex. This is what he thought of as he looked at the blood-slicked blade: a wet, throbbing phallus. In one afternoon, his father had introduced him to the utmost pleasure in life, and now mixed that gift with the most horrible deed any human could perform. This incongruent mix would haunt him for the rest of his life – he knew that, even then – but was powerless to stop it. Thirty years later – and four failed marriages due to domestic assault – proved there are forbidden elements of mankind that should never be revealed to a young, impressionable mind.

Julio held the blade out as he'd seen his father do, his hand shaking so much he thought he'd drop it. But, he didn't. He swung it down and struck the second man, hitting him in the shoulder, down to the bone. The scream covered Julio's arms in goose bumps.

'Again!' said Emilio. 'Quickly.'

Julio did as he was ordered. The blade flashed again, this time finding the man's neck, but hardly going through. The man tried to stand and run, but one of Emilio's men stuck out his leg and tripped him. As the man rolled on the ground, the bandana covering his eyes came off, and he looked up at Julio, his eyes pleading, blood streaming from his neck.

Emilio came over and squatted next to the man. He pointed at the man's throat with his index finger. 'Right across here, Julio,' he said, as if teaching his son how to cut firewood. Julio brought the blade down again. And again. It took several chops through bone and sinew to completely sever the man's head.

Julio turned, fell to his knees, and vomited. When he was able to stand up, one of the men assisted him and handed him a bottle of tequila. Julio took it and rinsed his mouth, then took another swallow that burned all the way down and filled his head with fire.

They had pulled the last man out of the van and placed him on his knees in the condemned man's position. He sobbed quietly.

Emilio looked at Julio and said, 'Again.'

Julio teetered over; sure he could neither raise the blade again, nor swing it hard enough to do what had to be done. But, the look on his father's face, the sneer, the disgust of having such a weak offspring, was so apparent, he did not have to hear the words. He found an anger inside himself, let it rise to a boil, and placed himself behind the man. This time, he raised the blade above his own head with both hands and, when he came back down, arcing it to the side, he put his weight into the swing. The blade was getting dull now and once again, it did not go all the way through. But, as the man fell to his side, Julio dislodged the blade, and without being coaxed this time, he swung it down again and again, until the man's head rolled off.

Emilio nodded to the other men and, without words, they took chainsaws from the van and cranked them up.

Julio wondered why they had not used the chainsaws in the first place then realized it was probably because his father wanted him to 'work' through his emergence as a killer. Now, he felt the transformation within himself and knew at that very moment he would never be the same. But, he would also never be like his father.

One of his father's men – a man whom Julio had heard being referred to as *El Monstruo*, The Monster – dismembered the bodies with the chainsaw and placed them in black plastic bags. He was a frightening presence, as wide as he was tall. His eyes were as black and lifeless as a shark's, set into acne-scarred skin. His other facial features were blunted and slightly out of place, as if the sculptor who moulded him left him in the kiln too long. His mouth hung open as if his nose did not take in air. As toad-like as he looked, his hands moved quickly with saw and blade; an efficient and experienced butcher. Once in bags, the parts were then placed into wooden shipping containers that, Julio later learned, to his horror, were shipped back to the dead men's families.

Emilio put his arm around his son's shoulders, grinning as if his son had just scored the final goal at the World Cup, and said, 'Okay. *Now*, you are a man. Let's get cleaned up. Those lusty whores in the house want more of you, I'm sure.' He beamed proudly as he said this, but Julio did not. Sex was absolutely the last thing on his mind at that moment.

EIGHT

It was Sara Logan on the phone. 'Good morning,' she purred.

Despite everything, his heart crept into his throat. 'Are you here?' he croaked. 'I mean, at the hotel?'

'No,' she answered. 'Still at the Gaylord Palms. We Feds like to stay at Marriotts. I keep the reward points and use them when I go on vacation.'

'Since when do you take vacations?'

'You're always on vacation when you love your job.'

'I wouldn't know.' Thiery rubbed his head, aching from lack of sleep.

'You should come up. I'm sure it's a wee bit nicer than your dive.'

Thiery ignored the invite. 'I don't know. This place is pretty sweet, if you don't mind cockroaches.'

'Eeeeyew,' said Logan. 'I've got a suite with a balcony overlooking a lake and a huge, very comfortable bed. I'm afraid I'll get lost in it all by myself.'

Thiery shook his head. The girl didn't give up. 'I'm sure you'll be fine.' Changing the subject, he asked, 'Anything new on your end?'

'With the school shooting?'

'Ye-es,' he said, managing to make the word into two syllables.

He closed his eyes and could see her as clearly as if she were still in the bedroom they shared years ago. Still standing in front of the window at her little fuck pad in Ormond Beach, pulling her then shoulder length hair up into a ponytail, the sweat of their exertions still glistening on her dark skin.

'I talked to the ATF agents last night,' she answered, a noticeable shrug in her voice. 'There's nothing for them here, so they're popping smoke and gone. Like you said – all amateur stuff on the explosives – probably couldn't get them to detonate without attaching a grenade. We've got Coody's hard drives. We overnighted them to our lab rats. I've got some people chasing down the numbers on the Weisz gun. So far, nada. And I'm collating a list of guns that the shooters had on them, and in their vehicle, and I'll run that through our database as soon as I can. My boss told me to stick around to represent our bureau and assist your department as needed. So, if you need forensic or lab work, or just old fashioned … *leg* work … '

Thiery again ignored her sexy punning.

'So, how are you?' Logan finally continued. 'The boys doing well?' she asked, straining to make personal conversation.

'Grown and out of the house now. You still married?'

She hesitated. 'Afraid so.'

He could have asked, 'why so glum?', or lent her a consoling ear, but he didn't. He heard a click on his phone, glanced at the incoming call, but didn't recognize the number.

Logan asked, 'Is that your phone missing a beat or mine?'

'Mine,' he said. 'Let's touch base later, okay?'

'Sure,' said Logan. 'And hey, thanks for not being a dick to me.'

Thiery clicked over to the second call without comment.

It was Chief Dunham. 'She's gone,' he said, dolefully.

'Who?' asked Thiery, wide awake now.

'The wounded teacher: Erica Weisz.'

'She died?'

'No, sir. She's just … gone. Left without checking out. I got a call from the Sheriff's office this morning. The hospital called them late last night.'

'Why did they wait so long to notify you?'

'Not sure. They had a deputy watching her last night, but he's a young guy and got distracted. Stepped away for a minute. They looked around the hospital for a couple hours, but couldn't find her, so they just wrote it up as a missing witness wanted for questioning. She hasn't been gone for twenty-four hours, and it wasn't reported by a family member, so it's not really an official missing person's case yet. They think she just left.'

'With a shotgun wound to the abdomen?' Thiery questioned. 'She'd have to be really scared of something. Maybe she's afraid of the trouble she could be in over having a gun?'

'Could be. Federally, schools are supposed to be part of the Gun Free Zone Act. Breaking that law, a person could buy themselves a whole lot of trouble, even if she probably saved dozens of lives.'

'I hear you,' said Thiery, his head beginning to ache from lack of sleep. He made a mental note to ask Logan about that when he had a chance. 'I'm heading over to the hospital now,' he said. 'Should be able to review the security videos. Could you do me a favour? Call the local PDs, and put out an APB on her? And let's do an Amber Alert, too.'

'Already got it written up. Just waiting for your okay.'

'Thanks, Chief. Know any place I can grab a quick bite?'

'Uh, you may have noticed there isn't much in Frosthaven, but there's Dutch's Diner in Avon Park on Main Street. That's about halfway to Sebring, where I'm at, maybe fifteen, twenty minutes from where you are. I could meet you there, if you don't mind company.'

'Not at all. See you there.'

Thiery arrived at the diner half an hour later. Dunham was already there, a cup of black coffee steaming in front of him. He smiled pleasantly, but he, too, could not hide the signs of fatigue. He stood and shook hands with Thiery.

'Get any sleep last night?' Thiery asked.

'Probably about as much as you.'

Thiery nodded. 'What's good here?'

'Everything. I like the Mustang.'

The place was fashioned with a retro look, like Mel's Diner from the old TV show *Happy Days*: black and white chequered floors like flags at race tracks; the breakfast counter was made from the grille of an old car; neon lights that read 'Ford' and 'Chevy' decorated the walls; the breakfast plates on the menu were named after muscle cars; the Mustang was 'a good chunk of corned beef hash grilled with two eggs'. Thiery was hungrier than that.

The waitress had pink dyed hair, earrings in her nostrils, and her arms were tattooed up to her neck. What skin still showed was as white as bone. She was friendly and attractive in an 'alt girl' way and as incongruent as the Pope in a strip bar. Most people in the area leaned toward cowboy boots and hand-tooled belts as their fashion statement. Thiery said he was starving and she suggested the 'Barracuda': three eggs, three links of sausage, three pieces of bacon, with biscuits and gravy.

The food came quickly, and Thiery went for it, eating as if he was still playing football in college, though he had to work out a lot harder to keep his weight down to what it was thirty years ago.

Thiery and Dunham ate without talking, the sounds of forks striking ceramic plates serving as the bulk of conversation until they were both finished, their hunger abated.

Sara Logan kept seeping back into Thiery's head, specifically, the memory of their discussion about why they couldn't continue to see each other. The anger. The hurt. One memory brought on another, until, inevitably, they turned to his wife's disappearance and all the doubts and regrets that brought.

'Why do you think she left?' Dunham asked.

'I don't know,' replied Thiery, momentarily thinking Dunham was referring to his wife. Refocusing, he pulled himself back to the present. 'Maybe she has an abusive husband or boyfriend looking for her. Maybe she didn't leave alone. Did you get a chance to talk to her at all yesterday before the ambulance took her away?'

Dunham looked sheepish, casting his eyes down. 'No. I'm sorry, I didn't. We were so busy yesterday. I still can't believe this happened here.'

'Don't beat yourself up. You had an emergency situation. Dozens of witnesses, wounded, and the dead to deal with. The parents of the children must have kept you hopping.'

'Yep. At one point I was sure we had more cars arriving than people. We got swamped.' He paused to reflect for a moment, and Thiery could see the sorrow in his eyes. 'We've got to make a better plan. There's been talk about all the departments in the county going under the Sheriff's department. The Sheriff has asked the county to almost double his budget.'

Thiery nodded, but added, 'You could have had a platoon of marines in here yesterday, and it wouldn't have made any difference. The damage was done and over by the time you and your men got to the school. As it was, you did a stellar job.'

Dunham looked out the window of the diner, his eyes wet.

'What do you think about the slow response time from the Sheriff's Office? How is it you could beat them there when their station is just a few blocks away?'

Dunham turned his focus back to Thiery. 'Don't know. I've heard their response times have been getting slower. I try not to stick my nose into everyone's business here, but I've also heard some of the guys saying they are trying to get more money for more men and equipment.'

Whispering, Thiery asked, 'are you saying you believe the Sheriff would deliberately slow his department's responses to increase his budget?'

Dunham looked back out the window and cleared his throat. 'I'm saying I'm a Police Chief in a small town, and I don't know everything, but I get wondering at times. There's a saying my daddy used to have about big government: "When elephants fight, the only thing that gets hurt is the grass".'

Thiery made a mental note to look into it, but, for now, he had more pressing issues. He grabbed his wallet and said, 'Let's head over to the hospital. I've got the tab. The state picks up my expenses when I travel. I'll let the governor buy us breakfast today, okay?'

Dunham nodded and wiped his eyes as subtly as he could with his napkin.

'You can follow me over. I better bring my car in case I get a call.'

In the parking lot, both men hesitated before climbing into their respective cars; Dunham seemed to have something else he wanted to say.

'When I talked to the hospital, they said the other lady was waking up,' said Dunham. 'You know, the receptionist?'

'Yeah? That's good to hear,' said Thiery. 'Maybe she can tell us something about this Weisz woman.' He stood for a moment, considering. 'Besides the teacher missing, you know what else is strange?'

Dunham shrugged.

'The age difference in the shooters. I mean, typically, if there's two shooters, like at Columbine, they're about the same age. Maybe went to the same school they attacked, shared the same vendetta. But, Coody is nineteen, and Shadtz was forty-one. What could they possibly have in common?'

Dunham looked at the pavement a moment before answering. 'They both liked to kill people?'

Moral saw the news as soon as he landed at Orlando airport. It was on the huge flat screen TVs that greeted him as he stepped off the plane.

'This just in,' reported THN's Gail Summer. 'One of the survivors of yesterday's shooting has disappeared.' Over her shoulder, a picture of Erica Weisz popped up. 'Erica Weisz, the teacher we now know used her own gun to shoot the intruders at Travis Hanks Elementary School yesterday, has vanished. Hospital staff stated she did not check out officially, and her absence was not reported immediately as staff spent several hours looking for her in the building and around the facility. When Ms Weisz did not return to her room after almost two full hours, the Calusa County Sheriff's Office deputy assigned to watch her room reported her as missing. The officer said he never saw her leave, and does not understand how she could have left with such critical wounds.

'In the meantime, to report on this unusual set of circumstances, we go back to Dave Gruber who has been standing watch at the hospital since yesterday's tragic shooting in which a dozen persons died. Dave?'

Gruber was rested now, his eyes bright, eager for breaking news, his blond hair perfect, immovable as a plastic helmet in the light breeze moving through the parking lot in front of the Emergency Room doors.

'Yes, good morning, Gail, and you said it right. This is an unusual set of circumstances, particularly when we consider Erica Weisz's injuries. With me now is Dr Harold Marsh, a trauma surgeon here at Lakeland Regional Hospital.' The camera panned and zoomed out, revealing a short middle-aged man in a white lab coat. 'Dr Marsh,' the reporter addressed the man, 'what can you tell us about Erica Weisz's injuries, and where do you think she might have gone?'

'Ah, yes,' the doctor began, clearing his throat, 'I can only say that Miss Weisz's wounds were initially life threatening. HIPAA law prevents medical professionals from discussing, specifically, a patient's medical history,' he continued, his comb-over hair catching the wind and flapping like a tattered brown flag, 'but I believe it is now common knowledge that her injuries were significant.'

Gruber persisted. 'Can you be more specific, Dr Marsh? We've learned she has a rather devastating abdominal wound. Can you confirm that?'

Dr Marsh blinked nervously, but felt he had to respond in some professional manner. 'I can confirm,' he began, 'Ms Weisz underwent a complicated surgery performed here at the trauma centre, which, at the time, stabilized her condition. I can also add that she should never have left our facilities, as her condition is still what we'd call critical. She needs additional care and follow-up treatment.'

'And can you speculate on where she might have gone, or why?' Gruber pressed on.

'No,' said Marsh. 'I cannot speculate other than to say it could not have been far. She is considered to be in a very vulnerable state and needs to return to the hospital as soon as possible. As for why she would leave the hospital, it is anyone's guess. We occasionally have these things happen, but not with one of our more critically injured patients.'

'Thank you, Dr Marsh,' said Gruber, returning his attention to the camera. 'There you have it, Gail. One of Erica Weisz's surgeons telling us she is in critical condition and should not have left the hospital. Now, we're polling people in the community this morning, and this is what some people are saying … '

The image on TV shifted to an overweight, whiskered man standing outside a feed store in front of a faded blue Ford pickup truck with a large bale of hay in the back. His southern accent was so thick they had to put subtitles in the banner below the shot.

'Uh, what some peoples are sayin' is dat dis teacher lady is a-scared she gonna get in trouble wit' da law, cuz she 'ez carryin' a gun. But, I can tell you, dat don't mean nothin' to anyone 'round here. Most of us in dis town believe we should have da right to own and carry a gun, an' we look at Missus Weisz as a hee-ro. If she hadn't a had dat gun, we mighta had a whole lot more of our chil'ren shot up an' dead. You ax anyone 'round here and dey'll tell ya, iffen we see her, we're a gonna shake her hand and give her a place to stay, iffen dat's what she need.'

A shot of another woman outside of a grocery store, her hair in curlers covered by a see- through polyester scarf. 'Well, I can't say why she left the hospital, but I hope she is okay. We all owe that young lady the lives of our children. I've heard some people wondering why she had a gun in the first place, because maybe it put the children in danger, but I say the proof is in the pudding. There were two gunmen that went into that school yesterday to kill our children, and now they are dead, or dying, but none of our kids is. How can you argue with that?'

Gruber was framed back on the screen, his mouth a firm line, his eyes smiling; *this stuff was just too good*. 'And there you have it,' he concluded. 'We have heard that some people in the community are not pleased that Erica Weisz was carrying a gun. There are a lot of questions about why she did and what kind of legal trouble she could find herself in for having that gun on school property, but most of the people we've talked to believe she did what was right. Now, we have also talked to the office of the superintendent of the school system here in Calusa County and they had a different reaction. They would not appear on camera, but they made this statement ...' Gruber read from a sheet of computer paper. 'The Calusa County School Board is aware that Erica Weisz probably saved dozens of lives at Travis Hanks Elementary yesterday. However, it is not the school's policy to allow teachers to carry guns, and this is a clear violation of our policies and of federal law. If, or when, she returns, she will be placed on administrative duty, pending an investigation of the circumstances.' Gruber looked at the camera as if he'd just read something as significant as the Gettysburg Address. 'Back to you, Gail.'

'Thanks, Dave. This just in: In Inverness, Florida, last night, a fifteen-year-old boy was shot to death by an unauthorized neighbourhood watchman ... '

Moral stuck a cigarette in his mouth, then remembered he was in an airport where smoking was prohibited. He kept it in his mouth, but put the lighter back in his pocket. *Why is she calling so much attention to herself?* he wondered. It was only going to make things worse, if not for her, definitely for him. He had to find her before the police, or the media, did. Of course, if the Esperanzas found her first, it might not look good for him at work, but it would certainly take care of his problems. He wondered if the Esperanzas were upset with him right now. They shouldn't be; he had done what he said he would. But, would that suffice? These guys did not think like most people. These guys were monsters.

NINE

The sound of bells woke her. Erica's eyes fluttered open, but she couldn't remember where she was. Then, it came back to her. She was in Lake Wales at the safe haven 'B' house. The bells were from the Bok Tower, heralding the bright, sunny day.

She was even sorer than she had been the night before. She tried to sit up, but it was too difficult. She had to roll out of bed, get her feet under her, and try to stand. Her efforts were feeble. Her skin was the colour of washed-out butterscotch pudding. Each step took effort on legs that felt like wobbly stilts.

There was nothing in the refrigerator, but, when she had first relocated to the area, one of her first responsibilities was to visit the 'B' haven and stock it with some dry provisions. There was coffee and cooking oil and powdered cocoa and eggs in the kitchen. A week's worth of MREs from a camping store in the cabinet over the stove. There were extra clothes, including another pair of Nike shoes in the bedroom closet. The bathroom was fully stocked with TP, toothpaste, hydrogen peroxide and, most importantly, several shades of hair dye. She would get to that later. Right now, she wanted to see how dehydrated she was. She sat on the toilet – her trembling legs gratefully giving up her weight – but she could not urinate when she tried. That answered her question.

Making it back into the kitchen, she started a pot of coffee, then retrieved the bag she'd brought with her from the hospital. She located a bag of normal saline, spiked it with the IV tubing, and tied a tourniquet around her bicep. She squeezed her fist several times, brought up a weak, thin vein, and stuck an eighteen gauge needle in. Dark blood crept into the plastic catheter, slowly, as though there wasn't much in her. She hooked up the tubing to the IV hub and opened it up all the way, then whipped off the tourniquet. She could feel the cool fluid filling her veins and giving her back some blood pressure. She poured herself a cup of black coffee, and sat at the kitchen table, having her liquid breakfast, until the IV bag and coffee pot were empty. She left the IV hub in her wrist with a preloaded heparin lock. Now, when she went to the bathroom, she managed to pee a couple of drops and was relieved her kidneys were beginning to work again.

Her hunger was kicking in. Before she made herself something to eat, she went to the bedroom and opened the closet. She pulled back the carpet, and found the floor safe. It had an entry system that looked like an old push-button phone, with several letters on each number. Erica typed the word 'MAGIC'. The safe opened with a mechanical whirr. Inside were new credentials, an encrypted satellite phone, the usual ten thousand dollars of 'escape' money, and another gun. This one was another automatic, but with a little more stopping power: a Springfield XD-S 9 mm, with a fourteen-round clip. It was heavier than the .380, but she might need the extra firepower. After she test-fired it without bullets, she loaded the clip and placed both it and the money in her purse.

The powdered eggs were fine, even without salt, and she made herself a second helping after she'd finished the first. The last time she'd eaten was yesterday morning, before the shooting at the school, and she'd only had time to have an apple on the way in. She was ravenous and thought about a third helping, but decided she'd better not overeat until she knew what condition her insides were in.

She took the bag of stolen medical supplies with her into the bathroom. She lifted her shirt and pulled the top of her panties down. A huge bandage covered the left side of her abdomen, from just below her rib cage down to just above her pubic area. Pulling at the edges of the sticky adhesive, she managed to remove the dressing. It was ugly. A giant swatch of dried orange Betadine coated her stomach. Inside this swatch was a grotesque three-inch line of stitches that looked like a hairy, black caterpillar on her upper left quadrant. She had hoped they would've been able to do a laparoscopic procedure if the splenectomy was partial, but it looked as if they had to do the full tilt boogey. She wondered how much they took because, depending on the answer to that question, she could approximate how long it would take her to get her red blood cell count back up. She was naturally anaemic; this wouldn't help.

The ugly orange swatch also contained over a dozen small incisions puckered up with one or two stitches in each where surgeons had removed the buckshot that had felled her at the school. Anger built up inside her as she thought about it. She wished she'd had a shoulder-held rocket launcher to blow those motherfuckers away. Recalling the little girl who had been grazed by one of the bullets made her blood boil and brought back unpleasant memories of another time, one in which she wished she could have made a difference.

Standing nude in the tub and using the peroxide, Erica scrubbed as gingerly as she could to clean the wound. Still weak, she showered quickly then dab-dried the area with some four by four gauze pads, let it air-dry, and covered it with fresh bandages. She used some cling film wrapped around her torso, rather than go back to the adhesive tape that had pulled off her skin when she had removed it. Her injuries and muscles were sore after she'd finished, but it felt good to be clean and have fresh dressings. She knew she'd have to keep up this routine if she wanted to escape infection.

One thing she had going for her was her physical condition. She'd been doing her own CrossFit programme of sprint running, burpees, mountain climbing, jump rope, and several hundred crunches, sit-ups, and other abdominal strengthening exercises almost every day for the past couple of years. She hoped that conditioning would help her heal quicker.

Filling a syringe with some of the Amoxicillin she'd stolen, she gave herself a dose using the IV hub she still had in place, pushing the drug in slowly over several minutes. Had she been thinking more clearly, she could've just included it in the IV bag, initially, but she forgave herself for that minor exclusion. She'd been through a lot in the past twenty-four hours or so.

Just the drive over from Lakeland was taxing. It wasn't that far, but it seemed to take forever, and she'd passed at least a dozen cop cars, worrying that each one might pull her over looking for the stolen car. At times, she had to bite the inside of her cheek to keep from passing out.

When she'd arrived at the tiny, turquoise-coloured cinder-block house, she'd almost passed it by. It was in a remote area in the eastern boundaries of Lake Wales. Like so many homes in Florida, its yard was overgrown; a US bank foreclosure sign barely visible among the knee-high weeds.

This was the prototypical house used as a secondary safe house, in case the primary location had to be vacated quickly. It was not intended to be used for a long period of time. Once an area is compromised, the target becomes vulnerable and has to be relocated, usually to a vastly different place in the US. Still, a secondary safe haven within an hour's drive was essential. If one had to flee the primary residence, they might well be doing so with little time or resources to take them further away.

This wasn't her first flight. The quick exit from Washington was not as traumatic, but it was no less fearful. The Washington house was a 'B' haven, too. She fled from Richmond and, before that, her first safe haven in Cleveland, after being whisked away from

Vegas. Had it already been three years? She suspected she'd been compromised in all of those places, too, but she didn't have proof.

The image of the gunman asking her name flashed back. She closed her eyes, recalling his face, his murderous intensity, and it became clear to her: he had come to the school, not as some crazed young man looking to bury his angst; he had come looking to kill *her*.

While she waited for her strength to return, she anxiously turned on the TV. The morning news shows – if you could call what they offered 'news' – were still on. She skipped past the pseudo-jubilant network hosts, their smiles wide and artificial as they moved from a brief summary of news to a new recipe everyone *had* to try. She came across the THN News programme that seemed to be doing a 24—7 cover on the story.

The anchor quickly went to an update of the school shooting. A grainy picture of her face, underlined with the words 'Hero Teacher Missing' accompanied the monotone monologue. The picture was soon replaced with one of the redheaded young man she had shot in the hall at the school. The photo revealed the pimple-riddled face of a troubled young man, though not as malevolent in appearance as when she had seen him venting his rage on the school. Under his picture were the words 'Shooter David Edward Coody Paralyzed.' This led into a story in which the reporter, Dave Gruber, stood in front of the home of Ellis Coody, the boy's father, and let him have his say.

With teary eyes, Coody Sr drawled, 'well, ain't none of us knowed what happened in that school, do we? We don't know what David was doin' there. Maybe he was tryin' to he'p those kids. I mean, most of them are poor black kids and Guatemalans whose parents are migrant workers in the fields around here, but I know he musta been tryin' to he'p out.' Coody, Sr looked back at the ramshackle home he and his son shared and rubbed his eyes, trying not to show his emotions. 'Yeah, he has guns and goes shooting and hunting, so that's why he had some with him. But, you tell me why a teacher in a public school had a gun. That's against the law, for sure. Maybe she endangered those kids having it. Either way, she's crippled my boy, and she needs to answer for it. If she wasn't guilty, why she run off? That's all I got to say.'

Not ready to let the golden interview end so quickly, and eager to incite a sound bite worthy of highlighting on the prime-time news, Gruber urged the man to continue.

'But what about your ex-wife and her husband found slain in their home?' the reporter queried.

Coody Sr turned, his eyes gleaming with anger. 'We don't know what happened there, neither,' he snarled. 'Now, get the -*bleep*- off my property!'

Back to the reporter. 'And there you have it,' he continued, his face a mask of faux concern. 'Ellis Coody, the father of the boy, David Coody, who doctors have said may be a quadriplegic, if he comes out of the coma he is in, asking what so many of us around here have been asking as well: why did Erica Weisz have a gun in a public school? What really happened there? And, finally, how come she fled the hospital? Back to you, Gail … '

Erica watched with her mouth hanging open, her mind reeling, astounded that a televised news programme would broadcast such an idiotic and incendiary report. The cowardly reporter didn't even press the issue of Coody Jr's dead mother and stepfather. It was insane. *It seemed like they were trying to turn her into the criminal here,* Erica thought. Once again, she felt that familiar anger begin to boil up, giving her the strength to get up and do what she had to do. She turned off the TV before throwing the remote across the room, then headed to the bathroom, looking for the hair dye.

Thiery and Dunham entered the room of Sally Ravich and stood quietly as a nurse finished tending to her. She was conscious, but in obvious pain, which seemed to subside after the nurse gave her a shot and whispered to her that she had company. Her eyelids fluttered, she took a deep breath, and nodded her head slightly.

The nurse handed her a pencil and a pad to write on, then turned to the two lawmen and said, 'She's going to have to write down her answers. Please don't press her too much, okay?'

'We won't,' said Dunham, then nodded to Thiery, giving him the floor.

Thiery tried not to react as he looked into Sally's face. Half of her lower jaw was gone. He surmised the teeth he found in the school lobby were once hers. It was a miracle she had lived, taking a gun blast to her face, but she was going to have a long, tough road of rehab ahead. He could see she had been a pretty woman before the attack. Now, her hair was shaved on one side, and her head was the colour of eggplant. He could imagine her eyes were once pale blue and lively. Today, the one he could see was filled with broken blood vessels, and doubt and fear.

Sally's head was heavily wrapped with gauze that occluded the other eye and the entire right side of what was left of her face, but her hands and arms were unblemished and she held the writing pad as if eager to tell her story.

'Hi, Sally,' Thiery began. 'I'm Special Agent Justin Thiery with the Florida Department of Law Enforcement.

She extended her hand. Thiery took it, gently.

'I know it is difficult for you to talk right now, so I will try to ask questions that will not require long answers. If you can nod, that's fine. If you want to write, that's fine, too. I would not be here bothering you if it wasn't extremely important. Are you up to this?'

Sally nodded.

'Okay. I'm not sure what you know, so I'll fill you in. First, because of your quick action when you turned on the PA system, many people were saved, including all of the children.'

Sally nodded and her one good eye began to fill. A red-stained tear ran down her cheek.

Thiery grabbed a tissue from a box near her bed and handed it to her. 'That was a brave thing you did, Sally,' he continued. 'You should know, too, that both of the shooters were shot. One is dead, and one is in a coma and may or may not live. In either case, he will never be a threat to anyone again.'

Sally exhaled deeply and nodded once.

'But, I don't want to talk about them right now. I want to talk to you about Erica Weisz. You are familiar with her, yes?'

Sally nodded her head.

'Good. Now, the troubling thing about Ms Weisz is, she was also wounded. She was here in the hospital, but now she is gone. We are not entirely aware of the circumstances of her disappearance.'

Sally's face grew concerned.

Thiery went on. 'Officers have been to her house, but she's not there. All of her belongings seem to be there. Her car is still in the driveway. There was a car stolen from the parking lot here at the hospital last night. We're not sure if she took it or not. We're hoping you might be able to help us find her. We know she only moved here about six weeks ago and not many people knew her. Did you know her very well?'

Sally raised her hand, palm down, fingers spread, and rocked it back and forth as if to say, 'a little'.

'Okay,' said Thiery. 'Do you know if she had a boyfriend or any other friends who she may have gone to, or who may have come here to get her?'

Sally shook her head side to side, emphatically.

'Do you know if she had family?'

Sally shrugged her shoulders weakly.

'Okay. Do you know where she came from?'

Sally scribbled three words on the pad and held it up to Thiery: *School Employment Records.*

Thiery nodded. 'We've looked. All her records list is an address in Washington, D.C. When we looked into that through the postal service, all we got back was another name: Harriet Blackstone. Did she ever mention that name?'

Sally shook her head.

'Were you aware of Erica ever having a gun, or carrying one in her purse? Did she ever mention owning a gun?'

Sally started to shake her head, 'No,' then wrote on the tablet again: *No. But always had her purse. Even the lunchroom.*

Thiery nodded as he read the note. When he looked back to Sally, he could see whatever the nurse had given her was beginning to take effect. Her eyelid drooped and she settled deeper into her pillow. Drool with a red tint dampened the dressing that covered the right side of her face.

Thiery smiled and took her hand again. 'Okay, Sally. We're going to leave, but I want to thank you very much for your help today.'

Sally regained consciousness for a moment and shook her head as if to say: I wasn't much help, then stopped as if she remembered something and held up a finger. She picked up the pad again and wrote: *Said didn't have a boyfriend. Never talked about family. And always wore running shoes, even with dresses.*

Thiery read the note and nodded. 'Well. That is unusual, isn't it? I mean the shoe thing. Huh. Okay, Sally. You get some rest. You've been a big help. I'm going to leave my card here on the night stand. You can have the nurse contact me if you think of anything else. Okay?'

Sally nodded, then her head fell to one side as she succumbed to the pain medicine.

Back in the hall, after they'd closed the door, Dunham said, 'I didn't want to bother you while you were talking with her, but I got a text from my admin coordinator at headquarters. She told me to call a Carol Dowling. She's the mother of one of the kids in the class. She says her little boy has mentioned something to her. She thought it might be helpful.'

Thiery listened, but his thoughts drifted to something that was beginning to needle him since he'd mentioned 'Harriet Blackstone' to Sally. As a boy, and even into his young adult life, he'd been fascinated with magic. He had regaled his parents and friends with card tricks and sleight of hand, and he'd shared that knowledge with his own children as well. In college, they had called him 'Magic Man' because everyone knew of his hobby; when he threw the football, they said he 'could make it disappear'. He had read about and absorbed the lives of all the great magicians, and was completely mesmerized by them. He knew their given birth names as well as their theatrical ones. For instance, Houdini, arguably the greatest magician and escape artist ever, was born Eric Weisz. Harry Blackstone, Jr, the son of 'The Great Blackstone' was one of the most successful magicians of his time. Both men were specialists in making things disappear.

Now, he was looking for a woman who had disappeared, and it dawned on him that her name sounded a lot like Eric Weisz, and the only name they found associated with an erroneous address she'd given on her employment application was also assigned to a 'Harriet Blackstone,' which sounded very much like Harry Blackstone.

Could that be coincidence?

'Excuse me, Agent Thiery,' said Dunham. 'Did you hear me?'

Thiery snapped out of it. 'Yes,' he replied. 'I'm sorry, I was thinking of something. Good. Yeah, we should go talk to the boy.'

TEN

Julio Esperanza had gathered his crew of hitters. These were people he could count on. People he had wanted to use before, but his father had advised against it. Emilio wanted Julio to keep a low profile, use someone with no name recognition in the national or international market. Someone who was expendable, and without links that could be traced back to them. That's where Shadtz had come in. The disposable killer. They'd had luck with this tactic before, but Julio knew lightning never struck twice in the same place.

Shadtz had been a badass, but couldn't hold a candle to any of these people, all of them experienced in their craft on an international scale. Maybe when he was healthy he could've, but that was why he'd taken the hit in the first place. An enforcer more than a button man, doing the occasional hit, but more often twisting fingers or cracking heads when someone was slow to pay their weekly 'protection' fee. He was a palooka, too: a heavyweight way past his prime and low in the IQ department. But, he was expendable and had no ties to the Esperanzas, so he got the job. And, as he was terminally ill, he also had one of the most desirable facets they were looking for: nothing to lose.

Now, with Emilio's trial set to begin again next week, they were down to the short hairs.

The school shooting might have been less obvious than the previous hit, but it had failed, and the fact was, this loose end had to be dealt with. All the other loose ends had been taken care of. But, not the nurse. She didn't know everything, but she knew enough to make the connections that would put Emilio away for the rest of his life. She'd worked for him – taken care of him – for eight years. In the first trial, she seemed almost hesitant to testify against Emilio, but, after what they did to her family, she wasn't going to hold back next time.

If the cops hadn't screwed up by using some inadmissible forensic accounting evidence, his father would still be in prison. But, some various pay-offs and a phalanx of high priced attorneys had fought tooth and nail and found the tiny glitches in the evidence chain from the first trial. Then, some testimony that should have been ruled hearsay was 'discovered', and finally, with at least three jurors coming forth to say they felt coerced by the district attorney's office, the judge allowed the appeal, and Emilio was set free, at least, temporarily. Money could buy freedom, at least, for a while.

Emilio could not leave Las Vegas, which was fine with him. He was ordered to be on house arrest, wear the ankle bracelet – the 'dog collar', he called it – and the place he'd chosen for his 'jail' was his penthouse suite in the Bellagio Hotel. Close enough to keep an eye on his holdings in Mexico, but far enough away to appear to be an old man living it up before his health, or the law, finally caught up with him.

For three years, his attorneys had been filing motions to delay the next trial. The judge in his first trial had since retired and moved to Florida – buying a beachside mansion that belied what a federal judge earns – so it was going to be a fresh start with nothing to jam them up. Except the nurse. Again.

One by one, the hit men had flown into Orlando. Julio had his driver pick them up and bring them to the hotel his secretary had booked for them: the Gaylord Palms. *What kind of name was that?* Julio wondered.

The first to arrive was De De Davies, a button man from Canada. Julio had used him before and had high confidence in him. He was a quiet but deadly monster, standing some six and a half feet tall. His shaved head blended seamlessly with his shoulders, the neck lost between. He had black eyes, slightly crossed, but no one kidded him about that. In spite of his horror-movie stature, he spoke eloquently with a deep, French accent, and was very good at tracking people and hacking computer systems; his huge sausage-like fingers dancing over the keyboards like spiders.

The Lopez brothers came in from Mexico City where they took contract work from every drug kingpin that wanted someone dead. And there were plenty. Alejandro was always Alejandro, never Alex, but Eduardo was Eddy. They looked similar, with their curly, black, coiffed hair, flawless coffee skin, and perfect ivory teeth that made them very popular with the ladies. But, they were as different as night and day when it came to killing.

Alejandro was strictly a gun guy, an excellent shot with pistol or rifle, but definitely a quick, distance killer. Eddy preferred knives and working up close. He enjoyed torturing his targets; take them out nice and slow, play with them like a cat messing with a lizard for a few hours. Take a foot off here, a hand off there. What was the hurry, after all? Once you were dead, you were dead. It was just too quick for Eddy and, while it made everyone uncomfortable around him, there were those who admired his particular skills. Julio Esperanza was one of them.

The last to arrive was someone Julio did not know well, but De De Davies had recommended her. Anichka Drakoslava had worked directly under General Ratko Mladic as an 'intelligence officer' in charge of interrogating Bosnian prisoners. She was an Albanian in origin and could speak seven different languages. She now lived in Venezuela where she'd been able to avoid prosecution for war crimes for some fifteen years. Her status and abilities were legendary among those who knew of her: the KGB, the CIA, MI6, and Mossad. Now, in addition to her unusual 'interviewing' skills, she also carried around a feeling of rejection that angered her and made her more dangerous than she had been previously. At five feet eleven inches tall, and trained in the Israeli martial art of Krav Maga, she was not a good person to have walking around, pissed off, unless you needed someone dead.

One by one, they gathered at the hotel, changed into swimwear and went to the pool, as directed. The Lopez brothers fitted right in, with their svelte physiques and South Beach looks. Anichka did, too. With her killer body and Eastern European accent, she was exotically gorgeous as she ordered a mojito at the pool bar. Davies, however, was a fish out of water. He looked like an overweight pro-wrestler as he sauntered by the crowded pool, his MacBook tucked under his elephantine arm. Sweat ran off him in rivers.

Julio met them at the bar.

'When do we move?' asked Davies, impatiently.

Julio looked him over, then glanced around to make sure no one was listening to them.

'There are a million law enforcement officers still swarming the area. And the media. We'll give them a few days. Americans have memories as long as their cocks: very short; so they will lose interest in this 'event' and move on.'

'Then why did you summon us so soon?' asked Anichka. Her voice drew the attention of the Lopez brothers, who obviously admired her in her tiny bikini. They immediately whispered a bet to each other on which one would nail her first.

Julio answered, 'I thought you might like to go to Disney World first.'

The Lopez brothers laughed. '*Si*,' said Eddy. 'Let's go see Mickey Mouse.'

'It's your dollar, *El Jefe*,' said Alejandro.

Anichka sneered, her eyes glinting in anger. She saw their macho Latino types in Venezuela every day and was not impressed. She liked her men a little more … strange.

'You watch the news today, Julio?' asked Davies.

'Not really. I don't watch much television,' Julio said, thinking of his father, who never stopped watching it, and whose phone calls he had been avoiding all day.

Davies snapped open his laptop and hit a button. The Internet headlines displayed a picture of Erica Weisz. 'Our target is on the run,' he said.

Julio sat up straight, looking intently at the small screen. He removed his sunglasses and ran his hand through his hair. '*Mierda*,' he said.

Gloria Shadtz got off of the plane in Tampa, rented a car with a GPS, and typed in Frosthaven, Florida. It was beginning to rain as she drove east on Highway 60. The road was long, two-lane, lined with cow pastures and tiny towns that grew up around the phosphate mining industry like old western mining towns that died slowly after their natural resources were depleted. Her emotions were mixed as she drove.

She hadn't heard from her estranged husband in almost two months. It wasn't unusual for him to stay away for weeks at a time, but he usually called to see how Randy was – their twelve-year-old son born with Down Syndrome – at least once a week, when he was out of town. Her husband no longer lived with her and Randy, but he visited his son regularly. In that respect, he was a good man. Being a guy who worked most often as a barroom bouncer, whom she caught diddling barmaids on enough occasions she finally threw him out, made him not such a great husband. Still, he provided for Randy, if not her, as best he could for a guy with a prison record and no real job skills.

Yesterday, Gloria had picked up Randy from the special education school where he spent his days after she'd worked at the bar where she'd met Frank a lifetime ago. She'd made dinner and was cleaning up when she heard Randy saying, 'Daddy's on the TV, Mama! Daddy's on the TV!'

The news was on. Gloria dropped her plate when the picture of Frank popped up, the anchor saying he was involved in an elementary school shooting. He had been shot by one of the teachers. She swallowed dryly, quickly changed the channel, and got Randy to bed, telling him that, 'Maybe Daddy is doing movies now.'

Then, a knock on the door. When Gloria went to answer it, no one was there, but a fat envelope that hadn't been there when she'd come home from work was placed on the stoop. She saw a man walking away quickly and thought she'd recognized him as one of Frank's bar buddies; a little guy they called 'Owl' because he stayed after everyone else left the bar and mopped floors to earn a drink.

She opened the package and almost fainted. There was a note that read, 'Use this to help Randy. I'm sorry I wasn't a better husband. Good-bye, Gloria. Frank.' Her eyes filled with tears as she counted the bills in the package. Fifty-thousand dollars, all in tens and twenties.

Gloria called her sister and asked if she could watch Randy for a few days. Her sister had not seen the news. Gloria heard her gasp as she shared the news that Frank was involved in a school shooting in Florida.

'Are you sure it was him?' she queried. 'I mean, what would he be doing in Florida, number one? And number two, why would he do something like that? He was a shitty husband, but I always thought he was pretty good with kids, especially Randy.'

'I ... I know,' said Gloria, sniffling. 'I don't understand it all. But, I need to go down there and see that ... he gets buried, or something, right?'

Sara Logan had just got out of the shower when her phone range. It was Miko Tran, a technician and wannabe field agent at the FBI's forensic lab who never failed to grab research requests when he saw them come in from Logan.

'Tell me something,' said Logan.

'Okay,' said a hopeful voice on the other end. 'Looks like we'll be able to piece that hard drive back together after all. We're starting to extrapolate some of the data. How are you, Special Agent Logan?'

'Good, good, good,' said Logan, impatiently, then, 'I'm especially interested in any emails you can find.'

'Of course, Agent Logan. It's part of our protocol now— '

'Then call me when you get your job done,' she said and hung up. She was frustrated, torn between calling Thiery to give him the good news and fantasizing about where that could take them. Their prior dalliance had almost destroyed her marriage and, worse, had hurt Thiery. He'd obviously been in love with her; she wasn't sure 'love' was the first thing that came to her mind about him when she recalled the nights they'd spent together. Thiery had filled a need in her that her husband could not. But Thiery had baggage; the two kids she had no interest in mothering. Still, when it ended, she'd lain awake too many nights thinking about his dark eyes, the wide shoulders, that chest with the hair she loved to run her fingers through.

Logan found herself breathing heavy, an ache in her loins, and decided she needed a cool shower.

ELEVEN

Thiery followed Dunham's car and pulled in behind him at the Dowling home. Dunham waited on the stoop until Thiery joined him, before knocking on the door. A woman with kind eyes opened it and asked them in. A tow-headed boy sat on the couch in the living room, his hands tucked between his knees. Carol Dowling introduced her son, Ricky.

Thiery stuck out his hand and the boy jumped up like a soldier at attention.

'Hi, Ricky, I'm Agent Thiery, and this is Police Chief Dunham.'

Ricky nodded as he shook each man's hand. 'Are you a *secret* agent, Mr. Thiery?'

Thiery smiled. 'No, I'm a policeman, just like Chief Dunham, but my department calls us agents.'

The boy sat back down, a quizzical look on his face.

'Can I bring you gentlemen some coffee?' the woman asked.

'No, thanks, Mrs Dowling,' said Dunham.

'Nor me,' said Thiery. 'We've been having our fill the past twenty-four hours. We don't want to take up too much of your time, so maybe we should get started.'

Mrs Dowling appeared a little hurt by their rejection, but waved her hand toward Ricky. 'Go ahead and tell the policemen everything you told me and your father last night.' She turned back to Thiery and said, 'I don't know if it will help, or not, but I thought what he told us was unusual, and you might want to hear it. I mean, you probably don't have a lot of witnesses to talk to, right?'

Dunham's phone rang. The ringtone was a Tim McGraw song. He excused himself, appearing embarrassed, and stepped out the front door. When he returned, he leaned in and whispered in Thiery's ear. 'That was the Sheriff. He told me he has a woman in his office that says she's Frank Shadtz's wife. Wants to know what we're going to do with his … ' He stopped, glanced at the boy, then, 'Wants to know what we're going to do with the deceased suspect.'

'They're doing an autopsy, yes?' questioned Thiery.

'That would be customary. He also said he has some more reports his officers compiled at the church yesterday. Witness reports; a few of the kids and the rest of the teachers in the school. Said nothing stood out, but he thought we might want them.'

'Okay. I'll need all of them.'

'Right,' said Dunham. 'If you're good here, why don't I go see the sheriff and this Shadtz woman. While I'm there, I'll collate the reports from all the agencies, have my secretary scan them and email them to you?'

'That would be a big help. You have my email?'

Dunham tapped his top breast pocket. 'Right here on your card.'

'Okay. Thanks, Chief. Maybe we can catch up this afternoon.'

'Sounds like a plan. See you later.'

Dunham excused himself, and Mrs Dowling walked him out.

Thiery said, 'Go ahead, Ricky. If it doesn't bother you to talk about what happened yesterday.' He took out his iPad, hit the settings button, then the record button, and placed it on the coffee table between his chair and the sofa.

'Oh, no,' said Ricky, his eyes going huge. 'It was scary, but it was kinda cool, too. Miss Weisz was so brave. She was like the Terminator!'

'Really?' said Thiery. 'Can you start from the beginning? You were in her class, right?'

'Yeah,' said Ricky squirming with anticipation. 'Mrs Miller was out again and … '

'Mrs Miller is your usual teacher?'

'Uh-huh.'

'I see. And how many days had she been out?'

'Gosh, she's been out a lot. I think it was three, no four days, 'cause she was out the Friday before, too. It was almost like Miss Weisz was our permanent teacher; she's been there so much.'

'You like her, don't you Ricky?'

Ricky shrugged.

'I do, but … '

'But, now you're not so sure? Because she had that gun?'

'Yeah. I still like her, but now I'm kinda scared of her.'

'That's understandable, Ricky. But, it sounds like she saved you and the other kids from the bad man.'

'Yeah.'

'Maybe she's not that bad. She's missing right now, and we want to find her, so we can talk to her about that. Anything you remember is going to be helpful.'

'Okay. Anyway, she came in and told us we had to silent-read this story, it's called *Sleepy Hollow*, and it's kinda creepy, because it's about this guy with no head who haunts this town.'

'Oh, yes,' said Thiery. 'It's one of my favourites. Just right for Halloween.'

'Anyway, we were just finishing it because we started it the day earlier. We were gonna make jack-o'-lanterns out of coloured paper after that, but that's when we heard the popping sounds, like firecrackers.'

'Only it wasn't firecrackers, was it?' said Thiery.

'No, sir. It wasn't, but it sounded like it.'

'Where were you sitting when you first heard those sounds?'

'I sit at the front of the class, right next to the teacher's desk, because sometimes I get in trouble, you know?'

'I see. And what did Miss Weisz do when she heard the sounds?'

'Okay, I remember it exactly,' said Ricky excitedly. 'She stood up and went to the window. I wasn't supposed to leave my seat, but I went to the window, too, and I heard her say something, like to herself.'

'Really? Do you remember what she said?'

'Yeah. She said something like, "Not again".'

'Hmmn,' said Thiery. *Not again. Why would she say that?* 'That seems a strange thing to say, doesn't it?'

'I don't know. I guess,' answered Ricky. He began wringing his hands and his words came faster, running together. 'Anyway, the intercom came on about that time, and we could hear the principal ask the men not to shoot the children, and one of the men said they were going to kill everyone, or something like that, and then there were sounds like explosions, and we knew it wasn't firecrackers then.'

Thiery glanced at Mrs Dowling, noted her eyes getting wet. 'Are you okay, Mrs Dowling?'

A tear fell. 'Yes … it's just … things could've been worse for us, obviously. I still shudder when I think how lucky Ricky … all of the children were. But … Dr Montessi and the ladies in the front office are … were so nice. I … just … ' She stood up and crossed the room to where a box of tissues sat, pulled some out, and dabbed her eyes. 'Please continue. You need to hear everything.'

'Okay,' said Thiery. 'Go ahead, Ricky.'

Ricky nodded. 'We all were really scared after we heard the shooting on the intercom. And we could hear noises down the hall. We heard a lady scream and Miss Weisz told us all to get in the closet, but we couldn't all fit. There was too many of us, so she started turning desks over and told us to get behind them. Then Mrs LaForge looked in the window and … and … she got shot.'

'Are you okay to keep talking, Ricky? I know this was very scary. If you need to, take a break.'

'No, sir. I can talk, but it *was* scary. I was hiding behind the desk with Miss Weisz, and I could tell she was scared, too. They started shooting through the door to our classroom. I forgot to tell you that Miss Weisz ran over and locked it, but, anyway, it didn't last long, 'cause the guy that came into our class had one of those guns like they use in *Black Ops*, you know, the Xbox game, like a military weapon, and it just tore the door right down.'

The boy stopped to get a drink of Gatorade that his mother had sat down in front of him. He gulped as if he hadn't drunk anything for days. It stained his upper lip red. After a moment and a deep breath, he continued.

'He saw Miss Weisz and he told her to stand up. Then, she tried to tell the man a fib and said we were all out on the playground, but he told her to, well, he said a bad word, you know, the 'F' word, and he told her to shut up. Then he asked her what her name was— '

Thiery stiffened and leaned forward. 'Wait,' he said, 'the gunman asked Miss Weisz her name?'

'Yeah. And when she didn't answer right away, he shot his gun around the room and it was so loud! He asked Miss Weisz her name again and, this time, she answered, but she told him her name was 'Millie,' or something like that. I knew she was still fibbing because I heard her and Mrs Wallace talking one morning and Mrs Wallace called her Erica, but I don't know why she said Millie.'

'Then what happened?'

'I peeked up over the edge of the pile of desks and I saw that man had taken off his mask.'

'Yeah? Did that scare you?'

'Yeah, I guess a little but not so much. He looked old, or sick, or something, He was sweating a lot. I could hear him breathe and it sounded like when I was a little kid. When I had asthma I sounded like that.'

'Like a wheezing?'

'Uh-huh.'

'Then what?'

'The man kind of smiled at Miss Weisz, and then Rachel came out of the closet and she was crying and her arm was bleeding.

Miss Weisz saw her, and went over to her and wrapped a cloth around it that she got out of her purse. The man with the gun was putting another one of those things in it … '

'A bullet clip?'

'Yep, that's it. I was watching Miss Weisz, and the look on her face changed. She looked like my mom when she's really, really mad. Then the guy with the gun started to point it at her again and she pulled a gun out of her purse and she didn't say 'drop it', or anything like that like they do on TV. She just aimed and fired. It wasn't as loud as the man's big gun, but it hit him, right here in the face.' Ricky pointed to the middle of his forehead.

Thiery stared at Ricky for a moment, trying to assess what he was telling him, but also thinking about how it might affect him later on in life. As a father, Thiery often considered how crime affected, not only the victims, but the eyewitnesses. He wondered if the school would provide grief counselling and made a mental note to check with the school board on their plans.

'Mrs Dowling,' said Thiery, 'I'll take that cup of coffee if the offer is still good.'

She needed that. Listening to her son describe how close he was to people shooting guns, getting killed, the little girl that could've been killed, the man that was killed, it was all too much for her. She said, 'Of course. I'll be right back.' Thiery could hear her sniffling as she poured the coffee. She returned; her eyes dry but red, her face drawn.

'Okay, Ricky,' said Thiery. 'You're doing very well. What you're telling me is very helpful. What did Miss Weisz do after that?'

Ricky took another sip of his Gatorade. 'Let me think. She was just standing there. It was quiet and some of the kids came out from behind the desk. A lot of them were crying, and the girls went to hug Miss Weisz. She was crying, too. Then, we heard more shots and Miss Weisz said, 'There's another one out there.' Then, she took her gun and told us to close our eyes and that it was going to be all right, but I didn't close my eyes like everyone else. I just kept watching Miss Weisz and I saw her walk over to the man with the gun and she shot him again. In the head. It … it was pretty gross. She saw me looking, and she told me to sit back down and she would be back.'

Thiery was amazed. He tried to picture what was, in his mind, this demure elementary school teacher calmly walking over and putting a kill shot into the gunman's head. This was not an ordinary action that might be expected from anyone, much less a school teacher in charge of a room full of seven and eight-year-olds. He found himself hoping he could meet her. He also found himself doubting this tragedy was mere happenstance.

So many questions now. Why would a crazed gunman ask the teacher her name before he planned to shoot her? What is the likelihood that Erica Weisz would have a gun in her purse and possess the willingness to use it? Was she expecting something like this? Was that even her real name? And the biggest question – where the hell was she?

Thiery pondered the fresh facts. Historically, when these mass murders occurred, investigators rather quickly gathered conclusive evidence pointing to the fact the gunman, or gunmen, were fanatics with some political message to announce, or a perceived slight to vindicate. That model didn't seem to fit here. A lot of things did not fit, and Thiery was beginning to believe something else was going on, something that suggested premeditation and planning. Lots of planning.

'Thanks for your time, Mrs Dowling, and you, too, young man,' said Thiery as he stood to leave. 'You've been a big help.'

Mrs Dowling walked him to the door. As he stepped out into the warm afternoon, Thiery heard Ricky ask his mother, 'Mom, is it okay if Seth comes over? He's got a new Airsoft gun and we want to play cops and robbers out back.'

Mrs Dowling gazed into Thiery's face as if she were drugged. Her lips trembled, and a tear ran down her face as she closed the door.

TWELVE

By the afternoon, news cameras recorded the angry crowds gathering in front of Travis Hanks Elementary School. On one side of the street, closest to the memorials of pastel-coloured teddy bears, flowers, and home-made posters expressing love and sorrow, people demanded this type of incident never happen again in the US. They carried signs and banners that read: TOO MANY PEOPLE ARE DYING BECAUSE TOO MANY PEOPLE HAVE GUNS!

Across from that group were crowds of people carrying signs – some misspelled – that read: OWNING GUNS IS A RIGHT, NOT A CRIME! DON'T LET A TRADEGY CAUSE ANOTHER TRADEGY-THE LOSS OF OUR CONSTITUTION! Within this crowd was a group of men adorned in camouflage wear and various baseball caps with embroidered slogans. Some were hunters. Some were simple rednecks. One man, in particular, was loud and opinionated, and drawing people to him like a fire and brimstone Southern Baptist preacher. It was Ellis Coody and, once again, the media was drawn to his vehement rhetoric like flies to shit.

'Hey, I think it goes without saying this is a tragedy,' he announced to a group of reporters, 'but if you're going to condemn my son for bringing a gun into that school, then you need to condemn Erica Weisz for having one, too.' Using the spotlight for his propaganda, he continued to try to avert blame from his son. 'I'll say it again: none of us knows exactly what went on in that school. We knowed there was some shootin', but who started it?'

'Mr. Coody,' interrupted one intrepid reporter, 'police reported your son was one of the men who attacked the school. Are you denying that?'

'You' damn straight I am,' he said, his already ruddy face glowing with heat. 'There isn't a single witness who states he saw my son shoot any of those teachers that died. Not a one. But, we do know that one of the teachers shot my son. Now, he's in a coma in the hospital, and where is she? If she didn't do somethin' wrong, why'd she run off?'

Jonathan Montessi, the husband of the slain school principal, stood on the opposite side of the street with the anti-gun group, lamenting the deaths of his wife and her staff. He was still in a daze, unable to come to terms with the sudden loss of his spouse of eighteen years and the violation of their school. He was sleepless, emotionally charged, and within earshot of Coody's blathering. With tears streaming down his face, he strode across the street and, without words, punched Coody Sr in the face. A brief melee followed, all caught on live television, chronicling the disintegration of the community. Police, standing guard by the school – which was still an active crime scene – moved into the crowd and tried to defuse the chaos.

Dave Gruber managed to break away and reassemble his camera crew. He reported back to Gail Summer and THN. 'Well, you can see, Gail,' he panted, 'as we noted yesterday, the aftermath of the "human tornadoes" encompasses not only the tragic loss of lives, it tears at the very fabric of this community. And, once again, the question is posted: where is Erica Weisz, the teacher who reportedly shot the two gunmen who entered the school yesterday morning and has now disappeared? Where did she go, and why is she running? Back to you, Gail.'

'Okay, Dave, thank you. Try to stay safe,' Gail advised. The camera focused on her concerned face. 'In other news, a case of road rage led one driver to shoot another in Atlanta today … '

Ellis Coody managed to extricate himself from the crowd, a few of his bubbas surrounding him, offering their sympathies and allegiance. They convened in the parking lot, leaning over the bed of his pickup truck, reaching into the giant Igloo cooler, digging into the ice, and popping open some Busch beers.

Coody Sr wiped the blood from his nose with the back of his hand, smearing a red trail across his cheek. It looked like war paint. 'Thanks, boys,' he said, addressing the group. 'I 'ppreciate you bein' here, showin' your support. But, I'm goin' to ask you to do me another favour. I got a friend in the Sheriff's Office that tells me a car was stolen from the hospital up in Lakeland last night, and they think that teacher probably took it. It was a black Camaro SS. There ain't a lot of places to go between Bartow and here, 'specially for someone what just got buckshot plucked outta their belly. I'm bettin', iffen we got a buncha eyes lookin' in the Lake Wales area, we could find a black Camaro. I'd sure like to find the bitch that put my boy in the hospital and turned him into a cripple. Anyone with me?'

A resounding, 'Yeah, man,' came from Coody's loyal friends, and they climbed into their mud-splashed trucks, gun racks prominently displayed in the back windows. Each of them called some of their friends, who, in turn, called more of their friends. Within half an hour, there were a hundred sets of eyes from Kissimmee in the north to Sebring in the south and from Yeehaw Junction to the east, back to Plant City in the west, all looking for the woman called Erica Weisz driving a stolen black Camaro. The official Sheriff's APB seemed like an afterthought.

Erica checked herself in the mirror – her new blonde hair was a startling change. She'd done a decent dye job, though the roots at the centre parting still showed dark, as did her eyebrows. But, it would do. She put on the jeans again and a loose-fitting, comfortable but nondescript blouse that would not draw attention, and a clean pair of Nikes. She just couldn't get away from those running shoes. Just in case.

Picking up the new cell phone, she considered calling Moral, but she couldn't get past the fact that he was the only person who could've known where she was. *Could she trust him?* This wasn't the first time she'd had reason to doubt him.

The more she thought about it, the more she was convinced that the gunmen had not come to the school randomly. She kept asking herself: *Why did that man ask my name? Would a crazed mass murderer do that?*

She thought of the man as he'd confronted her class, removing his mask, an act in itself that said one of two things: *no one here is getting out alive,* or *I'm not getting out of here alive.* It was a look of finality. She remembered the look on the other, younger man's face. It was not one of resignation like the older man. It was one of complete insanity, like the look in a mad dog's eyes.

Erica's mind swam incoherently, and she felt her eyes burn. A sign of fever, maybe? She felt her forehead with the back of her hand. It was warm. It would be a miracle if she didn't get an infection from the abdominal wound. She knew she should be in a hospital with a steady infusion of IV antibiotics, but she didn't feel safe there. She wondered: *Was it all my imagination?*

Digging into her purse, she found a notepad and wrote down some essentials she needed from the store. If she could wait until dark, when the roads and the stores were less busy, grab the few items she needed, and clean out the 'B' haven house, she could probably get out of the state by early morning. But then what? *Where would she go? Was any place safe?*

The notion that, if she could get to the main offices of the Department of Justice in Washington, perhaps she would be safe there. Get a new manager, a new location, a new start. But, she'd been in Washington before, and her 'haven' there had been compromised, too. Before that, in Las Vegas – when it all started – she had been surrounded by deputies, but, while they had kept *her* safe, she'd lost everything and everyone else.

Memories of that time slipped back into her mind like a shark creeping up from the depths while she floated on a volatile surface. She couldn't believe it had been three years. Fatigue swept over her as she tried to fight off those horrible images, but, before long, she found herself curled into a foetal position on a bumpy couch, drifting off to sleep while scenes of blood-splashed walls filled her mind.

The sound of tyres crunching over the shell-rock drive startled her awake. She wasn't sure how long she'd been asleep, but the light coming in the window had morphed into that salmon colour that is trademark to Florida sunsets. Her throat was so dry it felt like something was stuck in it, and it hurt to swallow. Her skin was hot and flushed, and she no longer doubted if she had a fever.

A car door slammed, and she sat up, her wounded side screaming at her for moving so fast. She managed to get up and hobble back to the room where she'd left her purse and the gun. She looked out the window of the living room where she had a view of the drive. There was a big, silver car behind the Camaro, but no one was inside.

Erica wobbled into the kitchen and looked out the window and into the backyard, but saw nothing. She remembered a small utility room in the back of the house, near the bedrooms, and rushed back to make sure the door was locked. When she got there, the door that led outside was open.

She knew she'd screwed up, even as she turned and found the man standing behind her. Her gun was at her side; his was aimed at her, the hammer pulled back ready to fire. He was saying something to her, but there was a persistent ringing in her ears, and her vision began to lose its focus. Her stomach reeled and began to empty itself, bile dripping from her slack mouth, the effort so strenuous she felt herself falling, striking her knees against the hard terrazzo floor, before coming to a rest against the side of a washing machine, its cold steel like ice against her face.

THIRTEEN

Thiery had met Sheriff Conroy, as well as a few other local police chiefs, at the makeshift command centre they had set up at the church. He collected the rest of the reports from the various agencies and thanked both of them for putting out the APB for Erica Weisz. He made a mental note that, if they were going to stay on the site past tomorrow, he would have them move in the Mobile Command Unit, or relocate to the Calusa County Sheriff's Office headquarters so they would not intrude on the church more than they had. Thiery wasn't thrilled with the idea of setting up a Unified Command System at the Sheriff's Office, so he sent a quick text to the FDLE Logistics Department to locate the closest MCU available.

Conroy still seemed to have a chip on his shoulder, but he did share the information with Thiery about the stolen Camaro and the hospital's security videos. Thiery had watched the security cam videos and seen a person he thought might have been the Weisz woman scurrying out in a white lab coat, as reported, but the camera angle did not extend into the parking lot, and the footage was grainy and not much help.

Thiery shared with them details of the meeting with the Dowling boy and also the news about the gunman asking the teacher her name. All agreed that was odd, perhaps unprecedented anecdotally, to say the least, in mass shootings.

After delegating a few more assignments and dismissing other departments less involved in the investigation, Thiery adjourned the meeting. He and Sheriff Conroy were parked next to each other.

'I didn't want to bring it up again in front of the others, Sheriff,' Thiery addressed the man as they approached their respective vehicles, 'but have you looked into the dispatch and arrival times reported by the communications office?'

Conroy looked up under the wide brim of his hat, his eyes flashing anger. 'Yeah, I did.'

'And?'

'And it was a mistake. They still use the old cardpunch system. They get a call, punch a time clock, dispatch the call, punch another time clock. Units go en route, they punch another time clock. They had a new girl working that morning, and she got behind in all the excitement and punched the cards late. That's all,' he ended, colour rising in his neck like a thermometer.

Thiery nodded his head. Hard to believe they still used an old cardpunch system, but they seemed a little behind the times around here, so Thiery accepted it. For now. 'Thanks,' he said.

Conroy said nothing, and they both got into their cars and motored away from the church; Conroy accelerating away in a huff while Thiery moved out slowly, accepting that he had a bunch of monotonous paperwork to wade through. He headed back to his hotel dolefully.

It was late in the afternoon, his room at the Sun Beam bathed in tangerine light, his eyes grainy from reading all the police and witness reports, when Thiery got the call from the governor.

'You want to tell me how come I'm the last dumb-ass in the state of Florida to find out the teacher has disappeared?' Croll spat through clenched teeth.

Thiery fought back a yawn. 'You want me to call you every time something new pops up down here?'

There was silence for a moment then words so angered they could only come out one at a time.

'No ... Mr ... Thiery ... just ... when ... it ... pertains ... to ... the ... fucking ... woman ... that ... the fucking President ... of ... the ... United States ... wants ... to ... meet.'

'Sir, you sent me here to do a job ... '

'Yeah, yeah. A job I guess I should have let Sheriff Conroy handle.'

'It was one of your sheriff's men who was watching her when she vanished.'

Silence.

Thiery began again. 'Governor, this thing is turning out to be something more than we thought it was. It's tragic enough it was another school shooting, but there seems to be more to it than that. Now, the media has blown it up into a gun control issue, and people are demonstrating in front of the school. You want to bring the President into that mix?'

'It's not what I want to do that matters, Thiery. It's what *he* wants, and he has called me directly and told me he wants to meet this woman. His press secretary is arranging an event for next week that will be publicized *internationally*. You know he is trying to push a gun control bill through the Senate right now.'

'I read the newspapers. I'm sure he'll get some sympathetic ears because of the shooting. But, I'm not sure how it will help his agenda to have a teacher who probably saved dozens of lives by using a gun.'

'So now, you want to help steer the President's policies?'

'Sir,' Thiery said calmly, 'I hear your concerns, and I can assure you I am doing the job I was sent here to do. But, before everyone decides who is the hero and who is the bad guy here, we should complete our investigation. You'd score major brownie points if you'd let the President know that. There's something hinky going on here, and it would behove him to stay away from it right now, until we have some answers.'

'Fine. Okay. Fine,' the governor said, though Thiery guessed the man was far from 'fine' with anything. 'I'll tell the President that we need more time, but you get this clear, Thiery: you don't make these play calls. We have a chance to get some national limelight on some of our concerns in Florida – low teacher salaries, shortage of police, rising crime rates – and we could blow it.'

Now, it was Thiery's turn to get pissed. 'I'll be sure to keep that in mind when I'm talking to the families who lost a loved one.' He paused to allow his words to sink in. 'If there's nothing else, sir, I've got a lot of work to do.'

The reply was a dial tone in his ear.

Thiery wasn't sure why he had blown up at the governor. Maybe he was burned out. Maybe he just didn't give a flip about the job, anymore. It had cost him a wife and took so much of his time away from his sons that, now that he could see 'the light at the end of the tunnel,' as the retirees referred to being near the end the career, it occurred to him that he'd missed the point. One has a job to support his family and, by doing so, form the bonds that keep them together. *What did he have now?*

He suddenly remembered that Dunham had said Frank Shadtz's wife had come to claim his body. He wondered how that was going. He hadn't heard back from Dunham since morning. He decided to give him a call.

'Oh, hello Agent Thiery,' said Dunham. 'How's it going for you?'

'It's going. I've gone through most of the reports. Talked to a few more witnesses. None was more helpful than the Dowling boy, though. Thanks for going over there with me. I think it made them feel more comfortable talking to me with your introduction. How did it go with the Shadtz woman?'

Dunham cleared his throat. 'Well, better than my meeting with the county sheriff.'

'Oh?'

'Yeah. Sheriff Conroy isn't being exactly cooperative. When I showed up, he was expecting you and asked where the – quote,

'Governor's boy,' unquote – was. I told him you were busy interviewing a witness, and he gave me a look like I just said something bad about his mother. I'm fairly thick-skinned, but it's pretty clear he resents me, and probably you, for taking lead over him.'

'I know. I saw him at the command centre. He'll have to get over it.'

'I suppose, but did you know he and the governor go way back?'

'I got a sense of that last night.'

'Anyway, I did talk to Shadtz's wife. Her name is Gloria. They have a son with some developmental problems and they are divorced, but it seems she was still carrying a torch for him. She's pretty upset.'

'Did she tell you anything useful?'

'Not too much. Says he's never done anything like this before, naturally, and that he was never a gun guy. Said he loves kids, so she can't imagine why he would've come down here and suddenly decided to go shoot up an elementary school.'

'Did she mention how he and Coody came to meet each other?'

'She never heard of Coody before last night.'

'I was afraid you might say that,' Thiery replied. *Another dead end.* 'Anything else?'

'Oh, yeah. When I couldn't get much help from the sheriff, I offered to take the lady to the coroner's office, and she said okay. She's really nice, and I could sense she wanted to tell me something. So, as we were driving, she asked me to pull over. She had an item to show me. So, I pulled over, and she reaches into her purse and pulls out a big fat envelope full of cash. She said Shadtz left it for her with a note that said he was sorry he wasn't a better husband and the money might help with their son.'

'How much was it?'

'Fifty thousand dollars.'

'Wow. That's a lot of money for someone who was a part-time bouncer.'

'That's what I was thinking, too.'

'She didn't know where he got it?'

'Not a clue.'

'How about the coroner? Anything newsworthy there?'

'You could say that. The coroner said he'd need a couple more days to complete the autopsy. Mrs Shadtz wasn't too happy about it 'cause she's got to get back to her kid in Chicago, so I asked him if there was anything he could do to speed things up. He asked if we wanted to have his brain studied, you know, like they do with some of the serial killers and mass murderers. I said that his wife still had the right to okay or deny that request. She said there was nothing wrong with his brain, it was his lungs that bothered him most.'

Thiery remembered the Dowling boy had mentioned something about how the gunman seemed to be having trouble breathing. *Wheezing like asthma*, Ricky had said. 'What about his lungs?' Thiery asked Dunham.

'That's what I asked,' the Chief answered, 'and you know what the coroner said? He said, his results weren't conclusive, but, as a matter of protocol, he had done an initial autopsy to save the bullets for forensic evidence. He said, as part of the investigation protocols, he had to remove the bullets from the body. He took them out of Shadtz's skull and, when he did, he found some lesions. He decided to do a preliminary look and opened the chest cavity. While he had Shadtz's chest open, he could see he had tumours all over in his lungs.'

'What kind of tumours?'

'Just a sec', let me check my notes.' Thiery heard pages flipping. 'Here it is,' Dunham continued. 'He called it metastatic lung cancer. He was pretty forthright, and the widow seemed to be able to take it, so I asked, could that be cured? And the coroner said, no, it is fatal. Shadtz would've been dead within six to eight weeks.'

Thiery sat up, now, his mind racing.

Dunham went on. 'Anyway, I took the lady for a coffee, and she said she needed a place to stay. I remembered you were staying at the Sun Beam and told her maybe she should stay there; maybe you'd like to talk to her. She said she would, and we left it at that.

Did she come up there? She was driving a rental. It was a late model, white Mercury Milan if you're looking for it.'

Thiery looked out the window. The parking lot was full, probably from all the media people in town, but he could see every car from his hotel room window. He spied the white Mercury.

'Agent Thiery, are you still there?'

FOURTEEN

Moral watched her sleep. When he'd placed her in the bed, she felt light, as if she were withering away to nothing, and her skin was hot to the touch. Maybe if he just waited, she would die on her own. That would solve all of their problems; she could stop running, and he wouldn't have to keep playing this deadly game.

Erica awoke to the sound of sniffling. She was fevered and her eyes burned, but she could make out the image of a man sitting in a chair next to her. It was Robert Moral. Trying to sit up, she found her hands had been secured to the bed's headboard with handcuffs.

'What … are … you … doing?' she asked weakly, her throat beyond parched.

Moral wiped his eyes with the back of his coat sleeve. His cheeks shone wet. He was drinking from a pint bottle of scotch. He leaned forward and tipped the bottle into her mouth. The liquid burned her cracked lips and sore throat, but allowed her to swallow.

'Why did you cuff me to the bed?'

Moral shook his head. His eyes bulged and a patina of sweat made his forehead slick. 'I need time to think,' he said.

'About what?' said Erica, still in a fog.

'About what our next step should be.'

The sip of booze helped wake her. 'How about getting me the fuck out of here,' she suggested, her anger coming back, but with a touch of fear. *What's he going to do to me?*

'It's not that easy,' he replied. 'It's going to take time to establish a new start. We didn't think this one would be compromised so soon. You shouldn't have called so much attention to yourself.'

Erica tugged at her binds. 'It wouldn't be compromised if someone hadn't told those guys I was teaching at the school. Did you do that?'

Moral glanced at her, but couldn't keep his eyes on hers. 'You don't know what you're saying,' he said. 'They were some crazed kids. One of them used to go to the school. Maybe he was bullied there. We don't know all the details, yet, but he was a nutcase. Played shoot 'em up video games all day, then hooked up with another nut, and they launched a raid on the school. It's happening all over the country every week now.'

'The man who came to shoot me wasn't a kid. He was a grown man.'

'What difference does it— '

Erica bolted up, but was held fast by the handcuffs. 'He asked me *my name*, Robert! Can you tell me why he'd do that, huh?'

Moral scrunched up his brow. 'I can't imagine— '

'Oh, shut up,' she cut him off again. 'Do you think I'm stupid, as well as naively trusting? It was the same as Washington, and the other places before that. My position keeps getting compromised. How is that, *Bob*?'

'I ... I don't know, Erica. I don't understand it, either,' he said, wiping his face with a yellowed handkerchief. 'We'll have to put you into a different programme.'

'Fuck that, Bob. I've got the emergency relocation money and another ID. Uncuff me from this bed, and let me get the hell out of here.'

He'd forgotten about the money. *Damn, there is a God*, he thought to himself. 'Okay, Erica, er, uh, Millie. You could make a run for it, but, without the agency's protection, how long do you think you'll last out there on your own?'

Erica nodded her head toward her stomach. Blood had seeped through her shirt. 'Yeah, looks like you guys are doing a great job, protecting me.'

'I'm sorry about that. I swear this wasn't because of us.'

'You don't think the Esperanzas were behind this?'

'I don't see how – '

'Shut up and release me!'

Moral stared at her, trying to come up with some excuse, some story that might make sense to her. *Maybe she was talking to a friend? Maybe there was a mole in the Marshal's Office?*

Fuck it. He didn't have to tell her anything. He thought about the money again. If he could use the cash to make *more* money, he might be able to get out of this, yet. Give him some time to think, sort things out. If nothing else, he could pay off that second mortgage and the credit cards. Maybe help his daughter get out of the trouble she was in. Thinking of her, of what she was doing now, always made him sick to his stomach. He felt an overwhelming anxiety overtake him. If he could only get the weight off his back, give himself breathing room. Sensing a plan, of sorts, gelling, he stalled her a while longer.

'My job is to keep you safe, Millie,' he said. 'I think it's best you stay here, and you won't if I take the cuffs off.'

'Quit calling me Millie. You never knew her.'

'Yes, I did. She was a brave woman.'

Erica stared at the ceiling, hot tears spilling from her eyes. 'If you were concerned about me you would get me medical treatment. What *are* you up to?'

'I'm not up to anything. It's my opinion you're a danger to yourself, and that's what's going in my report. I just need some time to set up a different plan. We need to find out what you're doing that's allowing you to be compromised. Now, where's that money?'

Erica glared at him. 'Fuck you, you piece of shit. Find it yourself.'

'You're delirious, Millie,' he tried. 'You don't know what you're saying … '

'Right,' she said, giving up. What could she do? She felt her heart beating in her throat. She was still dehydrated and needed more of the antibiotic. 'Then call in some cops to help us.'

'You know I can't do that. We can't compromise your identity and position.'

'Go to hell.'

Moral got up and began to look through the house. It was a tiny place, maybe nine hundred square feet under roof. It didn't take him long to find her purse. The money, stolen car keys, and her new ID were inside. He left the new identity – Christine Angel – in the purse and took the cash.

It was almost night, so the dog track would soon close. But, there was a Hard Rock Casino up in Orlando. If he could get there, double the $10K, or even turn it into a hundred, he might have some bargaining power. If he could make *that* much, he might even be able to *double* that, then he'd have the world by the balls. Suddenly, he was in charge, *electric*, on top of the world.

He stuffed the money packet into his inside coat pocket and headed for the door.

'Robert!' Erica yelled out to him.

He stopped at the door, his hand on the knob. 'Yeah?'

'If I can get out of this, I'm going to kill you, too.'

Moral felt a chill run down what spine he had left, and a lump of what felt like jagged ice pushed into his throat, his elation fell away. As he walked out to his car, feeling the lump of money pressing against his chest like the barrel of a gun, he murmured, 'I wish you would.'

The FBI's role in the school shooting was small. *Diminutive* was the word that kept coming back to Sara Logan as she waited to hear results from the forensic lab. She was bored and she didn't like to be bored, because it often led her into trouble. She'd been bored – with her job, with her marriage, with her life – a few years ago, when she'd met Thiery. The idea of a harmless (*who was she trying to kid?*) one time tryst seemed like something that might end that boredom, add some excitement to her life. Men had been hitting on her ever since she'd been in the FBI, opportunities were always there, but she'd resisted them, until Thiery. He was handsome, vulnerable – an easy target – and she turned up her sexy charm, drenched herself in alluring musky cologne, and gave it a whirl. Then – like an idiot – fell in love with the man.

Logan would never leave her husband; he was a contractor who afforded her a wonderful life and did not question her many nights away 'on assignment'. Like her, he did not want any children. That had been the problem with Thiery; his two sons. Not bad boys, but she didn't want to be mother to them. But God, Thiery was a match for her in bed. A guy who could finally keep up with her stroke for stroke, so to speak. She missed that as she went home to her husband, sixteen years older and well into slumberland by the time she slipped between the sheets.

In the end, she began to feel guilt, then shame, and she ended it, though she never openly declared it. Thiery had begun to ask when she going to get a divorce and she told him, with all the emotion of a cold-blooded killer, *never, silly – this has just been some fun*. The look on his face told her he wouldn't call again, and he didn't.

She tried to put him out of her mind as she idly plucked through evidence reports Thiery had emailed to her. One of them had a list of guns the shooters had used at the school, as well as the additional firearms found at Coody's house. The list had the make, model, calibre, and serial numbers.

Logan fed the list into the FBI's database of guns. It was a lark, really. She assumed the guns would be stolen or the serial numbers faked, but the database returned a hit almost immediately. It was a list of confiscated guns the Kentucky State Police auctioned off months ago. Logan couldn't believe it. Some cities were doing buy-backs and one-day amnesty programmes for folks with illegally obtained guns. But, in Kentucky, they were selling the damn things like hotcakes at a Sunday fundraiser.

Logan's mind began to race. *Federal law does not prohibit the transportation of guns across state lines unless, of course, the person moving them is a convicted felon.* She looked up Shadtz and Coody in the FBI's NCIC (National Criminal Information Center) and while Coody was a dead end, she found several convictions for Shadtz. She felt a slight adrenaline rush. *This case was going to be federal after all.*

She called Kentucky State Police, got hold of an admin branch manager who confirmed the weapons had been sold as a lot to a gun dealer licensed to sell in Vegas. Logan asked for the dealer's information. It was a pawn shop called Tito's Pawn & Guns, owned by a man named Tito Viveros. Logan called the pawn shop.

'Hello, this is Tito,' said a man with a distinct Mexican accent.

'This is Special Agent Sara Logan with the FBI in Florida,' she replied. 'I'm following up on some of the weapons we seized that we think might have come from your shop. I just need a few minutes of your time.'

'Uh, what?' said Viveros, feeling a sheen of sweat break out on his forehead and the back of his neck.

'It looks like you bought a collection of guns from the Kentucky State Police Department a few months back. Is that correct?'

Now, Viveros was in a full-blown panic. Fucking A he'd bought them. Sold them, too, to someone he wasn't supposed to be selling them to: a kid in Florida. But, it wasn't supposed to be able to come back to him. A federal agent who had set up the deal through the Esperanzas was supposed to take care of that. *Fuck!* he thought. *What now?*

'Can you speak louder?' he improvised, poorly. 'My phone, eet isn't working so well.'

Logan fumed. 'Don't pretend you didn't hear me. I need to know who you sold the lot to. You want me to fly out there and audit every record in your business? Think you could stand up to that?'

'I … I'm sorry, my Eng-leesh, eet ees not so good … ' he said and hung up. Then, he immediately dialled the man who had helped broker the deal: Julio Esperanza.

Julio recognized the number and did not pick up. He let it go to voicemail, then listened to the recording.

'Hey, *Jefe*. It's Tito,' he announced. 'Hit me back, man. The FBI just called. They were asking about that shipment of guns that went to the kid in Florida. I thought your guy was supposed to take care of that, man, make it a clean sale. If someone fucked up, it's not on me. I'll stall, man, but we might have some bad shit happening. Call me back, quick.'

FIFTEEN

On the way to the motel lobby, Thiery saw the perfectly chiselled and megawatt spot-lit face of Dave Gruber, along with his camera crew and a young blonde who chased Gruber around doing his make-up. Thiery avoided eye contact; he didn't want to talk to this cat right then.

Thiery manoeuvred revolving doors to reach the front desk of the motel, showed his FDLE identification to a young lady with active chewing gum, and asked for Gloria Shadtz's room number. Without hesitation, she pointed and replied, 'Number Four.'

It was long after sunset, and the concrete walk outside was dimly lit. Cool air moved in, lending Thiery a chill as he rapped a knuckle against the door marked with a crooked '4'. He heard shuffling noises inside, a chain latch clanking open.

Gloria Shadtz opened the door, pillow creases in her face, her eyelids swollen. *Must've cried herself to sleep this afternoon*, thought Thiery. Even lousy husbands need to be mourned he supposed.

'Hi, Mrs Shadtz. I'm Agent Thiery with the Florida Department of Law Enforcement.'

Gloria nodded and yawned. 'Oh, yeah. Chief Dunham said you might call on me.'

'I'm sorry to bother you, but I'm investigating the shooting at the school yesterday, and I'd like to ask you a few questions about your husband.'

'Ex-husband,' she chided, fingering her hair back, trying to make it look right.

'Okay.'

'It's nice out. You want to sit on the back patio? Maybe have a beer?' she suggested, touching her upper lip with the tip of her tongue.

'Out back is fine. I'll hold off the beer for now, though.'

'Suit yourself.' Gloria held up a finger indicating a minute was needed. She rooted around in the room's small refrigerator and came out with a six pack of Pabst Blue Ribbon. She closed and locked the door. Thiery kept up with her surprisingly energetic pace to the back of the motel where plastic chairs and tables sat around a pool whose surface was still and dark. Thiery sat in one of the chairs, instantly feeling its coldness seep through the thin fabric of his trousers.

Gloria opened an icy beer and took a quick swig. She pulled a cigarette from a pack of Camels and lit up. 'I'd offer you one, but you don't smoke, do you?'

'No,' said Thiery, smiling. 'How can you tell?'

'Your teeth are too white,' she said, smiling back. 'Frank smoked like a chimney.'

'Yeah?' said Thiery, watching her take another pull off the beer. He could see its amber colour, the drops of condensation running down the brown bottle like rivulets of sweat from a lover's body. He was parched and tried to think of when last he drank anything. He could almost taste the malty beer, thought about changing his mind and accepting her offer, but decided against it. One often led to another, then another. He had too much work to do. 'Tell me more about Frank,' he asked.

'What do you want to know?' Her voice a low rumble of gravel after a few pulls on the cigarette.

'Okay,' he said, thinking, *twenty questions it is*. 'Did he dislike kids?'

'No' she answered, exhaling a cloud of smoke. 'In fact, he was a fuck-up for the most part, but one thing I can say is he was a good father. We have a boy. Danny. He has Down Syndrome. He can be a handful, and sometimes I just don't have the patience. Frank always did. It was like they could communicate in a way I never could.'

'I see,' Thiery said as he took notes on his tablet. 'So, why do you think Frank would move down here, befriend a guy like Coody, and attack an elementary school?'

Gloria pushed her chin up and blew out a plume of smoke aimed at the stars. She shrugged and shook her head.

'Chief Dunham said Frank left you some money,' Thiery continued. 'Where do you think he got that?'

Gloria shot him a look of concern. 'You're not going to try to take the money, are you?'

Thiery thought about it. Maybe there were fingerprints. Maybe the serial numbers would yield clues. But, he said, 'No.' He could hear a sigh of relief in her next exhalation of smoke.

'Frank was something else,' she announced. 'If you would've seen him when he was younger. God, the ladies loved him. It was like he put Spanish Fly, or cigarette ashes, in the girls' drinks, you know, to make 'em horny? 'Cause they got hot in the pants real quick around him. I was one of them. Man, I fell for that guy. Put up with a lot of shit over the years, too. He wasn't a bad man; he just couldn't keep out of trouble.'

Thiery looked up from his tablet. 'What kind of trouble?' he asked.

'Well,' Gloria considered as she tapped ashes onto the cement pool deck between them, 'he was a bouncer for the most part, so he was always getting into fights, even when he wasn't at the bar. When he *was* at the bar, people were always asking him for drugs, so he got into selling grass and coke, and got busted a few times for that. Then he did some scut-work for some of the mob guys, leaning on people if they owed a loan shark, shit like that. I think you cops call it extortion. Hell, if you live in Chicago, sooner or later, you're going to be rubbing up against some made guys.'

Thiery sat up now, his interest piqued. 'Yeah? Do you think that scut-work would include a hit on someone?'

'You mean take a contract, like to murder someone?'

'Yes.'

Gloria thought about it for a few minutes, lighting another cigarette with the burning filter of the last one. 'If you would've asked me that a year ago, I would've said no. Absolutely not. He was tough, but he wasn't vicious. When he started getting sick, it was like I could see a fear in his eyes that wasn't there before. People do crazy shit when they get scared. But, he never owned guns that I knew of. He was a straight barroom brawler, a bare knuckles guy. I just can't see him as a hit man.'

'But, what if he knew he was dying?' Thiery asked. 'Would he do something like that if he knew he didn't have long to live? Maybe take a hit so he could leave you and Danny something?'

Gloria stared at Thiery as if she were in a darkened room and he'd come in and turned on the lights. 'Could be,' she answered. Then she considered the obvious. 'But, who would call a hit on a bunch of school kids?'

Thiery leaned forward. 'Gloria, I don't know what you know about the shooting, but none of the kids were killed. One was shot in the arm, but I think it was a mistake. I don't think Frank meant to shoot her.'

Gloria frowned. 'It doesn't make sense. Who would be the target then?'

'I was hoping you could tell me.'

'Like I said, I can't see Frank doing a hit.'

'But, what if he knew he was dying?' he asked again 'What if he thought it was the only way he could leave Randy something?'

Gloria drew deep on her cigarette and looked toward the horizon. A green glow, the last goodnight wave of the fading sun, held up the blackness of the rest of the sky. She wrapped her lips around the mouth of the bottle and chugged it back until it drained. The beer foam sliding down the neck of the bottle like dirty soap suds. She looked back at Thiery, her eyes wet. She nodded. 'He might do that. Who got killed there?'

'Mostly staff,' he answered, 'Mostly women. One man was killed, but he was an old Army veteran. I believe he might have tried to stop the shooters, playing soldier one last time.'

'God bless, but that's just crazy.'

Thiery looked at the ground. 'Yeah. I know. But, something about this school shooting doesn't make sense. These incidents are always tragic, but they seem to follow a pattern. A neglected, or bullied, teen isolates himself from society, then inundates his tiny world with violent video games and off-the-wall Internet exploration. They look for anarchists' sites, people who have a beef with the government, and so on. Finds out where he can buy guns and how to make explosives. Accumulates his weaponry and puts together some sort of crazed manifesto. Then he snaps one day and acts out on it. Coody fits that bill, but Frank doesn't.'

'I just can't understand why Frank would do something like this.'

'Did he ever mention Coody to you?'

'Never.'

'How about some of those made men you talked about; do you remember any of their names?'

Gloria scrunched up her face as if trying to remember was a physically painful experience. 'There was a family he worked for a couple times,' she said. 'They weren't mafia, though. They were Mexicans. Big time drug kingpins that had interests in Chicago, as well as other places. Sometimes they sent him out of town. New York. Vegas, a couple times. Usually, he was a mule for them, you know, carrying dope. Sometimes, he would catch a flight to say, Houston, then drive back in a huge cargo truck, or a tractor trailer. Once, he came home in a camper. He'd usually drop it at a warehouse or leave it in a parking lot and walk away. It was easy money. Let's see, what were their names? Es … Estero … Esquevero? No. Esperanza. That's it: Esperanza.'

Thiery jotted down the name. Then, he stood up. 'Thanks, Gloria. You've been a big help.'

'Okay,' she said. 'If you say so.' She lit another cigarette off the glowing butt of the last one.

'I'll make sure you get Frank's, uh, remains, as soon as the coroner is done with his report.'

An hour passed as he went over his notes. He was restless and his empty belly began to groan, so he grabbed his iPad and notes, along with the car keys, and started driving north. He wasn't sure why he'd headed in that direction, but he'd felt some comfort when he'd passed through Lake Wales the day before. Maybe he could think more clearly there than in the small rustic motel with a killer's amorous ex-wife and a TV reporter practically next door.

He wondered if the Bok Tower still played carillon music at night. He'd heard of an unusual, quirky-but-Zagat-rated restaurant near there called Chalet Suzanne. It was only about twenty minutes away. The drive would do him good.

Only five minutes later, he decided to call Jim Bullock.

'I didn't wake you, did I, boss?' Thiery asked when the man answered.

'Hey, Justin. Nah, you didn't wake me. I'm glad you called. The governor's been at me all day. Says he's pretty pissed at you.'

'I know. I'm sorry, Jim, but he's an asshole, and we just don't mix.'

'I should've known. I just thought I might be throwing you a bone. Maybe set you up to take my position.'

'I know that, too, but I've been putting some thought into it. To be honest, I'm not sure how long I'll stick around after you leave.'

'C'mon man, you're too young to retire.'

'I'm sure I could find something else,' he said, knowing full well he'd do no such thing. 'But, hey, that's not why I called.'

'Oh, okay. What's up?'

'Well, I thought I might take advantage of you being in Washington and ask you a favour. Actually two favours.'

'Sure, man. Go ahead.'

'This woman, the one that shot the school intruders, got wounded, and has now disappeared— '

'I've been following it on TV as well as getting personal and snarky updates from Croll.'

'I bet. Anyway, I've got an idea. It's just a theory, but there is something definitely hinky going on here. First, I can find no reason why she'd want to run or hide out unless something, or someone, was chasing her. There's a bunch of rednecks down here who want to put pressure on her for having a gun in school, but that's just fodder for the media.'

'So what do you think is up with her?'

'You're probably going to think I'm crazy, but I think she might be in WITSEC, you know, the Witness Protection Programme.'

'What? That's crazy. What are the odds of that?'

'Yeah, right? Here are some things that keep bringing me back to that idea: first, she just moved down here a few weeks ago. Hardly enough time to apply and get a job unless it was arranged for her. I've been going through her employment records from the school board, and it shows her date of hire, but no application or pre-employment physical, background check, or anything. So, I'm thinking it was arranged. I'd like to confirm with the principal, but she's dead.

'A few weeks after she arrives,' he continued, 'so does Frank Shadtz, one of the two shooters. He used to move dope for Mexican drug lords. I can't believe that was coincidence. Also, her name, Erica Weisz, that's a take-off on Eric Weisz, which was Harry Houdini's real name. When I tried to find out where Weisz came from, I came up with an address in Washington, but the name associated with that address was Harriet Blackstone, another nod to a famous magician, and there's no trace of her, either. Now, I know the US Marshals use various safe havens for their witnesses, and they set them up there until, and even after, they testify against whomever they're testifying against. Are you following me?'

'So far, yeah.'

'Okay, it could also explain why she had a gun with her at the school. I think it's still safe to say most school teachers do not carry guns to work. Maybe she has one because she *has* to have one to protect herself. It could also explain why she ran away from the hospital. If she is in the programme, at the very least she'd be worrying about the media attention exposing and compromising her. And, I think the Washington address was one of those safe havens when she was Harriet Blackstone. Something must have happened, and they had to move her down here.'

'So you want me to try to find this Washington address and check it out?'

'Yes. That's number one. Number two, don't you have a friend that works in the US Marshal's Office?'

'I sure do. A good friend named Ron Sales. He's pretty high up on the food chain, now, but we still get together now and then. You do know they have a policy precluding them from discussing any case, especially if it's active?'

Thiery knew. He also knew this fact could only hamper his investigation if what he was thinking was true.

His boss continued. 'They won't even talk to other law enforcement, state or federal, unless they need something from those agencies, and even *then* they are pretty cagey. We've dealt with this before. You remember the time that Cuban grocer down in Miami had his confidentiality compromised somehow? It was about seven or eight years ago. The marshals had us go in and pick up the guy, keep him in a hotel for a couple days until they could make other arrangements, but they never told us squat about the guy; where he went, what he'd done, or who was after him. I found out later but it cost me an expensive stone crab dinner at Joe's.'

'Yeah, I remember,' said Thiery, recalling how they'd been assigned to 'shepherd' an attractive federal judge from Tallahassee to Miami, who turned out to be the justice on a trial in which the Cuban grocer had been the primary witness against a human trafficking ring. The two of them had taken her to Joe's in Miami and after an hour of listening to Bullock's smooth humour and gobbling crustaceans and dirty martinis, the lady had given enough information for them to figure it all out. 'But, I know how charming you can be, too, and I'm hoping you can ask a few questions and see if I'm on the right track. Maybe he'll at least tell you about this magician connection, or if I'm barking up the wrong tree.'

'All I can do is try,' Bullock said, shades of doubt in his voice. 'But, you do know their agency has never lost a witness? It operates *that* good. At least that's their PR spiel.'

'I hear you, but what if it's crap? What if the programme was corrupted? Either someone got access to its confidential files, or *worse*?'

'What would be worse than that?'

'What if one of their marshals went bad? And don't tell me that can't happen. How many times have we seen some of the guys we've worked with go to the dark side? The temptation is always there.'

Bullock thought about it for a moment, chewing the inside corner of his mouth like it was gum. 'Why don't you give me that address, and I'll check it out. Then, I'll call Ron and see if he can meet for lunch tomorrow. Will that make you happy?'

'Make it a breakfast meeting,' he negotiated, smiling. 'And a big hug from you would make me happier.'

'Settle down, white bread. See, I kept telling you to find another wife. Now, you've gone sweet on me.'

Thiery laughed, 'I've always been sweet on you, man.' He and Bullock had become good friends in spite of the supervisor/subordinate relationship between them and they could always cheer each other up. Even on the bleakest days. 'Okay, boss. I'm going to text you the address. Let me know if Sales shares anything with you.'

'You got it. Be safe, pal, and let me know if you find that teacher.'

By the time he hung up, Thiery was crossing into Lake Wales. He could see the silhouette of the musical tower on top of the small mountain on which it was perched. It was silent, and Thiery was a little disappointed. But, the air was fresh and cool, and he felt a hunger developing. He punched in Chalet Suzanne on his tablet and got directions to the restaurant.

As he drove, he wondered where Erica Weisz might be at that moment and how she was doing. He also wondered what could scare someone so much that she would elect to run away from the hospital, the media, and the cops with a shotgun wound in her side.

In the Lakeland Regional Hospital, David Edward Coody opened his eyes for the first time since he'd been shot. It was dark inside his room, but he could hear the quiet *click-whoosh, click-whoosh* of the ventilator, and he could feel the air being pushed into his lungs, in time with the cadence of the machine. He felt the plastic tube sitting dryly in his trachea and wanted to take it out. Surely, he could breathe on his own. But, when he tried to reach up to pull it out, he couldn't feel his hand. He couldn't feel the other one either. He tried to move his feet, and that's when he came to the realization that he couldn't move anything below his neck. A panic seized him like nothing he'd experienced before. Vaguely, it occurred to him that this must be what the children at the school felt when they heard him and Frank start to shoot up the school and the teachers. That karmic thought brought him no peace, or reassurance, but intense terror.

That's when he began to scream.

SIXTEEN

Esperanza and his entourage sat in the smoky lounge at Rachel's 'gentlemen's' club, off of Orange Avenue in downtown Orlando. Most of the mismatched gang were in good spirits, fuelled by drinks and the thought of living on someone else's dime until their target was found. Not all were happy, though. Julio was frustrated. He thought all they would have to do was find the woman in the hospital and silence her. He'd brought in the contract killers in case they needed to bully their way in, or take out some local cops guarding her. Now that she was on the run, he wasn't exactly sure what he was going to do. He didn't dare reach out to his father for advice.

A girl with aftermarket boobs and a butterfly tattoo on her belly she'd tried to hide with some concealer make up – per the club's no tattoo policy – bent over their table as Julio was cutting into his very rare steak. The dancer's long blonde curls dipped into the bloody *au jus* on his plate.

'Wanna dance?' she asked rubbing her breasts against his shoulder, her breath reeking of garlic.

Julio gripped the knife he was using on his meat so tight his knuckles turned white.

'No. I want you to get your fucking hair out of my fucking food,' he barked.

The dancer didn't seem offended in the least, and never missed a beat as she drifted over the Lopez brothers and made the same enquiry, where she was eagerly invited to sit on their laps and rub their crotches with her butt. Eduardo nuzzled into her cleavage like an unweaned baby and began to nibble at the flesh-coloured pasties that covered her nipples per Orlando's stripper ordinances. You could be an 'exotic' dancer in the Mecca of Mickey Mouse but, like one of Disney's animated characters, you better not show your aureoles.

Julio had called his source several times, but the man wasn't answering. The tool had fulfilled his obligation by letting them know where to find the woman and lining up the gun cache purchase from the Kentucky State Police, but since the hit had gone sour and the woman was gone, who else might know where she'd disappeared to? They needed the asshole one more time.

As Julio gave up on the steak, watching Eduardo repeatedly try to slip his hand into the girl's thong, a thought came to him. He nudged his way over to Davies, whose shaved head reflected the club's multi-coloured strobe lights. Noticing Anichka sitting close to the giant – very close, with a necklace of hickeys on her throat – he wondered what was up.

'De De,' Julio yelled over the music into the big man's ear. 'You tapping that?'

The huge assassin stared at Julio with his crossed eye. It was as black and cold as onyx. He said nothing.

Julio backed off pursuing that line. 'Uh, if I give you a phone number, can you trace it?'

The big man looked back at him, his face like stone, as if the question was so simple, it didn't deserve being asked. '*Oui*' he grunted.

'Yeah?'

Davies smirked. 'It's child's play, boss,' he explained. 'But, I'll need my laptop.'

'Then, let's go,' said Julio.

He threw a couple of hundred dollars on the table and stood up. The rest of his group followed as if on command, the Lopez brothers unceremoniously dumping the tattooed dancer on the floor. Davies held out his hand to Anichka, who took it as elegantly as a debutante. They began pushing their way out of the crowd and back to the hotel, but not before Eduardo slipped in one more grope as he helped the dancer up and stuffed a twenty into her panties.

Moral started off great. On a lark, on his way to the blackjack tables, he'd hit the five dollar slots and pulled twelve hundred dollars out of the first machine after only two turns of the wheels. Three golden bells in a row. It was like cocaine: elation followed by the need for more.

The race tracks were closed on the east coast, but he found some televised races from California. He liked playing the ponies, but you had to bet big to win big. He laid down his slot machine take on a horse named 'Money Marshal'. It won and paid five-to-one. He made six grand, lost a couple of hundred on a few more bets, then decided he better go for the gusto if he was going to double or triple his money. He was feeling like a winner when he strode over to the tables, searched the floor for the best looking dealer with the biggest boobs, and pulled up a chair. Her platinum locks and crimson red lips would distract the other players, but not him. He was focused, bent on making that money, assured it would resurrect his soul.

On his first hand, he was dealt two aces. He doubled down and stayed at nineteen-on-one and got a face card on top of the other. He won both hands when the dealer took a hit on a fourteen and busted, pulling a nine. It was pretty unusual for a dealer to bust. Moral saw it as a sign, as gamblers tend to do, so he stayed put and picked up another forty-two hundred, playing two and three hands at a time over the next hour. When his luck started to go south – he lost about five hundred – at that table, he moved to another. But, he wasn't getting to where he needed to be, so he took a run at craps. This went on for hours, his confidence increasing, his heart pumping adrenalized blood into his head so that, in spite of downing at least eight highballs, he was as clear and focused as a rattler zeroing in on a field mouse. By 10:00 p.m., he had almost forty-five thousand dollars. He considered stopping, taking what he had, leaving on a semblance of success, going away with confidence. With the cash in his pocket he could face Esperanza. At least he had a bargaining chip.

He decided to take a break and think about it. He went to Velvet, a club with a live jazz band playing in the casino, and sat at the bar. He struck up a conversation with a guy in a loud jacket who said he was a local. Moral asked him if he knew where any *real* action was. He sure did. Some high rollers were holed up in one of the hotel's penthouse suites. 'Knock on the door,' he'd instructed, 'give 'em the password, "Horseshoe", and you got a seat at the table: five card stud, with a minimum five K buy-in.'

They rode up the elevator together, and the local man introduced him to some of the players: a bunch of out-of-towners, older fellas with sharp blazers, expensive cigars, overpriced watches, and lots of bling. There were a couple of hookers mulling about the table, too, giving neck massages. When you took a break, you could go to one of the three bedrooms in the suite and get a blow job. *Nice.* Booze flowed freely. Moral felt a warm glow envelope him like a soft, wet mouth. For now, *he was the man, the player, the winner.*

Moral had never been to Orlando. For a place that marketed itself as the premiere family destination in the world, he was amazed to discover how much of that action was clearly not family oriented.

Within ninety minutes, he'd lost everything. The guy with the loud jacket loaned him cash to get his car from valet. He hadn't even got a blow job. As he drove away from the casino, he felt lost, literally and geographically. Sweat soaked his armpits and seeped through to his plaid jacket. He could smell the sharp scent of his own body. His tie was loose, like a hangman's knot just before the trap door opens. His shirt collar was ringed with oil and dirt. Boozy bile ran up his throat and burned his mouth. Just when he thought he couldn't go on, his phone rang. It was *them*. To his surprise, he answered.

'I was going to call you,' he said, nervously.

'Yeah, right,' Esperanza snarled. 'I've been dialling you all day.'

'Work is crazy, right now.'

'Yeah?'

'Yeah, can't keep up … I've got to get down to Florida.'

'You're already here, *cono*.'

'No,' Moral lied, poorly, 'why would you think that— '

'Because I'm looking at your location on my laptop right now. Your cell phone helps.'

Shit, thought Moral. *Fuck it*. He'd roll the die again. Play it tough this time. No bullshit. Let them know this was the end. He couldn't keep this shit up.

'We're done, *jefe*. What's done is done,' He said, trying to sound bold but hearing his own weakness in the treble of his voice. He heard the man breathing over the phone. The sound made his blood run cold.

'Give me the address.'

'I … don't … '

'Give me the fucking address!'

'Nah,' he tried feebly. 'I don't even know what it is, yet. It doesn't happen like that. I've got to call my superiors, submit a report. There's follow up and red tape and— '

'Okay. I'll tell Amy you said hello when I see her. I'll tell her it could've been different, but you wouldn't let it happen.'

'Amy?' His breath halted. 'You're going to see Amy?'

'I am now. I just decided to finance her next film. I think we'll shoot this one down in Tijuana. We don't have to go through the American Motion Picture rating system down there, you know.

You ever see the shit they do with animals down there? I thought she might be done with that business, that *we* might be done with our business. But I guess not.'

Moral pulled over. He struggled to breathe. He opened the windows to get fresh air, but nausea welled up. He had to open the car door and retch.

He sat back up, the inside light casting a pall over him, the open door alarm incessantly dinging, dinging, dinging …

'Robert?' said a distant voice. Remembering the phone on the seat next to him, he picked it up, his hand shaking. He wiped the slick corner of his mouth with his jacket sleeve.

'O … okay,' he belched, the acidy bubble rising up his throat like anger. 'Where are you?'

SEVENTEEN

The bumper sticker on the Dodge Ram pickup read: 'You can have my gun when you pry it from my cold, dead fingers.' The man inside the cab ruminated on his choices. He knew the car in the driveway was the same one from the hospital, because he had the tag number. He could knock on the door and take the woman; he was carrying a gun, and she probably wouldn't put up much of a fight. Or, he could call his pal, Danny Coody, and tell him he located her. Or, he could do the 'right' thing and call the cops.

Coody might be a friend, but his son was as fucked-up as Hogan's goat. Always was. Didn't surprise anyone in town that the kid finally flipped out and attacked the school. When everyone else was out mudding with their gals, or drinking beer by the swim hole, David Coody was locked up in his darkened room with one of those video games. The only time he did go out with the guys was to go hunting, then the goofy fuck would shoot anything that moved – rabbits, crows, squirrels – and scare off the deer. No one asked him to go twice. Still, his dad was a friend.

He made the call.

Danny answered before the second ring.

'Hey bud,' the man said, not taking his eyes off the car in the driveway. 'It's Feller.'

'I knowed who it is. Wassup? It's late.'

Feller chuckled at his cranky friend. 'I'm up here in Lake Wales, sitting on the side of the road, and I got my eye on that black Camaro ya'll been lookin' for. Thought you might like to know.'

'You sure it's the right one? You know how many people been callin' me to tell me they found that Camaro?'

'You insult me, brother. You know iffen I tell you somethin', it gonna be fact. I'm lookin' at the tag, man.'

Coody rubbed his face and looked at his watch. Then, he thought of his only son, lying in the hospital, tubes stuck down his throat, a machine breathing for him. The doctor already told him he'd never walk again. The only good thing was that it might keep him out of prison. How could they jail a quadriplegic, anyway?

'All right, Feller,' he said, finally. 'Tell me where you're at. I'll be there within the hour.'

Harold, the shift supervisor at the Calusa County Sheriff's Office had received the tip from one of the guys looking for the black Camaro. They had basically put together a vigilante posse to go after the missing Weisz woman. Now, the makeshift posse were showing up with loaded guns, their tempers fuelled by booze. Harold wasn't comfortable holding on to that information. He called Conroy.

'I hope I didn't wake you, Sheriff,' said the supervisor.

'I never sleep, Harold. What's up?'

He told him about the posse.

'Thanks for the call,' Conroy said, 'but I'm well aware of the boys out looking for Miss Weisz. I hope they find her. We don't have the resources we used to around here, and we can use the help.'

Harold didn't know what to say.

'Don't worry about it,' Conroy continued, as if reading the concern on Harold's mind. 'If they find her, there's a couple guys in the group that'll give me a call. Hey, it'll save the department a bunch of overtime, right?'

Right, Harold thought. The mob was sure to save overtime. But what would be left of the girl?

Erica saw them alive again. They were sitting at the breakfast table, just like the last day she'd seen them, talked to them, and kissed them goodbye. She felt the familiar warmth that came to her every time she dreamed of them. She felt the love of family, of a good husband and a wonderful daughter who was just coming into her own at 14 years old. She felt the history of their life together: the Christmases, the birthdays, the nothing days when they'd lie by the pool and languidly reach over to pick up an iced tea, their hands brushing, touching, holding. The strength from something that simple seemed both impossible and forever gone to her now.

Then, her heart began to beat fast, as it always did when the dream turned into the nightmare. That sickening feeling as she pushed past the scores of cops – where had they been when they were needed? – and rushed into the house to find all the blood, her family and home ripped apart as if an animal had fed on them. And who could she take her anger out on? The man who had entered the house like a human tornado and killed everyone with no more aforethought than wiping his shoes off on the welcome mat before sticking the gun in his own mouth and blowing his brains out? She could rail at the sky for all the good it would do, just like victims of tornadoes or school shootings might do. In the end, nothing changed. The world kept spinning on its axis. Tides came and went. The sun still shone. The rain still fell. And people still died.

Erica woke drenched in sweat, panting, as if she'd come in from a 10 km run. It was night but she had no way to know how long she'd been unconscious. The handcuffs still held her prisoner to the bed, but she wasn't going to lie there and wait for someone to come take her life. With her toe, she'd managed to get the nightstand lamp turned on to better examine the rail on the headboard. It ran into the vertical stanchion that extended down and became one of the bed's legs. *What held it there?* She didn't see any screws or fasteners. Could it be simply glued?

She ran the handcuffs all the way to one side of the rail, then manoeuvred her legs up and placed her foot against the vertical wood stanchion. She gave it a kick. The effort pinched her side, and she winced back tears. She gritted her teeth and kicked harder while holding onto the horizontal part of the rail. Again and again she kicked, each time feeling as though her wounds were bursting open. Her breath came in ragged gulps, and she thought she might pass out again, but then she saw the rail had come about a half-inch out of the hole in the stanchion. Pausing to catch her breath, she mustered what strength she had left and kicked with both feet. The rail came out as the stanchion fell away, and the whole side of the bed collapsed.

She slid the handcuffs off the rail and slumped to her knees. Her side felt as if she'd just been shot again, and she reached down absently to rub where it hurt. When she used the same hand to steady herself against the nightstand, she noticed blood on it. She looked down at herself and saw her shirt was soaked with blood. *It would be easier to just lie down and let them come kill me*, she thought, instantly growing angry at herself for thinking it. How would she get back at the people who had ruined her life? *She needed to live!*

Pulling herself upright, Erica managed to get into the bathroom. She struggled out of her soiled shirt and was shocked to see how emaciated she'd become, and in only two days. She looked like a prisoner of war, complete with that gaunt look in her eyes that said, *I'm going to die soon.* She shook off the thought, soaked a washcloth with cold water, and gingerly applied it to her side. She carefully removed the bloody bandages and peered at the wounds. The stitches had torn loose on the largest incision and some of the pellet wounds were seeping reddish-clear fluid. She could smell infection.

She rinsed her face and body with cold water and patted herself dry; cleansed the wounds with peroxide again and applied new dressings. She found another clean shirt and began to look through her purse for the keys to the car when the beams from headlights flashed through the bedroom's jalousie windows.

She dropped on all fours and painfully crawled through the house, making her way to the kitchen. She rummaged through drawers and found a hefty knife. The edge of its blade was dull, but the knife was long and pointed.

More headlights shone through the windows. It seemed the quiet road where the new 'safe haven' was had turned very busy.

'We don't need everyone going to the house to get the woman,' Julio advised his team. 'A couple of you, De De and Anichka, why don't you stay here? Alejandro and Eduardo, you go take care of the girl. Shouldn't be difficult. My guy reports she's handcuffed to a bed. Said she's pretty sick, so you're just taking her out of her misery, okay?'

'Do you want us to bring her back here?' asked Alejandro Lopez.

Julio thought about it for a minute. His thoughts drifted back to that time his father had taken him to the beach house as a teenager then made him help behead some of his enemies. 'Nah. Just bring me her head, *si*?'

'*Si*,' said Eduardo Lopez, his face lighting up like a child going to Disney World. 'Can we play with her a little?'

Julio nodded. 'Sure, whatever you want. But, don't take too long. We have luck going with us right now. Let's keep it that way.'

De De was showing Anichka his Parabellum pistole, otherwise known as the German Luger, one of the most expensive and collectible guns in the world. It still retained its sleek, automatic lethality that made it look like a ray gun from the old *Flash Gordon* movies. She thought it was *beautiful* and sniffed its oily scent as if she smelled a bouquet of freshly picked flowers.

'I need to go powder my nose,' said Anichka, suddenly flushed.

'Inside or out?' Julio quipped. 'I got some really good blow in the bathroom.'

'No, I'm good. I'll be back in a few minutes,' she said, and slid out the door as quickly and quietly as a cat.

After an appropriate pause, De De said he was going outside to smoke a cigarette. Julio nodded and went back to business on the phone.

Anichka opened the door when De De knocked lightly. She pulled his jacket off and tried to push him back onto the bed. It was like pushing against a wall, but he went along with it and plopped himself down. She unbuckled his pants and slid them down, tugging at his underwear like she was skinning a buffalo. He was already erect and as huge as she remembered. She hiked up her skirt and impaled herself on him, filling her emptiness.

'We ... finally ... get to ... kill ... someone,' she said through her exertions.

De De looked up at her. She was small behind his enormous belly, but the energy she could generate was like a giant Cummings Diesel motor that, once cranked up, couldn't be stopped.

EIGHTEEN

Thiery finished his pan-seared sea bass and lobster bisque, and marvelled at how scrumptious the food was at this odd out of the way place. Chalet Suzanne was a quirky place; a pink palace in the middle of nowhere. The restaurant served food on mismatched dishes under a ceiling so low Thiery had to stoop down to walk through the place. The building sat so close to a lake it seemed as if it might tumble into the water and there was a trap door through which guests fed the turtles that lined the banks like soldier's helmets. There were pictures of presidents, astronauts, and Hollywood celebrities who had dined there over the years, set among various glass, ceramic, and pewter knick-knacks that lined the shelves. But, like most places in the area, business was slow, and he had noticed the 'For Sale' sign on the entrance door and the note that read: 'After eighty-three years, we are closing soon … ' Thiery couldn't help but feel the sense of loss for yet another *thing* that couldn't last. His life was full of those *things*.

Paying his bill as they closed up, he ambled past the grand piano, up the wooden stairs, and out into the night, still not ready to go back to the motel. He called Conroy to see if anything had turned up. Something told him he would have to ask or he wouldn't hear about it until he picked up tomorrow's paper. Conroy didn't answer. He called Dunham to check in with him.

'You're still up?' a hint of humour in his voice.

'Yeah,' said Thiery. 'Can't sleep knowing our primary witness is out, and we don't have a clue on where she might be. Thanks for giving me the heads-up on Gloria Shadtz. She gave me some info about her ex that might be helpful. I'll fill you in later. You hear anything else new?'

'Not much,' the police chief answered. Thiery could hear a television in the background, its volume set at a deafening roar. 'Talked to Conroy earlier. He's about as much help as tits on a boar, but I ... Hold on a sec.' Through the phone line, the background noise subsided. 'Sorry, couldn't hear myself think. Anyway, I know some of his guys. They told me they've got officers at the hospitals looking for her and a few wolf traps set up along the highway stopping cars.'

Thiery wondered if that was enough. Still, he was glad to learn they were doing something. 'Good,' he told Dunham. 'I asked him to do that, but I didn't get much of a commitment from him.' In truth, the guy had been outright stubborn in his defiance. But Dunham didn't need to hear that.

'I also heard there's some locals, friends of Coody's, that are looking for her, too. They know about that black Camaro stolen from the hospital last night.'

The recently eaten meal began to churn in Thiery's stomach. 'Damn it! You think they'll call the Sheriff's Office if they find her?'

Dunham hesitated, thoughtfully, before giving his best guess answer. 'No sir, I don't.'

Thiery breathed in deeply through flared nostrils, the sound of his own grinding molars echoing through his head. 'Think Conroy knows?'

'I'd bet money on it. He and Coody have a lot of the same friends.'

'Not good,' said Thiery, struggling to contain his growing anger, maintain his professional demeanour. 'Let's hope she goes back to the hospital. Anything else?'

Thiery's phone beeped before he heard Dunham's answer. He looked at the incoming call. It was Conroy. 'Hey Chief,' Thiery interrupted, 'the Sheriff is calling me back. I'd better see what he has to say.'

'Sure. Keep me in the loop, okay?'

'You bet.'

Thiery switched over to Conroy as he walked quickly out to his parked car. It was the last one in the lot and dew had already settled on it like the proverbial wet blanket.

'Good evening, Sheriff,' Thiery answered in his best *how-the-fuck-you-doin'* voice.

'Saw you called earlier and was getting back to you,' he said, his tone weary and obligatory. 'I got one tip from a teacher I know from the school. She didn't know Weisz well, but remembered she said something about going to dance once at a country bar up in Lake Wales. Thought I'd check it out tomorrow.'

What a coincidence, thought Thiery. 'I'm in Lake Wales now, Sheriff. What's the name of the bar?'

'It's a real winner,' he offered. 'Place called Highway 60 Saloon. Pretty rough. I'd keep my sidearm close.'

'That bad?'

'Last time I was up there was for a triple shooting, a couple years ago.'

Thiery thought about it for a moment. *Why was Conroy being helpful now? Was he trying to keep him away from his unauthorized posse?* 'Why would a woman go to a place like that?'

Conroy was silent, but Thiery could hear him breathing. 'I was just thinking,' the Sheriff finally said, 'maybe she likes to live on the edge, so to speak.'

Thiery considered the implications of Conroy's statement for a moment, then said, 'Or, maybe she had a gun.'

Thiery reluctantly left the charm of Chalet Suzanne behind and drove a short distance to the dive called the Highway 60 Saloon, not surprisingly located on Highway 60. He wondered how long it took the owner to come up with that original name. The wood planks that made up the exterior walls were grey, their edges peeling away from the studs. A beer sign glowed red, and the sounds of loud music reverberated through the walls. The handle on the door was sticky to the touch.

As soon as he walked in and plopped onto a stool – wary eyes watching him from every corner of the smoky, dimly lit bar – he overheard the topic of conversation: the school shooting. The place reeked of spilled beer soaked into the wood floor, and billiard balls clacked together as the neon jukebox played Tim McGraw. Girls in too-tight jeans with muffin top midriffs clung to their cue sticks like pole dancers.

Thiery liked places with local colour, even if they were, at times, less than aseptic. It was getting late but he had to see what might lure Erica Weisz to a place that would, in all likelihood house bikers and local rednecks. *Maybe she liked that type?* Who the hell knew? What chafed at him more, at the moment, was why had Conroy called him back to give him this information?

Thiery had been yearning for a drink ever since he'd turned down that lonely woman's offer for a beer earlier so *why not*? He was frustrated about the missing teacher. Without her, there was no way he was going to close this investigation. He could be living at the Sun Beam Motel for weeks, if not months. Stepping up to the bar, he ordered a Crown on the rocks with a lemon twist, and got a plastic cup, the booze with a little ice, and a chunk of brown-rimmed lime. *Close enough*, he thought, trying not to show his disdain. He hated plastic cups and old fruit served in dingy bars.

'You don't have glasses?' he enquired.

The bartender, a thirty-something, bottle-blonde with smoky eyes and a world-weary look offered him an answer. 'No, sir,' she said. 'They get broke in here.'

'But you serve beer in bottles?'

She smiled and shrugged. 'What can I say? It's corporate.'

You drink Kool-Aid out of plastic cups at a kid's birthday party, he thought. *But, hey, it's just a nightcap, right? Ask around, see if anything turns up. A quick drink and move on. It's not exactly the preferred dark wood bar with good company and some good jazz or blues.*

He tried not to be self-conscious about people staring at him. It was obviously a neighbourhood place, he was the new face, and his massive size didn't help. He tried not to listen to the alcohol-fuelled opinions of the citrus pickers, farmers, truckers, and bikers holed up in the bar like bats in a cave, most since happy hour. A football game was on, and he allowed himself a moment to get caught up in the action. He couldn't watch a game without thinking of his past on the gridiron. The memories came with a melancholy pang of self-doubt and the ever present question, *what if?* Still, he allowed the self-torture.

'You gonna nurse that drink all night, or you want another?' asked the bartender as she held up his near-empty cup. The plastic name tag on her tight, tank top read 'Gabby.' The side of her mouth turned into a crooked smile. She wore pale, pink, pearlescent lipstick and leaned over, her elbows on the bar top, her breasts brushing the caps of the chilled booze bottles.

Thiery smiled pleasantly while he pulled his phone out and thumbed through documents until he found the school board picture of Erica Weisz. 'I'm just nursing tonight, Gabby,' he answered. 'But, I was wondering if maybe you remember seeing my friend.' He held up the picture so she could see it.

Gabby squinted, then nodded. 'Yeah,' she said. 'On the news the past couple days, Sherlock. You a reporter?'

'No. Just nosey.'

Gabby shook her head but smiled. She leaned forward with the bottle of Crown and refilled his glass anyway.

Thiery smiled back and nodded his gratitude. 'You've seen her here?'

'Maybe.'

Thiery looked around the smoky, blue-collar bar. He figured a bartender might make about forty dollars on a good night serving the clientele. None appeared to be big tippers. Not enough to keep the lights on at the trailer, he supposed. He pulled a crisp fifty out of his wallet and slid it across the bar to her.

She looked up, pursing her mouth and widening her eyes. 'Drinks are only four bucks, and it's two-for-one night.'

''S'okay,' said Thiery. 'I'm rich.'

Gabby grinned at him and the fifty vanished. There was a customary bell behind the bar. She turned and rang it a few times, signifying she had received an ample tip. She spun around back to him, grinning ear to ear. 'I don't get to ring that bell much.'

'I'm glad I could help,' said Thiery, knowing it sounded corny.

She loved it. Leaning forward conspiratorially, she said, 'She came in here, that girl. Once. I was working. I remember, 'cause she had beautiful black hair, all glossy and nice, nice clothes, too, but she was wearing running shoes instead of nice flats or heels. I remember the poor thing don't know how to dress right.'

'You talk to her?'

'No, other than to get her a beer she ordered. It was one of those ultra-light beers. They taste like water, you know.'

'Anything else?'

Gabby shook her head. 'No. She just danced.'

'Who did she dance with?'

'That's the thing. She didn't dance with anybody. She just danced. Coupl'a guys hit on her, but she blew 'em off. She's here maybe half-hour, forty-five minutes, then left with a guy that came to meet her. Pretty girl.' She began to fill Thiery's cup again, but he capped it with his hand.

'Thanks,' he said. 'I'm good. Do you remember what the man looked like?'

Gabby smiled coyly. 'Like you, a cop,' she answered, 'but a lot older.'

'What makes you think I'm a cop?'

'You all look alike. Cops have sad eyes, like maybe they regret something they've done. He looked sadder than you, though; kind of a basset hound face. Hair was silver streaked, slicked back. Not as tall as you, but a good six feet. Suit and tie, maybe like a Fed?'

From a nearby corner of the room, a hawk-nosed man, long and lean, and red faced from the sun, was on a soapbox, his voice booming in spite of his emaciated look. As his voice rose, Thiery and the bartender couldn't help but glance in his direction. His creased leathery neck undulated as he spoke; his hands still greasy from whatever mechanical work he was doing, the scent of oil and baked-on sweat wafting off him. His long, grey-streaked hair pulled back in a ponytail. There was a long knife in a scabbard attached to his tooled leather belt. He wore Army fatigues, though it was obvious to Thiery he wasn't a soldier.

Beware of civilians wearing camouflage, thought Thiery. *No good can come from them.*

The recipient of the thin man's wisdom was a big man, as wide as he was tall, his pudgy face so fat it looked as if it might explode, his eyes bugging out like a bufo toad, his head pinched up into a cap that looked as if it might belong to a child, that was, if it didn't say: *Be Kind To Animals, Kiss A Pussy.* He ate up every word from the thin man as if he were listening to the governor himself, a bulge in the back of his lower shirt telling Thiery he was packing, too.

'Tha's right,' said the thin man, 'we don't know wha' happened inside that school an' who was shootin' who, but I cain't see no reason for that teacher to run off. Maybe one of those shooters was her boyfriend, an' she was fuckin' around, an' he came to make it right. Who knows?'

'Uh, huh,' said the fat one. 'See the picture of her on the news? I'd take a run at that. She's got that "come hither" look and I'd *cum* hither all over that.' He snorted and, hooking his heels into the rung on the barstool, managed to stand and grab his crotch, then perform a masturbatory gesture.

Gabby shrugged, turned away, and busied herself with wiping off the sticky bar.

The thin man tried to copy his buddy, and, in an attempt to situate his heels on his own stool while grabbing his crotch, lost his balance and fell backward. Some of his drink splashed on Thiery and a few other patrons at the crowded bar. Seemingly unhurt, the man sat up, still holding what was left of his beer. Noticing he'd made a mess on Thiery's jacket, the thin man pulled the wet bar rag out of Gabby's hand and headed for the detective's coat sleeve.

'Cool it, Mr Clean,' Thiery announced, pulling the rag out of the man's hands and passing it back to the bartender, while shooting the drunk a levelling a stare that would turn antifreeze to ice.

'Well, excuuuuuse me, sir,' he said moving into Thiery's space. 'It's not like you're at the opera tonight, right. You're in *our* bar, and sometimes it gets a little messy in here.'

'It's going to get a lot messier if you don't back away,' said Thiery.

He knew he should leave, but his frustration had grown and, with the two drinks in his system, his patience had diminished. He felt hot blood begin to well up from some place below his collar, rise up the thermometer that was his neck, and push against the back of his eyes. He turned back to the television, tried to cool down, but football was on and that sure as hell wasn't going to help.

The bottle stung for a second as it broke against the back of his head. He felt something warm and liquid ooze down his scalp and onto his neck. His vision began to pulsate, not from the injury, but from the unfettered anger that instantly swelled. Thiery stood up and turned, trembling from rage.

'Eeeyooou,' said the thin man. 'We got us a scrapper here, Jerry.'

Jerry, the fat one, squinted his eyes and approached the bar. Thiery couldn't tell if he was trying to look mean or just couldn't see well.

'Hey, man,' the fat guy started, 'I'm sorry about my friend here smashin' you in the head. You okay? Can I get you a towel or something? Oh, man, wait, are you …' The man paused to search for a name, then turned to his friend. 'Ben,' he grabbed the thin man by the arm and pointed at Thiery, 'don't you know who this is? It's Justin Thiery, the Magic Man from UF's Gators from, what, about twenty-five years ago? Where the hell you been man?' He was talking to Thiery again. 'Let me buy you a drink.'

Thiery said nothing. He finished the last of his drink, letting the ice clink against his teeth, the blood trickle down his neck. *Try to cool off, man*, he said to himself. *You might be off the clock, but you're never off the job.*

'You don't say,' said Ben, his baritone voice dripping sarcasm. 'I didn't know we had a rich celebrity right here!'

'Yeah, he was that quarterback, doncha 'member? He won The Heisman and the college pennant that year, but, when he went to the NFL, he couldn't cut it.'

'Yeah, I 'member now,' said Ben. 'They traded him off to the Jets, where he sucked like all those fuckers from New York do. Then after that it was ... '

'The Patriots!' the fat man interrupted with excitement. 'But, he never got past the preseason. Didn't have what it takes. Just couldn't cut it.'

He took a swallow of beer, and his tongue worked its way out of his mouth, across his tarter encrusted teeth and over his purple lips.

Thiery put down the plastic cup and turned his full attention toward the two drunks. It dawned on him that he'd been set up, possibly by the man who suggested he come in the first place: *Conroy*. Thiery didn't care. He'd grown weary of the local redneck mentality, including the one shared by Conroy and his minions. Their dumb-ass philosophies and backwoods way of doing business, none of which was helping the investigation, but hampering it. He'd grown up around people like this, who liked to think of themselves as simple country folk, but in truth, were ignorant opportunists whose only allegiance was to whoever bought their last beer.

'You've got a good memory, Jerry,' said Thiery. 'For a fat ass with a tiny head full of booze, you got most of it right. Guess you didn't remember the shoulder injury, but what the hell, at least you haven't forgotten your way to the trough.'

Ben's eyes went wide in surprise, his mouth a perfect 'O.' He acted as if he might turn away even as his hand dropped to his side and onto the handle of his knife.

Thiery did not hesitate. He reached forward and grabbed Ben's hand, his own grip like the jaws of an alligator. He squeezed until he felt something crunch, then angled the wrist up until the man went to his knees.

The fat one wiggled to a standing position, his porcine arms darting around his back. But, he was not quick or flexible enough. Thiery pushed Ben forward and let him fall face first to the floor, then grabbed a barstool by the seat and swung the legs into the unguarded face of the man's friend. The blow tore Jerry's cheek and snapped his head around, but he remained standing and, now, Ben was trying to rise from the floor and get back into the fray.

Thiery stepped forward, kicking Ben in the ribs, eliciting a scream that was high pitched compared to his booming speaking voice. Then, without missing a stride, Thiery continued his forward movement and spun, jutting his elbow up and into the face of Jerry, feeling the nose break like a cracker. Thiery spun him around and took the weapon from his belt. As suspected, it was a revolver. He opened it, took the bullets out, dumping them into his hand and putting them in his pocket. He walked around the end of the bar and tossed the gun into a sink filled with grey dish-water.

Gabby stood, staring at him, her mouth hanging open.

Thiery showed her his badge and said, 'I'm leaving, but you might want to call the police. These guys are apt to be a little pissed.'

'But *you're* a cop,' she said.

At that, he shrugged, straightened his jacket, and started to leave. He stopped, noticing Ben's attempts to regain his footing.

'Don't get up until I'm gone,' Thiery warned and walked out of the bar, past tables of people who had grown as silent as children in Sunday School.

He was just getting into his car when his phone rang. It was Chief Dunham again.

'Agent Thiery,' he greeted, 'something popped up on my radio before I could get home, and I knew you'd want to know.'

'What is it, Chief?' asked Thiery, cupping his hand around his phone to keep the sound of passing cars and the bar's country music from seeping in. He sat behind the wheel trying to think straight, brush off the bottle-to-the head assault, but the laceration was stinging like a bee sting.

'One of the guys looking for the car is also a friend of mine from church. He thought he was just helping out, but now he's had some second thoughts, so he called me. Says a bunch of the guys are carrying guns and drinking and whooping it up.'

'That doesn't sound like a good combination,' said Thiery. He found napkins from a fast food joint in the glove box and dabbed at the back of his head.

'He also said they think they've found that black Camaro up in Lake Wales. Are you still up that way?'

Thiery almost choked as he pushed the keys into the ignition. 'Yeah. Do you have an address?'

'I do. It's 10909 Guava Lane. It's in a residential area between Lake Rosalie and Lake Tiger.'

Thiery found his iPad in the glove box and made a note of the address. Wrote it down on his iPad. 'Are you coming up?'

Dunham was silent for a moment, then said, almost woefully, 'No. I better not. I got a call from the city manager tonight. He reminded me the Sebring taxpayers pay my salary, and I've got responsibilities here.'

'No shit,' said Thiery. 'I'll give him a call as soon as … '

'Thanks, Agent Thiery,' the Chief interrupted. 'But, don't bother. He's already talked to the governor, who indicated he had issues with the investigation, too. Said the lead was going to be reassigned to Sheriff Conroy. Thought you might like to know that, too. They'll make a press statement tomorrow morning.

Something about giving authority back to local law enforcement with jurisdiction over the school and putting the FDLE into an advisement capacity.'

Thiery felt his blood begin to boil. Again. He felt embarrassed, as if he'd done something wrong – or was it that old feeling of ineptitude creeping back in? He wasn't sure what to say to Dunham. 'Well, uh, thanks for letting me know first, Chief. I haven't been recalled as of yet, so you and I didn't have this conversation, okay?'

'What conversation, sir?'

Thiery smiled. Dunham was a good man, but in the wrong place. 'Thanks for everything, Chief. You've been a big help.'

'Not so much, but, if you need me, don't hesitate to call. I'd like to know why Miss Weisz ran. And, I'd like to shake her hand one day, too, just for keeping those kids safe.'

'You got it,' said Thiery. On his tablet, he tapped the map app and punched in the address Dunham gave him. It read: 16.6 miles, 24 minutes. He was sure he could make it in ten.

When the Lopez brothers got to Guava Lane, there were so many vehicles there they had to check the address again. There were only a few houses on the street to the left and a wide, open lake to the right. But, in front of one of the tiny cinder-block homes were about a dozen pickup trucks. In their rented, metallic green Chrysler 300, they felt out of place on the shell rock road dotted with potholes.

'Must be someone having a party,' said Eduardo, referring to all the pickups lining one side of the road.

They drove by the parked trucks, slowly, saw the address, 10909, but kept going. They found a cross street, hung a left, turned out the lights, then backed onto Guava Lane, so they could watch the house.

'What the fuck?' said Alejandro. 'These rednecks her friends?'

'I don't think so' answered his brother. 'Why would they all still be standing around outside?'

'Maybe they're undercover cops?'

Eduardo watched them through the streaky, lovebug spattered windshield. He could make out a group of men talking outside, leaning against their trucks. A few of them cracked open beers, and he saw them spitting long, brown squirts of chewing tobacco. 'I don't think so, *hermano*,' he said. 'These guys just rolled out of the turnip fields.'

Alejandro was the older brother, the thinker. Quiet compared to Eduardo, and more patient. He considered their options. They could go back to the hotel, but if they lost the target doing so, there would be hell to pay with the Esperanzas. They could do a full frontal attack, but he sensed these rednecks likely all had guns in their trucks; he'd seen some framed in the windows as they drove by. They might not be accustomed to using them on people, and he was sure he could mow half them down in minutes, but that was risky, too, and would draw unwanted attention.

As if reading his brother's mind, Eduardo said, 'I can sneak around back and take a look inside. If it's too dicey, we don't go in. If the woman is just sitting in there watching TV, we slip her out the back or take her down while these guys are out here finishing their beers.'

It was a waning moon, still bright, but clouds took turns blotting it out and plunging the scene into blackness. Except for the occasional glowing cigarette. Both brothers removed their sport jackets, tossed them into the back seat where the guns were stored. Alejandro still wore his tie. Eduardo kept his wide lapelled shirts open to nipple level, showing off his considerable bling and curly, black chest hair.

'What the fuck are they waiting for?' said Alejandro, just as one of the men stepped away from the others and began to move toward the house.

Sensing they were losing their moment, Eduardo said, 'I'm going around back. See what's up.'

Alejandro nodded. 'Check your weapon.'

Eduardo glanced at his gun, a 9 mm, sixteen-shot, Sig Sauer, with Night Sights and a Ti-Rant silencer on its muzzle that his brother had equipped for him. He patted his pocket and assured himself his other weapon of choice was still there – the ten-inch stiletto purchased in Italy where they still made them as true switchblades, unlike the knockoffs made in China and sold to gangbangers in America.

Alejandro looked at his brother, noting the scar on his ear he'd given him from one of their many fights as young, quarrelling siblings. In one melee, he'd slammed him into the corner of a heavy table and scarred his ear. But, Eduardo never told on him; he'd said he'd fallen down. That's what they both used to tell their parents when asked about their new wounds: they fell down. Now, though their killing styles were vastly different, they were the closest friends in the world, still covering each other's asses.

'Be careful, *mi hermano*,' Alejandro cautioned.

Eduardo smiled, slipped out of the car and darted across the road, skirting the shadows like a panther, crouching low, silent, and lethal.

Alejandro checked his weapons as well. He carried the same Sig as a backup, so he and Eduardo could easily trade ammo, but he didn't go anywhere without the semi-automatic Drako AK-47, with thirty-round clips aplenty. The Drako was small, like a pistol, really. If fired singly, it could have the accuracy of a sniper's rifle, or serve as a machine gun on auto. The gun was like an extension of Alejandro's arm. He checked the clip, slid the bolt back and forth, smelled the oily scent of the well-maintained gun. He checked the Sig, too, and the gargantuan, Ruger .44 Magnum Super Blackhawk with a ten and a half-inch barrel he liked to bring along. It wasn't practical. The weapon only held six shots and was heavy and cumbersome. But, if you needed some extra stopping power and a pistol that had more range, there was no equal.

Alejandro loved his guns almost as much as his *hermano*.

*

Ellis Coody told his buddies to wait by their trucks. He felt it was his duty to bring the woman out, seeing how it was his son that she shot. *Besides,* he thought, *these clowns would probably piss themselves if anything DID go down.* He made a show of checking the slide on his Colt .45 Double Eagle before shoving it into the holster on his belt. No one argued with him. He sucked in his gut, pulled up his pants a notch, and strode toward the house like a sheriff from an old John Ford western.

The house was dark.

Coody approached the front door and banged on it with the edge of his fist, rattling the jalousie windows across the front of the house.

Eduardo Lopez moved through the backyard, mixing with the shadows, a panther moving quietly in the shadows, taking advantage of the cloud coverage. He saw the back door and wondered if he could get inside, kill the woman, and slip back out before the rednecks knew he was there. He was going to try.

In the corner of the dark bedroom, Erica could hear her own breath and tried to hold it, so she wouldn't give herself away. She had seen the posse gathering across the road out front, heard their twangy exultations about 'Florida Cracker justice,' and cursed Moral, again, for taking her gun. Who was it that said, 'Never bring a knife to a gunfight?' Here she was, facing a makeshift militia with a dull kitchen knife. She thought of calling the police, just turn herself in and hope for the best, but, when she checked her purse, the phone was gone. *Moral had taken the fucking cell, too!* She was screwed.

She heard someone enter the house. Boots scraped on the terrazzo floor.

A light in the small living room came on, removing any shadows she might have hidden in.

'Erica Weisz!' he hollered.

She recognized Coody's voice from the news coverage.

'I knowed you're in here. Ain't nobody gonna hurt you. You just need to come with me and answer for some things.'

He slid the gun out of the holster as he checked the kitchen, then began to make his way toward the back of the house.

Erica saw Coody's shadow coming down the narrow hallway. She moved quickly out of the bedroom and slid into the utility area leading to the back door, where Moral had surprised her earlier. She began to turn the knob, trying not to make noise with the handcuffs dangling from her wrist, but felt some resistance, as if someone on the other side was turning it the opposite way.

On the other side of the door, Eduardo wondered why the doorknob resisted. It had begun to turn, then stopped, as if a ghost had grabbed it. He felt sweat trickle from his scalp and down his neck.

Coody moved down the hall and spied the opening to the utility room. He heard a metallic click. He flattened against the wall and inched toward the sound, edging toward the opening. He gripped the .45 in both hands, extended his arms, and aimed as he held his breath and jumped into the doorway.

Eduardo won the tug of war on the doorknob and pulled it open.

Erica fell through the open door and spilled out into the yard as Coody, surprised by the commotion, fired the first shot into the darkness, momentarily lighting up the claustrophobic utility room. The echo of the blast was deafening in the small space. The bullet missed Eduardo, who quickly drew his own gun and shot into the tiny room, the *thwick* of the silenced gun muzzle lighting up the tiny room a second time, long enough to see the surprised look on Coody's face.

'Wha'?' Coody grunted, feeling a heated pressure in his chest. He fired off another shot as he fell forward, shot through the heart, his forehead banging the side of the washing machine with a *gong*.

Erica removed her hands from her ears and looked up from the dew-dampened grass. She saw a flashy dressed Hispanic man, several gold necklaces glinting from his unbuttoned shirt, his pointy, basket-weave shoes in her face. A silencer on his gun.

The sound of people running through the front yard and crashing into the house sifted back to them. A door was kicked in and glass shattered, shoes scuffled on the terrazzo floor. Eduardo turned his attention to Erica, a grin stretched across his tanned face, a wisp of smoke dripped out the barrel of his gun. 'The Esperanzas send their love,' he purred.

Erica couldn't afford to hesitate. She lunged and jabbed the kitchen knife into Eduardo's thigh, feeling it hit bone.

He screamed as Erica jumped to her feet, grabbed his arm, and sunk her teeth into his wrist. Unable to maintain his grip, he dropped the gun, then backhanded Erica across the face, knocking her back onto the ground. He instinctively grabbed his stiletto with his other hand and flipped out the long, thin blade. It gleamed like a wolf's eye in the pale, grey light. Scooping the Sig off the ground, Erica rolled onto her back and pointed the pistol at Eduardo. He stopped as if evaluating the situation. She rose to her feet, careful to keep the shaking barrel pointed at her attacker. Before she could pull the trigger, Coody's posse arrived and discovered their fearless leader.

'What the fuck?' one of them yelled. Then, 'Hey, there's a guy out back.'

Someone flicked on the outside floodlight, simultaneously illuminating and blinding Eduardo. Erica was just outside the perimeter of light and took advantage of the distraction. She turned and ran on legs wobbly with fear and weak from feverish wounds. She stumbled forward, pushing her way through Brazilian pepper trees and crepe myrtle bushes that naturally fenced the backyard. Hearing another shot, she turned and peered through the foliage, just in time to see Eduardo fall to the ground. More of Coody's friends rushed into the backyard. She saw a flash of metal gleam in the yellow light as Eduardo, knowing he was done for, boldly threw his stiletto, striking one of the men in his protruding abdomen. The man looked at the blade as if wondering what it was, then raised his own gun, and shot Eduardo in the face.

Erica was transfixed, her mouth hanging open, gasping for breath. She heard more running, someone coming across the grass through the neighbour's yard. People began turning on porch lights and she could hear, 'What's going on out there?' and 'I'm calling the police.'

Alejandro burst through the bushes just a few feet away from her and, seeing his brother lying on the ground, half his face gone, went into a wild rage. There were a half dozen men standing in the yard when Alejandro opened up with the Drako. The weapon lit the night like a beam from a police chopper. Blood sprayed as his bullets found targets and they began to fall. A few of the wounded managed to get their guns out and began firing wildly at Alejandro.

Erica watched the elevating carnage for another few seconds, then turned to hobble away in the direction the last shooter had come from. She emerged onto the street, looked one way, and saw the balance of the truck posse running into the deadly house with guns drawn, rebel yells echoing into the chaotic night. She looked the other way and saw a car sitting at the corner of the next street, its door hanging open, the inside lights on. No one was sitting inside, and the motor was running. She limped toward it and jumped into the driver's seat, closing and locking the door behind her. Her wounds throbbed, the stitches pinched as if someone was pulling them tighter. The car's inside light faded out, and she sat in darkness and began to breathe again, her heartbeat pounding in her ears. She looked down and found the Sig in her hand, its barrel still warm. On the passenger seat was another gun, a huge one with a gaping barrel that looked as though she could fit her whole hand in.

Two jackets were strewn across the seat as well. She picked them up and checked the pockets. A fat cowhide wallet fell out with a *plop* in her lap. She opened it and found a Mexican driving licence that belonged to Eduardo Lopez. She squinted at the photo and realized he'd been the man who had pointed the gun at her in the backyard. Inside the billfold was a thick wad of money. She checked the second jacket and found another wallet filled with cash and an ID for Alejandro Lopez. *Killer brothers*, she thought. *How original*. So, now she had their money and their guns. With those, she could get anything else she needed.

A GPS screen was on the monitor on the car's dash. Erica looked at the screen and could see the route the car had taken. Her hands gripped the steering wheel, the handcuffs still dangling from one wrist.

The places where she was supposed to be safe from harm had all turned into places of danger. The man who was supposed to protect her had sold her out. She listened to the distant gunfire – acoustic shadows – again. The sounds of battle surprisingly much clearer, now, than when she was in the middle of it. Anger filled her, body and soul, as she closed her eyes. The faces of her loved ones floated by like the ghosts they were. She could not think clearly. She could not think at all, in fact, so she let her instincts take over; they told her to follow the route the car had taken. She was tired of running and hiding. Maybe the path would lead her to the men hunting her. If it did, then she could kill them, or die trying. She had nothing to lose. Nothing at all.

NINETEEN

Thiery made it to Guava Lane in just over twelve minutes. Headlights charged at him as he bumped over the dirt road, and a green Chrysler 300 sped past, careening close enough to knock his car's side mirror askew, then fishtailed onto the main road, and was gone. Thiery had caught a glimpse of the driver, a blonde woman, her eyes wide with fear, wrestling the car's steering wheel as if it were alive.

About a half-dozen men wearing either John Deere caps or straw cowboy hats with the edges turned down, raced between the house and a cluster of parked trucks along the road, guns blazing. Thiery caught one man in the headlights. The man turned and fired off a wild shot. Thiery ducked as he heard the bullet ricochet off the roof of his car. He braked, flung open the door, pulled his own weapon, and yelled, 'Police Officer! Drop your weapon.'

He was encouraged when, in the brief silence that followed, he heard sirens approaching. *Hopefully more cops with more guns and not the Johnny-on-the-spot county rescue guys who showed up with little more than a box of medical supplies.*

Ahead, the man in the street dropped his weapon to the ground as one of his friends appeared with his own gun. 'I got yer back, Sonny,' the newcomer declared, pumping a round into his shotgun, the barrel facing down.

'You level that weapon at me, friend,' Thiery addressed him, 'and I'll shoot you dead.'

'It's a cop, Bubba,' Sonny cautioned, his hands held high above his head. 'Best put yer gun down.'

Bubba slowly bent and placed the shotgun gingerly on the ground, his eyes never leaving Thiery's. As he returned to a standing position, he held his palms flat and facing forward.

'Your friends on the lawn, too,' Thiery nodded and gestured with the barrel of the gun. 'Tell them to drop their weapons.'

The men complied.

'Now,' Thiery said, holding his gun pointed at Sonny and Bubba, while continuously sweeping the rest of the crowd with his eyes, 'someone want to tell me what's going on here?'

The two men glanced at each other like kids caught writing on bathroom walls. A few of the trucks cranked up suddenly, and attempted to do three-point turns, trying to flee the small, tight road, rooster tails of dirt kicking up behind. One became stuck; another backed into a nearby canal in a scene that might have been comical if it weren't filled with weapon-wielding drunks.

Sonny spoke up, his breath coming in gasps. 'We was driving around lookin' for that gun-totin' teacher that ran away from the hospital, you know, tryin' to he'p out, 'cuz the cops and all are lookin' for her. But, when we got here, Ellis Coody went up to the house and someone … heh, hee.' He started to cry, much to Thiery's disbelief. 'Someone shot ol' Ellis,' he managed, before breaking down and sobbing.

'Coody's shot?' said Thiery. 'Where is he?'

'He's out back,' said Bubba. 'We called 911, but I think it's too late for him.' Then, almost like an afterthought, he added, 'There's a dead spic back there, too, and another crazy one with a machine gun.'

Just then, the fireworks inside the house erupted again, and Thiery immediately recognized the unmistakable sounds of a semi-automatic. What remained of Coody's posse abandoned position and, with an extreme lack of grace, dived behind Thiery's car.

'You men stay here,' Thiery ordered. 'Tell the cops what you told me when they arrive. If fire rescue shows up, tell them to stand back until we've secured the scene. Got it?'

The two men nodded, then lowered their heads as if ashamed.

Thiery grabbed a portable radio from a charger in his car and flicked it on. When he raised dispatch, he identified himself and gave them a brief synopsis, adding there were armed men on the scene and at least two men down. Call all nearby units,' he instructed, 'and have them respond *yesterday*, understand?'

He checked his gun quickly – a Glock 21, department-issued, .45 calibre, bad guy stopper – and felt for the two extra thirteen-round clips he carried on his belt. That gave him thirty-nine rounds. If he needed more than that, he thought, he really should retire. He ran to the house, hugged the first wall he came to, and cautiously inched around the corner. Bullets smacked the walls and chunks of cinder-block broke off the house like styrofoam chunks. He wished he had taken the time to don his Kevlar, but he was committed, now.

Peeking into the backyard, he saw flames coming from a gun at the perimeter like a tiny dragon spitting fire. A yellow light illuminated bodies lying about, patterns of blood soaking their clothing. Thiery watched for any signs of life, but didn't see any. That was good to know in case he had to launch a full bore attack; he wouldn't have to worry about civilians getting hit.

The dragon quit spitting fire. Out of the shadow and into the pale yellow glow of the porch light, a man emerged, carrying an assault rifle at the ready. Hispanic, tall, well dressed, with a loaded shoulder holster. He stepped out confidently, swinging the gun side to side, looking for, but finding no other targets. He nudged a few of the bodies with his elegant leather shoes. He stopped and lingered over the figure that looked like him. His shoulders slumped, a shiny streak visible on his face.

A dollop of sweat slid down Thiery's nose and dripped off. He could *hear* it hit the ground and hoped the other man could not.

He took a slow, quiet breath, locked his arms, and aimed his gun at the man with the assault rifle.

'Police officer!' he shouted. 'Drop the weapon. Now!'

The man sniffed and glanced up casually, letting his eyes focus. He rolled his head around on his neck, like a crazed bobblehead trying to form a thought.

Alejandro remembered a time when he and Eduardo had attended a birthday fiesta. They were ten and twelve. It was Eduardo's turn to put on the blindfold and strike at the piñata, a colourful *toro* so full of treats it had taken two men to hoist it on the rope that held it aloft.

Eduardo swung and missed. Twice. But on the third try, he connected, and the paper bull's stomach exploded open. Candy and treats rained down, reflecting the orange light of the late afternoon so they looked like sweet comets flying everywhere. Eduardo struggled to remove his blindfold. When he finally did, he had to scramble for what little candy was left. As he grabbed for the few remaining pieces, another boy pushed him out of the way and took the treats from him. Having witnessed the incident, Alejandro strode into the mix and punched the young thief in the face, spraying blood onto the other kids and the empty husk of the piñata. Then he handed the thief's candy to his little brother.

'Put down your weapon!' Thiery repeated.

Alejandro gripped his weapon, his finger tight on the trigger.

Thiery saw the man's arm begin to tense and knew he wasn't going to give it up. He did not hesitate. He was already locked in on his target: committed. His breathing stopped, held, and he applied the pressure on his own trigger. The round sparked off Alejandro's weapon as he raised it, then buried itself in his chest with a meaty *slap*. Thiery fired twice more, putting together a small triangular pattern in the man's chest. A bullet riddled genuflection: *Father, Son, Holy Ghost.*

Alejandro went limp and crumpled on top of his brother.

Thiery kept his gun ahead of him, ready to fire. He glanced around the yard as he approached the now dead Lopez brothers. He admired the Sig Sauer still in Alejandro's shoulder holster, the silencer sticking out the bottom. He checked the pockets for identification. None. This man wasn't part of some redneck posse coming to fetch Erica Weisz. Neither was the man with the uncanny family resemblance beneath him. These were professionals. The realization brought Thiery back to his original idea: the school shooting was more than it seemed.

There was no movement, save the tops of the crepe myrtles bending in the night's soft breeze. Thiery could smell sulphur and blood and spilled stomach contents. Over the ringing in his ears he could hear the last of the pickup trucks vacating the scene even as the wail of sirens grew closer. Apparently, Sonny and Bubba, and the rest of the posse hadn't wanted to stick around. He checked the pulses on each of the six bodies he found, including the one in the utility room: Coody Sr. They were as still as mannequins. He was sure he would not find Erica Weisz alive.

Thiery moved cautiously through the rest of the tiny house, though his gut told him he was alone, or at least, the only one living. He found the bedroom where Erica had been held captive. He saw the broken, scuffed rail on the headboard and wondered if someone had been tied or handcuffed to it. He checked the closet and found clothes and bloody running shoes. *She always wore running shoes.* Wasn't that what Sally Ravich had scrawled in her note? And the bartender had said the same thing.

In the bathroom, he found bloody dressings in the wastebasket, along with an empty IV bag, and Amoxicillin vial, syringes, and an empty bottle of Miss Clairol #98 Natural Extra Light Neutral Blonde. A thought flashed into his head. The woman he saw flying past in the Chrysler 300. He closed his eyes and tried to freeze-frame her face. The eyes had been wild with fear, the hair blonde, not black like her employee picture. But the shape of the face, the urgency in which she was fleeing the scene …

Who else could it have been? He cursed himself for not getting a tag number. He concentrated. *Was that a barcode in the rear window of that car?* That would indicate it might be a rental. If so, it could be traced back to one of the rental agencies. Even without the coded number, he could check for who rented a bottle-green 300 Chrysler. It would be time-consuming, but it might pay off with a name.

He was sure Erica Weisz had been there. He was also sure she was in bad shape and had to get out of there fast, because she'd left without clothes and medical supplies.

Then, he found her purse. Inside was a Florida driving licence with Erica's picture, next to the name Christine Angel. *Chris Angel. Another magician.* Thiery was now convinced his hunch was right. *Why and how would she obtain another identity so quickly if she wasn't in the witness protection programme?*

Blue and red lights flashed through the bedroom windows, and Thiery heard the squawk of radios. He walked through the house and out the front door, gun holstered, hands in the air displaying his FDLE badge. Several sheriff officers shouted for him to keep his hands where they could see them.

'I'm FDLE,' he announced. 'There are at least six men dead in the backyard. I think two of them were pros, here to kill the teacher involved in the school shooting yesterday.'

'Yeah?' came a familiar voice from outside the ring of light surrounding the cars and cops. 'Sure it wasn't a drug deal gone bad?' Sheriff Conroy stepped into the light as his men fanned out into the house and beyond. He was wearing a broad brim hat, his chest bowed out. He hooked his thumbs into his gun belt as he approached. In the man's body language, Thiery saw the insolence and confidence of a man who felt that, now that he was in charge, these kinds of shenanigans would cease.

'You can paint it anyway you like, Sheriff,' said Thiery, adding wryly, 'but the hitmen in the backyard weren't part of your approved vigilante posse.'

Conroy's radio crackled with the voice of one of his deputies giving the all-clear. He looked at the paramedics standing by and gave them a nod to go back. Then he turned his attention back to Thiery. 'I don't know what you're talking about, Agent Thiery. I didn't approve any posse.'

'You didn't stop it either,' he accused, 'and now a few of your friends, including Ellis Coody, are dead, and Erica Weisz is still missing. I'm glad you're taking over the lead on this investigation. I wouldn't want this egg on my face.'

'So, you've heard, huh?'

'Good news travels fast. Look, I'm fine with that. I didn't want to come here and step on toes in the first place. But, there's something more going on here than just the school shootings, and getting the community all riled up isn't going to help.'

'Well, I guess I know my *community* better than you do.'

'I know I would've had a fully armed SWAT in that school in less than ten minutes if my main station was located three blocks away. I can't imagine what would take sixteen minutes, Sheriff.'

Conroy scowled at him. Through clenched teeth, he said, 'Dispatchers don't always get the time exact. Sometimes there is a delay when they get too busy, like when a buncha calls come in at once. We're short-handed. Anybody can see that. You can audit the dispatch records if you're that anal about it. Isn't gonna change anything, now.'

'Oh, I'm that anal. I already requested the audit.'

Conroy stared at Thiery as if he were considering drawing his weapon on him. He bent slightly forward and spit tobacco juice on the ground. 'So what's this you were saying about hitmen?'

'Take a look for yourself, Sheriff. There are two dead men in the backyard that don't look like they're from around here. They've got weapons that pros use. One gun has a silencer. I don't know many people who use muzzle suppression devices that aren't hitmen, do you?'

Sheriff Conroy scratched a stubble of black whiskers on his chin. Thiery could hear it like someone rubbing heavy grit sandpaper. 'Can't say I do. Did you take any of them down?'

Thiery knew where he was going with the question. 'Your friends and one of the hitmen were already down when I got here,' he told the new man in charge. 'I shot the guy with the foreign-made assault rifle. I'll notify my boss and put myself on administrative leave, pending the internal investigation. So, it seems like I would've been stepping aside, anyway. It's all yours, Sheriff,' said Thiery, offering a mock salute before walking toward his car. 'Enjoy!'

'Gonna need a few more details about what happened here tonight,' said Conroy.

'I've got your card,' Thiery replied without looking back. 'I'll have my report completed and faxed to you before I go beddy-bye. See you on the news tomorrow. You might want to do something like put out an APB for a blonde driving a new Chrysler 300. Green. And it might be a rental. Oh, and thanks for that tip on the saloon. I confirmed Weisz had been there. Got to meet a couple of your friends, too. They were sweet.' He could feel Conroy glaring at his back.

When he fell into his car, it was as if someone had shot him with a tranquillizer dart. Rain drops appeared on his windshield, and he shook his head. *There goes the crime scene. Tough cookies, Sheriff.* Fatigue swept over him as the rain tapped, then began to beat, on the car's exterior. His adrenaline surge from the gunfight subsided. He wanted to drive back to the Sun Beam Motel and crawl into the sack. He even thought about calling Sara Logan. But, he let that go quickly. Nothing good could come from that tonight.

Still, he felt his loneliness like a wet woollen suit. It smothered him and made him doubt himself again, as he had for the past ten years. His wife's face flashed into his mind. He wished he knew where she had gone, why she had left him and their children. He never quit wondering if she was alive. Even after he'd reported her missing, after he had gone looking for her, leaving the boys with a kind-hearted neighbour for weeks, after he'd finally given up on finding her alive, nothing revealed itself. It was as if she'd vanished off the earth. He held out hope for the first year, or two. But, eventually, he had to accept she wasn't coming back.

If I couldn't find my own wife … He thought of Erica Weisz. *Can you get your shit together and find her? That's your fucking job, isn't it? Are you always going to think of yourself as a man who couldn't quite cut it? Couldn't cut the NFL, couldn't cut it as a husband. And, as a cop, couldn't find your wife? You can only make so many excuses …*

Thiery watched the blurred, flashing blue lights through the rain on his windshield, rubbing his tired eyes, considering his options. After a few minutes, he picked up his iPad and began to look up rental car agencies.

TWENTY

Thiery called Dunham on the way back to the motel. It was just after midnight and he was speeding down two-lane roads, wet and slick as black ice, the car windows open and drops of water sprinkling his face, refreshing him.

'He ... llo?' said Dunham, coming out of a deep sleep.

'Hi, Chief. It's Thiery. I'm sorry to call at such a late hour, but I could use some help. I know you were told to back off the case, but, if it wasn't urgent, I wouldn't be calling.'

'What do you need, Agent Thiery?'

'The Guava Lane tip turned into a big shoot-out. Six dead, including two guys I think were professional killers. And Weisz managed to slip past all of them, I think in a rental car. I need someone to check out the rental agencies, and see if they can find one that loaned a late model, green Chrysler 300. I know it's a lot of work ... '

'Yeah, it could be,' the Chief interrupted. 'Or, we might get lucky and get it on the first call. Don't get me wrong here, but don't you have people who can do that for you?'

'Well, it's a matter of timing. I, uh, I'm essentially off the case at this point.'

'Thought that wasn't going to happen until tomorrow.'

'I shot a man tonight.' There was silence for a moment, then Dunham spoke. 'Oh. I see. Who did you shoot?'

'One of the hitmen who came after Erica Weisz.'

'Did you see her?'

'Only in passing. And I didn't know it at the time. She was going out as I was coming in; I didn't put it together fast enough. But, I found where she had been staying, or held captive. I'm not sure about all the details, but I know she was there. The stolen Camaro was there. It was a small house outside Lake Wales. I found bandages, hair dye, and her purse. In the purse was a driving licence with the same picture, new name: Christine Angel.'

'Isn't that another magician's name feminized? That guy with the tattoos and all?'

'Yeah.'

'Hmmn, then your theory was right about her.'

'I think so. Can you help out? I don't want to get you into any trouble with your city manager.'

'Hey, I'm a law enforcement officer, first and foremost. Political whipping boy comes way after that. You need help with this case, you got it. I'll get started right away. You try to stay out of trouble for a little while, okay?'

'Thanks, Chief. I owe you big time.'

'Okay, then buy me another breakfast at Dutch's.'

Thiery smiled for the first time in a long while. 'You got it, Chief.'

It was after midnight and Sara Logan couldn't sleep. *Sleep is overrated*, she thought. All it did was bring her the same nightmare, the one where she, a long distance swimmer, would look up from her swim and find herself alone, in the middle of the ocean, no land in sight, no sense of which direction to go. An overwhelming fear would awaken her, and she would find her heart hammering in her throat, her body so drenched with sweat, it seemed she'd just emerged from the sea.

She wanted to call Thiery and let him know she had located the pawn shop in Vegas where the guns used in the school shooting had been purchased, but she was hesitant. She couldn't decide if that information was significant enough to wake him, or if the real reason she wanted to call him was to try to entice him into her bed. She turned on the nightstand light and picked up a Jodi Picoult novel she'd been reading for several weeks, but couldn't stay focused on the story, as her thoughts kept returning to Thiery.

She turned her laptop back on, thinking she'd attempt to make a dent in her never-ending flow of emails. The scheduled meetings and new directives and protocols. The titbits of reports that came from all over the nation about another Islamic terrorist cell caught making pressure-cooker explosives in Connecticut, or some neo-Nazis who were threatening to assault a gay rights parade in Nebraska, or some castor beans – the basis of ingredients to make ricin – seized in the makeshift lab of a former FBI research scientist who held a vendetta against the 'system'. All fun stuff and truly endless. *Crime and crazy never takes a holiday*, she thought.

Logan was picturing herself like a mouse running on a wheel that would never stop, her life passing her by like a missed bus, when the phone rang. She recognized the number of the forensic lab: Miko Tran, the agency's most thorough forensic IT specialist.

'Talk to me, Miko,' she said.

'Oh, uh, I was going to leave you a message,' he said, nervously. 'I'm so sorry, Special Agent Logan. I know it's late.'

'If I get any more beauty sleep, they'll be asking me to pose for *Vanity Fair*.'

'You're not upset with me for calling so late?'

'I'm getting a little irritated that you're dragging this out.' She heard Tran gulp on the other end of the line.

'Okay, I'll get to the point. Are you near your laptop?'

'Sitting right in front of it. But, please don't try to Skype me, or I'll moon you.'

'Is that a promise?' Tran asked, hopeful.

'C'mon, dude.'

'Okay, Special Agent Logan. We've been diligently retrieving data from the Coody hard drive. I now have in my overworked hands a list of email addresses with which Coody corresponded. We brushed through the occasional and infrequent ones, and focused on those that were repetitive and/or had attachments in them. I'm sending you one I think you'll find most interesting.'

The email Tran sent to Logan was from a Diceman1960@ hotmail.com. It read only: 'See attachment. Purchase will be arranged through Tito's Pawn & Gun, F.S. will deliver.' The attachment was the gun cache from the Kentucky State Police sale.

'Good work, Miko. "F.S."? Could that be Frank Shadtz?'

'Could be.'

'Who is Diceman1960?' asked Logan.

'We're working on that. The account was set up under a fictitious name through a public library in Texas. But, it's been accessed from several locations, including one in Washington DC. That's where the one I sent you originated from. We're trying to pinpoint that locale. The list had to be scanned in and attached though, so if we can find where it was scanned, we can find the person who sent Coody the list of guns.'

'What was the fictitious name?'

'Get this: *Wyatt Earp*. Mean anything to you?'

'Hmmn. Not really, but Earp was a lawman and a gambler," said Logan, pondering the possibilities. 'Maybe that's why the Diceman 160 moniker. Have to think about that one.' Good job, Miko. You might get a handjob for your efforts.'

'From you, Special Agent Logan?'

'Of course, not, silly' she said, and added with a chuckle,' but, I'll find a guy with nice soft hands.'

TWENTY-ONE

Thiery was pulling into the parking lot of the Sun Beam Motel when Dunham called him back.

'Hi, Chief,' said Thiery, 'that was quick.'

'We should play the lottery tonight,' said Dunham, the excitement in his voice noticeable.

'Yeah? Did we get lucky?'

'We did. I called my shift supervisor, and he told me they were slow tonight. They've been sitting around listening to the radio dispatches on your shooting, up in Lake Wales, so I had him put some people on the rental car. They got a hit at Enterprise.'

'Super. So, you have a name for me?'

'Yep. Alejandro Lopez. Know him?'

'No, can't say I do.'

'Enterprise makes a copy of their clients' driving licences, so I had them send me a copy. Lopez's DL was issued in Mexico. I'm going to text you and attach the image. Can you take it from there?'

'Absolutely. That's great, Chief. I can't thank you enough.'

'I'm holding you to that breakfast at Dutch's.'

'You got it, pal. Now, get back to sleep.'

'Yeah, sure. Stay safe.'

Thiery's iPad went *ting* before he was out of the car. He opened the message and looked at the attached file. He recognized Alejandro as the man he'd shot behind the house on Guava Lane. Dunham had also attached PDF files of the paperwork from the rental car agency. The paperwork required that the renter state which hotel he was staying at locally: the Gaylord Palms.

'No shit,' Thiery muttered.

Thiery finished cleaning the cut on the back of his head from the bar fight. It was a little tender, but didn't feel like it needed stitches. He'd had worse.

It was almost 01:00 a.m. but Thiery guessed Logan was still awake. She'd always been a night owl. He called her number.

Logan picked up before the first ring tone had stopped. 'Justin?'

'Yeah. It's me.'

'Can't sleep?'

'Haven't tried yet. Been a busy night.'

'Oh?'

'I need a favour, Sara.'

Logan smiled hopefully and looked at herself in the mirror. She was in her favourite lace teddy. Her nipples were pressed against the sheer fabric like flesh-coloured happy faces pressed against glass. She pulled at the points of her blonde tipped, spiky hair. She wondered if Thiery liked the new, short do. The thought came to her: *I wonder if he'd like to jumpstart where we'd left off ... would I?*

'Anything you want, Justin,' she said, embarrassed by the throaty sound of her own voice. *Jesus girl, control yourself! It can't lead to anything other than trouble.*

He hesitated, recognizing that sensuous change in her voice, trying to stay aloof. 'I was involved in a shooting tonight,' he said, ignoring her unspoken invitation. 'We were tracking the Weisz woman. She was in Lake Wales in what I think was another safe haven for WITSEC.'

'What?' worry now in her voice.

'Let me finish. I don't have proof yet, and if my hunch is right, I don't want to further jeopardize her, so I'm not going to say anything to the press. But, the governor made a big deal about putting the FDLE in charge of the case yesterday, so I'm going to have to say something to the media about why I can't be lead anymore. I'm going to say I'm on administrative leave pending an investigation into the shooting incident, which is true, but I'm also going to try to reach out to her through that press release.'

'What do you want me to do?'

'I want you to take over the lead on the investigation.'

Logan thought about it for a moment. If he was right about the WITSEC connection, and the guns were transported interstate by a convicted felon, it would make the case federal and give her a reason to take a more active role in the investigation. Still, she wasn't sure she wanted to put herself out there without authorization from her supervisor. Or, without getting something out of it.

'I suppose I could ... but it will cost you,' she said coyly, ashamed of her own longing but so caught up in it now, she knew there was no turning back. *Why not*, she asked herself, *we don't live forever*.

Thiery again recognized that familiar honeyed tone she used when she wanted him. 'C'mon, Sara. Quit fucking around. This is business.'

'Don't be a shit, Justin. Just once more, for old times' sake?' She closed her eyes and thought of him, his still athletic chest – she used to love to run her fingers through the hair like stroking a cat – his muscular shoulders and arms. The flat abs. The ... *everything*. A guilt trip as the image of her husband flicked into her head, his kind, watery blue eyes and familiar smile gazing lovingly at her. Then she pictured his leathered skin, the 'moobs' – the sagging man boobs – of a man that, while a saint, displayed their age difference like a failed monument of *if only*. But Logan pushed past those thoughts.

She felt her pelvis grow heavy with lust and shivered as if she'd been electrocuted. 'One more "roll in zee hay?"' she said, weakly, hopefully, referring to the Teri Garr line from Mel Brooks' *Young Frankenstein*. She and Thiery had watched the movie on a rainy afternoon at her Ormond Beach house.

Thiery couldn't help but smile from the memory. He could hear the waver in her voice, her breath almost ragged. She really had a problem, but what was he going to do? He shook his head, remembering how they were in bed, and found himself becoming aroused in spite of his reluctance to do so. Nothing good could come from it, but …

'Okay,' he said, relenting. 'I've got one of the reporters staying here at my hotel. I'm going to wake him up and give him an exclusive. I'd like you to be here when I do that. But, I need to call my boss first. I also need another favour from you.'

Logan was sliding into tight stretch jeans as he spoke. She pulled the teddy over her head while she kept the phone to her ear. She shrugged into a white button down shirt and looked around for her FBI windbreaker. 'Sure,' she said, trying to hide the anticipation in her voice.

'I'm going to text an attachment to you of the man I shot tonight. I think he and his brother, who was also killed at the scene, were hitmen. I don't know their connection to Erica Weisz yet, but they're out of Mexico, so I'm thinking there's some drug cartel involved. Can you run their names through your database, and see if you can find anything on them?'

'I'll get right on it,' she said, looking at her notes, 'but I found something of interest today, too. We traced the guns used at the school back to a pawn shop in Vegas. I tried calling the owner, a hump named Tito Viveros, but he acted like the connection was bad and hung up on me. I'm going to have some agents drop in on him tomorrow and see if they can shake something out of him. If Shadtz transported the guns from Nevada to Florida...'

Thiery cut her off. 'That makes it federal anyway.'

'Yup.' She was whispering as she trotted through the plush carpeted halls of the Gaylord, trying not to wake other occupants in the hotel but *so* eager to get with Thiery.

'Even better,' he said, trying to ascertain why she was speaking so low. 'This could lead us to something that would substantiate Weisz being in the WITSEC programme.'

'If she is, I should be able to find out.'

'I'm not so sure about that. The US Marshals are pretty tight-lipped about their witnesses.'

'So how did Mexican hitmen find Weisz in Bumfuck, Florida?' Logan asked, but a thought—something about Wyatt Earp, a *marshal*—crept into her head.

'Good question,' said Thiery.

'I'll be at your hotel within the hour. Is that okay?' She wondered if he could hear her heartbeat in her voice like she could in her own head.

'Yeah,' said Thiery, then almost reluctantly added, 'Thanks for the help. I look forward to … seeing you,' he added, trying to keep it cool and professional but knowing it wouldn't be.

He hung up, distracted. Logan did that to him. He'd forgotten to tell her that the dead triggermen might have been staying at her hotel, according the rental car agency lease agreement. *No matter, he thought, they couldn't hurt her or anyone else now.*

After the call to Logan, Thiery went to the bathroom, splashed some water in his face, and let it drip, undried, like an iceberg melting. He'd killed a man tonight; it wasn't the first, might not be the last. He stared, regrettably, at his reflection in the hotel restroom.

Then he called Bullock.

'Sorry to wake you, boss, but there's been an incident.'

Bullock sat up and sipped the water on his nightstand to lubricate his throat. 'When you say 'incident', Justin, it makes me uncomfortable.'

'Don't get riled, but I had to put a guy down tonight. You're going to have to place me on administrative leave for an investigation.'

'How is it you managed to kill someone while investigating a school shooting?' he whispered, trying not to wake his wife.

'Remember when I told you earlier that I had a feeling about Weisz and the WITSEC programme? Well, I'm almost sure of it, now. We tracked her down tonight, but missed. Then a couple out of country hitmen showed up at the place she was staying. Now, they're both dead and so are a few of the locals that came looking for her.'

'Jesus. Sounds like the wild west down there.'

'Oh, it's non-stop fun. Did I thank you for sending me down here?'

'Sorry, kid, but you play the hand you're dealt,' he said, sliding out of bed. He bumped down the hall on the way to the kitchen, rubbing his face to wake himself up. 'Speaking of WITSEC, I talked to Ron Sales, my friend from the US Marshal's Office, about meeting for lunch tomorrow, and he said he was up to his ears with some shit. So I pushed him on the magician thing you were talking about. Are you ready for this?'

'*Shoot*. Uh, my bad. Go ahead.'

'Smart ass. Anyway, he confirmed it. He said he couldn't reveal who was in the programme, but that there is a programme where witnesses are renamed after magicians. The idea is that they're supposed to *disappear*, you know, for a period of time. He also said there was another programme named after Hollywood starlets because, he said, "they're here one day and gone the next". And another one named after animals that are extinct. Clever, huh?'

'So there might be a Dorothy Dodo out there?' said Thiery, exhausted but somehow amused. 'Who writes their programmes for them, Jimmy Fallon?'

'I know, right?' Bullock hesitated. 'So, this shooting, it was justified, I assume?'

'Of course, Jim' said Thiery, a weariness seeping in. 'When I got to the scene there were already a half-dozen guys on the ground.

The perp, a guy name Alejandro Lopez, was firing off an assault weapon like he was going into Kandahar. Had to put him down. And get this, he shot and killed Coody's father.'

'The kid from the school shooting?'

'Same one.'

'Je-sus H. Christ. Now, who the hell can I get down there to take your place?'

'Uh, I've asked Sara Logan to take over as lead.'

'Oh, really? You getting back into that?'

'Trying not to,' he said, knowing full well he wasn't trying hard enough, 'but she is here and I needed her help. Besides, if this WITSEC thing turns out to be true, we're going to need her.'

'Explain that to me. I'm still not quite awake.' He found some coffee left over from the morning, poured a cup and put it in the microwave, then sipped it black as steam rose off of it.

'Well, she's federal. We can't seem to get behind closed doors at the US Marshal's Office, but she might be able to. If Weisz is in the programme, and some hit men came here to find her, it can only mean one thing: someone, like a US Marshal, has given her up.'

'Oh, man. You can't keep things simple, can you?'

'C'mon, boss. I didn't start this thing. I'm just trying to get ahead of it before the body count gets any higher.'

Thiery could hear Bullock sighing over the phone. 'Okay, let's make it official,' the boss said. 'At, let me see … as of 1:30 a.m., you are officially on administrative leave, pending the on duty shooting of a suspect. I'm guessing you won't come home to kick back and get some sun by the pool?'

'You got that right. On admin leave, I can still advise the lead agent in the course of an investigation, right?'

'Technically, yes.'

'Then that's what I'm going to do.'

'Okay, Justin. Do what you got to do. But, stay safe and try not to embarrass the department. Cool?'

'Like ice, boss.'

Thiery hung up just as he heard a quiet knock on the door. He opened it, and Logan rushed into the room. She ripped off her FBI windbreaker and, still wearing her shoulder holster, wrapped her arms around Thiery, practically squeezing the air out of him. Thiery had forgotten how strong she was from years of swimming. He tried to gently disentangle himself, but, when he looked down into her face, her eyes had that *do-me-now* look, her lips parted and wet. She rose up on her tiptoes and stuck her tongue into his mouth. His conscience tried to kick in, recalling: she'd dropped him before, the hurt, the guilt, his sense of loss, but it all fell away with that kiss, and the only thing that filled his mind now was the want for her.

A half-hour later, they were in the shower rinsing away the sweat of their exertions, trying to regain some professionalism, before they went to Dave Gruber's room to give him the exclusive.

TWENTY-TWO

The sun resembled a bloody egg yolk as it peeked up over the concrete and asphalt wasteland of Orlando, casting an ochre tint on Erica's already jaundiced face. She had reclined the seat of the Chrysler 300 and fallen asleep as she tried to summon the courage to go into the Gaylord Palms Hotel and find any accomplices of the men who tried to kill her, as if they were going to be standing around with signs around their necks that read 'BAD GUY'.

Through the night, Erica had followed the green line of the car's GPS. The trail had brought her to the gargantuan hotel sprawled out before her, detouring only once when she'd spied an all-night Walmart off I-95. She'd walked into the chain store carrying one of the Lopez brothers' jackets over her hands to hide the cuffs, though, looking around at some of the late-night shoppers, she realized none of them would've given two shits about a lady in handcuffs. In the auto parts department, she found a set of bolt cutters and, as nonchalantly as she could, placed them on the counter with an Arizona Iced Tea and three twenty dollar bills. The white-haired clerk with eyeglasses as thick as coke bottles didn't have time to give her a receipt before she was out the door.

In a dimly lit parking lot, she managed to get the chain that linked the handcuffs into the jaws of her new bolt cutters while balancing the cutters between her thighs. Then, she squatted down on the handles with her butt, hoping she still weighed enough to snap the links. She had to do a little bouncing, but she succeeded. Now, she sported a stylish stainless steel bracelet that looked exactly like one end of a handcuff. Biker chic. If only she had time to stop for a tattoo.

She got back on the road and continued following the route on the GPS that led her here. She stared at the entrance to the hotel, marvelling at its Disney castle-look, the winding entrance lined with expensive cars, and wondering what her next move should be, as she sipped the tea. The Sig was in her lap, feeling as if it weighed fifty pounds. It was well made, expensive, like an exotic sports car. She ran her fingers along the barrel of the gun, admiring its sleek hardness, its cool surface. She'd always hated guns, the deadly and final look of them. What they stood for. Their sheer criminality. Now, she looked at the weapon and felt her heartbeat speed up, not just in anticipation of using it in a firefight to avenge herself and her family, but because it was *attractive* in some odd way. Like the sports car, it was a symbol of speed, danger, money, and possibly death, and that no longer frightened her. It beckoned her.

Her stomach growled, and it dawned on her that she might not be doing her best thinking right now. She looked around and saw a Waffle House sign poking up from a range of palmetto bushes. She cranked the car and drove over. Looking into the glove box, she found some expensive wrap-around sunglasses and put them on. There was a little straw fedora in the back seat, and she pushed it onto her head and looked into the rear-view mirror. Yep, she looked like someone trying to disguise herself. But, she thought, a waitress at a Waffle House wasn't going to go out of her way to try to identify a missing person while earning minimum wage and worrying about how she was going to buy groceries for three kids. Besides, with the dye job, hat, and sunglasses, along with her newly acquired gaunt complexion, she looked like any other druggie creeping in for an end of night, eat-before-I-go-home-and-crash meal.

Erica pushed the pistols under the seat and went inside for breakfast. She ordered waffles, bacon, eggs over easy, coffee with cream, and a glass of milk from a red-eyed waitress who smelled like pot and had a tattoo of an angel on the back of one hand and one of a butterfly on the other. Her fingernails were chewed to the quick. She said she liked Erica's hat.

It was a lot of food. In spite of her hunger, Erica found she could not finish. Her stomach twisted in on itself like an eel eating its own tail, but she managed to keep the meal down.

She climbed back into the car and returned to the Gaylord. This time, she did not wait. She went inside, her untucked shirt covering the Sig nestled into the top of her pants, a round already chambered. She approached the welcome counter and told the man at the front desk she had been shit-faced the night before and lost her billfold with her room key. Removing her sunglasses, she widened her blue eyes. The young man was quickly lost in them, despite being at least ten years her junior.

'Your name?' he asked, hopefully, a gentrified southern twang in his voice. The name tag on his jacket read 'Cary,' and under that: 'Knoxville, Tennessee'.

'Lopez,' she answered.

He looked at a computer screen, frowned. 'Is that A. Lopez or E. Lopez?'

'A,' she answered calmly and without hesitation.

He quickly printed a new card and placed it in an envelope, scribbling her room number on the inside flap; Room 527. 'Is there anything else I can do for you, Ms Lopez?'

Erica smiled and dropped her eyes, then raised them back up. 'Thank you so much. I'll let you know.'

Splotches of red appeared on the young man's face as she turned away.

In the lobby, a huge flat screen TV caught her eye. THN was on, and the reporter she'd previously seen covering the school shooting was interviewing someone. She stepped closer to hear the broadcast.

'In an exclusive report you will only see here,' the reporter, Dave Gruber, was saying, 'we are interviewing Agent Justin Thiery from the Florida Department of Law Enforcement and Special Agent Sara Logan from the FBI. Agent Thiery, will you please tell our TV viewing audience what you told me a few moments ago?'

Thiery squinted into the bright camera light. 'Last night,' he began, 'while searching for Erica Weisz, the teacher who allegedly shot the two intruders at Travis Hanks Elementary School, a group of armed men stormed a house in Lake Wales. I believe Ms Weisz had been there and that these men intended to do her harm. Upon my arrival at the residence, I found several men had been shot, some were deceased, and one man, who has been identified as Alejandro Lopez, was firing an assault weapon. Per my duty as a law enforcement officer, I ordered him to cease firing and lay down his weapon. He did not comply and, instead, pointed his weapon at me, at which point I was forced to fire upon him. He was killed, as was another man we believe to be his brother. Before my arrival, they had shot and killed four other men. The names of the deceased are being held pending notification of their families, but we can reveal that one of those men was the father of David Coody, who was one of the gunmen shot at the school.

'At this time, and per my department's protocols,' Thiery continued, 'I am being placed on administrative leave, pending an investigation of the fatality caused by the discharge of my weapon. This was a witnessed, justified shooting. Still, under the circumstances, I can no longer represent the FDLE as lead on this case. Therefore, FBI Special Agent Sara Logan is taking over until further notice.'

The camera swung back dramatically to Gruber's face. The video clip had been shot in the wee hours of the morning and it was obvious that Gruber had just woken up. Pillow creases still lined his otherwise perfect face, and he seemed a little off his game. 'Uh, Miss, er, Agent Logan,' Gruber stammered, 'now that you're lead on this still evolving case, can you tell us what the FBI's primary concerns are? And where will the case go from here?'

Looking relaxed, her cheeks still flushed from the romp she'd scored with Thiery, Logan stepped into the light, and kept it short and sweet. 'I've been working with Agent Thiery for the past few days' she announced. 'He is a competent, professional law enforcement officer who's done a very efficient job handling this tragic and senseless crime. We are currently tracking where the guns used at the school were purchased and, of course, we're still trying to find Erica Weisz. To that end, Agent Thiery has requested to add one last comment.' Logan stepped back and, once again, Thiery looked into the camera.

'Erica Weisz,' he began, his eyes focused as if on her face, 'if you are in a place where you can hear this broadcast, I want you to know, I know what happened.' The camera man, at the urging elbow of Gruber, zeroed in on Thiery's face as he continued. 'I *know* what is going on. I *know* you're running to protect yourself. You don't have to run anymore. This is my personal cell phone: 850-256-1900. Please call. My department, the Florida Department of Law Enforcement, Agent Logan, here, and the FBI will protect you. So will I. You have my word. Please stop running and give us a call. If you are physically able to call us, you must do this as soon as possible, before other people are placed in jeopardy. Thank you.' Thiery stepped away from the podium.

'Wait a moment, Agent Thiery, can you explain that?' asked Gruber, coming after Thiery like a pit bull, his cameraman desperate to keep up. 'What do you mean by "you're running to protect yourself?" What, or who is she running from?'

'No further comment,' said Thiery, waving his hand as he walked away.

'Agent Logan …?' Gruber tried, but she waved him off, too.

Gruber, his eyes red from lack of sleep, stared into the camera and, for the first time since he'd been in broadcast journalism, had nothing to say. 'Er, uh, there … you … have it: the latest in this increasingly bizarre case; a case that started off as a school shooting, but has spawned other violence throughout this rural county in the heartland of Florida. We will keep you informed as we learn of any developments. Now, back to you, Gail ...'

Moral woke up and turned on the TV, glad to be alive. Oddly, the only reason he was still breathing was because Erica Weisz had managed to escape again. Even he could find slight humour in that she was named after Houdini, the world's greatest escape artist.

When he'd arrived at Julio Esperanza's room at the Gaylord the previous night, his tail metaphorically tucked between his legs, he'd been greeted by De De Davies, a mountain of a man who'd immediately thrown his arm around Moral's neck and squeezed. It felt like a python wrapped around his throat. Blood pushed into his head until he thought his eyes would pop out. He was beginning to lose consciousness when a local news flash reported the gun battle on Guava Lane in Lake Wales, along with the deaths of the Lopez brothers.

Julio quickly came to the conclusion that, with the Lopez brothers down, the woman had escaped again, and the only link he had to her – though it was a weak one – was Moral. He ordered Davies to let him go. Gasping for air as he writhed on the floor, Moral listened to Julio give him a pardon.

'Robert, I think you can hear me,' he calmly addressed the US Marshal, as if discussing interesting stock options he'd seen on TV. 'I was going to kill you tonight. Your usefulness has been questionable compared to your debt to my family. What you did for us three years ago alleviated some of that debt and gave us confidence in your ability, and your access to *information* has been valuable. Since then, you've become indebted to us again and again, with higher amounts each time. We've tried to let you work it off, but, aside from giving us the location of your so-called protected witness, you really aren't worth much to us. Do you understand what I am saying to you?'

'Ye ... yes,' Moral croaked painfully.

'Good. So you understand your value, and the best way to enhance that value is to either bring that woman back to us or kill her yourself. Do you understand?'

Moral rolled over and pushed up to his hands and knees.

Anichka had been watching the pathetic man with increasing agitation; being summoned all the way there for a hit that hadn't materialized had tested her patience. Her expenses would be paid, but, if not actually part of the kill, she wouldn't get a piece of the big bonus. All she was essentially doing was spinning her wheels. The only good that *had* come of any of this, so far, was screwing De De, again. That big Canuck could make her putty in bed. She strode over to Moral and kicked him in his ass, her kick going right into his rectum, causing him debilitating discomfort and humiliation. She fought the desire to kill him, just for being a loser.

Moral went spread-eagle, and the contents of his bowels spilled into his boxers. He lay there whimpering, the combined scents of liquor-stained hotel carpeting and excrement in his nostrils.

Julio laughed as though he was watching stand-up comedy. Davies looked at Anichka with renewed lust and admiration.

The following morning, Moral rolled out of bed, his ass still tender from the night before, a spot of blood in the fresh boxers he'd slipped into after showering, his head humming from emptying the room's bar of all its little bottles. But it felt good to be alive another day. Reaching for the remote, he turned up the volume as the latest breaking news report came on.

He wasn't worried about the overzealous FDLE agent. Guy looked like a former college football player who was handed a job to act like a cop. Big, not brilliant. But, he decided to look him up, see what his background was in case they ran into each other. He grabbed his laptop and Googled Thiery to see if anything popped up.

What a surprise. He was the cop whose wife went missing some ten years ago. *Could it be?* he wondered to himself. *Was the world really that small?* His mind raced, but he came to the conclusion it didn't matter. He rationalized his connection, made it jibe in his own head, and put it aside. 'Gamblers do that,' one counsellor had told him when he was trying to stop his addiction. 'They rationalize their failures.' *So the fuck what?* he'd said, leaving the counsellor's office that day, and on his way home, heading for a late afternoon poker game held in the back of a billiard hall.

Still, the FBI's involvement bothered him. They didn't usually tangle with his department, because they were aware of the importance of protecting a witness's identity, but they could get access to individual cases if they believed them to be part of an ongoing federal investigation. This was turning into just that.

'*Fuck!*' Moral muttered to himself, no longer as thankful to be alive as he was when he first woke up. He tried to remember when he had identified the Coody kid as a potential candidate for the school shooting and the hit on Erica Weisz. He had used an FBI-linked database – legal, due to the Patriot Act – that allowed federal investigators to scan a citizen's home computer when they searched for or purchased large amounts of guns, ammunition, chemicals, or explosives. Once he found young Coody and determined he was a suitable candidate, he'd approached him on an anarchist chat site called blackenedflag.org.

He learned Coody was looking for a huge cache of assault weapons, then toyed with him until the kid was practically announcing he was going to kill someone, a group of people, preferably, to show the liberal government it was powerless to stop him or anyone else from doing what must be done in order to, well, maintain order. It was all crazy gibberish to Moral, but it didn't matter. The kid was a gun-carrying nut bag with a chip on his shoulder, and all he needed was a little push. That had to have been three, maybe four, months ago.

Moral had found the auction the Kentucky State Police Department conducted, but learned one had to have a dealer's licence to buy the guns in a cache like that. He'd brought the plan to the Esperanzas, hoping it would finally make things good with them. Maybe they'd even loosen their grip on his daughter, or clean his slate one more time. They liked the idea and brought in the Vegas pawn shop guy to make the purchase from the Kentucky State PD. What was his name, Tito something or other?

The final piece had been scaring Erica Weisz out of her safe haven, first in Richmond, then the 'B' haven in Washington. That was easy. In Richmond, as in Cleveland before that, all he had to do was go into her place, ransack the drawers and closets a little and Erica was ready to run. But, in Washington, he'd gone a little farther. He'd fired a shot through her living room window as she sat watching an old movie one night. The downside of that plan had been his proximity to her place; as soon as the shot was fired, she called his cell. When it rang, he was sure she'd heard it. Instead of hiding like she was supposed to, follow escape protocol and get out of sight and away from windows, she had stepped outside. She'd actually looked around, forcing Moral to dive behind a hedge and hide for several minutes, while he tried quietly to talk her down and assure her he was on the way.

Meanwhile, he'd already set up her new place in Frosthaven, where Coody lived. A few more suggestions to Coody about why schools symbolized the epitome of government bureaucracy, wasteful spending, and the dumbing down of America, and he'd set Coody on a path from which he could not be deterred. Then, the Esperanzas had sent Frank Shadtz down to pick up the gun cache, befriend the troubled young Coody, and the thing was set. It was like putting a tiger into an enclosed cage with lambs. Sooner or later, that cat was going to go postal.

Moral tried to remember if he'd erased his hard drive on his laptop. Surely, he had. He wondered if Coody had. He remembered hearing on the news that the hard drives had been destroyed, but he still fretted over it.

On top of everything else, Julio Esperanza had declared Moral useless. *Fucker!* He had risked everything for their deal, and *they* had blown it. Shadtz was the problem. He might have agreed to do the shooting and the hit on Weisz, but he was no killer. Even though he was dying and they paid him good money, he must've hesitated, must've given Erica a moment to act. After all she'd been through in the past few years, a moment would have been all the time she needed. That woman had proven herself a survivalist time and again, and that was Moral's shortcoming, in the end: he hadn't considered what she'd turn into over time. He should have known; when you hunt something long enough, it fights back.

So, he was in a corner, pressure so intense he couldn't breathe. He had to find her and, this time, he would kill her himself. He had no choice now. She *knew* he had betrayed her. She might not have proof, but she knew. If he didn't kill her, the Esperanzas were going to kill him. So, it had come down to that: it was him or her.

Given the latest news broadcast, he knew he had to find her before the FBI did, before any more questions could arise about who she was and why, if she was in WITSEC, her location kept getting compromised. Without her, the investigation into the assault on Travis Hanks Elementary would fizzle, and the perception would be that it was just another school shooting that hurt the community, nothing more. No ties to him or the Esperanzas. She was the only one who could throw doubt on all that.

He tried not to think of the fear the Esperanzas instilled in him. It wasn't just because they were one of the cartels responsible for killing tens of thousands of people in Mexico over the past five years. It was because they *owned* him. From the time they'd approached him in the casino, when he was already underwater by some two hundred grand at the craps tables, they owned him. He had sold himself to pay for his addiction.

It had been Julio who'd first greeted him, bought him a few drinks, then boldly told him what he needed to do. *Wasn't it a thing he'd done before*, he'd asked, *a long time ago? Did he remember the first time his gambling habit had written a cheque his ass couldn't cash?* Moral had balked, telling Julio he didn't know what he was talking about. He'd walked away incensed, but trembling with as much fear as anger. Had his past indiscretions been so indiscrete?

Julio caught up with him a few days later at a local bar he frequented, and told him a story that went like this: One of Julio's associates had hooked up with Moral's daughter, Amy, in LA, where she was trying to be a movie star. He'd been helping her get into movies. He also got her hooked on oxys. Seemed she liked them so much, she was willing to do anything to get them. *Anything*, he'd emphasized. Julio showed him a video on his phone. The picture was small, but Moral recognized his daughter, even *with* the five naked guys all over and in her.

Moral went along after that. What could he do? Who could he turn to? They took care of his debt, but he soon managed to drive it up again. And again. Esperanza's men later *told* Amy it had all been a set-up, a debt collected because of her father. She never spoke to him again.

Now, the only time he saw his daughter was when he surfed the Internet looking for porn. She had got her wish and become a star, going by the name ImMoral Amy. She was known for her penchant for gang bangs – the more, the merrier. And, as much as he tried, Moral found he couldn't stop watching her. He'd drink until he couldn't see straight and watch her do things that, in spite of himself, aroused him, as well as his self-loathing.

Nothing the Esperanzas could have done to him would have been a more enduring torture. This was his miserable life.

Moral limped down to the lobby, a beaten man. Maybe he could get a boiled egg and a Bloody Mary at the bar. He ordered from a bartender who made the drink as thick as a salad, full of horseradish and celery sticks and booze. Moral took out his cell. He found the number to Erica's new phone and, after much internal debate and three shots of vodka to bolster his courage, dialled it. He heard it ring. Then he heard a phone ring *behind* him. He glanced across the lobby and saw a woman, with tufts of blonde hair sticking out from under a straw fedora, frowning at her phone. She looked like she'd just stepped off a Greyhound bus. He looked closer. Was that a handcuff on her wrist?

Erica looked up, still wearing the sunglasses. She spied Moral at the lobby bar as the elevator doors opened behind her. Her lips parted and her mind raced, trying to accept the conclusion she'd already suspected. Now, if there had been any doubt, it was gone. Why else would her handler be at the same place the hitmen had come from? She turned and quickly darted inside the empty elevator, her heart seeming to rise into her throat as if she would spit it up.

Moral was running toward her, shuffling across the polished lobby floor as if he were wearing an artificial leg, his ass throbbing from Anichka's kick the night before. He was still ten feet away when the doors closed.

As the car began to lift, Erica remembered the gun tucked into the waistband of her pants and cursed herself for not using it.

TWENTY-THREE

Thiery and Logan had fallen into bed after the interview with Gruber. They were exhausted and fell fast asleep.

Thiery was having a dream – an incredibly erotic dream – when he woke up. He looked over and saw that Logan's head was no longer on the pillow. He looked down and saw it under the thin bed sheet, bobbing up and down above his pelvis, the Bluetooth light on her ear phone still blinking off and on. It looked like a firefly doing jumping jacks.

'Oh,' he said, groggy headed. 'That's where the dream came from.'

Her phone vibrated and she stopped what she was doing. 'Yes? This is Logan. No, not now, let me call you back, I was just, uh, having breakfast.'

Logan, giggling, crawled up his chest, nibbling at the hair along the way, and popped out of the covers, playfully. 'Good morning,' she said and bent down to suck on his neck as she sat on top and pushed him inside of her. 'I made a call to an associate of mine early this morning and was waiting for a call back but, uh, uh … got…uhm…dis… tracted… uhm.'

'Uhmm,' turned into 'Mmmmm… My…God, MYGod, MYGOD!' as she came in less than three minutes. Thiery lasted a little longer.

'God,' she said, panting. 'Why did we stop doing this?'

'Uh, because you're married?'

'Oh, yeah,' she said, suddenly sobering from her lusty high. 'And you had kids.'

'I don't regret that.'

Logan sat up, pouting now. She shook her head. 'I … ' she began.

Thiery stopped her. 'Let's not get into that again.'

She wanted to. She wanted to talk about things that might bring a resolution – a happy ending, so to speak – but she knew he wouldn't go for it. 'Kids are gone now, right?'

Thiery rolled out of bed and pulled his pants on. 'Yep. And so is your timing.'

She pouted, trying to keep it light but sensing the after-sex fade. 'Don't be mean.'

Thiery reached down and kissed her on her head. 'I'm not. I just don't care to get my head fucked-up again, and you're pretty good at that.'

She smiled up at him. 'We'll always have … Ormond Beach,' she said, referring to her vacation home, a beach house fuck-pad.

He shrugged noncommittally at that. Then it was back to business. 'You get anything back on the Lopez brothers?'

She nodded, reluctant now to get back into work. She sighed and picked up her phone. There was an email from Miko Tran. Logan read it aloud.

'Alejandro and Eduardo Lopez. Interpol has a list of suspected hits in a half-dozen countries and ties to various drug lords in Mexico. Both brothers arrested several times, only Eduardo did time in a Chilean prison for a murder rap eventually downsized to a manslaughter charge because they couldn't prove premeditation. That was four years ago. Last known residence for both of them is a small town called El Salto, just outside of Guadalajara, but they are regulars in Puerto Vallarta, where they go to shake down female American tourists when they're not busy with contract hits.'

'Not anymore,' said Thiery, and smiled in spite of himself.

Logan smiled back, then twisted her mouth to one side as she thought of something. 'You got their name from the rental car company, right?'

'Yeah.'

'So, where is the rental car?'

'I told you, I think Erica Weisz escaped in it last night. I don't know where she would've gone. I'm hoping my boss can get some additional information from his connection with the US Marshal's Office.'

'You know, some rental car companies maintain GPS monitors on their cars.'

Thiery turned to her as if she'd goosed him and grinned. 'Yeah, I'm waiting to hear back from Chief Dunham on that. He was following up on the rental agency. Maybe got side-tracked. I'll call them.'

Logan inched over the side of the bed, wearing the white, now wrinkled, button down shirt and nothing else, her libido surging again. 'I think you're too tired, baby,' she said, running her hands up his stomach. 'And too pent up, poor thing.'

He smiled looking down at her, extricating her hands from under his shirt. 'Yeah, you're right. Thank you, doctor, for the assessment. But, I think I'm okay. Can we get a little police work done?'

'But, you're relieved of duty. You can't work—'

'*You* can. Let's go, Agent Logan. If this pans out, I'll owe you again. Deal?'

'Deal,' she said eagerly, jumping out of bed. 'God, you're easy.'

Thiery called the rental car company whose information Dunham had sent to him. He identified himself and asked about the car rented by the Lopez brothers. They located the records while Thiery was on hold, listening to a cheesy pop music knock-off tune chosen by some corporate lemming. They confirmed the rental contract.

'Do you happen to keep a location monitoring device on that car, like a Lo-Jack or GPS?' asked Thiery. 'In other words, can you find out where that car is currently?'

'We don't like to reveal that type of information, sir, but I understand this is an on-going police investigation?'

'Yes, that's correct.'

'That's fine. We do like to assist our law enforcement agencies when we can. Let's see, now. I'm currently showing that car at 6000 West Osceola Parkway, in Kissimmee.'

Thiery jotted it down with Logan looking over his shoulder.

She nudged him in the ribs. 'Hey, I know that address. That's the Gaylord Palms, where I'm staying.'

Thiery thanked the man at Enterprise and turned to Logan, a quizzical look on his face. 'So were the Lopez brothers.'

This time, it was Logan who dropped the playfulness. She finished buttoning up and sliding into her shoulder holster. She took out her gun, a Glock 22, .40 calibre, and checked it out, sliding the clip out then back in, checking the slide before placing it back in its holster.

'Let's go find your girl, Agent Thiery.'

'Okay, but can we brush our teeth first?'

'I've got chewing gum. Let's go.'

When they got to Thiery's car and started to get in, Logan said, 'No way. This thing smells like an ashtray. Let's take mine. Follow me, big guy.'

They walked briskly to a Porsche Cayenne sitting at the edge of the parking lot, away from other cars.

'Nice,' said Thiery, getting into the car. 'Another Porsche.'

'Tried to get you to come over to the FBI years ago, Justin. They pay better.'

She cranked, then over-revved the German motor, grinning, as the tyres barked on the pavement.

Thiery called Dunham as Logan began making some calls of her own.

'I'll have to rain check you on that breakfast, Chief,' said Thiery. 'We think we found where Erica Weisz might be.'

'Thought you were on admin leave,' said Dunham.

'I am, but I'm assisting the FBI. They took the lead over for me.'

'I saw that on THN. FBI agents are better looking than I remember them.'

'Yeah, some of them are even women now, Chief.'

'You don't say. Well, let me know if you need any help.'

'You were already a big help. I called that rental car company you found, and they have GPS locators on all their cars.'

'Cool. They never got back to me. Must've been shift change when I talked to them. Hey, wanted to run this by you – I heard Coody, Junior was awake and talking – I thought I'd go see if he has anything to say.'

'Is that going to upset your city manager?'

'Too bad if it does. As first officer on scene, I still have an obligation to complete my report, and I can't do that without talking to one of the suspects, if we have one. Seems we do.'

'I hope it doesn't get you into hot water, but I'd like to get a copy of that interview when you're done.'

'No problem. I'll record our conversation and send you a copy as soon as I have it transcribed. One last thing. Remember we were wondering why more of the male staff weren't shot at the school? Well, I was looking through the security videos and found an outside view. It showed three men I've identified as Ed Bremen, Tim Cress, and Randy Perry. They all worked there but ran out and hid in a tool shed behind the school when the shooting started.'

Thiery felt anger bubble up from his stomach, then let it settle. *Not all men are meant to be brave.* 'Thanks,' he said. 'At least Jim Swan, the janitor, made a stand.'

'And that teacher. You let me know if you find her. I'd like to talk to her myself some time. Gotta be a story there, right?'

'I'm sure. You got it, Chief Dunham. And thanks again.'

When he hung up, Logan was wiggling her eyebrows at him. 'Guess what?'

'You got me. Spill.'

'I asked the young man at the front desk if anyone checked in matching our description of Weisz. He said no one with that name, but this morning a woman came in, seemed pretty strung out, wearing what looked like a handcuff bracelet. Came in saying she lost her purse last night and gave him the name of a guest staying there, so he gave her a room key.'

'And?'

'And the guest was *Alejandro Lopez*. The guy you put down last night.'

'This just keeps getting weirder. What do you think about getting the Orlando PD over there?'

Logan scrunched up her brow while she chewed the inside of her cheek. 'I don't know,' she said. 'This woman seems pretty gun shy. If she saw black and whites rolling in, she might be out the back door and gone again.' She looked at her wristwatch. 'I can get us there in twenty minutes. Trust me?'

Thiery squinted at her. 'No … but that's one of the things I like about you.'

Logan reached over and squeezed Thiery's thigh, then let her hand drop to the Cayenne's shifter and slammed the car into passing gear. It was early morning, the traffic light, and Logan dodged around the few cars on the road like a NASCAR driver.

Thiery's phone rang. He looked at the number calling, but did not recognize it. He picked it up and said, 'Hello?'

The caller was silent for a moment.

Thiery repeated, 'Hello?'

'Agent Thiery?' asked a female voice.

A chill went down Thiery's back and he sat up, his stomach, suddenly, inexplicably knotting up. 'Yes, this is Justin Thiery, with the FDLE.' He looked at Logan and she knew.

'Huh, hello. This is Erica Weisz. I think you've been looking for me … '

TWENTY-FOUR

Dunham greeted the Calusa County deputy guarding the entrance to Coody's room. He told the deputy who he was and what business he had there.

'Trying to wrap up my end of this thing. Got it covered if you want to grab some coffee.'

The deputy allowed him into the room.

It was dark, other than a blue glow from a silent television in the room. When his eyes adjusted to the darkness, Dunham saw Coody lying there, staring at him. It made him uneasy, but he tried to remain professional as he approached him.

Coody's face was swollen, his bright red hair combed back from his scalp giving him the appearance of an overripe tomato ready to burst. Some flowers were next to him on the nightstand and Dunham wondered who would be so concerned with a man who had gone into an elementary school with a cadre of guns and the intent to kill as many people as possible.

'Good morning, Mr Coody,' said Dunham, removing his flat-brimmed hat. 'I'm Chief Dunham from the Sebring Police Department. Has anyone read you your rights?'

'You mean Miranda rights?' his eyes darting toward Dunham. 'Am I being arrested?'

'Yes, to both questions.'

'No.'

Dunham put a small digital recorder on the nightstand near Coody and turned it on. Just to be on the safe side. He read him his rights before he began the interview, then opened with, 'I'd like to ask you some questions about your involvement at the Travis Hanks Elementary School.'

'My *involvement*?' Coody said, his voice harsh, his face reddening with the exertion of talking. 'I wasn't just involved. It was *my* plan.'

'So, you are admitting that you did, wilfully, gain access to the school and premeditatedly shot innocent people?'

'Innocent? I don't think so, but yes, I planned the event.'

'The event?'

'Yes, that's how we talked about it when we discussed it.'

'You and Frank Shadtz?'

'Yeah. But, Frank was just a mule, really. He brought the guns in.'

'I see,' said Dunham, surprised at the young man's willingness to talk so openly. He leaned over and pulled a cord to crack open the blinds. Slats of lights striped Coody's face and caused him to blink.

'Is this the part in the movies where the cop shines the light in the guy's face to make him talk?' Coody grinned, showing his yellow teeth. His sour breath created a fetid cloud around his head.

Dunham resisted the urge to spit in his face. 'Were there any other people involved with the event?' he asked.

'Maybe,' said Coody, coyly. 'Some people I talked with online in chat rooms. People that encouraged me to act on my beliefs. You won't find them, but believe me, there are a lot of people who think like I do, who applaud what I did. I'm not alone.'

Dunham heard the grandiosity that Coody was trying to lend his cowardly act and something occurred to him. 'Do you take any medicines for your condition?'

'What condition?' Coody asked incredulously. 'Fuck you, pig. You can't ask me about my medical background.'

'I can if it helped influence your crime. Hey, by the way, no one has called me a pig since I was handing out speeding tickets almost ten years ago. Thanks for the nostalgia.'

Coody said nothing.

Dunham stepped closer, trying not to inhale Coody's odour. He looked at the tubes going in and out of his body, so much effort to keep him alive. The bed tipped side to side, one way, then the other, to keep his blood from coagulating, Dunham assumed. *What a waste of a human being,* he thought, then asked the question everyone wanted to ask.

'Why did you do it?'

Coody blinked his eyes, his anger seeming to fade as he reflected.

'I … It's like, one day you think about it. Another day, you are buying some ammo, or a new gun, and you think about it again. Then you start to think about it every day. Like a kid wishing for Christmas to come. Video games don't do it for you, anymore. Neither does shooting the neighbourhood dogs and cats. You drive by the school and watch these entitled kids with their shitty parents who spoil them and treat them like they're something so, so *special*. And the dumb-ass teachers who drag themselves into their boring jobs and try to act like they care about these little fuckers. It's all just one big fantasy land. People who really don't like each other, acting like they do. I can't stand the pseudo caring, the fake people who go through life acting as if they are living it, when they are all really dead already.'

Now Dunham was really creeped out. He didn't know what else to say or ask. *What do you say to someone who is so insane, anything they tell you will just be a crazy diatribe that makes sense solely to them?* He wasn't a cruel man, but he felt his anger rising like a festering boil, so fevered it could lance itself. He cleared his throat. 'I bet your daddy bought you your first gun, right?' he asked, his tone bitter.

Coody's eyes darted to the Police Chief's face. 'Yeah, he did. Gave me a Colt .45 western revolver when I was fourteen. We used to hunt together all the time. My stupid fucking mother didn't like it. Hated guns. She was a whore. She left him for another guy, and my dad suffered for it. But, she got what was coming to her, too.'

Dunham nodded his head, his jaw muscles flexing. He used to hunt with his father, too. The commonalities with this sick kid ended there. *I'd like to take this bastard out of his misery,* he thought. Put his pistol against the fucker's head and save the taxpayers the hundreds of thousands of dollars it would take to convict, then house, a homicidal quadriplegic. Instead, he reached over and turned off his recorder, and said:

'Your father was shot last night when he tried to hunt down the woman who shot you. He's lying over at the county coroner's with a tag on his toe, along with that same stupid look you have on your face right now.' He leaned over, closer, and whispered, 'For every person you killed at that school, I hope they come back as an itch on your head. You think about that when you get one and wonder how you're going to scratch it while you're lying there like a carrot with your arms hanging by your sides like limp dicks.'

Coody's eyes were wild with fright and frustration as Dunham turned and strode out of the room, resisting the urge to slam the door behind him.

Julio Esperanza's phone rang and, distracted by the view out his penthouse window, he picked it up without looking at it. He regretted that for the rest of the day. It was his father.

'Could you fuck this up any more than you already have?' asked Emilio.

'Papi—' Julio tried.

'Shut up. Just tell me you have the woman and the problem is taken care of.'

'We are getting close.'

'I'm coming down there.'

'But, you are sick,' Julio argued. 'The trip will be rough on you, and you know the kind of trouble you could get into.'

'I don't care. If it's the last thing I do, I'm going to kill that woman. I might kill you too, you useless *maricon*.'

Julio's lip curled in anger as he tried to think what he wanted to say to his father, the man he had loved, hated, emulated, and feared his whole life. There was a knock on his hotel room door. He lowered the hand that held his cell, without breaking the connection. Julio went to the door and opened it. It was Moral. He was panting as if he'd run several miles, red-faced, his grey streaked hair stuck to his sticky pate. A dollop of sweat rolled off his nose.

'She ... she's here,' he managed.

Julio frowned at him. 'Who?'

'The woman. Erica, or Millie, whatever you want to call her. The Adkins woman. I just saw her in the lobby.'

Julio slowly brought the phone to his face. 'Papa? Did you hear that?'

'Yes. Who was that?'

'Moral.'

'Ok,' he said, his icy voice coming through clinched teeth. 'Try not to fuck this up. You get that woman. You hold onto her. I'm going to come there and personally kill her *and* that fuck-up, Moral. I'm bringing *El Monstruo*. Do you understand?'

For a moment Julio thought he might faint. Since the day *El Monstruo* had used his chainsaw on the men he had been forced to behead, Julio had feared him. *El Monstruo* knew it and so did Emilio. Even his father did not frighten him as much as this hulking man with ice for blood.

'Ye ... yes, Papa. Whatever you say.' He hung up the phone and turned to Moral. 'Are you positive it was the woman?'

'Of course,' said Moral. 'She's dyed her hair blonde, but it was her.'

'Why would she come here, to this hotel?'

Moral frowned at Julio. 'I ... well, I have no idea. The local law enforcement's put out an APB on her. Said she was driving a stolen rental the Lopez's were using. Maybe she used it to find her way here. I dunno. Was that your father on the phone?'

Julio stared at Moral, his face still flushed from the heated conversation with his father. His eyes shone wet, like a child who has been scolded.

'Yes,' he said finally. 'He's coming here unless we kill the woman first. He's bringing … a man. One who has lived in my nightmares … forever. He's not a man you'd want to meet.'

Moral felt panic creeping up his spine like some parasite that had found itself into his body and was eating its way toward his heart. 'That's not a good idea,' he pleaded. 'There's too much media attention now, too much at stake. He'll stand out here like fucking Madonna. If he's seen at all, the least he'll get is violation of probation. They'll lock him up until his trial. You have to stop him.'

Esperanza shook his head. 'I cannot tell my father what to do. The only way I can stop him, stop *them*, is if we kill the woman now.'

Moral swallowed, his Adam's apple riding up his long neck like a bubble rising through a viscous fluid. He knew if Emilio Esperanza came there, it would mean they had not completed the task he had given them and that would mean he had been worthless to them. If you were worthless to Emilio, you were already dead.

'Then, let's do it. Once and for all, let's kill this bitch.'

Moral's tone gave Julio some slight comfort. Perhaps he was right. Maybe he could get this thing turned around. Maybe he could make his father proud of him, perhaps for the first time. Maybe, he could even save himself, because he was sure, if his father did come to Florida, he would kill him, too.

He called Davies.

'*Oui, monsieur?*' Davies replied.

'Quick, De De. Find Drakoslava. The Adkins woman is here, in the hotel. We have to find her and end this today. *Now*. Come to my room, and we will spread out and look for her.'

Something suddenly occurred to him as he hung up the phone. He thought he knew why the Adkins woman was there. *She had come there to kill him*. The thought lifted his heart for some reason. It was funny in some perverse way, and he smiled as his confidence grew. *It was like a mouse hunting a panther,* he thought to himself.

She was giving him one last chance.

'Miss Weisz, where are you now? Are you safe?' Thiery asked. He pushed the speakerphone button on his cell so Logan could hear the conversation.

'I'm at the Gaylord Palms Hotel in Kissimmee, just outside Orlando.' She sounded out of breath. 'No, I am not safe.'

'Okay. Is there security nearby—?'

'Please, just listen. My real name is Millie Adkins. I am a witness in the WITSEC programme.'

Thiery glanced at Logan and winked. Logan returned the gesture with a thumbs-up and pushed the Porsche up to one hundred-twenty. It flew like a hovercraft.

Erica continued. 'My controller is a US Marshal named Robert Moral. I have reasons to believe Moral exposed me to the people I've testified against.'

'Who are those people?' asked Thiery.

'Emilio Esperanza. He is a drug lord from Mexico. I was his nurse for eight years. It's a long story, but you and the FBI agent, what was her name? Logan?'

'I'm here,' said Logan.

'You two can check it out. The US Marshals will not tell you anything unless you convince them I'm in danger.'

Thiery was jotting down notes with a stylus on his iPad. 'Okay, Millie,' said Thiery. 'We will be at the hotel in five minutes. Can you stay hidden until we get there?'

'I … I'll try… '

Thiery could hear a knock on the door in the background. The woman on the phone held her breath.

'Millie,' said Thiery. 'Do not answer that door. Move into a safe place, bathroom or closet, and whisper which room you are in.'

He heard her breathing again. Then, a man's voice.

'Erica? *Millie.* Are you in there?' A man's voice. Edgy, desperate ... A pause. Then, a fist banging on the door. 'Millie! It's Robert. I heard you in there. You need to come out now, if you want to live. The Esperanzas are in this hotel. I tracked them here. I can protect you from them, but you must come out, now.'

'I'm in 527,' she whispered.

''K,' said Thiery. 'Don't answer that door. We're pulling in now.'

There was an abrupt sound of the door being kicked once, twice, and the crack of the doorjamb splintering. Then, the sound of gunfire.

TWENTY-FIVE

Bullock sat across from his friend Ron Sales, the Associate Director of the US Marshal's Service, at the Lincoln Waffle House on 10th Street in DC. They had been friends for years, having met in the police academy two long careers ago. Bullock had stayed in Florida while Sales had gone on to take a job with the Feds. They'd vacationed with each other's families when their kids were young, but the responsibilities of their careers had curtailed visits until they only saw each other now and then, more often at law enforcement conferences than in the comfort of a friend's home.

Now, Bullock found himself losing his patience as he tried to extract information from Sales. He found him to be cagey, speaking generally rather than providing the specifics Bullock – and Thiery – needed. He held up his hand, stopping his friend mid-sentence, the rattle of the diners' forks and coffee cups on flowered, white ceramic plates lending their conversation some privacy.

'Look, Ron,' Bullock said. 'I know you have to maintain a level of confidentiality, but I've got my best man working on this school shooting and the investigation that has come out of that. I'm concerned about him and this woman he is trying to find. I'm going to be blunt. *I* don't believe we had a random shooting by some pissed-off kids in black trench coats whose mommies didn't hug them enough. From what Thiery has found, the evidence seems to point back to your department.'

Sales looked across the table at his old friend, a quick flash of anger in his eyes.

'I ... understand, Jim, but just as you have obligations to your department, I have commitments to my organization and the people we protect.'

Bullock leaned forward, trying to keep his voice down, his nose twitching as if he were trying to keep his glasses on the bridge, an involuntary thing that happened to him when he was losing his cool. 'If this woman is one of your witnesses, you guys are doing a shit shoveller's job of protecting her.' He continued in a harsh whisper. 'She's already been shot. She leaves the hospital because she doesn't feel safe there and goes to another one of your so-called safe houses and almost gets killed *there* by a bunch of gun-toting rednecks and some Mexican hitmen.'

Sales stared at him for a moment and sipped his coffee. Both men quit eating. 'How do you know it was a safe house?'

'C'mon, Ron,' said Bullock. 'We're cops, too. The Lake Wales house was owned by the same bank that owned the house that was the last address for Weisz in DC, and the same one that held the title on her current address in Frosthaven. We looked them up, and she hadn't leased, or purchased, those houses. *Your* department did.' He watched Sales' face turn red.

'Okay,' Sales said with resignation. 'Okay.' He rubbed his forehead with his fingers, kneading it like dough, unable to look into his lifelong friend's eyes. 'Jim, it's our job as US Marshals to underscore the importance of our witness protection programme, and for the public to see us and WITSEC as infallible. We have to have people trust us implicitly or we would never get people to testify against organized crime. You get that, don't you?'

Bullock looked at Sales warily. 'I understand what you're saying. I understand the significance of the programme. But, as any person with common sense could discern, there is no way your organization could go all these years without a fuck-up. Some fly in the ointment. C'mon, Ron. Law enforcement officers gossip as much as anyone. I've heard stories ... '

'Maybe you have, but there's never been anything in the media. There's never been any ... proof. To the public, we're still golden. And, we have to stay that way. Do we understand each other?'

Bullock scowled at Sales but nodded an affirmative. There was a television installed in the corner of the restaurant. THN was running the footage of Thiery and Logan talking to Gruber outside the Sun Beam Motel. Bullock had already caught it in his room before leaving to meet Sales. He glanced at it over Sales' shoulder, but said nothing.

'First, you need to know that yes, Weisz is one of ours. Has been for years. I can't disclose her real name, so please don't ask. She was part of the Magician Programme I talked to you about briefly yesterday. She's testified already against a significant and very dangerous drug lord, a kingpin from Mexico. So, you're probably right about the hitmen. But, I just can't believe the shooting at the school would be due to a compromise by one of our agents. Especially the marshal assigned to her.'

'What's his name?'

Sales shook his head. 'I'm sorry, Jim. I can't tell you that. It could compromise everything.'

Bullock had to loosen his collar; he felt his blood pressure rising. 'Wouldn't you say this witness has been compromised? Whether it was your agency's fault or not, this girl is out in the open now. If your guy had his shit together, he'd have gotten her down into a hole already.'

'He's trying. It's just— '

'Just what? Maybe it's just that she doesn't trust him anymore. Maybe she shouldn't. If she's had to move so many times, it's obvious someone is dropping the ball, at the very least. Worse case scenario, your guy has compromised himself— '

'No,' said Sales, shaking his head vigorously. 'That doesn't happen to our people.'

'Oh, really?' said Bullock, exasperated. 'You're all popes and preachers, huh? Well, let me tell you, Ron. Popes and preachers do bad things all the time. Now, you sit here and look me in the eye, and tell me your man is golden. You tell me this cat never gave you any reason to doubt his character, his motivations. You tell me that right now, and I'm outta here. I won't say another word. But, if you can't tell me that, we need a different game plan. And quick.'

Sales chewed on one of his knuckles as he considered his next words carefully. His eyes blinked rapidly, and he drew a deep breath. 'There was an incident about ten years ago,' he began. 'And yes, it gave us some doubt about the man. He was the lead marshal providing protection for an inside man named Eric Gazmend, connected to the Albanian Mafia in New York. He was supposed to testify against one of the head honchos, a mobster named Andre Kadriovski. We couldn't get him on racketeering, so we thought we'd go for the old standby, tax evasion.'

'I've heard of Kadriovski,' said Bullock. 'He's still in operation, so I think I know how this story goes.'

Sales nodded. He seemed weary and rubbed at his eyes. 'Anyway, we had his accountant, Gazmend, and we had him in a corner. We do what we have to do to get these guys to come over to our side, and some of it isn't pretty. We knew he had a girlfriend. The mistress was an old flame Gazmend couldn't let go of. He didn't seem to care if his wife found out about her, but the mistress was married, too, and she didn't want her husband to find out about him. So we used that to leverage his testimony against Kadriovski. Our man was assigned to his case and was handling it well, point by point, no mistakes. Then, the bean counter goes to dinner with his woman friend to a tiny, little, presumably very private, Albanian restaurant in New York. The owner kept it open after hours just for Gazmend, so they had the place to themselves, you see?'

Bullock listened, but said nothing.

'They ... didn't make it. We had three guys covering Gazmend. Everything had been quiet and we had other people doing twenty-four hour surveillance on Kadriovski and his key players.'

'But, there was still a hit?'

Sales nodded. 'Yep. Took out Gazmend and his lady friend and two of our guys. But, one of our men survived.'

'Without a scratch?'

Sales nodded. 'He fired back, the restaurant owner confirmed that, but the shooters were all wearing masks and no one was ID'd. We had doubts about the deputy, but his story held up. We assigned him to desk for a year or so, had internal take a look at him. But, after a year, our HR department came around and told us he'd made some complaints that we hadn't charged him with anything, so we put him back on the streets. As far as I know, he's had a good, long, and at times, distinguished career.'

'What was the name of the woman killed in the restaurant?'

Sales smiled, the Cheshire cat returned. 'We weren't sure. She had an assumed name, also Albanian, we thought. The newspapers reported that she was killed at a restaurant shoot-out, and printed the name we had, which was something like Magnolia, or Mangola. First name, Andrea, or something like that. Truth is she wasn't identifiable; took a shotgun blast to the face.'

'You guys didn't notify her family, or anything?'

Sales shook his head. 'I know it sounds shitty, but she wasn't important to us. We knew she was a side fling for our accountant, but that's all she was. NYPD was the lead on the homicide investigation and they didn't take it anywhere. With our witness dead, we lost the sure conviction we thought we had. Essentially, he got away from us. Without Gazmend, without eyewitnesses who could ID the shooters, we couldn't prosecute. We tailed Kadriovski for months, waiting for him to slip up, but he never did. After that, he vanished.'

Bullock sipped at his coffee. It was cold. 'So, that's that?'

'I know,' said Sales. 'You wanted more, but I don't have it. I'm so far up the ladder now, so removed from the field; I only know most of this, because you asked me to look. You knew I would eventually tell you what I knew, out of our friendship, but what I've told you is all I can share. The mission of our department demands we fly under the radar with some of these cases so we don't expose other witnesses to the bad guys. You *know* that. Not to be disrespectful, Jim, but I can't believe someone in our organization would be corrupt and last as long as this man has.'

'*Can't* believe, or *won't*, Ron?'

'C'mon, Jim. I didn't have to share any of this with you.'

Bullock squinted at his old friend, noticing for the first time in years how much he'd changed. 'Yeah, you did. You knew I'd really stink up the place if you didn't.' He let Sales chew on that for a moment. 'Can you at least send another marshal down to keep an eye on your man? If nothing else, maybe he could shadow him and assure things are on the up and up?'

Sales breathed out heavily and looked out the window. It was bright but cold and a wind whistled down the street like a sigh. He looked back at Bullock. 'I'll see what I can do.'

'Fair enough,' said Bullock, standing to leave.

Sales stood up as well and reached for his wallet.

'I got it,' said Bullock, trying to remember if he'd taken his blood pressure medicine that morning …

Sales looked at his watch. 'Oh, man, I'm late. Jim, it was good seeing you. Wish it was under better circumstances, but this *will* work out. You just watch. It'll all be fine.'

Bullock nodded, shook his friend's hand, and said nothing. As soon as Sales was out the door of the restaurant, Bullock called his secretary, an efficient woman who had been with him for some twelve years.

'Good morning, sir,' she answered. 'How is Washington?'

'It's cold, Dawn,' he said abruptly. 'Listen, I need a favour. Get some people in our research department to look into something for me.'

'Go ahead, sir,' she said, a pad and pen poised at the ready.

'Have them find out everything they can about an Albanian mobster named Kadriovski, and his accountant, a guy named Gazmend, who was hit in a restaurant in New York about ten years ago.' He took the time to spell the names for her, then went on. 'There were some US Marshals killed at the scene, and a woman. See if they can confirm the woman's name: possibly Mangola, Andrea, and that could be an alias. There was a US Marshal that survived the hit, too. See if they can find out who he is. Have our guys work with the FBI on it. The Feds like to play in their own sandbox but aren't necessarily bed buddies with the US Marshals. Tell them it's connected to an active case in which one of their agents, Special Agent Sara Logan, is working with one of ours. This is urgent. Priority is Number One. You got all that?'

'I sure do,' said Dawn, her tone never less than melodic, as if she were scribing a grocery list Bullock was reciting. 'Just trying to work out that "bed buddies" statement for our investigative team, but I'm sure I can find the right phrase.'

Bullock thought for a moment before giving her one more piece of information. He felt guilty as he cleared his throat and said, 'Have them look into Ron Sales, too.'

'Ron Sales, from the US Marshal's Office?'

'Yeah.'

'O … kay. But, don't you know him personally, sir?'

Bullock hesitated before answering. 'I thought I did.'

'Yes, sir,' she said, diplomatically. 'Probably prudent to make calls rather than send emails.'

'Thanks, Dawn,' said Bullock, recalling why she was so valuable to him and the department. 'One more favour, too.'

'Go ahead, sir.'

'Book me a flight out of here as soon as you can get me on the next one. I'm not staying here.'

'Too cold, sir?'

'Nope. I just can't take the politics anymore.'

TWENTY-SIX

Millie Adkins – there was no sense in pretending she was Erica Weisz anymore – glanced back at Moral. He was hunched over, framed in the doorway, grimacing, his pistol lying impotently about five feet away, holding his arm, clutching at a bloodstain that grew under his hand.

'Millie,' he called her, using the name she'd gone by her entire life, before becoming enmeshed with this den of snakes. She stood staring at him, her mouth agape as she still struggled with the realization that Moral was one of the bad guys. The gun felt hot in her hand, a faint wisp of smoke curling out its barrel. She raised it and pointed it at his head.

'Millie,' he repeated, pleading, 'don't ... please ... Millie! You've got it wrong!'

'Then why are you here?' she screamed. She wanted to believe him, believe *in* him, or anything that could give her reassurance, make her feel not so alone. 'With *them*?'

Moral sensed a glimmer of hope. Maybe he could bullshit her one more time. 'I'm not with them. I tracked them here ... you were right. Su ... somehow they found you. I ... *we* need to move you again.' Then, trying for one more ounce of sympathy, he tried, 'I can't believe you shot me ... '

But, it didn't stick. Even if he were telling the truth, she was done running. 'Where are they, Robert?' she said, her voice icy, almost mechanical. 'And how many of them are there?'

Millie heard the 'ding' of the elevator stopping on their floor. She stepped past Moral to see who would emerge from the car, hoping it might be a tourist, or better yet, a cop. Her heart stopped as she watched an antique gun, like one of those a German soldier would have in an old World War II movie, extend from the elevator's doors, the end of its long barrel encased in what appeared to be a homemade, cylindrical housing that she knew to be a silencer. A round face peeked out of the door, one eye squinting.

Millie raised her gun and fired. The head and gun tucked inside the elevator instantly, as the bullet ricocheted off the stainless steel doors. She heard them begin to close again. Millie glanced back at Moral who was trying to stand, his face ashen. She looked up and saw the 'Exit' sign that pointed to the stairs. Her choices were to stay and try to shoot it out with the man on the elevator, with Moral free to put a bullet in the back of her head, or to run for it and hope the cop and the FBI agent were already downstairs. She felt outnumbered in spite of Moral's wounded arm. She decided to run for it, the hollow but prophetic quote, *A good run beats a bad stand any day*, creeping into her head.

She made for the exit, kicking Moral in the hip as she passed him. Moral stumbled to the floor again, cursing her as she flew by and scrambling for his gun. She kicked it further away from him. She grabbed the steel push handle of the exit door, just as she heard slapping sounds above her head, seeming to emanate from behind the patterned wallpaper. She glanced up to see holes as big as fingers appear in the wall. The 'Exit' sign exploded, raining red plastic shards on her as she pushed through the double doors, legs like rubber, and began her descent.

As she took two and three steps at a time, her side aching like an abscessed tooth, she heard sounds like thunder and realized it must be coming from the giant bald man running down the hall, coming after her.

Thiery and Logan entered the lobby of the Gaylord Palms, went immediately to the front desk, and told them to notify hotel security that armed gunmen were in the hotel, and to call 911. A manager appeared immediately, his plastic name tag identifying him as Noel. Noel demanded an explanation. Thiery and Logan showed him their identification. To their surprise, Noel immediately called his chief of security and told him to perform a lockdown with all guests ASAP, this was not a drill. Clear the pool and bar areas, he'd instructed, place men at all egresses. Noel pointed out to the agents that it was an enormous hotel. They would do the best they could.

Millie burst through the stairwell's ground floor exit, emerging onto the far east side of the building. A sign on the wall with an arrow said 'Lobby'. She was half way down the hall when she heard the stair doors bang open behind her; sounds like rocket-propelled wasps flew by her head.

Julio Esperanza and Anichka Drakoslava stepped out of the elevator into the lobby. They were both fully dressed, but wore hotel robes to help conceal the weapons they were carrying. His was a Taurus, 'The Judge' model, loaded alternately with .410 shotgun shells and .45 calibre bullets. Hers was a beautiful little Makarov, 9 mm, sleek and stylish, with armour-piercing rounds, their black, pointed bullets like the lethal heads of coral snakes.

Moral had called Julio and told him the 'target' was headed for the lobby and that he would meet them there. Thirty seconds after their arrival, Moral whirled into the lobby, his gun in one hand, his other arm hanging loosely at his side, blood soaking his jacket sleeve from hem to hand, his lips quivering in pain and anger. He didn't see Millie, but he saw the two agents talking to the hotel manager at the front desk and recognized them from the news. He glanced at Julio and Anichka and nodded.

Millie rushed into the lobby, De De Davies following a few yards behind, a fleshy tsunami pushing after her, his gun extended in front of him like a lance. Between the concierge and transportation desks, while mulling around, waiting for someone to address their needs, hotel guests scattered as the melee burst down the hall. Overhead speakers boomed the announcement:

'Attention guests, this is an emergency. Please vacate the common areas immediately and return to your rooms. I repeat, this is an emergency; please return to your rooms and await further instruction.'

Patrons already angered and curious as to why security guards were rushing about switched from mild irritation to panic and terror when they saw Moral clutching his bloodied arm. *What's happening?* was the common thread as hotel guests clamoured to exit the building, scurry back to their rooms, or dive under tables and behind chairs.

Thiery saw Millie first, but prudence dictated an authoritative response.

'Law enforcement officer!' he called out in his best shut-the-fuck-up voice. 'Everybody down!' He drew his weapon, and the OK Corral was reborn.

Millie turned to the sound of Thiery's voice and screamed, veins distended in her thin neck like hoses ready to burst. 'It's me, Agent Thiery. Millie Adkins.'

'Put down your gun,' Thiery ordered.

'I … no … I can't,' she pleaded, peering over the bodies scattered about the floor.

'Put it down, now,' he said calmly, but forcefully.

Millie leaned against a column in the lobby. Her hands shook as she steadied herself with one and crouched to place the gun on the floor with the other. Thiery believed he saw more anger than fear in her eyes. Suddenly, a chunk of the column blew out and sprayed her with plaster dust as Davies sighted his gun at her and fired, his silencer-muffled gun spitting repeatedly. Millie threw herself to the floor and crawled behind the column. The gun stayed in her hand.

Logan turned and spied Moral and his bloody arm. She drew her weapon and aimed it at him. Moral shouted in a panic, 'US Marshal!' He laid down his gun and held out his badge. Logan quickly scanned the rest of the lobby with her gun, one eye closed, looking for the next threat. Without looking at him, she ordered, 'Stay face down, Deputy, until we can get this sorted out.'

'Sure,' said Moral, but as soon as he saw Logan was distracted by Davies, he quickly and quietly retrieved his gun and crawled away.

Thiery and Logan drew down on Davies as he approached the centre of the lobby, a surprised look on his face, like a bull that successfully made its way through the chaotic streets of Pamplona, only to discover an arena of death at the end of its run. His tiny eyes went wide as he looked around, trying to decide who he should shoot first.

Julio and Anichka took advantage of the distraction and circumvented the cavernous lobby. They stepped over the costumed guests, some of whom had begun to cry, some lying in puddles of their own urine, helpless in their panic. They managed to manoeuvre behind Thiery and Logan, as Moral inched forward, as if to help his fellow law enforcement agents. He retrieved his gun and appeared to aim it at Davies.

Logan did not fire a warning shot. She was an incredible marksman; she and Thiery had gone to the shooting range on various 'dates,' and she always outshot him. She fired a single round into Davies's head, throwing a piece of it across the lobby like a discarded pool towel. Davies stood for a brief moment as if waiting for someone to tell him to die. The last thing he saw was Anichka, his ferocious and relentless bed partner, staring at him aghast, her mouth open and round, like it was when she slipped into bed with him in the middle of the night. He fell like the columns Samson pulled down on the Philistines. Some of his brain spilled like red, wet Play-Doh onto the gleaming marble floor. He twitched, and curled into a pitiful foetal position.

From under her terry robe, Anichka pulled her Makarov and shot Logan in the back. The agent let out a small shriek as if she'd been goosed. She and Thiery looked at each other, as if one had played a joke on the other; an unbelievable prank. Logan smiled, let out a small laugh and specks of blood followed it to her lips. She went down on one knee. Thiery grabbed her arm, easing her to the floor as Anichka continued to fire.

Two security guards burst onto the scene, their inadequate .38 Specials blazing like old cap and ball guns, with no direction and no defence. Glass and ice sculptures adorning the lobby exploded as bullets filled the air but none found their target. Anichka took the hapless guards down almost as an afterthought.

Julio and Moral spied each other simultaneously, and nodded. This plan had gone to shit but, with a little luck, they might still be able to escape. Julio slipped his gun back under his robe and began to slink toward the rear exit of the lobby.

Moral crept over to Thiery and Logan like a crab. 'There're more shooters going out back,' he said, though no one was listening. 'I'm going after them,' Turning to address the empty lobby desks, he yelled, heroically, 'Someone call 911. We need a doctor!' Then he scuttled toward the same exit door as Julio, fleeing into the rear parking lot.

Millie managed to pull up her knees to steady her shaking hands. She closed one eye, aiming at Anichka's chest, and slowly squeezed the trigger. She hit her in the leg.

The wound seemed to startle Anichka, and she stopped her forward assault. She looked down and saw the hole in her thigh. Blood wasn't coming out, yet, but it felt like she'd been whacked with a cutter Mattock. Her stomach rolled, and she felt as if she was going to puke.

Millie fired again. This time, the round hit the woman in the white robe in the centre of her chest. She seemed to disintegrate, the bullet exiting her back as easily as if it had gone through an offal-filled styrofoam cooler. She fell back, sprawled out like a broken doll.

Thiery heard the last shot, looked up to see the dead security guards, the dead bald giant, the dead woman in the robe. All the carnage had happened in less than a minute. Hotel guests stuck to the floor like quivering leeches covered in ice and glass and splotches of other people's blood. Gun smoke hung in the air like ghosts looking for a place to stay. Thiery turned back to Logan.

'Sara … ' he said, lifting her head, trying to make it easier for her to breathe.

Millie slipped over silently, the gun in her hand so big it made her seem small. The artificial lights of the lobby cast her faint shadow over Logan. She watched as Thiery tried to comfort his partner. She felt the need to help, but was also driven by her now seething hatred of Moral, of Esperanza, of every witless killer she had encountered, and there had been so many. Police and fire rescue sirens screamed into the parking lot. Through the windows, she saw the Orlando Police Department and Orange County Sheriff deputies hurrying toward the front doors of the lobby, guns drawn. Her world spun but one idea locked in her head.

'The US Marshal is one of them,' she said, robotically, almost under her breath. 'I'm going to kill him.' Then, she turned and walked toward the exit where Moral and Julio Esperanza had disappeared.

Thiery watched her leave, knew he should follow, but quickly turned his focus back to Logan. She was staring up at him.

The corners of her mouth twitched as she tried to smile. 'Glad we got one more roll in zee hay … lover.'

Thiery smiled and said, 'Me too.'

She coughed. 'Better go after her. She's gone through a lot to end up … like this.'

'No. I'm staying with you, till the medics get here … '

Logan smiled, pink frothy bubbles formed at the corners of her sensuous mouth. 'I … I'm going to be fine,' she gargled. 'Get … her out of here. This thing is too fucked-up. Give her some down time before … ' she coughed again, harder this time, 'before the media circus begins.' She pulled a set of keys from the pocket of her pants. 'Take my car. The keys to the beach house are on the ring.'

'I ... can't,' said Thiery, Logan's face blurring as he looked at her.

'Go,' she ordered. 'Get out of here, you fucking hayseed, or I'll never give you another BJ.'

Thiery laughed, even as a tear fell from his eyes, even as Logan died, her glazed eyes fixed on his. He watched as the pupils grew large, as if widening to see what new place beckoned her. Her tanned skin blanched and a red-tinged bubble formed on her lips, then popped as her last breath left her body. Her grip on his hand slackened and he laid her head down, gently.

A rage built in him and pushed back his sorrow. He stood up and turned, machine-like, his feet taking him toward the rear exit. All these dead people and he hadn't shot one of them. He was going to change that.

He ran into the parking lot and saw Millie walking quickly down a sidewalk, one arm extended, the gun leading the way. Ahead of her, he saw the US Marshal leaning over, talking through an open window to a man in the back seat of a black Lincoln sedan, a driver revving the motor. He could make out the face of the man in the back seat; he'd seen him in the lobby talking animatedly to the marshal. The man in the white terry cloth robe; Thiery thought he'd been a guest asking Moral what was happening. Now, Thiery recognized him as the man with the woman who had shot Logan in the back. If he had any doubts about Moral's complicity, they were now gone. With his gun in hand, he started jogging.

Moral looked up and saw Thiery running, then noticed Millie marching toward him, too. He pulled his gun, trying to hold it steady with his injured arm. The car window on the passenger side of the car opened and Julio held up a pistol, pointing it at Millie, who seemed not to notice, or perhaps didn't care.

Shots rang out again, and Thiery saw stalks of banana palms falling behind Millie as she continued her slow but steady charge.

She returned fire until the gun clicked on an empty chamber. Still, she kept pulling the trigger.

Thiery yelled at her. 'Take cover, Millie. They're going to kill you!'

A headlight exploded on a car next to her, and jolted her out of her trance. She threw down the empty gun and withdrew another from her waistband, then ducked behind a different parked car. Thiery ran toward her, laying down cover for both of them. Now, Moral was shooting at them, as well as the two other men in the car.

Suddenly, the Lincoln's tyres squealed and reversed as plumes of white smoke billowed up. The driver pointed the car toward Thiery and stuck a gun out the window as he accelerated toward him. The man in the back seat continued firing, too. Thiery had no choice but to duck back behind the car with Millie as windows shattered and the sounds of bullets boring into metal surrounded them.

The car sped past them, out of the parking lot, allowing Thiery a quick glance around. Moral stopped firing his weapon as a group of Orlando PD rushed out of the building. Moral held up his badge and laid down his gun. He ran to the cops, pointing in Thiery's direction, talking hurriedly.

Thiery hunched back down next to Millie, who shook her head.

'So, you're the cavalry?' she asked, leaning against the car, breathing rapid and shallow, wincing from the pain of her wounds.

'That was the idea,' said Thiery. 'Was that Esperanza in the car?'

'Yeah,' said Millie. 'One of them, at least. The son. I testified against his father a few years ago. It cost me my family. Then, his lawyers got it thrown out. I'm supposed to testify against him again next week.'

Thiery nodded. No wonder they turned up the heat. 'The marshal, I think you said his name is Moral? He's out there talking to the PD. What can you tell me about him? In one sentence, or less?'

Millie looked at him for a moment, then said, 'One sentence? *Needs to die.*'

At that, she withdrew the giant magnum pistol, leaped up, and extended her gun arm across the hood of the adjacent parked car, ready to fire.

'No, don't!' cried Thiery as he jumped up and pushed her.

The powerful recoil caused the gun to fire high. From the corner of his eye, Thiery saw the cops go low, take cover, and return fire. The gunfire sounded far away and puny, but the bullets hitting the car next to them sounded like hot rivets slicing into soft metal. A tyre was hit and exploded, parts of rubber peppering them. The car leaned to one side, diminishing their barricade.

'Great,' said Thiery as he pinned her down with his body and considered his options. He could give up his weapon and hope they didn't shoot him. It would take some time, but he should eventually be able to get them to hear his side of the story. *There were witnesses in the lobby, after all, right?* But, Moral would probably convince them they should hand over his 'protected witness'. He was federal, so the local PD would probably comply. Even if for a little while, it would give Moral the time he needed to finish Millie off. Whether he would get away with it or not was immaterial; Millie Adkins would finally be dead.

Above, the shooting abated. Beneath him, Millie felt so thin, so worn out, but her initial resistance hinted at a determined fierceness still in her. It was probably what had kept her alive for so long.

'You up for one more run?' he asked as he rolled over and released his hold on her.

'I keep my running shoes on,' she said. Thiery glanced at her feet, remembering what Sally Ravich – the secretary who had half her face blown off at the school – had told him. *She always wore running shoes* ... Now, he knew why.

'Okay,' he said. 'There's a grey Porsche SUV just around the corner. We're going to make a run for it, get out of here until we can sort this out.'

Millie seemed to mull it over for a moment. 'Okay' she said, finally. 'No one has believed me so far. Why would they now?' She seemed to be reassuring herself. 'Let's go.'

'Follow me,' he said, 'and try not to shoot anyone.'

TWENTY-SEVEN

Gail Summer summoned an anxious look as she stared into the camera and into the eyes of her many viewers. 'This just in,' she began, 'within hours of our reporter on the scene, Dave Gruber, submitting the following report, we have heard an FBI agent, possibly the one in this story, was killed in Orlando, Florida this morning.'

The video clip of Thiery and Logan talking to Gruber at the Sun Beam Motel in the early morning hours was shown again: the plea Thiery made for Erica Weisz to call him; the statement that Logan was now in charge of the case as Thiery stepped down on administrative leave pending an investigation of the shootout the night before in Lake Wales.

Gail Summer continued, 'we are getting reports from Orlando that Florida Department of Law Enforcement agent, Justin Thiery, who had been investigating the school shooting in nearby Frosthaven, was involved in a shoot-out at the Gaylord Palms Hotel. A guest that was checking in took this video with his cell phone. We must warn you, though, some of what you are about to see is very graphic.'

A jerky video image played across the screen for all of America to watch. The view was from the floor where the guest had obviously taken refuge. It showed Thiery crouched and Logan firing at Davies, glass breaking, a smoke alarm screeching, set off by the gunfire. Logan getting hit in the back and falling. Thiery going to her side. People running for cover and finally, Millie Adkins, standing up and shooting Anichka Drakoslava.

'Of the three people you see being shot in this video,' Summer went on, 'two were foreigners, a man and a woman. Their identities are being withheld pending further investigation, but the other victim has been identified as FBI agent Sara Logan, the Special Agent who was supposed to take over the lead on the school shooting investigation. It is unclear who shot her and who will now lead this investigation that continues to vex authorities. Now, we are going to look at the video again and freeze one frame … there it … is … '

The video played forward until it showed Millie Adkins standing and shooting Anichka. Summer continued, 'there, that woman who shot and killed one of the foreign tourists is believed to be Erica Weisz, the teacher who was, herself, shot in the tragic attack on Travis Hanks Elementary just two days ago. She vanished from the hospital where she was recuperating. She and Agent Thiery have now both disappeared and spurred a statewide manhunt. Only moments ago, we interviewed Calusa County Sheriff Alton Conroy.'

Dave Gruber held the microphone to Conroy's face and asked, 'Sheriff, what do you make of this new turn of events in this perplexing and seemingly expanding case?'

Conroy squinted into the camera. 'I have to say, I don't know why this feller was sent here in the first place. We were doing fine, trying to pick up the pieces and pull this community back together. The state sent this investigator down and, if you ask me, that's when everything got worse. We still aren't a hundred per cent sure what happened in that school, but it should've stopped there. Now, more of our good citizens have been shot and killed, while this Thiery guy goes poking his nose around.'

Gruber pressed for more. 'So you feel Agent Thiery has botched this investigation?'

'Well, I hate to throw another law enforcement officer under the bus, but it seems we would've done better without him. We need to talk with that teacher, find out what she knows and why she's running from the law, and it appears Mr Thiery blew that chance for us.'

Conroy started to turn, but Gruber got one more in. 'Sheriff, one more thing. Is it true you will be taking over as lead on this case, and if so, what will be your first order of business?'

Conroy looked at the ground for a moment, as if considering spitting out some of the tobacco juice in his mouth then deciding against it. His eyes went back up to the camera, a determined look fixed in his countenance. 'The governor himself called and put me in charge. My first order of business is to apprehend those I feel are responsible for the carnage wrought on our community. The governor has reassured me that any and all means of support will be provided. In the past, we've had our hands tied by financial constraints, and this community has suffered for it. But we're moving forward, now. Today, we take back our streets, our schools, our safety, not only for our small town, but for everyone in 'Merica. It's time we stand our ground! God bless us all.'

A crowd of onlookers pressed in around the camera crew – and the prophetic sheriff – turned local hero. All let out a cheer.

Sally Ravich held her husband's hand as he helped her walk the length of the hospital hall. Besides the horrendous facial wound, the rest of her body was fit, and her doctor wanted her to get out of bed more often. Get some exercise, move some endorphins around, make her feel better. Her biggest obstacle was her mental well-being, rather than the physical recovery of her gunshot injuries.

'Are you ready to try the stairs, Sally?' asked Harold, Sally's husband of twenty-eight years. He tried not to stare at the side of her face still covered in bandages.

Sally nodded, her one good eye levelling with his, revealing the determination to do this task. Their steps echoed off the ochre-coloured, institutional walls, like the teeth of a giant clock clicking away time.

The couple moved up the stairs, one flight, then another, until they arrived on the final floor. Harold pushed open the 'Exit' door and entered the hall leading to other patients' rooms. They had performed this exercise routine for a couple of days, now. Knew the layout, and where the nurses were, if they needed help. But, Sally didn't need help walking, or getting around; she was way past that, she needed to get her head straight, and, without words, had managed to get Harold to understand. And because he did love her still, after all these years, the ups and downs of any good marriage, raising a family together, all the emotional, financial, and logistical struggles they'd overcome, he could make that commitment without any hesitation.

They moved down the corridor, saw the Cuban Sheriff's deputy stationed outside one of the rooms and, at the nurses' desk, a young and curvy Latina from Puerto Rico. The Ravichs strolled up to her station, and Harold made a request. 'Hey, Shakira,' he addressed her, 'why don't you make me a cup of that coffee, like you do for Jose over there?' He nodded toward the guard.

Blotches of red appeared on her neck as though she was having a niacin reaction. 'My name is Linda, sir,' she corrected the man who, to this point, hadn't revealed his ignorant, racist side, 'but that coffee, there, is left-over from this morning.'

'Just make some fresh, J-Lo,' he said, releasing his grip on his wife's hand. Due to her injuries, Sally still couldn't talk. Seemingly embarrassed by her husband's abrupt and abusive manner, she slowly and silently distanced herself from him.

The nurse's mouth hung open as she tried to form words that might assuage the man's rudeness without making too big a scene. After all, he was taking his ailing wife for a walk, and she didn't want to upset a patient who had arrived only a few days ago with half her face shot off.

Noting the escalation unfolding before him, the deputy stood up.

'Fuck it,' said Harold. 'I'll get the damn coffee myself.' He darted around the counter, invading the nurses' station, hell-bent for the coffee pot.

'You can't come back here, sir,' the nurse advised, now quite agitated.

The deputy moved in. There was honour to be saved here. And pride. As he crossed the threshold of the nurses' station, his attention wholly focused on keeping the peace, Sally disappeared down the hall.

'Sir,' addressed the deputy, 'what is your problem?' He was six feet two-inches tall, with shoulders wider than some doors allowed, courteous and handsome and chivalrous in an old-fashioned way.

Harold picked up the coffee pot. 'Just getting some coffee, Miguel. Or maybe it's Ricardo. You know, like Dick. Mind your own business, *comprende*?'

It was the deputy's turn to grow red-faced, and he began to grind his teeth. 'Come out from behind that station, sir. Now.'

Harold ignored the lawman, rummaged through cabinets until he found styrofoam cups, and poured himself a coffee. The nurse moved away, her eyes wet.

Sensing a disturbance, the floor manager emerged from a nearby office. 'What's the problem, here?' she asked.

Seeing her chance, Sally Ravich quietly entered the dark room the deputy had been assigned to guard. Once her one good eye adjusted, she focused it on the marvel that dwarfed everything else in the room, specifically, the bed that rocked slowly back and forth like a baby's cradle. It reminded her the killer was just a kid. Still, she inched quietly over to bed and tapped the young man on his forehead.

David Coody's eyelids fluttered, then slowly opened. His eyes widened as he stared into the half-bandaged face of a woman. She looked like a mummified zombie, and frightened him. Unfolding a piece of paper and holding it up so he could see the words she'd scribbled, he read: 'DO YOU RECOGNIZE ME?'

Harold turned around and noted the floor manager had arrived, adding to the small but intense gathering of hospital staff. 'Ah, finally someone I can relate to,' he spoke to the woman with the clipboard. 'You must be the person in charge, eh? Gotta be a tough job keeping these tacos in order.'

'That's it,' the deputy said, lunging forward.

Harold raised his arms, as if gesturing to give himself up, then dropped the coffee pot. It burst and splattered everyone with hot coffee and glass.

The deputy grabbed him and shoved him against the wall. 'I don't know what your problem is, old man, but we are done here.'

'Not quite,' said Harold calmly, smiling like an idiot.

David Coody frowned at the spooky woman in his room. She turned the note over in her hands and let him read the other side: 'I BROUGHT YOU SOMETHING FROM TRAVIS HANKS ELEMENTARY SCHOOL'. His moderate fear gave way to instant horror.

From beneath the hospital-issued gown, she removed a gun: a small, easily concealed Ruger LCP. Made from glass-filled nylon mated to hardened alloy steel, it weighed only 9.4 ounces and carried six-in-the-clip and one in the chamber. She planned to use them all.

Sally removed her bandages, revealing the vacancy where the other half of her face used to live. Young Coody's eyes filled with terror. He tried to scream, but his throat was dry, and his diaphragm no longer pushed breath through his lungs as efficiently as before. Despite painful efforts, he managed nothing more than a squeak.

The sound reminded Sally of a rat, and made it even easier to squeeze the trigger. Her little gun fired again and again, sending bullets like flesh-eating termites into his chest, knowing he couldn't feel them, but wanting to inflict as much damage as possible in the few seconds she had. His paralyzed torso jolted with each shot, as if he were being spanked. Down to her last two rounds, she fired into his rat mouth. The last she sent with a delicious fervour into his brain.

The deputy heard gunshots, remembered his orders, and released Harold, screaming 'Shit!', as he ran into the unguarded room. He found Sally standing next to Coody, the gun lying on his bloody chest, a tendril of smoke still curling from the barrel. Her hands were in the air and she was smiling with the remaining half of her face.

At the nurses' station, Harold apologized to the Puerto Rican nurse and the rest of the staff. 'If you have a mop,' he offered, 'I'll clean up this mess.'

TWENTY-EIGHT

Thiery's phone rang. He had steered off I-4, knowing his fellow police officers would have the interstate covered with the Florida Highway Patrol, and driven north along tiny Highway 17, until it ran into State Road 40, then banked east. He'd be in Ormond Beach in less than a half hour. Thiery looked at the caller ID and answered. The timing couldn't have been worse but Thiery felt he had to answer in case his kids had seen the news.

'Hey, Owen,' he greeted his son. 'How ya doing?'

'Doing great, Dad. I'm up here with Leif in San Francisco. Partyin', you know?'

'Sounds … fun,' he said, relieved. They hadn't seen the media coverage that was making him out to be either an inept cop, or a rogue lawman gone crazy. 'What's the occasion?' Thiery asked, looking out the car's window, watching the green blur of the trees – life – passing by, as Millie sat in the passenger seat, staring blankly ahead.

'You sitting down?'

'Uh, yeah.'

'I got engaged, Dad. I'm gonna get married!'

Thiery was speechless. 'I, uh, that's great, son. Who … are … who's the lucky girl?'

'C'mon, Dad. Susie, remember?'

'The girl you were dating when I came out last time? What's it been, six or seven months?'

'It's been over a year … '

'That's still such a short time … '

'Dad, you always told me I'd know when it was the right one, right? And she is the right one. She's perfect!'

Sure, he thought. *Like a young man of twenty-five knows perfect. At that age they were ALL perfect.* Thiery caught himself gripping the steering wheel so tight, his hands looked skeletal. Dots and smears of Logan's blood patterned his shirt sleeve. *Who am I to question or advise anyone on marriage or relationships?*

'I'm happy for you, son,' he finally said. 'I … congratulations.'

I hope you'll be better at it than I was.

The words were left unspoken, but, for what remained of the Thiery family, the subject of marriage always conjured the memory of the boys' mother. The *missing mother* subject was still a sensitive spot, like the crack in the glass of the picture they'd kept hanging in the living room for five years. There were just the three of them, and someone had broken the picture and put it back on the mantle overnight. No one claimed responsibility. Later that night, he heard the boys talking in the bedroom, before they knew he was home from work, and young Leif told Owen, *I think Dad was drunk last night and broke the picture of Mom …* Thiery knew, or thought he knew, he hadn't done it. The doubt and denial still lingered.

'You want to talk to Leif?' Owen interrupted his father's thoughts. 'He's kinda hung over,' the boy explained, 'but still eating everything in the house, while leering at my fiancée.'

Thiery forced a laugh at the joke but regretfully declined. 'Uh, Owen,' he stalled, 'can you give him my apologies, and tell him I'll call him back? I'm kind of in the middle of something urgent right now.'

There was a moment of silence that echoed disappointment.

'Sure, no problem,' the formerly excited young man replied. 'He probably wouldn't make much sense right now, anyway. We hit it hard last few days down in Cabo. You okay, Dad?'

'Yeah, I'm … fine,' he lied. 'Just busy with work. Speaking of, I've got to get back to it. Always nice to talk to you. You guys enjoy yourselves, but try not to party too hard. I'll give you a call later, and we'll talk some more, okay?' And then he remembered the big news. 'I'm really happy for you,' he added. 'And proud.'

'Thanks, Dad. Love ya. Later.'

The phone went dead, but Thiery replied, anyway. 'Love you, too.'

He turned his full attention back to the road and breathed deeply, his eyes wet.

'Are you okay, Agent Thiery?' asked Millie.

He looked over at her, almost as if he'd forgotten she was there. 'Yeah. Yes. That was my son calling.'

'I gathered. I couldn't help but hear. He's getting married?'

Thiery nodded, but couldn't speak with the lump in his throat.

Millie was silent for a moment, then said, 'Congratulations, Agent Thiery … '

'Please,' he said, swallowing, 'call me Justin. And thanks.'

'Can I ask where we're going?'

Thiery had to think about it for a moment. He glanced at the sky as if trying to get his bearings. Its liquid blue shone through clouds that looked like gauze bandages.

'I'm … I thought it best to get you away, sort some things out. Agent Logan has … had … a house in Ormond Beach. It's a small, old Florida beach town. No one is there, and I know it's safe. It's not far. I'm going to call my supervisor when we get there. Get him to respond a team out to us and bring us in safely.'

Millie nodded slightly, but he noted her hesitancy. 'Will it be people you know?' she asked.

Robert Moral let the paramedics clean and dress his wounded arm, which turned out to be nothing more than a two-inch laceration. He'd had to think quickly, so people would believe his answers to the questions they'd asked, such as why he was there, why he was wounded, and where the missing teacher supposedly under his protection had gone. In short order, he came up with a fantastical tale that stretched the boundary of rational thought, but, given a gullible and willing television audience, could be plausible. It was a gamble, but that in itself, was what made it even more attractive to Moral. He had been in the business long enough to know, if the television reported it, people – even other law enforcement officers – were willing to believe it, as if God had told them, Himself.

Gail Summer could barely keep still behind the anchor desk as she blurted out the latest live report from Orlando, Florida. 'In a bizarre twist to the tragedy at Travis Hanks Elementary School in Florida,' she almost giddily read from the autocue, 'we have reports and footage of a shoot-out that left several persons dead at a popular resort in Orlando, Florida. At this time, we do not know all the details as investigators, themselves, are still trying to put together exactly what happened, but it appears that the teacher, Erica Weisz, who shot the school intruders and was, herself, wounded, then vanished from the hospital for the past two days, was tracked to the Gaylord Palms Hotel in Kissimmee, Florida. Witnesses report the scene was ground zero for a bloodbath that may have included international hired hitmen, and has cost the life of at least one FBI agent. That agent was Sara Logan, the same woman who, just this morning, took over the investigation of the initial school shooting from FDLE Agent Justin Thiery, who officials now say has fled the scene with Erica Weisz, the wounded teacher.' Summers hesitated, her throat obviously dry from her round-the-clock reporting. She rubbed her neck and a hand reached into view to place a cup of water on her desk. She drank deeply and dramatically, conveying the sacrifice she was making for her viewers, then continued. 'At this point, it is unknown if she left willingly with him, or was abducted, or the other way around. This is an alarming report and we must caution that some of the footage you are about to see is graphic.'

The shaky, handheld video taken by one of the tourists in the Gaylord Palms lobby was replayed as Dave Gruber reported live from the scene, his image, from the shoulders up, displayed in a tiny box in the corner of the screen. 'Gail, this footage is raw,' he explained, 'but we've obtained a copy from one of the hotel residents who wished to remain anonymous. You can see the video tells its own story. If you watch as our technicians slow it down, you'll recognize Agents Thiery and Logan involved in a gun battle with persons who some law enforcement officers are saying were possibly hired hitmen. Others say they were simply tourists trying to defend themselves when the shooting started.'

The video played out, again and again, slowing, backing up and going forward. The carnage lasted only a couple of minutes, but long enough for viewers to watch in awe as windows were shot out, bodies fell, and blood coated the floors of the hotel lobby.

The camera turned back to Gruber, who was now interviewing a US Marshal on the scene, one whose arm was held in a sling and bandaged, his coat slung over his shoulders. Sheriff Conroy stood next to him as if they were old fraternity pals.

'I'm here now with US Marshal Robert Moral,' Gruber introduced the injured man. 'He stepped in to help with this strange and evolving case and, in doing so, placed his own life at risk. Sir, you've obviously been wounded, so, first question, are you okay?'

'Yes, thank you, Dave,' Moral replied. 'I'm fine, unlike my friend and associate, FBI Agent Logan. My department and I, of course, send our heartfelt condolences to her family and vow to find her killers and bring them to justice.'

Gruber was eager as he pursued the interview. 'And can you tell us who the suspects are that were involved in this melee?'

'We are still trying to piece this investigation together,' Moral answered, 'but I can say, from my own involvement, there may have been an organized crime syndicate involved here. We have reasons to believe the Albanian Mafia from New York might be connected. It's too early to say for certain, but it appears that, possibly, Erica Weisz may have been involved with them.'

Gruber dived in, took the bait, and went past the buoy with it, gut-hooked. Flexing his jaw muscles and, with a determined countenance that revealed his search for the truth (i.e., entertainment value), he asked, 'Sir, do you think this Mafia connection might have something to do with the school shooting a few days ago?'

Moral took a deep breath, then added solemnly. 'We're looking at all possibilities. But, yes, there might be a link between these awful tragedies. This is an ongoing investigation, so that's all I can say at this time.'

Sheriff Conroy stood close to Moral, nodding, giving affirmation to this new conspiracy, and credibility to Moral.

'Just one more question, sir,' Gruber blurted out.

Moral stopped and looked back, impatiently. 'Quickly, please.'

'Reports from some witnesses say FDLE Agent Justin Thiery may be with Erica Weisz. Can you tell us why that would be, if the reports are true?'

Moral pursed his lips as if pondering the question, though he had been anticipating it since agreeing to talk to Gruber. He returned to the imaginary 'X' on the ground, where Gruber had instructed he stand, earlier, and replied. 'Well, there's really only two reasons he would be with her, the obvious one being that she may have forced him to go with her as a hostage.'

'And the other reason?' pressed Gruber.

Moral acted as if it was difficult for him to say, but mustered and continued. 'The other reason is that he may, somehow, be involved with her and whatever criminal enterprises she is involved with.'

'Are you saying it's possible Agent Thiery has compromised this investigation?'

Moral started to answer, but Sheriff Conroy butted in. 'In my opinion,' he started, stepping in front of Moral and speaking into Gruber's hand-held microphone, 'Agent Thiery, at best, has shown incompetence since he showed up a couple days ago. He lacked the leadership to head this investigation and, at the very least, his ineptitude has compromised this investigation. That's all I got to say.' At that, Conroy and Moral disappeared into the command post, leaving a very excited Gruber to his report.

The well-groomed reporter turned his attention again to the camera, wiggling like a chihuahua when the postman rings the doorbell. 'There you have it, Gail,' he concluded. 'We heard from the lead investigators on this case that, what began as a school shooting, may now have ties to organized crime. And, once again, the teacher – the woman known as Erica Weisz – who seems to have come from nowhere and who has been evading authorities since the school attack, has gone missing. She is, seemingly, the key to this investigation. Back to you, Gail.'

'Thank you, Dave.' Summer reclaimed the broadcast and the camera. 'What an incredible story. It's like something out of a movie, really. We'll get back to this with live coverage in just a moment. But, first, we have breaking news from California's Silicon Valley: today, a disgruntled engineer, fired last week from his job at the ChipStart Corporation, returned to his former workplace and shot six co-workers with a semi-automatic weapon. More on that when we continue after this commercial break … '

TWENTY-NINE

'My daughter would've been finishing high school,' Millie was saying, her tone blank. Thiery had found lavender tea in the kitchen and boiled water in the kettle Sara kept – *had* kept – on the back burner of the stove. Millie had calmed considerably since they'd first shut and locked the door behind them. But, in spite of having settled into the corner of a comfortable couch, in what appeared to be a safe place, her hands shook as she sipped the tea.

They had arrived at Logan's small beach house in the Silk Oaks section of Ormond Beach some thirty minutes earlier. It was a tiny, but meticulous two-bedroom hideaway, decorated with seashells and locally produced art, mostly depicting mermaids, ocean vistas, and dolphins. The walls were pastel greens and coral pinks. The floors were terrazzo and cold underfoot. Candles were grouped here and there around the house, and Thiery had lit some to help remove the slight musty scent that crept into the house after being shuttered up for a while. It felt like a cosy bed and breakfast and, to Millie, a momentary slice of heaven.

'This was your friend's house?' she asked.

Thiery nodded and looked away.

She saw him swallow dryly. 'You came here ... with her?'

He nodded again, not sure what to say. But, he tried to deflect the conversation away from him. 'Tell me what happened,' he said, clearing his throat, rising from the high-backed, wicker chair across from Millie and shuffling, *sans* shoes, to the kitchen. He looked in the refrigerator and found bottles of water, white wine, and beer. He opened two beers, returned to the living room, and handed one to Millie noting she was still quivering.

'This might work better than the tea,' he said.

'Thanks,' she replied, after swallowing a generous gulp. 'I needed that.' Then she added, 'It's a long, terrible story.'

Thiery nodded and sipped at his beer. 'I need to know it. I need to know *everything*, including whatever you can tell me about Moral. Are you up to it?'

'I'm ... so tired,' she said, slinking further into the couch. 'But, I guess can tell you.'

'Please,' he urged, returning to his seat. 'And don't leave out details.'

A breeze off the ocean pushed some brittle sea grape branches against the kitchen window, making a sound like bony fingers tapping on glass. Thiery noticed the muscles in Millie's thighs tighten, her breath catch, and her eyes go wide with fright. He could see the colour in them, now. They were that blue the ocean turns as it goes from shallow water to deep. And, though her skin still had a post-surgical putty colour that accentuated the violet crescents under her eyes, he could see she was beautiful.

'It's just the wind, Millie,' he said, placing his hand on her knee and feeling it tremble. 'Go on.'

'Well,' she said, regaining her composure. 'Where to start?' She closed her eyes and began. 'Okay.' Another breath. 'I was a nurse for Emilio Esperanza for almost eight years. I'd gone from hospital work to private duty nursing when my Jilly – my daughter – started school. I could control the hours better, and Mr Esperanza was very nice, always letting me off when we had a family emergency, or for holidays. He lived in a penthouse suite in one of the Vegas casinos. My family and I lived in north Las Vegas. It was a short commute, so it worked for me, for us. Emilio became very comfortable with me, and meetings he should have held behind closed doors were often held while I was present, as if I wasn't there, or not important enough to be thought of as a problem.'

'You heard things? Like about his business?'

'Oh, yeah.' He sensed in her tone and in the awkward way she almost chuckled at the thought that she'd heard far more than she ever wanted, or would reveal. 'He was part of the Guadalajara drug cartel,' she continued. 'They make money producing drugs in Mexico and distributing them in the US. But, his real genius is in the money laundering; he reinvests, in real estate, stocks, commodities, *et cetera*. He felt he was so far removed from what would be considered criminal, he became very casual about it. He would talk to associates and loosely refer to the drug business as, 'the Mexican interest', but I knew what he meant. Not at first, when he was more secretive. But, after a few years, he … trusted me.'

'What happened?'

She took another swallow of her beer before she went there. 'My husband – his name was Nick – was a professor at the University of Nevada. He taught American History, as well as Latin Studies. He didn't make much, but he enjoyed his work. Emilio was so fascinated by an American who was so well versed in Latin history and culture, he invited Nick over, and we all had dinner together. This happened a number of times and, while Nick suspected Emilio was a criminal, he still admired him. They developed this fondness for each other, talking about both US and Mexican history after dinner, smoking cigars. It made Nick feel important. Eventually, he came to me and told me he had been getting advice on investments from Emilio. I told him my boss wasn't the best person to rely on for that sort of advice, but he insisted every transaction they had performed was legit.'

'But, it wasn't?'

'Of course it wasn't,' she said, matter-of-factly. 'And, unlike Emilio, who had an army of high-priced attorneys and accountants who knew how to hide his money, Nick had only the dream of making more money. Before I knew exactly what was happening, Nick had accumulated hundreds of thousands of dollars. And he was stupid about it, buying me expensive jewellery that I never wanted. Promising Jilly the world. Then, it all came apart. First came the IRS. Then, as they began to sniff around and saw the ties to the Esperanzas, the US Marshals became involved. The Esperanzas were some of the "straw buyers" that the ATF was trying to track with that failed programme they were calling Operation Fast and Furious. Emilio had never been *convicted* of a crime in the US, but he had been arrested several times in Mexico. He seemed to come and go with impunity down there, because he had been paying off officials to ignore the fact that he was a known criminal. Eventually, the Organized Crime Drug Task Enforcement Force, directly under the supervision of the Attorney General, became interested in my husband's financial history.'

'Wow,' Thiery remarked. 'The people involved with the scandal around Project Gunrunner? The ATF was trying to stem the flow of firearms into Mexico but it backfired on them. I think I know where this is going.'

She shook her head. 'You can't imagine the heat they put on us. But, my husband knew, in spite of all the deals they promised, he would never live to go to prison, so he kept his mouth shut, and they just kept turning up the heat for him to give up Emilio. *And Emilio knew*. I still worked for him, too.' Her hand trembled as she raised the beer to her lips.

'My God, how could you do that? You must've been terrified.'

'I didn't know what else to do. If I just quit one day, he would know why. I felt trapped. Then, they arrested Nick and began procedures to convict him for insider trading and unreported income. They threw around figures of him being in jail from thirty to fifty years, or more.'

'Did he fold and give up Esperanza?'

Millie looked down at her hands and rubbed them together. Her breathing became ragged and Thiery saw a tear catch the light from the flashing windows and fall into her lap. 'Nuh ... no. He didn't fold. *I did*. They came to me and asked if I wanted to keep my husband out of jail. Keep my family together. Of course, I did. They asked what I knew and ... God forgive me, I told them. I told them of offshore bank accounts, places I knew he was manufacturing his drugs, some of his associates' names. I told them everything I thought might give them what they needed, to keep Nick out of jail.'

'When did you quit working for Esperanza?'

'Not until they told me I could. It was difficult. I could tell Emilio knew what was going on. He asked me all the time, in his subtle way, and told me that governments lie and that, if Nick was in trouble, I should tell him and he would get us out of the country to a safe place. He had his men check me for a wire when I came to work. I was so confused and scared; I didn't know what to do. I put the fate of my family in the US Marshal's Office, and in one marshal in particular, Robert Moral. He was my handler. They placed us in WITSEC, so now Emilio knew. He called me one last time. He said he knew I had betrayed him, then he hung up. No threat spoken, but his voice chilled me to the core. I knew I had made a mistake. I ... should've just let Nick go to jail, do his time, but I also felt, if there was a chance for me to help him, save my family ... do what was right ... ' She trailed off and took another gulp of beer, emptying the bottle.

'Where did they hide you?'

'We were moved from state to state, primarily throughout Ohio and Virginia, and each time, I felt, *I knew*, our position was compromised. I couldn't prove anything and, of course, Moral was always there telling me it was my imagination while he would reluctantly move us again. This went on until the Attorney General had his case put together. It was tough, especially on Jilly. Then, they brought us back to Vegas to testify. It was exhausting, but I was too deep into it by then. And that's when it happened. The third day I was in court, testifying, Emilio looked at me, as he had every day. I hadn't seen him for a while, and his health had declined. He looked like the guy from that old show, *Tales from the Crypt*, very creepy. Up till then, he had just glared at me, expressionless. But, that day, he smiled. And *I knew*. It was as if I had a premonition and could actually *hear* when … when they killed my family.'

She broke down crying. Thiery placed his hands on her shoulders, trying to comfort her even as she crumpled into a small form, as though she was shrinking from the pain of her memories. Thiery wished he could channel his strength, a strength that had come to him from his own loss so many years ago.

'You don't have to finish all in one sitting,' he said.

Millie nodded, weakly, 'Yes, I do. You said you needed to know everything, and I need to tell it.'

She paused before going on, getting her thoughts together, steeling herself so she could survive the telling of her tragedy and, by doing so, relive it and perhaps exorcise the pain from her soul. 'The day he smiled at me in court,' she continued, 'I stopped talking. I … I could see his teeth … I know this sounds crazy, but, I swear I could see his teeth AND his eyes … *shining*. I told the prosecutor I couldn't go on, that I needed to get home. They were not happy with me. They tried to tell me everything was okay, but I knew it wasn't. I swear I could *hear* them screaming, crying. My husband had told me once about a phenomenon, commonplace during the Civil War, called *acoustic shadows*. It's … when a battle is raging and people near the fighting can't hear it, but people far away, sometimes miles away, can hear it clearly. And that's how it was. I imagined I could *hear* the attack on my family. I pleaded with my handlers to take me home so I could check on them. They told me I was only having an anxiety attack, and asked, if they called and checked, would that be okay? When they *did* call, I could tell on their faces it had already happened. Waiting to go home that day was the most horrible thing in the world. I hated those people for that. When they finally drove me home, I saw the horror for myself. It was the worst day of my life.'

'You don't have to share details.'

'But, I do. You *have* to know. Who else will know? Moral? No, I *want* you to know.'

Thiery thought of his own loss. It had been more subtle, but as he realized his wife was not coming home, the sensation was like a permanent nausea that crept into his stomach. He awoke each day with it, and went to bed with it each night, along with the persistent feeling of being worthless, of failing again, just like he had with the NFL. 'Okay,' he told her. 'Go on. I'll grab us another beer.'

She resumed after he returned with fresh drinks. 'When we got to our "safe place",' she said, 'there was blood everywhere: at the front entrance, down the hall that led into the living room, where several agents were dead, and into the rooms where my family was. A single man had entered the house. He was in full body armour and had several guns. He had methodically killed Nick and everyone in the house, including my Jilly. He'd shot her … in her beautiful face. After he'd shot everyone he turned the gun on himself. She was fourteen. The man had no history of doing anything like that, no criminal background at all.'

She stopped for a moment, gasping, trying to breathe through her pain and, finally, continued. 'Later, they did an autopsy on the man and said he was a terminal cancer patient. They could never link him to the Esperanzas, even though they were sure the cartel had hired him. Of course, I couldn't continue with the testifying. I was in an emotional coma, I guess. But, it was over. And I felt I had caused it all. I had made the wrong choices. I tried to play by the government's rules, following the advice of their *experts*, and it had gotten my family killed. The prosecution tried to convict on what they had, but they failed. Most of their "evidence" was tossed out of court, simply because it was not complete enough.

They tried to make some smaller charges stick. In the end, they just didn't have enough.'

'How long ago was that?' he asked.

'Over two years now.'

'And, they've kept you in hiding since?'

'Of course. But, they haven't done a very good job of that, either, have they? Each time I moved, something would happen, and I would know I was compromised. I always wondered why. I followed their advice, kept a low profile. Still, every time, something would happen: a break-in at my home, or phone calls where the caller just breathed heavily into the phone. A stray bullet came into the house, once. Moral tried to tell me it was just a "side effect" of the neighbourhood they had placed me. It was a suburb in DC, not the best neighbourhood, but I didn't believe him. And that is when I began to suspect *he* was the problem; he was the one continuously compromising me. I don't know why. I had no proof. But, since the shooting at the school, I'm convinced. I think he is indebted to the Esperanzas, somehow, just like my husband was. I believe he has a gambling addiction. I've watched him play online poker when sitting watch over me. He was always checking newspapers for track information. I think the Esperanzas have been controlling him for a while, now, and it's only a matter of time before he, or they, get to me.'

'And I think you're right,' Thiery agreed. 'We saw him at the hotel. Why was he there, if he isn't working with them?'

'Exactly. I think he went there to meet them, tell them where I was. I think he sent the killers to the house in Lake Wales.'

' Let's think … What's his story going to be? He'll probably say he was tracking the Esperanzas, because he felt they were a threat to you. It's a viable story.'

Thiery glanced at Millie. She looked empty, as if she'd told her sins to the priest in the booth and now awaited penance.

'You know,' said Thiery, after stumbling onto a small epiphany, 'that's why I ran with you: I couldn't take the chance they might give you to him.'

She reached over and patted Thiery on the leg, tears running down her face, dripping off her chin. A reassurance of trust, perhaps for herself as much as for him. How long had it been since she could trust anyone?

'I'm so sorry about your friend, the FBI lady,' she consoled.

Thiery nodded, but said nothing.

There was a brief period of silence, throughout which Thiery and Millie took turns staring blankly out the window, looking for answers they knew would not come.

'Now what?' she asked the inevitable question.

He wanted to give her a great answer, give her something to encourage her after all she'd been through, but, he couldn't. 'I ... I'm not sure,' he replied. 'But, I need to make some phone calls, and I don't want to use my phone. I turned it off so no one could trace it, but I have to talk to my boss.'

'Is he a man you can trust?'

Thiery looked into her eyes. He could see – and understand – why she could not trust anyone, anymore.

'Yes' he assured her. 'He's a good guy.'

Millie nodded and reached across the cushions of the couch for her purse. 'Here,' she said, producing a flip phone, 'use mine. It's a WITSEC phone. It needs to be charged, but it can't be traced.'

Thiery took the phone from her, and sipped some more beer. It was warm, and he'd lost his taste for it. Plus, he reminded himself, he needed to keep sharp. It might be a while before he could arrange the help and protection they would need. 'Why don't you try to get some rest?' he suggested.

Millie looked up at Thiery and the slight, but reassuring smile on his face. 'Okay,' she said, feeling a sudden wave of gratitude.

She stood, found a restroom, and showered, feeling for the first time in years that she could do that and not worry about someone tearing down the curtain and shooting or stabbing her to death, like in *Psycho*. She stumbled into the bedroom, asleep on her feet, and fell into a bed that held her like a mother's arms. There were still demons out there, and she would deal with them, later. For now, the demons could go fuck themselves.

THIRTY

A mobile command trailer was set up in Orlando in the parking lot of the Gaylord Palms. Inside were the chiefs and assistant chiefs of all the local police departments: Orlando PD, Orange, and Calusa County Sheriff's Offices, even Chief Dunham from Sebring sat in. Now, agents from the FBI and backup deputies from the US Marshal's Office joined the assembly and an IAP – Incident Action Plan – was formulated.

Moral gave a debriefing of events, making them up as he went along, an army of law enforcement officers with no reason to doubt the veracity of his story bobble-heading along. He pulled information out of his ass, using the past history of the New York Albanian crime syndicate as the target bad guys and completely leaving the Esperanzas out of the equation. If, or when, it was discovered he was fabricating the story, he would simply claim his intel must have been bad and adjust the truth from there.

Sheriff's deputies and local PDs would be in charge of roadblocks and, if a hold-up site was identified, would be tasked with going door to door. The US Marshals and FBI would head research and planning. A target area of one hundred miles was set up, and a statewide APB was issued for Logan's Porsche Cayenne. No one mentioned the black town car Julio Esperanza and his driver had used in their escape. The local cops were the first to adjourn and hit the roads, a majority of them with itchy fingers, eager to take down someone who may have killed an FBI agent.

The Assistant Director of the US Marshal's Service phoned Moral, who was all too eager to fill him in on current events. Assistant Director Ron Sales listened to the report as he peered out the window of his Washington, DC office. It was mid-afternoon, and he'd had a busy morning. Sitting next to him, listening along via speaker phone, were Denise Germain, Assistant Director of Investigations, and Michael Cammarata, Assistant Director of Witness Security. Moral was not aware of their presence. Sales wanted it that way.

'What's going on down there, Robert?' Sales had asked.

'One of my birds has flown the coop, sir, and she's caused a lot of trouble doing it,' Moral had replied. The air conditioning in the mobile command trailer was set to freezing, but Moral's collar was soaked with sweat, his tie loose to allow him to swallow better, which he did abundantly, though his mouth was as dry as an exhaust pipe.

'That's Erica Weisz, yes?' Sales asked.

'Yes, sir.'

'She was supposed to testify against the Esperanzas next week, right?'

'Well, yes, sir,' Moral answered, 'but, uh, I don't see them involved here, sir. I ... believe Kadriovski's people are our real concern.'

Sales looked at his fellow assistant directors, his eyes silently questioning them. Germain shook her head, meaning, 'no way', Cammarata shrugged his shoulders.

'Why do you think that, Robert?' prodded Sales.

Moral cleared his throat and searched for the right lie. 'Because, one of the shooters shot in the lobby at the hotel was a known hitter from the Eastern European block,' he remembered. 'Name is Anichka Drakoslava.' He said it slowly, as if reading it, and as if he hadn't heard it dozens of times before. 'Maybe you can have intel look her up.'

'You're sure about the Esperanzas?'

'I really don't see a connection here,' he pleaded as much as offered confirmation. The back of his shirt was soaked as if he'd just completed six sets of tennis with the Williams sisters on a clay court in August.

'Hmmmn,' Sales murmured. 'Wonder why the Albanians would want her? Especially if they knew she was testifying against the Esperanzas. Seems they would appreciate the competition taken off the field.'

'Can't say, sir.'

'And you told the media, you think this FDLE agent, what's his name, Thiery? You think he's dirty?'

'It's just a hunch, sir,' Moral answered. 'I can't even begin to say what his involvement is, but both he and the Weisz woman were shooting at me when I arrived at the hotel. She even managed to wing me, sir.'

Sales could barely contain his scorn for Moral in front of the ADs in his office. 'That's too bad, Robert,' he consoled, trying to make it sound sincere. 'Hope it heals up quick. Maybe we should bring you in, get you some medical treatment.'

Moral protested. 'No, sir,' he said. 'I'd like to see this through. I'm in it pretty deep, now. I know the players and would like to wrap it up, find my witness, and see what her involvement is. It's really my responsibility, sir.'

'What brought you down there in the first place?'

'Well, when Weisz got shot at the school, I felt it was my responsibility to come check on her, change her safe haven, if I needed to. I moved her to Lake Wales, but it was compromised, too. Couple of pros from Mexico hit it but were killed on the scene.'

'And how did that compromise happen?'

'Again, sir, I don't know. I think Weisz might have been working with one of the syndicates, maybe.'

'Uh, huh,' Sales responded, acting convinced. 'Okay, then, Robert. You've got some field people down there, now. Why don't you stay in the command post, let them do what they need to in the field. You kick back for a bit; maybe advise the locals what we need from them. One of our directors will be down in a few hours to help you sort things out. Okay?'

Moral was chewing on the inside of his mouth and almost bit a hole through his cheek. 'Uh, sure, sir. Whatever you say. But, I'd like to get out there and see this thing through.'

'I understand, Robert, but you've already been wounded. You're doing a hell of a job. Now, just sit back and advise till we get there. That's a directive, Bob. Have I made myself clear?'

'Okay, sir, uh, hey listen, it's still pretty busy here. I've got to debrief a few more agencies, so I'll sign off for now.'

'Sure, sure. We'll see you soon.' Sales hung up and looked to his associates. 'Well?' he asked them. 'What do you think?'

'Should we speak openly, sir?' asked Germain, and nodded toward a man sitting silently in the back of the room.

Sales acknowledged Miko Tran. 'Of course,' he answered Germain. 'Agent Tran has the highest security clearance. He also brought us information about "Diceman1960". Care to comment on that, Agent Tran?'

Tran sat up and took a deep breath before answering. He was a young, smartly dressed professional; his jet black Asian hair was perfectly groomed, and surrounded what could've been a male model's face: high cheek bones set in a triangular face with a complexion that was flawless. His dark, intense eyes were still red after hearing of Sara Logan's death. But, true to his word to her, he had doggedly pursued the identity attached to the email address of "Diceman1960".

'I was able to go through his office PC this morning, sir,' Tran stated, 'and hacked into his home computer. On that hard drive, I found links to emails from "Diceman1960" to the email address of David Edward Coody through an anarchist site called "blackenedflag.org". I also found numerous searches for gun caches, including one that located the cache for sale from the Kentucky State Police auction. Some of the guns used at the Travis Hanks Elementary School shooting were from that cache.'

Germain looked at Sales. 'That answers my question,' he said. 'Why don't you continue, Agent Tran?'

Tran nodded. 'I found hundreds of links to various gambling sites Robert Moral used. If I may use conjecture, I would say it's not beyond the realm of possibility that he is an habitual gambling addict, which might be a motive for his questionable actions. Additionally, it appears he enticed Coody into buying those guns and assaulting the school.'

He held up a printout of a compilation of emails addressed to Coody, whose address was Apocolypsangel13. 'From "Diceman1960",' he announced before starting to read. *'Dear Angel, You are right in your thinking. Schools, such as the elementary school near you, produce the little monsters that become our obstructive government and inept leaders, those who embrace liberal ideas and foment anarchy with their complacency. They do not deserve to breathe the same air we do ...'* Tran looked up from reading. 'Shall I go on?'

All three of the directors shook their heads. 'Thank you, that won't be necessary, Agent Tran,' Sales answered on everyone's behalf. 'If you could leave copies of your findings with us, we'll be in touch if we need further clarification. Of course, we ask that you not discuss this case with anyone outside your direct supervisors, especially not the media. Will you agree to that, sir?'

'You have my word,' Tran answered, then he nodded, stood and brushed the folds out of his perfectly tailored suit, and left the room.

He had more information, but he didn't disclose it. He didn't know any of these people and wasn't sure which ones he could trust. If some of the other information he uncovered was accurate, it could lead to other assumptions, perhaps other conclusions.

Until he could confirm what he'd found, he was going to have to play his cards close to his vest, so to speak. Logan would've been proud of him.

In Tran's absence, Sales turned to Germain and Cammarata. 'You two get down there and stop Moral,' he directed. 'As quietly as you can. This doesn't need to be a media circus any more than it has been already. Understand?'

'Of course,' answered Germain.

Cammarata nodded. 'Yes, sir'

'Get him out of there, and let the local authorities take over the investigation, such as it is. We need to pull up stakes and slink back into the woods.'

Germain and Cammarata left the office. It was late in the afternoon, but Sales hoped they could get down to Florida before the news pressed Moral for any more statements. *God damn*, thought Sales. *What a fucking mess!*

Reluctantly, Sales picked up the phone and called Bullock.

'You wanna tell me something, Ron?' Bullock answered.

'Jim,' he began, 'would you be satisfied if I told you it's complicated?'

'Ha! What isn't?' he replied. 'Just use small words, you know, for us dumb state cops down here in Florida?'

'You were right,' Sales told his old friend, 'he's dirty.'

'You mean that Moral guy? The one who's been on the news all day trashing my agent?'

'The same. But why did your man run?' Sales asked. 'Why didn't he stay on the scene and tell the other cops who he was and what was going on?'

'I don't know,' Bullock answered. 'I haven't talked to him, yet, but I trust him. I'm sure he had his reasons. Maybe he didn't have proof. Maybe he was afraid Moral would take the woman into his custody and, by the time it was all figured out, Moral would've killed her.'

'I'm sorry, Jim. We've all learned a lesson on this one.'

'Really?' Bullock asked, leaning forward in his worn desk chair as he wadded up a sheet of paper and tossed it in the trash can across the room. 'What would that be?'

'Things like no agency is beyond reproach,' he explained. 'And that, sometimes, we need to look at ourselves, outside the good work we think we do, and run some assessments.'

'Sounds like you're preparing a press statement.'

'I understand how that might upset you, Jim, but that *is* part of my job. And it's a job governed by the Department of Justice and the Attorney General, who, in turn, rely on the President for direction.'

Bullock shook his head. 'Save the campaign speak, Ron. I just want to get my man out of hot water and back home safe. Can you send me everything you have? On Moral, this Erica Weisz woman, and the Gazmend hit where this all started.'

'I … can't do that, Jim,' he said, reluctantly. 'You must know that. Some of this information is extremely sensitive, especially relating to the drug cartel in Mexico that she was testifying against. Some of that shit goes up to the AG's office in case you haven't been watching the news.'

'What I know is that, if you don't send it to me, so I can make some informed decisions, I'm going to the media and telling them there's a scumbag working for your department who's responsible for this whole tragedy, and I'm going to do that without the polish you're trying to put on this thing.'

Sales thought about it for three seconds. 'Okay,' he agreed. 'But, I'm going to ask you as a friend, Jim, please let us make the statement. We've got to inform the AG, and he might want to talk to the President about this before the media gets it. Last I knew, the President still wants to come down and meet the Weisz woman.'

'Fine,' Bullock said. 'I'll let you do the talking head thing, but I want the background on this guy ASAP. I want to bring my man home. He's been through enough, already, and so has your witness. You want me to take the guy into custody?'

'No,' said Sales, forcefully. 'I've got two directors going down there to do that. Please, just cool your jets and let us clean up our own mess. Can you, please, do that, Jim?'

'Okay. Sure.'

'I'm sending the file to you by email, right now. Call if you have questions. And, Jim?'

'Yeah?'

'Thanks for being a friend.'

Bullock hung up without saying anything. He turned on his computer and waited for the file to appear. *Why does he need to talk to the Attorney General before this goes public? What's he not telling me?* Before he could further ponder his many questions, his phone rang. It was the governor. *Shit!* Not now.

'Hello, Governor,' he answered, trying to churn up a pleasant, buttery voice, but failing.

'Hi, Jim,' said the governor. He sounded subdued, almost humbled. 'How's the thing going with Thiery? I saw some coverage on the news. Is he okay?'

'I think so,' Bullock said, then repeated. 'I haven't talked to him today. My understanding is that he has the woman with him. Turns out she's in WITSEC.'

'WITSEC? What's that?'

'It's what the US Marshals call their witness protection programme. Seems the deputy assigned to watch over her gave her up to the bad guys.'

'Oh my God, Jesus,' Croll said, then breathed deeply as if he was just punched in the stomach and tried to catch his breath.

'Are you okay, sir?'

'I should say not,' Croll said. 'Haven't you seen the news?'

'No, sir. Can't say I have.'

'Last week, my goddamned Lieutenant Governor was caught up in some scheme to defraud people who thought they were donating money to help veterans. Today, I walked into her office here, and she was giving head to one of our interns.'

Bullock searched for the right words. He settled on, 'Hmm … you don't say. That must've been … awkward, sir. Must be causing problems with her husband, huh?'

'I guess you could say that, seeing how the intern was another woman!'

'Uh, oh.'

'Yeah,' the governor agreed, 'and, now that I walked into that shit, I have to report it, or it will come back on me. What do you think the media is going to make of that?'

'I'm sorry, Governor. I can see you're not in a good place.'

'I should say not,' he barked, then realized he'd ventured off-track. 'I was, uh, calling, because the President still wants to come down to do something at the elementary school. Of course, I told him he would have our utmost cooperation and assistance, but there's all this crap on the news. It makes it look like a bunch of morons are running the state. And what about the missing teacher?'

'She's with Thiery now,' Bullock answered, 'and I'm sure he'll bring her back to us, safely. Maybe you should tell him we're still investigating the case, because some leads have taken us on another course.' He heard a click on the phone.

'That's my other line, Commissioner,' Croll announced. 'Please do me a favour and try to get this thing settled, so I know we can make the President happy, *capiche*?'

THIRTY-ONE

Julio Esperanza had his driver take the back roads and stick to the speed limits. He had no reason to believe he was being followed, but he wasn't taking any chances. He had a conundrum though; he wasn't sure where to go or what to do at that particular moment. His heart was still racing, not so much from the shoot-out a couple of hours earlier, but from the thought of his father coming down there. He could hear him now: *Could you have fucked this up any more than you already have?*

And he would be accompanied by *El Monstruo*. Julio pictured the giant man staring blankly at him as he pulled the starter cord on a chainsaw and hungrily eyed his neck.

They drove to the small town of Eustis, a tiny piece of central Florida that billed itself as 'a friendly hometown and a destination for arts and culture', though it was better known for being home to several young Goth types who, years earlier, had come to believe they were modern-day vampires. Dressing in black and occasionally slurping each other's blood, they'd grown bored one day and killed a gang member's parents, beating them to death with a crowbar. Still, it was a pretty little town, and Julio felt some solace as they pulled into the parking lot of Haystax. As if being directed by a higher power, they discovered it was a Mexican restaurant, and Julio, in spite of his shot nerves, was hungry.

He was about to exit the car when his father called. He answered the phone, his hands trembling. Suddenly, hunger was the last thing on his mind.

'Where are you?' his father demanded.

Julio looked around in a daze, the bright Florida sun blinding him. 'Nowhere,' he answered hesitantly, not being a smart-ass; despite knowing the name of the town and the restaurant, he actually didn't know where he was.

'Did you see what Moral did?'

Julio gulped, his throat dry from fear. 'I … I'm not sure what you mean, Papa.'

'Turn on that little computer phone you have and check out the news. You two have made a mess of this whole thing. I gotta say, though, that dumbfuck Moral actually did something right, for once.'

Julio found the THN app on his Droid phone and watched the video of Moral's interview, finding his breathing easier the more he watched. 'He's pointing them toward the Albanians,' Julio said, returning to the conversation with his father.

'*Si*,' said Emilio. 'I'm not sure that will be good for him, but it takes the heat off us, for now. Do you know where the woman is?'

'No, Papa. We're working on it. She could not have gone far. With all the cops looking for her, she will probably lay low. We will find her. I promise.'

'You're goddamn right we will. How much heat do you have on you after that display in the hotel lobby?'

'So far, not much,' Julio answered, relieved to pass along at least a shred of good news. 'I think Moral covered for us.'

'Good. I am flying into Jacksonville. Pick me up there.'

'Orlando is probably closer.'

Emilio shook his head. 'It's also closer to where the heat is now, wouldn't you say?'

Julio shrugged. 'Yes, you are right, Papa. I'll pick you up in Jacksonville.'

'And find a comfortable place for us to stay,' Emilio added. 'It doesn't have to be one of the five star places you like. I'm not going to be there long, twenty-four hours at the most. If I'm absent from here longer, the Feds will know. Find a place and we will go there and make plans to end this, quickly, once and for all. Do you understand?'

'Of course, Papa. It is done. I will handle it.'

Emilio thought of a smart-ass retort, but did not say it. He was sipping some very nice bourbon as his private Learjet zoomed toward Florida like a missile. He didn't want to spoil the moment. He'd had a run in with the Albanians some years before, and he was finding some pleasure in how Moral had managed to throw the suspicion toward them. In fact, he found it quite amusing. 'I'll call when we land,' he said, and ended the transmission on his satellite phone.

Julio sighed, feeling better about things, overall. He stepped out of the icy air-conditioned embrace of his car, into the humid heat of the parking lot, and invited his driver to join him for lunch. He hoped the joint offered a big, fat burrito. He loved them covered with salsa, sour cream, and avocado. If it came to it, he would choose a burrito as his last meal. Though his father had sounded like he was in a pleasant mood, he was bringing *El Monstruo* with him. That meant someone was going to die and, if history was truly an indicator of the future, he would die in a most horrible way. Julio entered the door of Haystax, his mouth watering at the thought of diving into a loaded burrito, his mind working hard to ignore the possibility it might be his last.

Thiery watched the news reports, particularly THN's interview with Moral. If he'd had any doubts about the guy, they were gone. What he'd told the media was pure, unadulterated bullshit. Unfortunately, as far as Thiery knew, only three people were aware of that: himself, Millie Adkins, and Logan, who couldn't help them, now. He wondered if she had completed any reports, or if her investigation into the gun cache used at the school shooting was in a place where someone could find it and put things together. Probably not. That only happened in the movies: the clever investigator who somehow pulls all the pieces together and magically concludes the investigation. There was no magic here. Only one crooked tragedy after another and too many people had paid for it.

Millie's breathing in the other room was loud and slow, he knew she was in a deep sleep. She wasn't snoring, but, at the end of each inhalation, he heard a fleshy click as her tongue fell back against her throat, then a pause, followed by a slow gush of exhaled air. Thiery was tired, but he'd only had a couple of bad nights of sleep. Millie had several years' worth.

He turned his phone on, just for a minute, to check calls. He noted Bullock had left messages, voicemail, and texts. No surprise there. He'd surely heard the news reports, and, while he was smart enough not to believe them, he would be wondering what – and where – his agent and friend was. He saw his sons Owen and Leif had called him back. They'd probably seen the news, too, now and wondered a few things themselves, like why their father hadn't told them about the case and his involvement. But, he'd kept lots of things from them over the years. Maybe too much. He turned the phone back off, so it couldn't be traced.

He needed a shower to wash off the stench of blood and gunpowder. Walking to the bathroom, he passed Millie, lying across the bed like a broken doll. He tried to imagine what it would be like to lose one of his sons, the constant worry of any parent, but had to put it out of his mind. He felt an overwhelming sense of loss for this unfortunate woman who had gone through so much.

The shower helped wash away his shifting emotions, though the image of Logan's lips bubbling with blood kept creeping back into his mind, accompanied by a sense of guilt and remorse. He wondered how her husband was doing, and quietly mouthed a prayer for him to any God who would listen, anymore.

After attending Episcopalian service for years with his young family, he had stopped going after his wife's disappearance. Now, when he looked at a church, all he saw was an ornate building housed by people who seemed to need something he was no longer capable of giving. He'd struggled with his faith ever since his NFL gridiron gig faltered. While speculative sports reports attributed the loss of his career to his shoulder injuries, or more often his 'lack of talent,' it had been more than that. Simply, NFL advertisers didn't want a quarterback who looked to the sky and genuflected after every successful play. Coaches, agents, and managers told him to stop doing it, but he was full of the spirit, then, and ignored their demands. In turn, they began to look at him as a prima donna who would not take direction, ignored his renewal contract, and played him on the field less and less. 'One nation, under God … ' seemed like nothing more than hot air from a Bible Belt America that wanted everyone to be faithful, they just didn't want you revealing it in public. Hypocrisy was as much a part of the American culture, now, as crooked politicians.

Thiery stepped out of the shower and dried off, pushing his negative thoughts to the back of his mind the same as he had done for years. He looked his clothes over. His pants were still okay – a little scuffed in the knee from diving behind a car – but he needed a shirt. He tiptoed through the bedroom, again, and looked in the closet. Logan and her husband had left some clothing there, and he rummaged around until he found an oversized Florida Gator football jersey. He was surprised, since Logan was an alumna of Florida State University, and seemed to love to goad him with her allegiance to the Seminoles. He found sandals and swimming shorts that fitted, too, if he cinched them up. The outfit would serve as a makeshift disguise when he went for food.

Millie heard the hangers rattling and opened her eyes. She wasn't sure where she was and thought the sounds of the hangers were wind chimes. Then, she spied a shirtless man with droplets of water still on his muscled back, looking through the closet. The sight frightened her, at first, and she gasped before realizing it was Thiery.

He turned and watched her eyes focus. 'I'm sorry,' he whispered. 'Didn't mean to wake you.'

Her eyes drifted over his still bare chest and made him self-conscious, though Millie, who hadn't slept with a man since her husband was murdered, didn't mind. She noted the scars across his shoulder; typical football player wound, probably a torn rotator cuff.

Thiery slid the jersey over his shoulders, caught a glimpse of himself in a full-length mirror on a nearby wall, and had a momentary flashback to his college quarterback days.

'Oh, my God,' Millie gasped behind the hand she'd brought to her mouth. 'I thought there was something familiar about you. I haven't had the time to figure it out. You used to play college football, around … '

'Forever ago?' he jumped in.

'Yeah,' she said. 'I was a cheerleader in high school and used to watch all the college games with my dad. They used to call you "Magic Man", because you could make the ball disappear when you threw a Hail Mary! You were … awesome.' She watched as Thiery's face blushed. 'I'm sorry. I didn't mean to embarrass you.'

''S'okay. I get that every now and then.'

'What happened? I mean, how did you get into law enforcement?'

Thiery shrugged. If she watched him back then, she probably already knew what had happened. There was the short stint with the Broncos, until he tore out his shoulder. That kicked off a series of trades: to the Jets, who kept him benched as a second-string quarterback, then the Patriots for try-outs, then down to other, lesser teams as damaged goods. After a few years, the offers quit coming. That was the cover story, anyway. No one would believe the truth in the current "politically correct" world.

'It's a long story,' he said, dropping the subject. 'I thought I'd go find us some grub. Maybe we can talk about it over dinner. There's a Weber out back. I could grill some steaks. Unless you're a vegetarian or something.'

'We're going to stay here?' she asked, her eyes wide, quizzical.

Thiery nodded. 'I think we should, at least for a day or so. Saw on the TV that Moral has already gotten to the media and spread some pretty thick bullshit about us. I need time to get things straightened out with my boss and the FBI.'

'Are we in trouble?' she asked, swinging her legs off the bed. The effort made her dizzy, and Thiery noticed.

'Not too much,' he said, sitting next to her on the bed. 'I mean, I think Moral's story is going to fall apart real quick, as soon as anyone has the time to research it. For now, it would be best if we took a breather. We're safe here. You okay with that?'

Millie nodded, then bent forward to put her head between her legs, overcome by a sudden wave of nausea. 'Safe,' she muttered. 'I don't know if I'll ever feel *safe* again.'

Thiery placed his hand on her neck and kneaded the small spot between her shoulder blades with his thumb. He wondered when she'd last eaten. He could feel the bones in her neck and thought of a frail, vulnerable bird.

'How are your wounds?' he asked, surprised how comfortable they were with each other after meeting during a moment of such violence and bloodshed.

'I'm … healing,' said Millie. 'There was some infection, but it seems to have cleared. Just kind of weak, right now.'

Thiery gave her a small shake and laugh. 'Most people who are shot tend to stay in the hospital a little longer.'

She looked up at him and smiled. 'If I would've stayed at the hospital, I don't think I would still be alive.'

Thiery stood and said, 'I'm glad you are.' The instant the words came out, he felt he was being too forward, and his face blushed. He changed the subject. 'I'll be just a little while,' he said, staring bashfully at the floor. 'There's a store down the road. Do you need anything special?'

She lifted up her shirt and looked at the wounds healing, slow but sure, on her abdomen. 'Maybe fresh bandages?'

He raised his head but looked away from her raised shirt. 'Already on my list.'

Turning to leave, she grabbed his hand and stopped him.

'About how long do you think you'll be gone?' she asked. 'You know, just in case there's a knock on the door.'

He looked at his watch – *three o'clock* – then picked up his wallet and dug around. He handed her his card. 'Shouldn't be more than a half hour at the most. If it's more than that, call this number. The man's name is Jim Bullock. He's my boss. Tell him everything. You can trust him. But, try to stay here. It really is the safest place for us right now.'

'Okay,' she said. 'But, can you leave me a gun?'

THIRTY-TWO

They knew.

Moral splashed cool water into his face in the restroom of the command post vehicle, trying to quell his growing panic. He looked at his image in the mirror. He was a mess. Nothing new there; he'd been lending himself that assessment for years. He knew his weaknesses and the shitty fabric from which his morals were made. He could make no excuses. Simply, he was unable to control his addictions. But, it was the end of the road now. The way Sales had talked to him made him realize something was up. How much they knew, he wasn't sure, but he knew *they knew* he was up to something.

He explored his options, his chances, as any man who'd wasted away his life gambling would do. Gambling is always about exploring options, while inwardly thinking you know the outcome. He could give himself up. *A good attorney could say I did the things I did because of addiction. Might still do time, but wouldn't be forever, right?*

Fuck that. Who was he trying to fool? They would probably give him the needle for what he'd done. Especially the thing with the school. Seemed pretty fucked-up, now. At the time, it seemed a good way – maybe the only way – to get the Esperanzas off the hook, and he had to do that or he'd already be feeding the buzzards off a deserted highway. Eliminate the key witness against them, and they could walk. Julio had brought in Shadtz, who was perfect: a guy with nothing to lose. They'd done the same thing when they took out the Adkins family. It was almost a trademark for the Esperanzas to use a guy who had no future. But *he* had brought in the crazy kid on his own. Recruiting Coody might have seemed like a gamble (*But hey, he liked that!*), but Coody hadn't been the problem. Millie Adkins was the problem. She wasn't supposed to survive the school shooting. Now, he was fucked. Unless ... *unless* ... he, or the Esperanzas, could get to Adkins and Thiery first.

Moral envisioned a blackjack table, full all the way around, everyone's money and cards laid out, and everyone busted. But there he was, counting cards, double-downed, two face cards showing, two face cards down. His piles of chips stacked a foot high, and him hiding behind them, like a wall, *a barricade* that protected him from loss. The dealer with twelve showing and having to take another card. He could bust like everyone else at the table. In Moral's mind, he could see the guy sliding the card out of the deck, the colours of a face card peeking out like lacy underwear sticking out of the tiny cut-off jeans on a Vegas hooker's ass.

He could be smart just one more time, he thought. Like when he was young and untainted. Like when he was a good cop. Before he'd found his evil muse of cards and dice and smoky casinos. The erotic sounds of ceramic poker chips clinking together, like the sound he and the devil made as they toasted with diamond glasses, sealing their deal, drinking the blood from his own veins. *Here take my daughter, too, while you're taking my soul.*

He went to one of the computer monitors on which they had uploaded the hotel's security videos, and watched the video of the shoot-out in the lobby over and over again. When it came to the part where Thiery bent down to check on Logan, Moral zoomed in and focused. *What were they doing? What was she saying to him? What was that she handed him? The keys to her car, right? That was the car they'd sped away in, going where?*

He looked through the notebook he'd been using to act like an investigator doing his job. Someone had given him Logan's personal information when he'd called the FBI in Miami to tell them she'd been killed in a shoot-out trying to save a protected witness. Her home number was listed in the information. Moral picked up the phone, like so many dice he'd rolled, and made the call. Maybe he'd get lucky.

'He ... hello?' came a man's voice, filled with sadness. A sniffle followed.

'Mr Logan?' said Moral. 'This is Deputy Robert Moral with the US Marshal's Service. I'm sorry about your loss.'

'Th ... thank you,' said Logan's husband, stifling a sob. 'Did ... you know her?'

Moral could hear the tinkling of ice in a rock glass. *Poor bastard was probably getting sloshed right about now.* 'I was *with her* when she died, sir. She was one hell of a woman, and I mean that with all due respect.'

'Yes, she was,' said the man on the other end of the line, before he broke down crying, again.

'I'm so sorry to bother you at this very trying time, sir. As you know, we are still trying to apprehend her killers, and I thought of something you might be able to help with.'

'Sh ... sure,' said Mr Logan. 'Whatever I can do.'

'Okay,' said Moral, looking around and lowering his voice. 'One of the men that fled the scene took Agent Logan's car and I was wondering, is it possible, that her car has a locating device on it?'

'Yes, sort of. It has the PCM service, sort of an OnStar type thing. If car is stolen or in an accident ... ' he said, his voice slurred, trailing off.

'Yes, sir. That's it. Can you give me information on the car, like the VIN number or anything like that? This might be very important, or I might be chasing my own tail, but, if you'll give me that number, we'll check it out, you know, just in case.'

'Of course, Deputy ... what did you say your name was?'

'Moral, sir.'

'Yes, Deputy Moral, anything that might help. Do you have something to write with?'

'Yes, go ahead, please.'

Logan's husband gave Moral the VIN and the phone number for Porsche's Communication Management programme, then asked one more thing. 'Deputy Moral, will you make me a promise?'

'Yes, sir, I'll do my best.'

'Will you promise ... ' he said, his voice full of emotions and booze as he broke down again. 'Promise you'll kill them when you catch them?'

Moral nodded to himself. 'Sir,' he began his answer, 'ordinarily, I wouldn't make that kind of promise to a victim's family. This time, I'm going to. You have my word, sir. I'll take care of that.'

He heard the man sobbing as he hung up the phone. He called the PCM service, gave them the Porsche's VIN, and identified himself as a US Marshal hunting a fugitive. The service was able to find the car in Ormond Beach and gladly gave him the address.

Moral excused himself, telling the mass of lawmen in the command vehicle that he needed to go have a smoke. He walked out into the parking lot, stopped, lit a cigarette, continued to his car, got inside. He looked back the way he came, and no one had followed. He called Julio Esperanza as he started the car.

'Hello, Bobby,' said Julio, sounding almost happy.

'Eh, hey Julio. Your father here yet?'

'Oh, yes. We are together staying at a sweet little hotel we found on the beach at, uh, ... hey, Jose, what's the name of this place? Oh, yeah, Vilano Beach, just north of St Augustine. Did you know St Augustine is the oldest city in the United States?'

'Uh, yeah, everybody who lives in Florida knows that, but can we skip the history lesson for a minute? Tell me, is your dad going to kill me?'

'Kill you? No! As a matter of fact, he's quite pleased with you right now. He's been watching your interview on THN, and he thinks what you did, throwing the heat toward that Albanian mob, was brilliant, *amigo*.'

'Really?' said Moral, gaining some confidence. He tweaked the rear-view mirror so he could see his face. He saw hope there and managed to smile back at himself.

'Yeah, man. It's cool. Everything's cool. We just need to catch the woman, and that cop that saw us together, too, and take them out.'

Moral switched his phone to speaker and looked up a map of Florida, to see where Crescent Beach was in relation to Ormond Beach. 'Have I got news for you, Julio; you are practically in the same town.'

'Same town as what?'

'Not what,' he said, 'who, as in Millie Adkins and the state cop. They're in Ormond Beach. It's maybe an hour from you.'

'No, shit!'

Moral heard Julio speak to someone in Spanish. When he came back on line, he asked, 'Are you going to meet us there?'

'That's what I was thinking,' Moral answered. 'I think I can get there quicker. I'm already on the road and headed that way, now. Looks like if you come south on A1A, you'll run right into it. Why don't I give you a call when I get there? We'll meet some place and go in together.'

'What about cops and the FBI?'

'Not a problem. Locals are watching the interstate, and the Feds are researching Anichka and De De. They already know the Lopez brothers were hitters and connected somehow with the other two. And the story I told about the Albanian mob, they're searching for connections there, too. But, like the pirates say, "dead men tell no tales", right?'

'Riiiight,' Julio answered. 'Okay, *mi amigo*. We will meet there and end this thing, once and for all.'

Moral hung up and, for the first time in days, began to feel he could win this thing. Yes, some explanation would be required. But, if no one was left to refute what he said, he'd never be more than a suspect. *Just like the last time.* He'd be done with the Esperanzas, and he could take some vacation time and cool off. Without that debt hanging over his head, like the sword of Damocles, he might actually enjoy some time off. Take a cruise, maybe a little gambling junket, and blow off some steam. *Yeah*, he thought, *I can actually win this thing.*

George Dunham sat hunkered down in his unmarked cruiser and watched Moral talking on his phone. He saw him look around, start his engine, and pull out of the parking lot. Dunham thought it was odd, seeing how Moral was the go-to guy for the media, now, spouting his version of what was transpiring and spreading that crap about Agent Thiery. Hell, Dunham knew that wasn't true. *And if that wasn't true,* he wondered, *what else about US Marshal Robert Moral was bullshit?*

Dunham cranked his car and followed Moral, making sure he stayed several car lengths behind.

THIRTY-THREE

Gail Summer of THN was working overtime. She'd carried her morning broadcast into an afternoon news update, took a couple of hours off for a quick salad and a strong martini, then went back to reporting the news, of which there was seemingly no end to gun-related headlines. Her face was bent over a stack of reports, even as the news director gave the '3-2-1, you're on the air,' signal. She looked up and appeared to momentarily forget where she was. The pause was tantamount to a death knell on televised air time, but the intrepid anchor used it to dramatize the already dramatic story.

'Earlier today,' she began, 'David Edward Coody, the alleged shooter at Travis Hanks Elementary, was shot dead by one of the school's surviving victims. Administrative assistant Sally Ravich, who herself had suffered a critical, disfiguring wound, gained access to Coody's hospital room and shot him, point-blank, while the guard posted outside the room was reportedly preoccupied with a disturbance. A spokesman for the Calusa County Sheriff's Department said Mrs Ravich was arrested and charged with first-degree murder, though she will be allowed to stay at the hospital pending her own recovery, under an armed deputy guard.

'The woman said to have initially wounded Coody as he allegedly launched an assault on the school, substitute teacher Erica Weisz, is still missing and now presumed dangerous after she was involved in yet another shoot-out with law enforcement officers at the Gaylord Palms Hotel in Orlando, Florida. You may recall she is also suspected of participating in a gun battle last night in nearby Lake Wales, Florida, where Ellis Coody, the father of David Edward Coody, was shot to death, along with several others.'

The overworked anchor brushed back a strand of hair from her Botox-filled brow and continued. 'Also in Florida last night, a self-appointed neighbourhood watchman, twenty-seven-year-old Gary Penn, followed someone he described as "a suspicious black male" in a small residential community in Destin, a town usually known for its attraction to spring breakers. The two men argued and eventually fought. The suspect, a fifteen-year-old student named Chaz Freeman, was shot and killed after Penn pulled his weapon, an FMK 9 mm, semi-automatic pistol.'

She continued, wearily, 'Sales of guns, particularly, semi-automatic handguns and assault rifles, have skyrocketed since the elementary school shooting in Frosthaven, Florida. Gary Penn purchased the gun he used against Chaz Freeman just yesterday.'

Millie watched the news broadcast from the couch, a gun in her lap and a glass of white wine in her hand. The name Erica Weisz seemed foreign to her now, unreal, as if they were talking about someone else. *Could that really have been me that shot those men?* She closed her eyes and shook her head in disbelief. It didn't seem possible. Still, she couldn't help but feel the world was a hopeless place ruled by violence, and the fact that he who had the biggest weapon, the fastest trigger, and the most common ruthless element of kill or be killed, was always the victor. That included her.

When Thiery returned, Millie looked up at him blankly and asked, 'Need any help with the groceries?' It sounded like a rote comment she might have used a thousand times when routines were a comfort to her, when her family was alive.

Thiery smiled, crossed the room, and sat the two bags down on the kitchen counter.

'Nah,' he answered, 'got just the two bags, but thanks.' He smiled. 'Can't remember the last time someone offered to help with bringing in the groceries.'

The comment brought a long stare from Millie. She brought the wine to her lips and sipped it.

'Did I say something wrong?' he asked.

Millie shook her head. 'No. It's just ... I've been inside my own head for so long, I ... I haven't thought of other people, you know?' She paused, then stood to help with storing the provisions. 'Are you still married?' she asked, meaning to make light conversation, while simultaneously fearing she'd done the opposite. When Thiery didn't respond immediately, she grew more convinced of the latter.

They finished unpacking the bags. He'd bought lunch meat and bread, fresh fruit, milk, eggs, beer, bottled water, and steaks for the grill. The refrigerator had been stocked with a few things, like margarine and condiments, and some seasonings were left in the cabinets.

He eventually replied, but only with, 'That wine cold?'

Millie nodded, opened a cabinet, pulled out a stemmed glass, and poured a drink for him. She opened a window in the kitchen and the scent of ocean air filled the room. She let the slow breeze flow over her face and imagined the waves lapping gently at the nearby shore. It brought her a rare moment of peace.

Thiery sipped and grunted pleasantly. 'No,' he finally answered. 'I'm not married, anymore. My wife skipped a long time ago. She did have the heart, though, to leave our two boys.'

'You raised them on your own?' she asked. When he nodded, she added, 'Wow. That's tough.'

'It was a challenge,' he admitted, 'especially the teen years. You know how it is ...' he caught himself – recalling she had lost her daughter just as she was entering her teens – but too late. 'I'm sorry. I shouldn't have ... '

"S'okay," Millie replied. 'I asked the question. Go ahead. Please. Unless it's too much.' She was standing next to him in the kitchen; his hands were flat on the counter as he leaned against it. Millie placed her hand on top of his to encourage him to talk. She noted how masculine it felt compared to hers, how powerful. It made her feel safe.

'Her name was Adrienne,' he continued. 'She was the daughter of eastern European immigrants who owned a successful dry cleaning business in Brooklyn. She grew up to be an accountant, then moved to Florida. We met when she did my taxes. Dating, marriage, two kids, all seemed great, except my job kept me away from home. It caused … a disconnect between us. When her father died, she started spending more time in Brooklyn, supposedly to help her mother, but sometimes I wondered. Then, one day she dropped the kids off at school and disappeared.'

Thiery looked down into Millie's face. It was upturned, her eyes focused on his; a look of genuine interest was there, and he pictured that look as she must've appeared to her students. It was a caring face, a lovely face, even more so now that she'd rested a little. He pulled a chair out for her at the dining table, then took one for himself.

'She left me a note,' he went on. 'It said she needed time to sort things out, so I gave her time. After two months, I went to New York. When nobody answered at her mother's apartment, I checked with the police and learned her mother had killed herself several weeks earlier. I knew, then, something had happened to Adrienne. She would've called to pass along news that big. I tried to look up an old boyfriend she'd kept in touch with, but he was dead, too. Killed in a restaurant shooting, of all things. I kept looking for Adrienne for two more years. Thought she might have used her maiden name, Manjola, but there was nothing. After a while, I stopped looking.'

Millie sipped her wine and sighed, looking at the floor as if she'd dropped something. 'I can't imagine a woman leaving her children,' she said. 'How long ago did she leave?'

'Ten years,' he answered. 'The boys are grown, now, becoming who they are going to be. One's a firefighter and the other is in the Navy; both in California. But, they were at a tough age to lose their mother, especially without a reasonable explanation. I wonder how it's going to affect them, sometimes, in the long run. I mean, they seem okay. You never know.'

'Well,' she smiled and attempted to point out a silver lining, 'your oldest is getting married, right?'

'Yeah.'

'So, maybe they're okay. I'm sure you must've been, *are*, a good example for them.'

'I'm not so sure about that. For a while, I drank too much. I wish I could've been more patient, not so … I don't know. Strict, maybe.'

'It's hard to play good cop *and* bad cop,' she semi-joked.

'Hey,' he said, changing the subject. 'Let's eat. I'm starving.'

Thiery lit the charcoal outside and grilled the steaks, while Millie made a simple salad. She continued sipping wine, but Thiery decided to lay off. Though he felt safe for now, he knew he should keep watch, just the same.

'Hope you don't mind the steak cooked medium," he said, 'freaks me out when there's blood oozing from the meat.' He immediately wished he hadn't said that, considering what she'd been through.

'That's fine,' she said, her attention elsewhere.

Thiery was ravenous, but Millie took small bites, conscious of her mending abdomen. He made a pot of coffee after dinner and began to clean up. She tried to help, but, noting the lines of pain tighten around her mouth, he told her to sit down and relax, he would finish up.

He joined her on the couch a few minutes later, a cup of coffee steaming in his hand. They looked, first, for updated news reports. Finding none, they settled into absent-mindedly flicking through the channels, eventually finding the old black-and-white, Bogart–Bacall film, *Key Largo*.

Millie fell asleep. While Thiery sipped his coffee, he felt her body slowly collapse against his side until her head came to rest upon his shoulder. She felt warm against him as the evening air came in with a slight chill. He turned off the TV and leaned his head back, letting the edge of the couch massage his stiff neck. A creeping melancholy settled over him as he thought of the times he and Sara had met here. The pang of loss he'd been denying himself grew in the pit of his stomach. He breathed deeply to overcome the feeling.

As if her nursing instinct responded unconsciously to his pain, Millie snuggled in closer. He could smell the scent of shampoo in her hair; feel the soft heat of her breath against his neck. Feeling her shiver, he placed his arm around her shoulders. She snuggled in tighter.

They sat like that for a while, until Thiery leaned his head back again, his breathing slowed, and began to drift off, himself. A dream materialized in his head, or perhaps it was a memory, a jumble of things that either happened or, perhaps, he wanted to happen: he and Sara were driving, coming back from yet another illicit rendezvous. She looked over at him and placed her hand on his leg, moving it up just as the car she was driving sputtered, lost power, and drifted off the side of the road. They should have been upset, but Sara saw it as an opportunity to spend more time together. They were still on A1A, the beach was deserted, and she had a blanket in the trunk of the car.

'C'mon,' she summoned.

Thiery got out. 'But what about the car?'

'Don't worry,' she said. 'I'll call Porsche's Communication Management system. They'll send someone out.'

Thiery sat up with a jolt, pushing Millie back and mumbling, 'P ... C ... M.'

Millie mumbled, 'what?' through sleep-thickened lips.

He gave her a throw pillow and encouraged her to lie back down. 'I've got to check something,' he said. She could see worry in his eyes. He wasn't sure if the new Porsche had PCM, specifically. And, sure, it had only been a dream. But, it couldn't hurt to check. He grabbed the car keys and stepped outside.

Poking around the dash and instrument console, he found the owner's manual and opened it up. Right away, he found the header, 'PCM' and a list of its services. At the top of the list was 'stolen vehicle recovery.'

'Shit,' he said aloud, now fully awake. *They can find us.*

Rushing back into the house, he tried to keep his voice calm as he watched Millie sit up, a look of concern on her face. 'I still need to call my boss,' he said. 'I'm sure he's going crazy trying to figure out what I'm doing and why. Is your phone charged, yet? You said it was a sat-phone that can't be traced, right?'

'Yeah,' she answered groggily, 'supposedly doesn't have a GPS locator. At least, that's what Moral told me. Who knows if that's true?'

Thiery pondered her words for a moment, then said, 'Let's find out.'

Bullock consumed the report Sales forwarded. It was mind bending. Each time he read over it, he picked out something new, and he had gone over it five times already. It had been compiled by Special Agent Miko Tran. He'd done a thorough job putting together both a dossier of Robert Moral's career and personal life, and a comprehensive report on the Gazmend hit, where Moral had been assigned.

The reports showed Moral had been a supervising field agent and personal handler for Millie Adkins, *aka*, Erica Weisz, assigned to protect her from the Esperanzas, major league players in a Mexican drug cartel she was testifying against. Most interesting were pages of email correspondence between "Diceman1960", Moral's moniker, and "Apocolypsangel13", the address used by David Edward Coody.

'Motherfucker,' grumbled Bullock from the desk of his home office.

'What's that, hon?' his wife, Helen, called from the kitchen.

He felt his face flush; he never cussed in front of his wife. 'Nothing, dear,' he replied. 'Just reading about this guy who was talking smack about Justin on the news today. The US Marshal.' He flipped back to the part that kept gnawing at him: the pages on the Gazmend hit. The report mentioned a woman had been killed during the shoot-out. Her name was Eva Monroe. Bullock remembered Thiery mentioning the US Marshal's methods for code-naming protected witnesses, as in using jumbled names of magicians and Hollywood stars. *Eva Gardner?* he wondered, and *Marilyn Monroe?*

'Is he going to be okay?' Helen asked, noisily putting dishes away in the cabinet.

'Who?' murmured Bullock, deep in thought. He saw Tran's notes next to the Eva Monroe report. The note read: *Gazmend's fiancée. Recently changed name from Adrienne Manjola to Eva Monroe?*

'Justin,' said Helen.

'Justin?' said Bullock, lost in his thoughts. Then, something emerged, something from the era when he and Thiery had spent time together, when their families had spent time together; when Thiery and his wife seemed happy. He sat up and reached for the sweet tea Helen had made fresh earlier and gulped it to the bottom, until the ice smacked him in the teeth. The sudden chill wasn't the only thing that made him shiver.

'Honey,' he said, surprised at how feeble his voice sounded. 'Do you remember Justin's wife's name?'

Helen entered the office, drying her hands with a dish towel and shaking her head as she noted her husband's intense scrutiny of the papers on his desk. After thirty-plus years of marriage, his stamina and persistence still tickled her. 'You know what time it is?' she asked, stepping behind him. His answer was more of a grunt than anything in either the positive or negative. She tucked the towel into the waistband of her apron and started rubbing the knots out of his shoulders. 'Justin's wife?' she recalled his earlier question. 'You mean Adrienne?' she asked, peering at the documents splayed across his desk. 'What are you working on?'

'Do you remember her last name?' he prodded. 'Her maiden name?'

Helen had an incredible memory, so she was surprised this one stumped her. Continuing her work on the troubled muscles in her husband's shoulders, she focused on recollecting conversations she'd had with Thiery's wife. They'd spent hours – entire days! – on the beach together with the kids. They'd created photo albums and scrapbooks and shared recipes. She was so pretty, and a very sweet lady. Helen considered their relationship a close one. She'd been shocked and devastated and a range of other emotions when Adrienne left Justin. Eventually, though, the only emotion that had stuck was anger.

'I haven't thought about her in years,' she admitted to her husband. 'What *was* her maiden name?' she thought aloud. 'Let's see. Manning? Mangold?'

'Could it have been Manjola?' asked Bullock.

'That's it!' said Helen, smacking her husband on the back for answering his own question. 'Why? What are you looking at?'

Bullock swivelled his chair around to address his wife. The look she saw on his face almost frightened her.

'What is it, Jim? You look like you've seen a ghost.'

His mouth moved, at first without words. Then he whispered, 'I have.'

THIRTY-FOUR

Betty's A1A Diner had an all-you-can-eat fried fish dinner special on Thursday nights. It drew every kind of person, from the elderly – patrons who typically launched early, snail-like assaults and arrived in walkers with tennis balls for feet – to bikers, who came in groups of a dozen or more, their 'scooter trash' gals perched up proud on the Harley's 'bitch pads'. They came in loud, but were usually friendly, drank more beer than ate fish, and stayed till closing, often helping to put things away and clean up at the end of the night.

Moral pulled into the parking lot, his stomach growling. He couldn't remember when he'd last eaten. He had driven by the Logans' beach property and saw the Porsche parked on the side of the house. He called Julio and almost choked when Emilio answered, his voice croaky and menacing, a voice that still held authority.

'We are almost even, Señor Moral,' the old man said.

'Ye … yes sir,' responded Moral, trying to swallow with a throat pinched with fear. 'I was telling Julio, I thought they'd be here, and they are. Are you coming down, too?'

'Of course,' Emilio answered. 'I don't want it fucked-up again. Where are we meeting?'

'There's a diner on A1A, called Betty's,' Moral said as he glared up at the glowing neon road sign. 'It's down the street from the, eh, *targets*.'

'Julio says we'll be there in fifteen minutes. I'll see you then.'

'Yes, sir,' Moral answered, trying to discern if he'd heard menace in the elder Esperanza's tone. *Could it all really be over tonight?* he wondered. *Could it ever be over?*

Seated in the silent car in the diner's parking lot, he considered all he'd lost: his integrity, his self-worth, hundreds of thousands of dollars, and, of course, his daughter. He thought of what she'd become, and rationalized: maybe a porn star was what she would've become, anyway. Most young women who go to Hollywood to become movie stars never realize their lofty dreams. *Could I be solely responsible for her sleazy outcome?* He'd watched her 'films' many times, and it seemed she enjoyed what she did for a living; she was certainly enthusiastic. For a moment, he wondered why he watched so much. When the simple truth came to him – that her movies turned him on – he shut down all related thoughts before he had a chance to hate himself. He handled all negative thoughts – *truths* – that way, especially ones that added to his self-loathing, like thoughts and criticisms of his gambling habit.

He pocketed his phone and retrieved a back-up pistol from the glove box. After securing his weapon in its low-profile shoulder holster and ensuring the car was locked, he shuffled into the diner, sat at the bar, and ordered a beer. The cold hops and barley concoction felt like heaven bubbling down his throat. Out the front window of the restaurant, the ocean sparkled, illuminated by the full moon. It was a nice view. Then, a long car crept into the parking lot, moving like a shiny, black alligator pulling its weighty reptilian body up and onto shore.

The driver's door opened first. A tall man hopped out and rushed to open the rear door for his passenger. Emilio emerged slowly, like a poisonous gas escaping a ruptured container. The driver was slim and quick, his hair slicked back over his tanned face. 'Thank you, Jose,' Moral read Emilio's lips as he recognized the driver who enabled Julio's escape from the Gaylord.

Julio popped out next, followed by another, unfamiliar man. He was squatty and wide, wearing dark wrap-around sunglasses despite the hour, his mouth a lipless straight line that underscored hollowed, acne-scarred cheeks and a predatory bird nose. The man pulled his jacket closed, though it wasn't that cold. His fingers twisted at the buttons, quickly, efficiently, silver skull rings on each digit winking in the light cast through the diner's windows. *Must be the man Julio called El Monstruo,* he thought. *Name fits. Ugly fucker.*

Moral felt his heart pick up its pace. *How had it come to this?* A federal law enforcement officer hanging out and colluding with some of the world's most dangerous criminals. *Well, it had begun a long time ago, hadn't it?* Once you accept that you are willing to do anything to keep your habits, no matter how atrocious they are, you learn that unreasonable decisions come easier each time.

The men drew attention as they entered the packed restaurant, but only momentarily. The hostess told them in a polite country twang that it would be a few minutes if they wanted a table. Spying Moral as he hailed them over to the wide open bar, the gentlemen thanked her, anyway, and seated themselves. Moral nodded to the Esperanzas. No one shook hands.

Betty's only served beer and wine, but everyone was fine with that. Seeing they had Pabst Blue Ribbon on tap, Julio ordered a round of four PBRs. The bar was separated from most of the dining area, and the bartender worked as a waitress, too, so they could talk without worrying about being overheard. There were a few bikers sitting at an eight-top nearby, talking loud while their tattooed gals rubbed up against them distractedly, like cats in heat. No threat there, either.

Emilio got to the point. 'Where are they?' he asked, squinting, as the cold beer went down his gullet. Behind him, *El Monstruo* stood cleaning his nails with a stainless, folding hunting knife.

Though feigning indifference, he listened carefully to every word in their conversation.

'Around the corner,' said Moral. 'Not two minutes away.'

'You are sure?'

'Not a doubt,' Moral answered. 'Just drove by before I came here. Lights were on, and I recognized the car. How do you want to do it?'

Emilio looked around, an old, expert killer surveying the landscape, weighing the circumstances, planning the strike like one of the non-native pythons that were taking over the Everglades, with no natural predators to stop them. 'We'll park the cars down the street,' he said. 'I'll stay in the car with the driver. You go in the front, *El Monstruo* will go in the back. He's wearing a vest. You should be, too,' he pointed at Moral. 'Julio will stay on the road and watch for any runners. If you can get the woman without killing her, bring her to me. If it's too much of a problem, just take her out. Then, we leave. You go south, we go north. You and I are done after that. Even. What you tell your people is up to you. Any questions?'

Moral shook his head. 'No.'

'Then, let's get this over,' Emilio commanded as he stood. 'Julio, get the bill.'

Sales' phone rang. He saw it was Assistant Director Denise Germain calling him, and he knew it wasn't going to be good news.

'Hello,' he said wearily.

'Sir,' she replied, calmly, 'I'm afraid I have bad news.'

What a surprise. Sales looked at his watch, an old instinct he held from working in the field. When something significant to an investigation happened, like finding a dead witness, he would later need to note the time on his report. 'Go,' he told her.

'Moral is gone,' she said. 'We got to the command post in Orlando. Some of the law enforcement here said they thought he'd just stepped out, but we can't find hide nor hair of him.'

'You tried calling his phone?'

'Yeah. Nada.'

'What about the witness?'

'Cammarata is checking leads,' she answered. 'All we know for sure is that she left with the FDLE agent, the cop named Thiery.' She paused for a moment and added, 'We think that means she's safe.'

Sales sighed, painfully. Chest pain; maybe from angrily shovelling down his food earlier; maybe he was having a well-deserved heart attack. He reached into his drawer and opened a bottle of Pepcid Complete and chewed a couple, the pink chalky stuff running down his throat like drywall. 'It's a sad day in hell when we have to worry about one of our witnesses because of one of our deputies,' Sales admitted to Germain. 'I should've had someone arrest him, but who wants to arrest a federal lawman, right?'

'Right,' she agreed.

'Okay. Keep on it and keep me in the loop. I'll contact IT and have them track the GPS in his department-issued phone, along with any calls he's made, and get back to you directly. Unless he's thrown it away, it might lead us to him. I'll check with Finance, too, and see if he's using his department card for rentals and so forth. From what I've seen on his credit report, he's probably using our card exclusively. In the meantime, I'm going to put out an alert to every marshal in the area and the FBI. We'll cover the airports, but I don't think he'd try to fly.'

'We can do that from down here, sir …' Germain offered.

'Thanks,' Sales told her, 'but I can get it done without the red tape. We need to do this fast for damage control. I already look like a fool for not pinning this guy down before now. I don't know what the fuck he's thinking, trying to flee from a department whose primary job is running down shitbags like him.' He paused for a moment to belch away a sour stomach.

'What's that, sir? Didn't quite hear you.'

'Nothing, sorry.' He cleared his throat. 'Hold off on alerting the local PDs until I tell you. I've got to call the Attorney General and catch him up on what's going on.'

'I'm sorry, sir. That's going to be a tough call.'

'Yeah, thanks.' Sales hung up the phone and stared at it a long time before picking it up again, and calling the AG. He chewed a few more Pepcid and chased them down with a gulp of gin as the phone began to ring.

'Hello? Who is this?' asked Bullock.

'It's me, Jim.'

'Justin, you okay, man?'

'Yeah, for now. Just wanted to touch base with you quick. I'm using a sat-phone they gave Erica Weisz, *aka* Millie Adkins.'

'You're with her?'

'Yes. Long story,' said Thiery, glancing at Millie, a feeling of ineptitude sneaking back into his psyche. *I should've gone to the local police, or to the FBI office just north of Orlando-hell, I drove right past it. What was I thinking?*

'I know some of it ... and some other things you should know.'

'Look, Jim, I don't know if they can trace this phone or not, so we need to be brief.'

'Understood,' Bullock said, 'but I have to tell you something—'

'Okay, in a minute. Right now, what I need you to know is that I was right. About Millie Adkins being in WITSEC, about her handler being tied with organized crime. He's dirty as they come, Jim.' As he spoke, he kept popping the bullet clip in and out of his gun, flicking the safety off and on.

'We know, Justin. His people know, too. They're heading down to arrest him. Evidently, Sara Logan and one of her colleagues, an agent named Miko Tran, started looking into this guy, eh ... Moral. They found stuff, Justin. This isn't his first time going off course. I think he helped with the Adkins family hit while she was testifying against the Esperanza family. The gunner they used with that hit was dying of cancer, too, just like Shadtz. They use people with nothing to lose. These killers don't expect to live out the hit.'

'Then, why did they use Coody? He wasn't terminally ill.'

'No, but Moral came up with the idea to make the hit look like a school shooting. He needed an angry young man with an axe to grind, and it seems there's no shortage of them.'

Thiery thought about it, adding it all up. 'Makes sense. It's sick, but it does help with motive.'

'The Feds all know,' said Bullock. Special Agent Miko Tran found Moral's emails to the kid, enticing him to become an anarchist. He also arranged a gun cache purchase from the Kentucky State Police through a pawn and gun shop in Vegas.'

'Uh huh,' agreed Thiery. 'And Shadtz made the pickup, came down here, befriended Coody, and made the hit. But, they weren't counting on Adkins fighting back. I don't know if Moral was planning on using this fictitious Albanian mob concoction to draw blame away from the Esperanzas, but that seems like what he's doing now. I need you to know that.'

When Bullock fell silent for a moment, Thiery asked, 'You still there, Jim?'

'Yeah, man. I'm here, but there's something I have to tell you, too.'

'Be quick. I just found a stolen vehicle recovery system in Logan's car. If Moral knows about it, he could already be on his way here.'

'Okay. I wasn't sure how I was going to tell you, but ... you have to know this piece. When I said Moral had done this before, it wasn't just Adkins and her family. He did it about ten years ago. You see, he *did* have a connection to an Albanian mob. A guy named Kadriovski, a big player in New York being investigated for racketeering. He had an accountant name of Gazmend who was turning state's evidence against him ... '

Thiery cut him off. 'Did you say Gazmend?' He felt his heart jump into his throat.

Bullock felt his eyes begin to burn. He knew he wouldn't have to say much; Thiery was one of his sharpest agents. 'Yeah, Justin. Gazmend. He, uh, well he knew Adrienne … '

Thiery's mind raced and spun; the facts too difficult, too crazy for him to accept. And yet, he already knew they were true. 'Gazmend was Adrienne's former boyfriend from college,' Thiery disclosed. 'What … what are you telling me, Jim?'

'Okay,' said Bullock, dolefully. 'The reason you couldn't find her when she left, Justin, was because she had changed her name and—'

'And what, Jim? Please tell me … is she …?'

'The reason you couldn't find her, Justin, was because she had changed her name and … she was killed, too, in that restaurant shoot-out. You were looking for a person that, well, was no longer here, brother. Can you understand, Jus'?'

Thiery was silent as he tried to catch his breath. He'd begun to hyperventilate as soon as Bullock had mentioned Gazmend, New York, and Adrienne. Because, *he knew*. He had always known. Because, even if she had left him, she wouldn't have stayed away from the boys. Not forever. Now, it all made sense.

'Justin, you okay?'

'Nah. I'm not, Jim. I … I have to think … '

'What you need to do, man, is stay safe. At least until the US Marshals have rounded up this Moral and got him to sing on the Esperanzas. Until then, you and Adkins aren't safe. You understand? Now, tell me where you are, and I'll send an extraction team to you … '

Thiery was standing in the small dining room of the beach house, looking out the window, his vision blurred from the emotions of what Bullock was telling him, when he saw the first car go by, driving very slow. The windows were tinted, but he thought he recognized the car. When the second car went by, he could make out Moral's silhouette, looking up toward the house.

'Shit,' Thiery uttered, snapping off the lights. 'It's too late, Jim. They're *here*.'

'What?'

'Listen,' he spoke calmly and clearly, 'I'm at 16 Sunset Road in Ormond Beach. Call for help, Jim. We're going to need it.'

'Wait,' said Bullock, but the phone had already gone dead.

THIRTY-FIVE

Adding the lies Moral was spewing to the media to what Thiery had already told him, Dunham knew Moral was dirty. You didn't have to be a rancher to recognize bullshit when you saw it. He called his assistant chief, told him he was off the clock, and asked him to cover for him if the city manager called. Then, he slipped into his Kevlar vest and followed Moral all the way to the east coast, watching him, a desperate man completely devoid of his surroundings, oblivious of anything beyond a singular purpose.

Chief Dunham saw Moral meet the group of shady looking men at Betty's diner, watched them through binoculars while perched on a quiet shoulder on a section of A1A by the beach. They hadn't sat at a table. It was just a meet, with a purpose, no dinner or drinks with old pals, no hands were shook. No one smiled, least of all the grim-looking tank of a man wearing too much big city bling for a fellow cop, or anyone who followed rules.

Dunham waited until they came out. He tried to call Thiery several times, but understood why he wasn't picking up. Thiery didn't want to be found. The small town police chief from Sebring wasn't sure if Moral and his new friends were going after Thiery, but he was bet-money sure they were up to no good.

Moral and his amigos got into their cars and drove, slowly, quietly, letting the cars idle their way a couple of blocks north, finally turning into the residential community of Silk Oaks.

Dunham waited a few minutes, drove by the street they turned onto, passed it and turned onto the next street, Sunrise Road. He parked in front of a darkened house with a 'For Sale' sign sitting in the overgrown lawn. The street ran parallel to Sunset Road where Moral and the others had parked. He checked his pistol. He still carried the gun they issued him ten years ago, a Smith & Wesson .357 magnum, six-shot, double-action revolver. He was a good shot, and the gun had stopping power, but it was slow to reload and not the best weapon of choice in an extended gunfight.

He popped his trunk and pulled out the one item he'd treated himself to over the years: a Mossberg 500, 8-shot, pump-action, 12 gauge shotgun, with Ghost ring fibre-optic front sight and tactical slide. It weighed just under seven pounds. The department never would've sprung for it, but his loving wife of twenty-one years told him to pick one out for Christmas one year because she, 'didn't want him standing there with a pop gun, while the bad guys had those semi-automatics out there robbing gas stations and general stores'. He loved her for that, especially now, as he hefted the weapon in the pale night light, its dull, flat black winking at him like a promise. He knew the weapon was loaded, because he kept it that way.

As quickly and quietly as he could, he made his way between the vacant house and across backyards, praying no dogs would give him away. After passing a few houses, trying to guesstimate where Moral was parked, he heard a car door clunk shut, then two more, followed by the sounds of hard-heeled dress shoes scuffling along the pavement. He peeked out between the slits of a shadow-box fence and saw three men, one of them Moral, walking hurriedly down the road. They were all openly carrying guns, emboldened by the sparsely populated street lined with several vacant houses.

Dunham watched them approach a darkened house then stand in front of it for a moment as if contemplating their attack. The squatty man with the black suit and shiny bling slipped away from the others and disappeared into the shadows as he rounded the back. Moral walked confidently up the drive toward the front door, as if he had just arrived home. The last man, a tall guy in a fitted suit, remained at the end of the drive behind a parked Porsche Cayenne, cradling a short automatic rifle like a deadly baby.

Inside the house, Thiery had pushed a fresh clip into his Glock and handed Millie his BUG, or back up gun: a Beretta Tomcat .32 calibre, with a seven-round clip shoved up its tiny butt. The gun was small but accurate and with little recoil. Most importantly, it was the only other weapon they had. In the darkened house, they had slid the heaviest furniture against the doors, in the few seconds after Thiery noticed the cars cruising by. He hoped Bullock had made the 911 call for him and that police were on the way. But, in a small town like Ormond Beach, he could only wonder how many cops they could send and how long they would take. If it took more than a few minutes, it wouldn't matter; they were outgunned and outnumbered by people who had no other reason to be there than to make sure he and his companion were dead.

'Millie,' Thiery whispered harshly, 'hide in the bedroom. If they get past me, kick the window out and run.'

She shook her head. Her face looked like a fragile ceramic figure, one where the artist's intended expression of fear had somehow turned to anger in the kiln. 'I told you,' she said, 'I'm not hiding anymore.'

'But, you *need* to survive and we might not … '

'Shsssh,' she said and held her finger to her mouth. 'I won't. If I get a chance to kill one of these bastards before I go, it'll be worth it.'

Thiery saw the determination in her eyes and realized there was no sense in arguing. No matter the consequences, the scene was set. Even if it was going to be the Alamo. He nodded and extended his hand. She took it and squeezed. It was no 'one for the Gipper!' pep talk, but it was good to know they were in this together. Gripping their guns, they stood ready for a fight. They peered out the front window of the living room, their faces glistening with nervous sweat.

The front door knob clicked as Moral tried to open it.

Thiery tried to aim his gun at him through the small, frosted window in the door, but couldn't get the right angle. He considered shooting through the door when he saw headlights coming down the road from A1A. He glanced at Millie, who nodded her confirmation that she'd seen them, too, and mouthed, *'Thank God!'*

Julio calmly laid his rifle against the mailbox as if he were depositing a benign UPS package and stood with his arms crossed as the car slowly rolled up and parked in front of him.

Moral sidestepped off the front stoop and slipped into the shadowed carport, unseen.

A big man got out of the car and approached Julio. Thiery recognized him as a neighbour he'd seen earlier mowing his lawn. He stepped into the car's headlights and said, 'Evening, sir. I'm part of a neighbourhood watch here in Silk Oaks and—' Before the man could finish, Julio unfolded his arms, produced a small semi-automatic pistol with an attached sound suppressor from inside his jacket, and shot the man in the head. He quickly picked up his rifle, hurried to the cruiser, turned off the lights and engine, and, in an exaggerated whisper, called out to Moral, 'Hurry!'

The cold-blooded shooting happened so fast Dunham was taken aback. His mouth hung open in surprise as rage filled his head like a thermometer heated to bursting. 'No!' he yelled as he ran forward, pumping the shotgun and firing, laying down a barrage of shot as thick as a swarm of killer bees.

Julio took cover behind the car, aiming loosely and returning fire in the direction of the shotgun's muzzle blast.

Thiery flicked on the porch light. He wasn't sure who the cavalry was, but he thought some light might help them target

Moral. Within seconds, other houses along the small street lit up as residents, stirred by the sound of gun blasts, began to investigate.

From the temporary safety of the carport, Moral thought about his plan of attack. *They might expect me to come through the door, but what about that window? One more roll of the die; could I get in and get off one more shot without taking one myself? What the fuck do I have to lose?*

Thiery was holding his aim on the door when Moral flung himself through the front bay window, shattering glass and firing wildly as he rolled across the floor. The gunfire was deafening in the small living room, and the space was lit up like strobes at a KISS concert. Moral kept rolling and took cover in the kitchen.

In the backyard, *El Monstruo* took advantage of the distraction out front and, using the tip of his hunting knife, quietly pried open the lock to the back door.

From inside the waiting car, Emilio watched the gunfight with trepidation. 'Jose,' he called to his driver, his voice high and dry with fear as he watched his plan deteriorate before his eyes. 'Go,' he instructed. 'Get Julio and bring him back.'

Jose opened his mouth to say something, but Emilio didn't give him a chance.

'Even if he's dead,' Emilio continued, 'get him. We can't be found here. Go. Quickly!'

Millie stood up, framing herself in the now glassless window as, outside, Julio turned his attention back to the house and sprayed bullets across the front of it. Plaster exploded into powdery dust, curtain rods flew off the wall, as street light filtered into the room.

Thiery saw Millie standing, exposed, arms extended, gripping the pistol, but obviously confused as to which way to point the weapon. He jumped up and grabbed her, shielding her body with his own, drywall dust clogging their eyes and nostrils. Pushing her down the hall, he paused once to shoot back toward the kitchen, where he'd last seen Moral. He needed to use his dwindling ammo efficiently, but also wanted to keep the heat of return fire going.

El Monstruo leapt from the shadows of the hallway and onto Thiery's back, shoving the blade of his knife into his shoulder. It hit bone and stuck.

For a moment, Thiery felt as if he was back on the gridiron, like he'd just completed a touchdown pass. The huge, block-like man who used to be his college coach was there to slap him on the back. But the slap was hot and piercing, to the point where it knocked his breath out, and the squatty man was a black and deadly bear, metal glinting off its claws in the dark, its face shining, baring its teeth as it tried in vain to extract the knife, so it could strike again. Gunfire continued to echo from the street and into the house like cannon fire. What had Millie called the sounds, again? *Acoustic shadows* …?

The pain caused him to drop his gun, but he pushed Millie forward as he turned toward his attacker. She stumbled into the bedroom and twisted back, aiming her gun at the knot of men grappling in the narrow, dark hall, trying to get in a shot without hitting Thiery.

El Monstruo gave up trying to free the knife and, instead, pushed one meaty hand under his jacket to free his gun: a well-used, nickel-plated, snub-nosed Smith & Wesson Airweight .38 Special, with the serial numbers filed off. It was well worn, as evidenced by the black-taped grip, and designed to be used up close, as *El* liked, which typically meant against someone's head. He drew quick, but the big cop was quicker, gripping *El*'s hand in his own and crushing it against the small gun. He tried to pull the trigger, but the man's huge hand covered his so completely he couldn't get his finger inside the trigger guard. In desperation, he launched an explosive left against the giant cop's head. He felt a knuckle break.

Thiery used his height to his advantage, bending at the waist and plying down on his wide-shouldered attacker, pushing him back, but taking a punch that caused his vision to jiggle wildly, and his ears to ring. It pissed him off, and he was too big an opponent to piss off. The pain of the punch and the knife piercing his back brought a rush of adrenaline that fuelled his rage. Thiery grunted like a bull gator and headbutted the man, then he did it again, then again. Each time, he could smell the man's skin and his greasy hair tonic wafting into his nostrils.

The force of a headbutt from a man with a neck that squeezed into an eighteen-inch collar was like being hit in the head with a twelve-pound sledge. *El Monstruo* felt his legs turn to rubber, his grip on the gun loosened. He could no longer feel his crushed hand and, when the giant finally released it, the gun fell to the floor with a metallic clatter.

The brief respite allowed Thiery to glance back at Millie, and he yelled, 'Get out the window and ru … ' He was cut off as *El Monstruo* grabbed him by the throat and began to squeeze.

Thiery clenched his colossal hand on his attacker's neck. The man didn't have much to grab onto; it was as if his head had emerged like a fetid mushroom from his muscled shoulders. He managed to wiggle his fingers between the man's chin and chest, and his grip pinched like a hydraulic vice. Like the bull with the picador's lance that boils its blood and fuels its charge, Thiery's strength was bolstered to an unreal level from an overdose of adrenaline. He grit his teeth and felt the man's tight neck muscles weaken, then felt a satisfying 'pop' as a gush of hot, beery breath pushed into his face. The man went limp. Thiery wasn't sure if he'd crushed his windpipe or broken his neck, but he didn't care as he released him and let him crumple to the ground.

Glancing up again to search for Millie, he was relieved to see her slipping out the window, gun in hand, waving him toward her. As he struggled to his feet, he heard her scream, 'Look out!'

Thiery turned his head as Moral pulled the trigger. There was an earth-shattering explosion and a bright white light that turned a dull red, then maroon. Then the world went black.

THIRTY-SIX

Julio Esperanza never stopped to identify the shit stain who'd fired the shotgun, leaving several buckshot pellets in his thigh, but the return fire he'd laid down from his AK-15 had stopped whoever it was and left him bleeding in the street. He sprayed the house with another clip and reloaded before limping toward the front door.

He approached cautiously, careful not to brush the door, now a mass of splinters barely hanging on by its hinges. Inside, the place looked like the surface of the moon: dark, quiet, and with crater-like chunks missing from the walls. The flashes of light that had earlier illuminated the struggling figures had subsided, as had the screams of those within. He wasn't positive, nor did he care, who was still alive, but he was determined to make sure they were all dead. If that included *El Monstruo*, or Moral, so be it. He never cared for the fuckers anyway.

'Moral!' he hollered. No answer. He reached inside and flipped on the light switch. The living room brightened, revealing a lump dressed in black, stretched into the room from the hallway. He looked closer and saw it was *El Monstruo*, staring up at him, his face still shining from its sweaty exertions. His eyes were bulged and bloodshot, his mouth gaping open, revealing gold caps and yellowed teeth. The place smelled of something burnt, mixed with the scent of blood powerful enough to be palpable on his tongue, like smelting copper.

Beyond *El Monstruo*, Julio could see the big state cop he remembered from the lobby of the Gaylord, sitting upright against the hallway wall, his head tilted over on his massive shoulders, his face a mask of blood, a sticky clot at the edge of his hairline where a bullet had entered. *So where the fuck was Moral?*

'We have to go,' an urgent, familiar voice broke the silence and startled him. Julio whirled around to see Jose the driver had come up from behind.

'Scared the shit outta me, man,' said Julio. 'Where's the woman?'

'Don't know, but your *padre* says we need to go.' Jose looked at Julio's leg. 'Man, you're bleeding. Bad.'

Julio looked down. He hadn't thought it was so bad. Looking now, he could see his pants were soaked red from the crotch down. For the first time, he felt ice creeping up from his feet to his belly. When he swallowed, it was dry, his tongue sticking to the roof of his mouth. He and Jose had retreated no further than the front doorway when, from outside, shots rang out again.

Pop. Pop. Pop. Unreal. Like firecrackers.

Jose looked surprised when tiny holes appeared in the pressed white shirt he was wearing. It seemed like forever before the blood began to flow, though only seconds passed. He looked at Julio, appeared to try to smile, then fell forward onto his face.

'Sonofabitch,' screamed Julio, just as a shadow – a small, feminine-looking shadow – ran across the front yard, firing its popgun in his direction. He felt a slap to his chest, then another to his face, as he tried to raise his weapon. The assault rifle was suddenly very heavy, and he struggled to hold it. The weapon fell from his hands, and he stumbled back onto the porch as Millie stepped into the light, holding a small pistol. Her mouth was trembling, tears streaming down her face, leaving white streaks in the dirt on her cheeks.

The irony of a life that intimately blended violence with sex – ever since that beachside trip with his father – was not lost on him but it was just a notion as his consciousness slipped away. Julio went to his knees as if in prayer, his mouth spilling blood and teeth.

With a throbbing head and a touch of justified satisfaction, Millie watched as he fell forward onto Jose, and died. She was about to go back into the house and check on Thiery when she heard, 'You're done, Millie.'

She spun, her gun pointed at Moral, and fired. But, instead of emitting a loud *bang*, the pistol whispered an impotent *click*.

'I knew you had to be empty,' Moral said, smiling, as if his comment was charming.

Knowing her options for escape were limited, Millie lunged forward, trying to grab Julio's weapon before Moral could shoot. Before she was able to stretch far enough to reach, she felt the cold barrel of the US Marshal's gun against her head. Closing her eyes, she waited for the explosion that would end her life. Instead, she heard Moral hiss, 'Let's go,' as he gripped her neck, guided her to her feet, and pushed her ahead of him toward the dark street.

As he shoved her down the road toward the parked cars, he noticed people standing on their porches, watching cautiously. Most of them were older retirees, a few hunched over on canes, some with flashlights trying to peer into the road. They walked past them; it seemed to take forever from Moral's point of view.

'Get inside,' he commanded as he continued shoving Millie down the narrow neighbourhood road. 'I'm a law officer, and this is a dangerous crime scene. Police are on the way.' A few residents moved cautiously inside, though many stood their ground.

Millie screamed, 'Help, he's going to kill me!'

One man, with grey brush cut hair and faded military tattoos on his forearms, stepped forward, coming down his drive, boldly. He had a handgun at his side. 'Hold up, sir. We need to know what's going on here.'

Another neighbour yelled, 'What are you doing to that woman?'

Moral fired his gun into the air. 'Drop your weapon and go inside, or the next round will be for you. I'm a US Marshal, and

I am *ordering* you inside. This woman is a dangerous fugitive. Now, get back inside!'

The man laid his gun down and inched back, slowly, toward his home. Others followed.

Moral continued with Millie, shoving her ahead. She stumbled and he pulled her up by her hair and prodded her with the gun barrel. The street was eerily silent as they reached the Esperanza car. Moral opened the rear door and pushed her in.

Millie plopped onto the back seat and looked to the darkened gargoyle seated across from her. And, next to Emilio, sat a small but deadly, lightweight Kel-Tec PF9, 9 mm, single stack, seven in the clip and one in the cartridge, pistol with a rubber Suregrip, and nickel-plated barrel. It gleamed in the low light like the smile on Emilio's reptilian mouth.

'Hello, Millie,' Emilio said. 'You've been so much trouble.'

Moral slid into the driver's seat. 'We need to go. Get this over with.'

'Where's Julio?' queried Emilio, calmly. 'And Jose?'

Millie proudly answered, 'They're dead, you piece of shit. *I* shot them.'

Emilio's face twitched, then he shrugged, turning down the corners of his mouth. He struck out quickly, like a coiled snake, and backhanded Millie across her face. He turned to Moral. 'What about when they find them?'

Moral turned to face him, his arm across the back of the seat. 'They won't find us. And they won't find her. There's no connection to us. It was dark out there. No one saw us clearly. Julio takes the fall – he was acting on his own – and there's no one to refute it. We're *golden*.'

'What about your car?'

'It's not in my name, and I wiped it down before I went into the house.'

'Then, let's go,' Emilio said. 'We finish this somewhere else down the road.'

'Agreed,' said Moral, and turned around to start the car.

Millie tried to shake off the blow from the old man but her vision was still rattled. She had come too far to die now. *If she could come up with a distraction then jump from the car …*

Thiery woke feeling as if his skull was cracked. Little did he know it was. He'd smashed helmets before when he was sacked, but it had been nothing like this. He felt his head with a sausage-fingered hand and thought he felt something sticking out along the scalp line. It felt wet and squishy and, somewhere deep inside the fog of his thoughts, he decided he shouldn't play with it. *It might be brains.*

The lights were on in the room, and the brightness helped stir him. He remembered a sense of urgency; he remembered Millie, and his heart sped up, pushing blood back through his limbs, waking him. *Where was she? Was she still alive, or had they gotten to her?*

'Miserable fuckin' bastards,' he mumbled to himself, his tongue feeling as though it belonged to someone else. But the words didn't sound right. The words said, 'Mizz-fu-tids.' He pushed himself up using the wall, and nausea washed over him like a wave. There were two of everything; two dead men lying in front of him, two knives with blood on them, two overturned couches, two doors that led out of this charnel house. *Now, which one to choose?*

C'mon, you big tough quarterback, he thought to himself, incoherently. *You've got another quarter to go in the game, and the other side is winning.* He stumbled toward the splintered front door, trying to call Millie's name, but it just came out, 'Moo-ryyyrrrrgh,' like the bellow of a gut-shot elk. He leaned over and vomited, and the effort made little molecule-looking things dance in front of his eyes like microscopic bees. He waved them away and took a deep breath as he plodded forward, telling himself, *move one leg, now the other,* but he noticed one of them was dragging. Looking down and noticing one of his feet was pointed in to one side, as if it was dislocated, he concluded some neurological damage had occurred. He assessed himself further and observed that the hand on the same side as his limp foot was curled inward, too. The words of some comedian from long ago drifted into his head: *must be 'dain-bramage'*. He didn't remember the knife wound in his back, or much of anything, except that there was an urgent matter to attend to.

Thiery made it out into the yard where the world began to spin, and he fell into dew dampened grass. It felt surprisingly refreshing as he stared up at the stars and watched them move about like a giant monochromatic kaleidoscope. If there *were* urgent matters, they would have to wait while he figured out if he was truly going to fall off the earth.

Disturbed by a tapping on his window, Emilio turned and uttered a surprised gasp as he stared at the bloody hand on the other side, pointing a Smith & Wesson .357 magnum. The hand was shaking, some of the fingers were missing, and the small man attached to it, aiming the weapon, was wavering, trying to stand erect on a leg that was missing at least a kneecap.

'Get out of the car,' Police Chief Dunham ordered. 'You're under arrest.'

Emilio smiled, as if he were merely an old man sitting in his car, minding his own business. *Move along, nothing to see, here.* He shot a warning glance at Millie before sliding the window down and lowering his gun so Dunham couldn't see it. 'What's happening, officer?' Emilio asked in his best 'surely this is all a misunderstanding' voice. 'I was just sitting here and heard all the commotion … '

Enough light filtered into the back seat for Dunham to see Millie. He knew without asking, without ever having met her, she was the teacher. This was the woman who had shot down two intruders who'd entered an elementary school Dunham's children had once attended, a person who had survived several attempts on her life, someone who had come too far to be taken away by this creepy reptile; the old guy was obviously trying, but experience had taught Dunham it was nearly impossible to convey innocence through eyes with predatory slits that emanated evil as ancient and fatal as a cobra.

'He's got a gun!' screamed Millie. Dunham didn't have to see it. He fired the .357 through the glass and into Emilio's head. The bullet hit at just the right angle to take off the top of his head, and send it flying out the shattered back window.

Millie threw open the door and rolled out onto the ground, covered with tiny cubes of glass, her ears ringing intensely from the gunshot.

Moral jumped out of the car, gripping his gun, and fired. He hit Dunham square in the chest, his breath gushing out of him with an audible 'ugh'. The impact knocked him back several feet, and he slammed against the ground and did not move.

When Moral looked back for Millie, she was gone. He looked up and saw a pale figure in the distance, running down the road.

'Shit!' he said, and started running after her. 'Stop ... you ... fucking ...' he began, already winded, but knowing he had no choice but to continue after her, and the distance was growing.

Millie ran east toward the ocean, toward what she hoped would be freedom. She thought of stopping at one of the houses along the way, hoping she could get in before Moral caught up with her, but she feared Moral might just kill her would-be benefactors as well, or maybe they would just give her up. Either way, he would win.

The wound in her side screamed with each pounding step, but she didn't care. She wanted to be away from it all, even if she just got to the ocean and threw herself into the surf. Even if she drowned, she would do so knowing the Esperanzas, especially Emilio, were dead. Moral would be alive, but how could he explain all that happened? She could accept death knowing that, at least, he would get caught.

Still, she ran as though she wanted to live.

Thiery heard the shots in the street and rolled over nonchalantly to see what was going on. He watched hypnotically as Millie ran by, followed by a scurrying Moral, a moment later. It was the image of Moral that awoke his short-term memory. *That's the fucker who shot me*, he thought, feeling his anger return. He let it give him strength, let it push him to his hands and knees, then onto wobbly legs that took one step, then another, and another, until he found he was actually able to trot. His numb side was beginning to come alive again and, while it felt as if a million needles were undulating along that side, it also gave him back some muscle control he sorely needed.

As he galloped unevenly, he came across an object in the road: Dunham's pump shotgun. Part of the pump mechanism was missing, likely splintered from a round from Julio's rifle, but when Thiery pulled it back, the gun ejected an empty cartridge, and he heard another slide into the chamber with an almost eager *clink*. He looked up and saw Millie dart across A1A without looking, illuminated by headlights of passing cars that beeped horns and yelled obscenities. Moral was about fifty yards behind, but he was forced to hesitate as a small but steady stream of cars passed.

He used the time to close the distance between them, his long legs functioning better with each step, his old gridiron pace coming back, an imaginary goal line just ahead.

Millie had disappeared over the sea oat-covered dune and, within seconds, Moral did, too.

Thiery got to A1A and could hear sirens coming, saw blue flashing lights at a distance down the road. But, they weren't going to make it in time. He heard a shot ahead and prayed he wasn't too late. Mounting the dunes, he hurled himself quickly over the side so he wouldn't be silhouetted against the road, and forced his eyes to adjust to the dark shoreline. The bright light of the stars helped, and he could see Millie running north along the surf, her feet kicking up foam as she splashed forward. Moral had stopped and was carefully aiming; his arms locked-out tight as he slowly squeezed off one round, watched where it hit in relation to Millie, then adjusted, and fired again.

Millie went down and, at first, Thiery thought she might have been hit, but she must've only stumbled, because she got back up and moved into the ocean at a diagonal. She was going to make a swim for it, he thought, or duck under water. Neither strategy would work for very long. Moral's aim was getting closer, kicking up little geysers of water each time he pulled the trigger.

'Drop it, Moral!' he ordered, levelling the shotgun at him, panting, his head reeling from the effort of the run and his wounds.

Moral twirled like a Peeping Tom that just got caught looking into a window. His arms were lowered, but the gun was still there.

Thiery fought off the bees that reformed in front of his eyes and the nausea that was returning and tried to steady the shotgun that seemed to be growing heavier by the second. He walked slowly toward Moral. 'Said … put … it … down.'

Light reflected off the ocean, perhaps it was an illusion brought on by loss of blood, but to Thiery, it looked like stage lighting. For a brief moment, he could see Moral's face as clearly as if the sun were coming up over the horizon. He saw his expression change from worried concentration to a benign, almost goofy smile.

'Do you remember a woman named, Adrienne?' asked Thiery, his tongue still thick and occluding his speech.

'Who?' said Moral, almost grinning, his grip tightening on his pistol.

'In a restaurant, about ten years ago. New York. She was with a man named Gazmend.'

Moral's brow was furrowed, but smoothed as the memory came back. *Yeah, he thought, that was the beginning. The start of the downhill run, the fear of being financially underwater, the relief that there was a way out, if only he didn't mind giving up everything that mattered.* Moral shrugged. He couldn't muster any more sympathy for the man in front of him than he could muster for himself.

They could both hear sirens growing closer, now, and a helicopter was looming over the street where people lay dead in the previously quiet community.

'That was *my wife*,' continued Thiery. 'Now, put that fucking gun down.'

Moral nodded his head, but didn't release the gun. 'She was screwing around on you,' he told Thiery.

'That didn't give you … the right to kill her,' he mumbled, weakly. A blood vessel behind his eye began to make his vision look like a pulsing, red light.

'You got it all wrong, Thiery,' Moral said, stalling, weighing out one last gamble, one last throw of the dice, wondering if, *maybe*, there was a way he could win *one last time*. 'You need to know the truth. If you'll let me explain … '

Thiery knew Moral was trying to distract him until he could make his move, talking shit until Thiery passed out, or fell over dead. *How much longer am I gonna last, anyway, with a knife wound in the back and a gunshot wound to the head?* He saw Moral draw a deep breath, his elbow start to bend, but didn't wait for him to move. He tightened the shotgun against his shoulder so it wouldn't kick too hard, and pulled the trigger.

Moral took the blast midsection, and it seemed to cut him in half as he was kicked back into the surf.

Thiery could see his eyes, wide with the recognition of death, dim out, like the lights of a boozy, sweat-scented, casino, blinking out as the gamblers shuffled off at closing, their pockets and hopes empty.

Crumpling to his knees, Thiery dropped the shotgun and rolled onto his back on the sand, allowing its cool, granular embrace to comfort him. He could see the star formation of Orion, ever the hunter, ever the fighter, behind the kind and pretty face of Millie Adkins as she stroked his face, gently, with her nurse's touch. He closed his eyes and felt his body float up and into the stars.

THIRTY-SEVEN

Four Weeks Later

Thiery's doctor began to decrease the thiopentone that had kept him in a drug-induced coma for a month while his brain healed and the swelling subsided.

He awoke several times over the next few days. Initially, he opened his eyes to see a lovely woman who seemed recognizable, but whose name he could not remember. Her hair was its natural colour now, with a few incongruent streaks of grey poking through on one side, where that childhood swing injury had healed. She smiled at him, squeezed his hand, and gave him, with the doctor's permission, a tiny sip of water. Then he was off to that foggy state, again, that allowed neither comprehension nor creative dream sequences, just a mental limbo.

The next time he woke up, his hand was curled in what he initially thought was a bird's nest, then the 'nest' moved and below it was the face of his oldest son, Owen, his curly hair grown out and a ragged beard outlining his jaw. Leif, the younger, was standing behind him with his usual gum-showing grin. The woman was there again.

'Wha ... ' Thiery croaked, his throat dry. The lady gave him another sip of water. 'Why are you guys here?'

'We thought you might check out,' replied Leif, ever the smart-ass. 'We were hanging around, waiting for that big inheritance.'

Owen nudged his brother in the ribs. 'Just checking on you, Dad,' he said. 'How do you feel?'

'Ha,' he chuckled, not without discomfort. 'I feel like someone kicked a field goal with my head.' He noticed one of those stainless steel trapeze bars hanging from a chain above his chest. He reached up, noticing how pale and small his arms looked, grasped the bar, and pulled himself up a few inches with his good arm. The woman practically flew to his side and assisted.

'Th ... thanks,' he said. Trying to focus his eyes, he looked at her and added, 'I know you, right?'

She smiled. 'Enough to almost get yourself killed for it.'

He smiled lopsidedly at her, 'Millie, right?' Then added, 'you look like you were worth it.'

Her face blushed, and she looked at his sons. 'Some people come out of anaesthesia crying. Some people wake up making jokes.'

'I don't think he was joking, Millie,' said Leif.

They kept it light that day. Getting caught up, filling him in. A nurse came in and brought horrible hospital food. The boys promised him a pizza with meatballs if he could 'keep that crap down'. Later that night, they smuggled one in.

His surgeon stopped by the next day and told him he was healing as he should. He went over the injuries: a small crack in his skull where the bullet had 'bounced off' ('hard head,' Leif had added), and his scapula was cracked from the knife wound. He'd had some swelling in his brain, but it was under control. He would probably need balance therapy when he walked again, which the doctor encouraged him to do as soon as he felt up to it. 'Might experience some double vision, initially,' he'd said, along with a ringing in his ears, but that should pass. His shoulder would actually take longer to heal and require physical therapy to regain motion and overcome the muscular atrophy.

'Maybe you can actually beat him arm-wrestling, now,' said Owen to Leif.

They all had a chuckle.

The boys stayed around a few more days to assure themselves he was on the mend, but Leif had to get back to the Navy base in San Diego and Owen back to the fire department in San Francisco. Owen needed to save vacation time so that he could go on a honeymoon in a few months. He expected his father to be there to see him off.

When Millie excused herself to visit the ladies' room, the boys both grew serious and each took up a place on either side of his bed.

'That one is a keeper, Pops,' said Leif, raising his eyebrows up and down comically.

'You think?' said Thiery, remembering those blue eyes as the first thing he saw when he woke up.

'Don't know how much you remember, Dad, but you got him,' said Owen stoically, his jaw muscles flexing.

Thiery looked quizzically at his sons. 'Who?'

Owen glanced at Leif, who said, 'The bastard who killed Mom.'

'I did?'

'Yeah, Dad,' said Owen. 'Commissioner Bullock was here when they first brought you in. He stayed a few days after we got here and kinda filled us in.'

'Yeah?' Thiery said. 'I don't remember everything. Can you fill *me* in?'

'The Commissioner said he was coming back in,' said Leif. 'Maybe he should do that. He's got more details than we do. But, we, both of us, just wanted to say … ' He got choked up and couldn't finish.

Owen did it for him. 'We wanted to say you're the best father we could've hoped for. And that we never doubted you. We love you, Dad.'

Thiery tried to lighten it up. 'Hey,' he addressed Owen, 'don't they have grooming standards at the fire department?'

'Yeah, I know,' he said, stroking his beard. He bent over and hugged his father, as did Leif.

As if on cue, Bullock walked into the room, carrying a Tupperware container that barely concealed the scent of home-fried chicken.

'Unhand that man, you trolls,' said Bullock. 'And don't you dare make a pass at this chicken. I'm armed.'

'Hey, Chief,' said Owen. 'You're just in time, we gotta catch a plane.'

'Okay boys,' Bullock said. 'It sure was good seeing you. I'll try to keep this guy entertained.'

'Good luck,' joked Leif. 'See you at the wedding.'

All said their good-byes, and the boys left, Thiery looking after them fondly, but with tears in his eyes.

'God, they're almost as big as you, man,' Bullock commented. 'You must be proud of them.' Getting to the matter at hand, he added, 'How are you feeling?'

Thiery dabbed at his eyes with the corner of his bed sheet. 'Like I lost the game.'

Bullock laughed. 'No, you didn't. Fact is, you put down a real piece of shit.'

'Moral? How much trouble am I in for that?'

'You're clear. Millie Adkins was the witness and Moral had a gun. We already had an administrative hearing; interviewed residents in Ormond Beach, and our forensic people were all over the scene. The FBI's report ties it all together.'

'Can you help *me* tie it together? I feel like one of those new kids in school who's missed a semester.'

'How much do you recall?'

'Most of it, now,' Thiery answered, 'but that last day, when we went to the beach house, is like a dream with parts missing. It gets all jumbled.'

Bullock spelled out the events of the beach house shoot-out: who got who, how, where, and why.

Thiery closed his eyes and tried to remember. Bits and pieces flashed into his head, but it made him dizzy, so he let it go for the time being.

'The boys said I got the man who killed their mother.'

'You don't remember our conversation that night you called me?'

'Not that much. I remember something about the Albanian mob ... '

'That's right. I don't know how much you want to hear right now ... '

'Fill me in, Jim, or I won't get any rest.'

'Okay,' he said, 'but I think you knew, already. Adrienne had that old boyfriend in New York – the guy she went to school with – Gazmend?'

'I remember the name.'

'He was an accountant, like her. When she left you, she hooked back up with him. Eric Gazmend was already assigned to the US Marshal's WITSEC programme. Adrienne wasn't a witness, but she had ties to one, so they allowed her in, even though they weren't married, just so he'd cooperate with them. They gave her one of their contrived Hollywood starlet names, Eva Monroe, and she legally changed it. She was trying to hide from her husband – you – a cop. She knew if she kept her name, you'd find her in no time and, if you could find her, the mob probably could, too. Unfortunately, the guy who was supposed to protect Gazmend was Moral. Adrienne just happened to have the bad luck to be out with him when the hit went down.'

'Jesus. How did you put that together?'

Bullock smiled. 'I didn't. *You* did. I remembered you had told me about your theory, that the marshals were using code names of famous magicians and old Hollywood stars to rename their protected witnesses. Seemed pretty silly at the time, but you know the Feds. I mean, they named that fiasco down in Mexico "Fast & Furious", so they are not beyond some drama, you know?'

'Hmm,' said Thiery, confused, but curious. 'So, now what? Does Millie have to go back into hiding?'

Bullock shook his head. 'We don't think so. The Esperanzas' organization is falling apart. The old man ran it, and the son might have tried to keep it going, but he's gone, too.'

'What about the shooting at the school? That community?'

'They're recovering. The Feds owned up about Moral being a dirty marshal, but they're keeping the details vague. They sure as hell don't want the public to know the school shooting was any more than a random school shooting, and that, not only did Moral secure the weapons, he spent several months on an anarchist chat line talking a crazy kid into doing the deed. Moral arranged the purchase of the gun cache from the Kentucky State PD through a licensed pawn shop in Vegas, owned by a guy named Tito Viveros. Viveros bought the cache for the Esperanzas, who then hired Shadtz, a man dying from cancer, to bring them to Coody. Logan's FBI buddy, Miko Tran, got Viveros to sing like a bitch; that was the ribbon on the gift. Oh, yeah, one last thing.' Bullock handed him a newspaper. Thiery read:

CALUSA COUNTY SHERIFF RESIGNS UNDER INVESTIGATION

In the wake of the Travis Hanks Elementary School shooting, an investigation into the delayed response of the Calusa County Sheriff's Office has revealed that officers had been ordered, according to several deputies questioned, to delay their responses to certain calls. Sheriff Alton Conroy allegedly had been trying to manipulate response times in order to get more funding for his department. Conroy's attorney has stated the allegations are false, but a number of officers within the department have already given statements to the Florida Department of Law Enforcement ... '

The story continued for several pages, but Thiery put the paper down and rubbed his eyes. 'You know,' he said, 'I hate this business.'

'I do know,' Bullock responded, 'but you're good at it, Justin. And, you're *honest*. We, the state of Florida, need you. Hell, I'll say it, even the US government needs you. Now, you've got a lot of time to recover, and you need to think about coming back when you do.'

'Not likely, sir.'

Bullock had his hands over his ears. 'Sorry, man, I can't hear you. You should know, I've slowed my retirement, just a bit, until you can get better and maybe reconsider your future. I know the governor would like you to take over— '

'Oh, I'm sure about that.'

'No, really. You missed the President meeting with Millie Adkins. He said he was going to nominate her for the President's Citizen Medal for saving those kids at the school. Said he was considering you for an award, too.'

'The President of the United States?'

'Yeah,' said Bullock, laughing. 'That's the one. I told him you didn't need an award 'cause you already have the Heisman.'

Thiery shook his head and laughed weakly. 'You're too much, man.'

'That's what my wife says,' Bullock joked. 'Hey, I have to go. Tallahassee calling. You get better and come see us, okay?'

After Bullock left, Thiery closed his eyes for a moment to digest it all. He finally settled down, drifted off, and never heard Millie Adkins come back into the room and take up her station next to him, where she'd been for the past several weeks. She was, after all, still a registered nurse.

When Thiery's doctor released him about a month later, Millie was there. She'd offered to help look after him while he recuperated. She had nowhere to go and nothing she had to do. Thiery didn't mind; he needed the help and enjoyed her company. She was easy to talk to and quick with a smile or a laugh. Her injuries were well on their way to being healed, but he still felt that, in some way, she needed him as much as he needed her.

Bullock had driven Thiery's truck down before his friend was released. The fabulously restored 1958 Chevy Apache, with its beefy rounded fenders, massive grille, and dual headlights, appeared to have a gruff face, not unlike its owner's. Thiery gave Millie the keys and asked her to pull it around as he waited in a wheelchair at the hospital's entrance.

The eggplant-coloured truck rolled up in front of him, and he smiled hearing its familiar and comforting, *glub, glub, glub*. Millie got out shaking her head. 'You couldn't possibly drive anything from this century, could you?'

'Nah,' he grinned, 'too much plastic. But, hey, it is an automatic with aftermarket air-conditioning.'

'Wow,' she feigned adoration, 'you sure know how to spoil a girl.' She helped him into the truck, then got into the driver's seat.

'Which way is the best way to go, sir?' she asked.

'We could go straight up I-75,' he suggested, 'then over on I-10 to Tallahassee. But, would you mind taking a drive down to Sebring, first? It's only about an hour, and I want to check on a friend.'

Millie smiled. She knew which friend and she needed to see him, too, to say thanks. She pushed the gas down and was surprised at how responsive the old truck was.

'Like music?' Thiery asked.

'Anything but country,' she replied.

'I hear that.' He found an alternative rock station and they cruised south to George Dunham's house, stopping to buy a six-pack of cold beer at a convenience store, before pulling into his driveway.

Dunham was sitting on the porte cochère outside a bone-coloured clapboard house with Kelly green shutters, in the shade of a giant oak tree. His leg was in a straight cast. He shook Thiery's hand with what was left of his: the pinkie and ring finger were gone. He made a joke of it, holding up his remaining fingers as he greeted, 'Peace, brother.'

Thiery and Millie sat down on a swinging love seat and rocked slowly back and forth. When Dunham's wife, Sherry, joined them, introductions went around. No one was averse to drinking a beer, even though it was barely after twelve noon.

Millie thanked Dunham for saving her life and risking his own. Had he not hobbled over to the car window when he did, Emilio Esperanza would've shot her, driven away with Moral, and they would've won.

'But, they didn't,' Dunham reminded her. 'I have to say that was one of the most satisfying shots I ever made, and I did it with this hand!' He held up the peace sign again. 'The fastest two fingers in the south!'

They laughed and chit-chatted. Dunham's wife brought out snacks. After a while, Thiery and Millie excused themselves. It had been good to see the Chief, but Thiery wanted to get home, and Millie just wanted to feel the breeze blowing in the side vent window of the old Apache truck, feel free and finally, safe. Everyone promised to stay in touch, as people do when they've shared a common disaster.

Sometimes they do.

They took their time on the drive north to Tallahassee, choosing the small roads, catching Highway 19 that would take them up the west coast of Florida where they could watch the sun as it slowly dipped into the Gulf of Mexico.

'My son is getting married in San Francisco in a couple months,' said Thiery. 'You wanna go?'

Millie felt the warmth of the sun on the side of her face and smelled the healing salt air wafting in from the sea.

'We'll see,' she said, reaching over and taking his hand, rubbing her thumb over his knuckles, noticing the bruises fading from purple to yellow. She picked up his hand and kissed it, feeling the coarse hair on the back of it brush her cheek, like a loofah sponge.

She smiled at Thiery and nodded. 'We'll see.'

Acknowledgements

Thank you to my beta readers: Lisa MacMillan (x 2!) especially for the advice on school teachers and how they relate. Varsha Chandra, for her in-depth review and advice on my antagonists – good call. Louis Lara, for your perspectives. A special thanks to James O. Born, author and advisor, for your information on firearms, law enforcement, and support over the years.

Thanks to all the editors who worked on this book: Ramona DeFellice Long, Dawn Scovill – a special thanks for kicking me with those pointed cowgirl boots in the you-know-where. The editorial staff at HarperCollinsUK: Kate Stephenson, for your developmental advice and for taking a chance on me. Janette Curry for your work on copyediting and schooling me on how you do it in the UK.

And thanks to my readers whose allegiance keeps me working. Without you, I would not be.
~PK

KILLER READS

DISCOVER THE BEST IN CRIME AND THRILLER.

SIGN UP TO OUR NEWSLETTER TO KEEP UP TO DATE WITH OUR LATEST BOOKS, NEWS AND COMPETITIONS.

WWW.KILLERREADS.COM/NEWSLETTER

Follow us on social media to get to know the team behind the books, hear from our authors, and lots more:

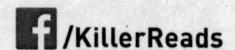

/KillerReads   /KillerReads